Also by Stuart Gordon from Macdonald

ARCHON
The First Book of the Watchers

THE

HIDDEN WORLD

The Second Book of the Watchers

Stuart Gordon

Macdonald

A Macdonald Book

First published in Great Britain in 1988
by Macdonald & Co (Publishers) Ltd
London & Sydney

All characters in this publication are fictitious and any resemblance to real persons, living or dead, is purely coincidental.

British Library Cataloguing in Publication Data

Gordon, Stuart, *1947–*
Hidden world.
I. Title
823'.914[F]

ISBN 0-356-15421-1

Typeset by Leaper & Gard Ltd, Bristol, England
Printed in Great Britain by
Redwood Burn Limited, Trowbridge, Wiltshire
Bound at the Dorstel Press

Macdonald & Co (Publishers) Ltd
Greater London House
Hampstead Road
London NW1 7QX
A Pergamon Press plc company

Dedicated to the memory of Francis Rath
A philosopher and friend in stony places

Contents

Western Sea
6
Panting Cliff
5
Lodge of the 9 Doors
Lake Village
4
The Ford
3
THE FOOL'S JOURNEY

MAP 1
The Grove
1
2
The Whole Place
Estuary of the Narrow Sea

Toulouse
Laurac
Fanjeaux
Montréal
Limoux
Pamiers
Foix
Montségur
Tarascon
Tabor
Caves (Gate of the Stone)
R. Ariège
River Aude
Ax-les Thermes
PYRENEE
Puigcerda
LANGUEDOC
Ariège Region

Béziers
Carcassonne
GULF of LYON
River Agly
Perpignon
River Tet
S
River Tech
MAP 2
Scale in miles
0 5 10 15

Prologue
The Shift

Diane Joyce dreamed that her shabby room in Edinburgh was filled with light, and that a great voice spoke to her from the heart of that light.

Diane, it said, *How can we tell you this without misunderstanding?*

Every ten thousand years or so your planet – we Elohim call it the Hidden World: you two-legs living on it call it Earth – goes through a Shift.

So long as certain powers of the spirit remain beyond your society's material vision, a Shift will always involve violent displacement of the Earth's axis of rotation and slippage of the outer crust over the molten interior. Electric storms, earthquakes and lava flows assault the lands; poisonous gases and ash veil the sky and choke you air-breathers; climates change instantly. Displaced ice-caps – the centuries-long build up of their weight is one of the chief factors contributing to a Shift – melt rapidly so that after the fire comes flood, killing most of you, leaving the rest in such amnesiac shock that all knowledge is lost, leaving later generations nothing but regressive myths of guilt and God's violence.

Understand: each Shift arises from millennia of increasing stress, in the body of the Earth itself; between Earth and you life-forms that walk, swim or crawl on it; and again, between Earth and its life-forms and the dynamic astral sea through which it swims round its star.

Each Shift is the inevitable outcome of that energetic imbalance in the nature of things without which no life or separate forms can ever develop.

Please see: not only your world is subject to this process. In every world the energies of rotational imbalance periodically cause devastation. Life-forms on the planet must learn how to channel those energies ... or die. Your role (few of you know that now, the end of your 'twentieth century', a new Shift — the Seventh — is due) is to exalt mind over matter. Now listen:

Your world — any world — provides earth from which intelligence sprouts and may ripen. But ripening can't come without realising the link between violent, bestial thought, word and deed, and violent, bestial consequences. To convert Shift-energy into flowering, the planetary life must first 'grow up'. This has been achieved on many worlds whose beings have evolved their lower natures so that, when the Shift comes, they're ready to play their part in the Great Work known to us as 'The-Knowing-of-All-by-Itself'.

But some worlds are recalcitrant. Your world is the most recalcitrant of all. Many of our best minds have not only been lost in the heat and passion of its gravitational turmoil, but actively perverted. Six times since our first intervention long ago (we bred Neanderthal to produce a new two-legs you call Cro Magnon) the Shift has returned with all of you still unready. After the sixth failure many of us wished to end the project and let you — as some of you might put it — 'go to hell'. But some thought you worth one more chance. So after the sixth Shift (do you recall Atlantis?) we sent a new mission. Soon it was corrupted like the others before it. So that for millennia now a war has been going on — one fought in many lands and times; spawning your civilisations, religions, philosophies. It's a war to see what the war's about, before it's too late to see anything. It's a war we Elohim fight to help you break free of Hidden World weight.

Why do we help? Because we must. We are bound by our own choice. If we fail to help, then we too will fall back into the traps of time, death, gravity, pain and selfishness — into evil. And so — this war sees many battles fought from the First Days to the Last of this Seventh Age.

It's because of one of these battles we come to you.

Diane, Sam your husband and Chrissa your daughter were born to it. So were you ... but you were the one left behind. You saw them vanish. You had to live on. We know your despair, Diane ... but you must fight it ... because they still live, and they may return ... but only if you can help.

Be ready, Diane. Be ready.

Then the Presence left her ... but when she awoke in the morning, to the grey cold light, Diane Joyce did not believe what she had dreamed ...

First there was Sam. Alias Shem the Fool. Seized into another age and placed, witless and naked, in a garden of delights where he spoke with the birds and beasts and knew nothing of men and women — especially not women.

Yet there came the time when She who'd seized him decided he must awake and begin the work for which She'd brought him back to this age.

And so his innocence ended . . .

'Her Fool's awake! That madman She snatched from the mists during the battle for the Whole Place! She returns with him now to the Whole Place! They say it took the death of a man and the gate of a woman to awaken him; they say now She'll drive back Azazel and his brood, for he awakes with the power of the Last Days! For that's where She sent him! The awful Last Days, when the earth rocks! She sent him there, and now – why look at me like that? Why doubt me? Everyone knows it's true – She's been seen with him, going to the Whole Place to give him what She has!'

The news spread quickly through the island. From the lands of the Lady Tiy it ran west, to the lodges of those who called themselves the Free Men, and further, to the bald wet mountains dominated by Azazel and his legions. Soon all knew She'd dispersed the clan which had guarded Her Fool during the sleep of his wits. They knew blood had been spilled. The Wild Women had killed a man, Hoel, who'd tried to kill the Fool for besting him in love. 'Fool himself!' Her Children whispered uneasily round their deep forest hearths. 'For this we invaded the isle and fought Azazel and died at the Whole Place? Who is this Fool? What does She want him for? Is he a halfling, born of An and El like Herself? Can he drive Azazel back and wake Her from Her cruelty? Or is he just a Fool we'll die for?'

Who knew? Azazel, who'd sworn to destroy the Lady and them all?

West of border battlefields where men died cursing, amid hills where snow lingered and the raven hovered, on a high ledge of the Panting Cliff mad old Azazel lay dreaming in a pool of ice-water (yet he groaned at the heat of it) and used Long Sight to spy secretly on Her. 'Oh Sisster Tiy!' he mumbled, 'I know your plan, and where you seized your Fool! Ah, and his beautiful little daughter – you're scared of her!'

Yet he was alarmed: amid his dreaming he sent orders to his armies: 'I WANT THE WHOLE PLACE AND THAT FOOL IN MY HANDS BEFORE THE MOON IS OLD!'

The news went south and east as well, crossing the Narrow Sea to the shores of the Endless Land beyond. And it was in a port looking over grey waters to the white-cliffed isle that Dion, a traveller, first heard of the Fool's awakening – and knew as soon as he heard of it that it was why he'd come so far to these Hyperborean lands.

He was a small dark man of early middle age, with curly black hair and a self-assured manner. He wore dusty sandals and a stained, hooded woollen cloak, and his bulky canvas pack stayed strapped to his back as he sat in the dark smoky corner of a dockside tavern. And as he listened to the dirty, grizzled seaman who told him the tale his lips curled slightly up and his deep blue eyes twinkled, as if to say: *A good tale, my friend – now tell me another!* Then the seaman – off the red-sailed ship with its cargo of tin now unloaded – scowled dangerously and burst out: 'Why look at me like that? Why doubt me? Everyone knows it's true – She's been seen with him, going to the Whole Place to give him what She has!'

'Easy now!' Dion smiled and lifted a hand. His fingers were long and delicate. 'Forgive me, but who is this Lady?' – though he knew very well.

The sailor's eyes widened.

'You haven't heard of … Her?'

'Her name would help,' said Dion, still smiling.

'We cannot speak Her name!' The man clutched at something – an amulet, perhaps – in a grubby leather pouch around his neck. 'She has many names, She's … She's … Sir, *surely* you know! She's one of the … '

'One of the Old Ones.' Dion nodded. 'But *which* one?'

The sailor shot him a hard look. 'Why do you ask? Who are you?'

'I've never been to these parts before.' Dion shrugged. 'It's the curiosity of a nobody, nothing else. But tell me: is she beautiful?'

'Who can say? Her face is masked, so as not to blind us.'

'How kind of her!' Dion no longer smiled. 'But – *is* she kind?'

'Kind?' The man blenched, looked down. 'Yes, yes, She is … kind.'

'I understand you perfectly,' said Dion gravely. He nodded over the grey seas towards the distant white cliffs of the island to the north. 'And from what you tell me, she has you hard at war against – what's his name? Azazel, did you say? And you said – correct me if I'm wrong – "*Now She'll drive back Azazel and his brood.*" Does this mean that her powers and forces have proved inferior to his … thus far?'

The sailor raised his wooden mug and drank violently, not stopping until the mug was empty. With an ugly backwards glance at the stranger he went for more. When he returned he slammed the mug down on the rough table so that the brew foamed over and dripped to the earth floor.

'Now listen, whoever you are! It's plain you're to be pitied; you know nothing about Her or you'd never dare to speak as you do, so I'm giving you the benefit of the doubt. Listen! These are Her powers! First, She can both hear and see us as we sit here now – so take care!' And as Dion eyed him with interest the man bit his lip and clutched his amulet again, then went on in a lowered voice. 'Listen! Her powers are many! She can raise the dead and transform Herself into bird or beast – or, if She wishes it, transform any man who displeases Her into a . . . snake, or a . . . '

'An ass?' Dion suggested helpfully.

'The ass? The ass is loathsome to Her.' Again the man drank hard. 'Now listen before you doom yourself! This lady can pull down the skies and make the earth shake. She has the Long Life. She has the power of the Gates and knows the future. Indeed, it's said that Her Fool . . . '

'The one who's been awakened?'

'Yes! It's said that long ago She sent him to . . . '

'The Last Days. So you said,' agreed Dion, his blue eyes growing so brilliant that the sailor could not meet them. 'Yet isn't it odd that, with all these powers, she should have to contest any war at all? This Azazel must be as powerful, in his own way.' And he nodded, his gaze seeming to retreat inward, and when he spoke next it was as if he spoke to himself. 'I think,' he said, 'I must meet this Lady and her . . . Fool.' He looked up. 'You sail again today? You will give me passage?'

The sailor grinned as he finished his drink. He eyed the stranger up and down, his gaze lingering on shabby clothing and dusty feet.

'And how will you pay for your passage . . . My Lord?'

'Pay?' Dion laughed with such easy, spontaneous joy that every head in the place turned. He untied his pack and from it withdrew a finely carved seven-stringed lyre. 'This is how I'll pay. Now, *you* listen!'

Then, smiling remotely, Dion began to play . . .

Part One

Trial of Darkness

I was told that the Chinese said they would bury me by the Western Lake and build a shrine to my memory. I have some slight regret that this did not happen, as I might have become a god, which would have been very *chic* for an atheist.

The Autobiography of Bertrand Russell, Vol. II: 1914–1944, Ch. 3

1.
Zoe and Boann

'PREPARE THE WOMB-HALL FOR A SOWING TONIGHT.'

The voice rang in Zoe like a bell. With a start she awoke, dry mouthed and nervous, in the darkness of her subterranean cell in the Whole Place. Daily for fourteen years since the age of seven she'd attended the Lady; she was a woman now … *but I still fear Her*, she knew, grimacing as she rose to light the lamp. *Why do I feel I've sinned every time She catches me asleep? I'm not a guilty child or a slave any more. I have needs too!*

These were unguarded thoughts; a confusion of awakening over which Zoe still had little control. They were dangerous thoughts too. She knew it.

Quickly she splashed her face from a bowl in the corner, rubbed her teeth with a hazel twig to draw away the staleness of night, brushed her long black hair, and took up a bronze clasp which, shaped as a figurine, showed the Lady bare-breasted, a flail in Her right hand, an ear of corn in Her left. 'I hear you,' Zoe told Her urgently. 'It will be done.' Then, her severe face softened by anxiety, she drew on a black unbelted robe, bound her hair in a topknot, fixed it with the clasp, blew out the lamp and left her cell in the dark but restless heart of the Whole Place.

The passage outside was empty. Rough and black, it writhed through the rock like a frozen serpent from entry to depths of the inner system. For a moment she listened. The system carried sound so well that she'd hear any whispering fifty yards away with perfect but eerie clarity – this was part of the design: to impress supplicants with the oracle's pedigree as a Gate to the Other Worlds. Zoe knew all that ... and though now she heard nothing, still she seemed to hear the Lady's voice. '*It's not enough,*' She'd told Zoe bluntly, '*for people to know that here the dragons war! They may know it, but they have to see it before they believe it. Child, listen! The spirit is not visible in the world. To be seen it demands a cloak to show its outline in acts and effects. In this temple we offer a drama of acts and effects to those who come to us. By arresting images we help them to understand. And they must understand! Soon! Or Azazel conquers all!*'

Zoe shivered again. Such odd advice! *She sounded sad; I could have sworn She was ... scared?*

This thought too she crushed. With a frown that embraced her entire form, like a dark wing she swept up the silent curve, her only company the soft echo of her feet as she followed by feel the billowing, generations-smoothed rock floor. She came to Third Arch, after which smoky torches, sconced at intervals on the gleaming featureless wall, lit the way with lurid flickerings of red on black. She passed the heavy wooden doors of the Painted Room (the torch outside it unlit: no supplicant locked there alone with the horrors last night) and the doors entering to the Waters of Forgetting and the Waters of Memory; underpassed the heavy wood carvings of Second Arch, ascended a final stretch, and through First Arch emerged into the temple's outer precincts at the rocky, wooded base of the Whole Place.

At last the soft summer daylight received her.

Blinking, she eyed the courtyard. Not a soul in sight. 'Boann!' she muttered, and over the sandy court she strode past the black double cube of the Divining Stone to the major-domo's untidy office. Tally-sticks and rods for measure were piled in heaps, but Boann wasn't there. 'Never when you need her!' said Zoe crossly, and turned past the well and outer precinct dormitories to the kitchens by the timber palisades of the outer wall.

'Where's Boann?' she cried fiercely at a kitchen-boy lazily stoking the fires. The child, a mute, nearly jumped out of his skin. Shaking his head he shrugged furiously. Zoe glared at him. 'Just because She's away people think they can laze!' she snapped, ignoring how the previous afternoon she herself had slipped into the woods for an hour with Doney, helping him to forget the war's most recent pain. Scowling, she whirled away and returned to First Arch – a jagged, narrow vertical slash in the rock – and at the mouth to the inner domains she ran straight into Boann, emerging.

Boann gasped and recoiled. Zoe did not. The major-domo, a raw-boned grey-haired woman with heavy jowls, quickly folded her arms and hooded her eyes. Zoe smiled. *You have no talent and will always be a clerk!* said Zoe's smile, and Boann's glinting eye said she knew and resented it.

'I've been looking for you,' Zoe said steadily, 'The Lady ...'

'So you're looking for me! That's rich!' Boann laughed and stood firm, arms folded tighter. 'And what do you think I've been doing?'

'Poking your nose where you shouldn't!' Zoe refused to drop her gaze, yet she felt uneasy. 'You're not supposed to enter the inner precinct!'

'I was looking for you ... with a message from Our Lady,' Boann explained in a gently venomous voice. 'She spoke to me. In my dream.'

'Oh.' Zoe, crestfallen, did not show it. *What's She up to, talking to this fat lump?* 'Well. Yes. Likewise. We're to prepare the Womb hall.'

'You mean *you* are!' Boann's grin said: *Rather you than me!* 'I have my own instructions. From Her. She'll be here at sunset. With the Fool.'

'Quite,' Zoe agreed reluctantly, and for a moment wanted to burst out with: *But what's going on? What IS all this? Where will it lead us?* And she saw the same need in Boann's eyes ... but the moment passed with nothing said. 'Well. So long as we each know what we're doing, I suppose ...'

'Child, you're not the only one She speaks to!' Boann's angry grin grew broader. 'By the way ... I hear Doney got hurt. A spear in the thigh, isn't it? Nothing ... *serious*, I hope?'

'You sad person!' whispered Zoe, and swept into the inner precincts, grey eyes blazing. *You wait, Boann! You wait!*

But duty came first. *The Womb hall!* Through First Arch Zoe returned to her inner world as her angry sense of violation began to fade; through Second Arch, past the Painted Room and the Waters of Forgetting and Memory she went, breathing more calmly as the depths took effect; through Third Arch into darkness. She took a torch and continued past her cell. The passage narrowed, sloping steeply down to Fourth Arch by way of a flight of uneven steps. The deeper she went the more her anger at Boann was replaced by the austere calm of duty ... and by apprehension. *The Lady here tonight with Her Fool? I've got a lot to do!* And her thoughts grew nervous. On she went past forks in this deeper darkness until, with torch held high, she wriggled through Fifth Arch, the Cervix, and dropped to the unseen floor below. There was no way back up for those who did not know the Quiet Door. On she went, preoccupied with details of oil, incense, food and offerings to be prepared. Yet anxiety would not let her be.

Our Lady's changed since the Fool came, she thought. *She's so angry so often; sometimes it's almost as if She forgets Herself. As if She hates Herself for depending on this Fool to do something She can't.*

Zoe shivered, not only because of the dank wind that whispered up from the river in the depths below to sigh against her legs. For a moment she stopped, staring into the blackness, lips parted, eyes wide.

Five years ago! But still so sharp she saw that misty violent day atop the Whole Place, her ears assailed by shrieks, her sight by the bloody lances of light piercing the swirling fog. Azazel and his ugly brood! She hissed to see the Lady pinned down by the hairless blue giant – old Azazel himself. *And he'd have had Her,* Zoe knew as she dismissed the vision. *And we'd have been dead or worse, sucked into him! But the idiot sprang from nowhere, out of the fog, out of the abyss between the worlds, witless and wailing! And Azazel was amazed and let Her throw him off! The Fool won it for us! Now the Beast marches on us as we did on him ... but the Fool has his wits back, and the Lady wants the Womb-hall prepared for tonight ...*

So Zoe shivered as she came down to the River of the Dead, down to a series of steps that, carved from the dripping black rock, ended in Sixth Arch and a landing stage. Stooping, for the jagged roof was low, she groped in her pouch for the coin and in a low voice she called out:

'Ferryman! Ferryman! It is I, Zoe, the Servant of the Lady!'

The muffled sound of oars approached out of the darkness. Not for the first time Zoe reflected: *I would not want to come here without the Lady's protection. I would not want to be a man in this place ...*

And when the shadowy craft came, the Lady's servant embarked and went on over the River of the Dead, and on the far side she went deeper, deeper and deeper still, until at last she came to the Womb-hall ...

Throughout that damp summer day preparations for the Lady's return continued. Late in the afternoon, with cloud drifting in from the west, Boann arduously climbed the narrow path that spiralled up the heights of the Whole Place. When at last she reached the top she was red faced and blowing, acutely aware that neither her weight nor her age had diminished. But it was the first time she'd ever been up on her own – it was something she'd promised herself – and the view from the high, bare, rocky summit was such that it almost made up for her fury at Zoe. In fact she felt oddly gleeful. *Poor Zoe! Under my feet now, fumbling beyond the darkest of the Arches! Serves you right! Let the eagle fly and the worm crawl, I say!*

The Whole Place was a single crag, conical, deeply fissured, volcanic in origin, not typical of the gently swelling rise and fall of the wooded lands about. To north and east low forested ridges rolled far to horizon haze; on clear days (but not today) the sea could be seen to the south; to the west – like tumbled limbs of giants asleep – rose mountains where even now armies were fighting and dying. With a grim eye Boann fancied she saw blood in the cloud above those distant, dome-like hills ... then with a grunt shrugged it off. 'Just the sun painting the air,' she muttered, turning to what lay below. Squinting, she made out the ant-like figures of people gathering in the temple's outer precincts and beyond the Gardens along the Serpent-Way from the east. But beyond that – Boann frowned, her feet and eyes hurting as she strove to make out what she'd been told was there ... that subtle sculpting of the land which, radiating from the Whole Place for miles to every point, the Lady had undertaken long ago.

Why can't I see it? she wondered painfully. *I know it's there – She did it long ago, before the Mad One drove Her out; before She found us in that foreign land; before She made an army of us and brought us back here.*

But Boann knew why she missed the meaning, let alone the whole design, of what lay all about. Stare as she might, her prosaic outer precinct eyes would never resolve the varied landscape elements of the view into the high whole picture which some – *like Zoe!* – apparently saw so easily. It upset her to know it yet still not see it, how the land around the Whole Place formed a vast glyph centred on this peak and its depths below. To create it, rivers had been diverted, earth-walls laid, snaky roads set out, groves planted, stone circles and menhirs erected at crucial points of the system. Still she could only see practical things as she cast her critical eye about. *Are the people in order along that flank? Those fields look ragged!* Not even from this height could she discern the inner pattern of pentagram and hexagram united within the squared circle, no more than she could make out the thirteen birds and beasts of the zodiac written in the land round the perimeter of that circle. She knew these occult forms were there, defined by hedge and tump, river and road and grove; she knew they helped to focus and increase the power spiralling between earth and heaven through the Whole Place and the Gate which had brought the Fool ... but for the life of her she could not see it or even feel it! *I lack insight*, she had to admit. *I'm a stolid lump! To me a river's a river, a road is a road! I know the Gate's here, I stand in it – but to me it's just bare rock.* And she clenched her teeth, taken by her hatred for that impudent, arrogant child – *Zoe!* 'Why should she have the Sight that I lack?' she cried out aloud, tears in her eyes. Then, staring at the hard rock between her feet, she relaxed and even smiled. 'But why should I want it?' she murmured in sudden complacent relief. 'That poor child! Her gift takes her away from the sun. Today she's deep down in the Womb-hall ...' – she shuddered at the thought – '... and she'll pay if her preparations are imprecise. All I have to do is organise people efficiently and keep the tally on things ... and I thank the Lady for that!'

Far below a horn blew a prearranged signal. She started; she looked east ... and saw colour and movement on the Serpent-Way, winding through the forest. *It's Her! Are the people in place? Yes, it looks all right!* But for just a moment before she left the summit of the Whole Place she frowned again at the landscape. No. Prosaic. She saw only fields, gardens, and the moving shadow of approaching rain, turning sparkling green to a sombre dullness. With a shudder she looked west. The mountains were masked ... but through the cloud scarlet beams splayed down like bloody amputated fingers.

So Boann hurried back down to the hustle and bustle where juniors swept roads, laid tables, erected awnings and argued about their place in the ranks of those privileged to stand in the outer precincts and greet their Lady – their Red Lady of Battle, their Green Lady of Healing, their Great White Sow, their Lady of the Nine Heights – now returning home with Her newly awakened Fool, Her mystery-man from the Last Days ...

Yet a soft and misty drizzle began to fall as Boann reached the ground and the horns blew loud, announcing the Lady's approach. Eyes met anxious eyes, and many looked west, not east. The horns sounded not triumphant at all, but filled with melancholy foreboding as the rain stiffened and cloud from the west thickened over the Whole Place ...

2.
The Half-Free

Amid those storm-flayed western hills Deru the half-free crouched behind a rock high up a slope, sniffing at the smell – woodsmoke? – that blew up from the horror taking place at the ford in the rain-drenched valley below.

Gawky in drab green cloak and cap, Deru was untypical of those calling themselves Free Men. Tall and thin with untidy straw-coloured hair, his face, with lantern jaw and beaky nose, was saved from sourness by laughter lines around his wide-set, mismatched eyes – one sober grey, the other a startling green. But there was no laughter in him now; his face was white with shock, and his exhaustion was forgotten, though he'd travelled hard since leaving the Lodge of the Nine Doors to return to the Lady's army. It was only two days since he'd deserted his post as a guide to report to the Council. Now he was back, persuaded by Taishi, but too late, and now as the pungent smell drifted up from the carnage below a huge fear seized him.

This must be the start of it, he thought dismally, recalling the uproar last night in the underground lodge. For the Elders, responding to news of the Fool's awakening, had chewed the Toad and flown to the subtle world, and on return had immediately convened a general council.

It was Taishi the Seer, craggy face stark in torchlight, who'd spoken.

'We are the Free Men who remember the Elohim who brought

us knowledge and the Long Life so long ago,' he'd declared. 'Now! What do we see in the subtle world tonight? We see that the armies of Tiy and Azazel gather for final battle! We see that this Fool's awakening is no tiny pebble tossed in a pool, but a mighty rock, creating waves that may wash us all away ... and not only in this age! These waves wash all the way to Last Days. We must choose sides in the war approaching. We cannot sit here in our raths and hide from Azazel! We must resist him, and fight for this Fool, and for Tiy's slaves, lest their fate becomes our fate too!'

Discussion had followed the uproar. Decisions had been taken. Taishi had prepared those known as the Singers for a mission which he would lead. And then had persuaded Deru to return to the Lady's army and carry on his work as a spy. 'We wouldn't ask if it weren't a crisis,' the Elder had said. Now, remembering this, Deru laughed wildly, tipping his cap as if it were Taishi and not something far worse he saw below him. 'I know I'm just a half-free!' he cried angrily into the rain. 'Clearly my place is among these *slaves*, and not among *cowards*, which is what they call you!'

Of course he'd said none of that to Taishi. Instead, he'd bowed submissively then set out again, pausing only to see his mother, Mogan.

'It's all my fault!' she'd wailed, as usual. 'If I hadn't let that dirty slave have his way with me you'd not have been born half-free!'

'That's true, mother. But here I am.'

'Yes, my son. But the girls won't look at you! And you despise us! It's your father's blood! Those poor beasts!' She'd shot him a dramatic, tragic look. 'They only live fifty years or so, they have little to lose. We do! The Long Life's too valuable to throw away! We who remember the El and An ...' – she'd started to weep – 'know it, but ... you, my son, you – Oh how I've paid for the idiocy that bore you into this sad Hidden World! It breaks my heart to see you going off again. Can't you settle down? Must you risk the Long Life just because Taishi knows how to get you to do dirty work nobody else will do? Guiding the slaves of the Watchers? Have you no pride? As for Taishi, he must be mad! Why anger Azazel by opposing him? Is Tiy any better? Do you want us all to die like ... like slaves?'

'Mother,' he'd said, 'you can call it dirty work, but Long Life is long misery if we don't see sense. The Elohim abandoned us. Now we have to deal with it by ourselves.' And he'd smiled, not too kindly. 'Fool yourself if you must – I'll follow the nature I inherited.'

Now, lurking in the rain as the pungent smell strengthened, Deru gaped at the slaughter of one set of slaves by another, and raged at his half-free nature, for in the agony below was no sense, only horror. The thickly wooded spot where he hid was cut by steep bramble-choked gullies which ran down to the river-ford, this side of which waited the ranks of Azazel's army – watching motionless. At first Deru couldn't understand it. Not so much as an arrow was being shot. But on the far bank, massacre was taking place. Through the wind and rain Deru heard the men of the Eagle Regiment screaming; he saw them stagger, break ranks, and fall in their hundreds without anyone laying a finger on them! There in the mud they writhed, clutching their skulls, kicking their legs in ever-more frantic convulsion until – through the mist he couldn't be sure he was seeing straight – their brains exploded and they died. But not all of them fell rightaway. Large groups of insanely roaring men were cutting each other to pieces without any self-defence as others, wailing, hurled themselves into the river and were quickly swept away by the swollen brown waters, In a few minutes a thousand men – the cream of the army; men Deru had led to this place only days earlier – were reduced to less than a hundred, with every man for himself, only a few squads maintaining any sort of order as they pelted away from the slaughter, slipping through birchwood and sliding through bog, mad eyes reflecting the horror they fled. Many were naked, most had lost their weapons ... almost all had lost their minds.

Amid all this the opposing army did not even cross the ford.

In their ranks and on their horses they stood or sat and waited, and from his height through the grey pall of rain Deru rubbed stinging eyes and wept to see how they laughed and joked as the Regiment massacred itself. *What is it?* he cried to himself, bending under a suicidal despair. *What have they done? What can I do now? I should kill myself!* For an urge to hurl himself off the rocky slope had seized him with sudden overpowering force. He stood up, resolved to die ... then checked, frowned, sniffed, wiped his streaming eyes ... and almost too late realised: *Not wood-smoke, no, but ...*

It came drifting slowly up from the charnel house like a fog of blood: the subtly foul invitation which had blown into the brains of those now dead. *Don't you want to die? How sweet to die! Die now, and never fear again!* It was a clammy whisper, subliminally ingratiating ... and even as he knew it and with a convulsive shudder rejected it, Deru knew that only the least hint or eddy of it had accidentally reached him on the wind.

An old magic newly applied, he thought as the suicidal urge lessened and then, at last, departed. But it left him deeply depressed as with great difficulty he turned his gaze on the backward ranks of Azazel's army, and made himself look …

He saw seven giant shapes in a circle round some contraption.

Azazel's sons! He hissed at those dim monstrous shapes in the rain. They looked human at this distance, but …

'You foulness!' he spat, throwing two crooked fingers to his head to make the horns that ward off evil. 'It was always a dirty fight! You used the light-lances, you shifted shape and sacrificed men by the thousand, you proved you are truly slaves … but this … this …'

And he realised dully: *It's not the horror of death. It's worse. What do I do? If I go back now they'll do me for desertion. They might even think I set it up. Unless* … And through the rain he stared as the survivors of the Eagle Regiment fled away over the war-ruined land, across pastures empty of sheep or cattle, trampling fields which would see no harvest for years to come. *Maybe the rain's merciful*, Deru told himself as he stood with a sigh. *It hides our shame from heaven!*

So, with no clear idea what else to do or where to go, the half-free man went to share the misfortune of slaves. With fatal lack of prudence he followed them. Still muttering in shock he slid down a gully away from the enemy, waded the river (struggling chest-deep, but in his distress he hardly knew it), and followed four sodden men in flight through dripping green woodland and up thorny pasture. Maybe he was as dazed as they, for when in exhaustion they fell into the shelter of an overhanging rock he did not notice or pause, but came blundering among them. Before he knew it, they had him down on his back with a knife at his throat, their teeth bared and their eyes mad above him. They wore scarred black leather jerkins and breeches, but they'd lost their boots and thrown away their useless shields and swords. A hand snatched the cap from his head.

'What's this?' hissed a broken-toothed face. 'Meat for supper?'

'Naw!' jeered another, pinching Deru's ribs. 'Too stringy.'

'Looks like one of those stuck-up Free Men bastards!' spat a third.

'Izzat a joke?' The first drew blood with his knife. 'Too short. Too ugly. Too stupid looking. If he's a bleedin' Free Man I'm Our Lady.'

Oh Shining Ones! Deru found himself praying. *I don't want to live forever but I wouldn't mind a few more years! Give me back my tongue!*

But they were about to cut his throat on a general principle when their sergeant, a haggard man with exhausted eyes, frowned in sudden recognition. Deru tried to smile, but the blade at his windpipe kept him quiet.

'I've seen 'im,' said the bloodstained sergeant with remote interest, 'in the camp. Native guide. Halfer. Brought us to the ford, he did.'

'Guide? Halfer spy, more like!' spat the first man, and drew a second line of blood across Deru's throat. Mad eyes bored into Deru's mismatched pair. 'Led us into it! Led us straight into that ... into that ...'

But he couldn't say it, he couldn't speak of the horror, and the hand that held the knife trembled more fiercely than before, as if he might stab himself before Deru, who writhed and with his eyes implored the sergeant. 'Ga ... ga ... ga!' he spluttered. One of the men laughed without humour, but the sergeant sighed and began to cry. 'Would I be here if I'd betrayed you?' Deru croaked, and the sergeant shrugged. 'Cut his throat, boys,' he sobbed. 'Cut the bastard's throat!'

'The Lady!' Deru croaked. 'Her Fool's awake! He'll lead you to victory against those monsters. You'll revenge your comrades. But you must let me live because I alone know how to ...'

The man with the knife trembled in the rain.

'Her and 'Er bloody Fool! It's because of them we're dead!' His face twisted, he raised the knife and was about to plunge it into Deru's throat when they were attacked by three angry knights of Azazel's cavalry.

This body of men regarded themselves as an elite, but as night fell they were out in the rain and furious. No proper fighting all afternoon, and then Bortibel's orders to go and 'mop up' survivors! 'Mop up?' Sauriel their leader had bellowed in his older brother's purpling face. 'Are you mad? Listen, Snotnose, so the Old Man put you in charge today, but don't push the cavalry around! An elite force does not, as you put it, *mop up!* Get me?' Bortibel won the argument (after all, he had won the battle), but the cavalry took their time crossing the ford and, once over it, ignored the writhing charnel heaps. Instead they split into small bands to ride down survivors. These three were such a band; already they'd cut down a dozen mad stragglers, and now, spotting the men under the rock, they came in at a confident canter, drawing bloody swords and slapping them ringingly against their metal-studded leathers. They were short and swarthy, dark of hair and eye; they rode up through the mists shouting jokes and insults. They expected no trouble. Neither did the four about to die. Forgetting Deru, they leapt sluggishly to their feet and gaped at their fate. *Now's my chance!* Deru realised. *The mist!* Quickly he got up behind them. But instead of running or snatching his own short blade from his belt, he poised himself on his left leg, shut his right eye, and flung out his left arm, finger extended, at the oncoming horsemen, pointing at each in turn as in a high-pitched singsong voice he delivered the *fith-fath* spell:

'Fath-Fith! Fith-Fath!
Will I put on thee
Fith-Fath! Fath-Fith!
A fog-mantle from the sea!
From Boar, from Sow,
From Bull, from Cow,
From Cock, from Hen,
And from One to Ten
A magic cloud I put on thee!
Fith-Fath! Fath-Fith!
These curses from my rath!
Fath-Fith! Fith-Fath!'

The results were extraordinary. Deru began his chant as the three horsemen rode in with raised swords; in despair the four soldiers ran at them as the half-free hurled his finger at each in turn. And he hit them with confusion. Each in turn reined in and wheeled round, facing the others with perplexed, frightened looks, blinking and peering about in the swirling wet mists. For the men they meant to kill had completely vanished. A white veil had descended on their eyes. 'What's this?' one shouted hoarsely as Deru cried the curse – and a second later the sergeant was up behind him, cutting his throat with a sobbing cry. His men took heart from this: within a minute the other two had been hauled off their horses and hacked messily to death.

Deru, exhausted, shut his mouth. When the killing was done and they'd stopped whooping, the soldiers turned to him as he lowered his arm and leg, and opened his right eye. For a time, getting back their breath, they just gaped, until one muttered in disbelief, 'That was bleedin' Free Men magic!'

'So?' Deru said, overcoming his weariness and shock that the spell had actually worked. 'You see? I didn't betray you! So my mother's Free, but my father was one of you. I serve the Lady's army,' he went on fiercely, 'because I don't love the Free Men! Why should I? I'm not a coward! I'd rather take my chances with *real* men – like you!'

The sergeant sighed and scratched his bloody, tear-stained cheeks.

'You saved our bacon,' he admitted. 'No doubting that.' He eyed the other three. 'What d'you say, boys?'

'I'll lead you safe back to base,' Deru insisted. 'You won't do it without me. I know the ways that Azazel's creatures can't bear to walk.'

The four muttered together and decided they had nothing to lose.

'Okay,' agreed the sergeant, 'but no tricks!'

So Deru, his back tingling in fear of a knife, led them into the night along a slope and down a gully. Curses came from a thicket ahead; they froze – but it was only three more poor demented devils like themselves, wilder with fear than rage. Deru crept forward, calling out soothingly until the men emerged, shaking. In this way twenty men were found and calmed enough to fall, not quietly, in line. Their brains were still on fire. 'Get them to gag each other!' Deru begged the sergeant, but the man began weeping again. Yet the rain drowned the worst of it, and soon Deru realised that they were alone in the night: the enemy had retired to feast.

For hours through the storm he led them, head angled as he loped easily through deep woods and along steep paths. But he sensed he'd made a big mistake. *What happens when we get there?* There were shouts at his pace; several times men turned on each other, and two men deliberately walked over cliffs. Yet late that night the survivors safely reached the camp.

Up a final smooth slope they trudged through the rain to the palisades around the main gate. Torches flared; a challenge was issued. The sergeant stepped up, identified himself, and was called in alone to report. 'I'll do my best for you,' he told Deru gruffly. 'Look after him, boys.'

Soon all, including Deru, were admitted. Inside was chaos. The camp was in ferment with incoherent rumour of the disaster. Reserves had been sent forward, but nobody knew what to do about the death-wish weapon, so it was not openly mentioned. Riders had left for the Whole Place in hopes the Lady might know what to do, but fear was thick, and the return of these ragged survivors did little for morale. In the canteen Deru got a bowl of broth and many hard looks; nobody talked to him until an hour later he was called before a field tribunal. The faint hope he brought into the lamplit tent soon vanished: he was charged and condemned on the spot as a deserter and spy, and told he'd die at dawn. The officer commanding wore a filthy bearskin, had melancholy eyes, and shrugged at Deru's protests.

'It might as well be you as anyone,' he said wearily.

'What do you mean?' Deru was outraged. 'I saved the lives of twenty of your best men! And the enemy weapon, I know what it ...'

'Quiet! You used Free magic. Plus you're a spy and a deserter.'

'I am innocent of those charges!' Deru roared. 'Listen, I ...'

'Aren't we all?' asked the officer. 'At least you'll be out of this lousy mess. Be thankful. A short life's better. Right. Next one.'

Deru shrugged miserably ... and then, oddly, found himself smiling.

'How are you going to do it?' he heard himself ask.

'Do what?' The officer, who had dismissed him, looked annoyed.

'Kill me.' He heard himself say it. 'How will you kill me?'

The officer leaned back and yawned with frustration.

'Do you really need to know?'

'It involves me,' said Deru with a wild laugh.

'Oh. Ants and honey if the weather's good. Impalement, if it rains.' Embarrassed, he tried to smile. 'Not my policy. I'd make it quick, but the men need to get their minds off what they've been through. Understand, it's not personal, but we must keep morale up.'

Deru felt confused. 'Killing me keeps their morale up?'

'You're a half-free,' said the officer. 'That's enough.'

'You're a poor stupid slave,' cried Deru. 'I keep trying to tell you, Her Fool's awake, and I know how the weapon they used can be ...'

'I earn my pay!' shouted the officer, slapping down his hands on the table, 'and that's what I'm paid to do! Now stop bothering me!'

Deru managed to grin as they dragged him out. He shouted and roared that he knew about the new weapon but they gagged and bound him, then threw him into a waterlogged trench along with others sharing his good luck. He didn't sleep at all that long night ... and at dawn it was still raining ...

3.
Tiy's Fear

Along a curving misty-wet avenue flanked by heavy oaks and standing stones the Lady Tiy came out of the wild wood on a palanquin carried by four sweating porters. Her people lined the route She took. Their heads were bowed. Many were on their knees. Only a few dared look at Her where She sat, Her great height draped from head to toe in the Gown-of-the-Feathers-of-many-bright-Birds; Her blinding face hidden by the golden mask She wore.

But the Fool who shambled behind they eyed freely ... resentfully ...

Tiy betrayed no doubt as She neared the Gardens. Yet the rain from the west was so grey; trees loomed out of the mist along the Serpent-Way like the ghosts of dead warriors, and She felt the nervous prickling that always meant bad news. Again into the depths of the emerald ring She wore on Her left hand She looked and tried to find Her army ... but the depths were cloudy, revealing nothing. It depressed and frightened Her.

As for Shem, shuffling behind Her, his eyes boring into her back, his thin dark face twisted in mockery ... again the fear swept Her.

Why is he angry with me? She wondered. *I'm cruel? Did I trick him? How? What did I do? Is it that girl Ailma I used to wake him up? But I did her no harm; she'll suffer no more than any other woman! Then, because of Hoel? But Hoel asked for it! If he'd killed Shem ...*

'SAMJOYCE!' the fool suddenly cried in a raucous voice. 'My name's Samjoyce, folks! Step right up and talk to the Last Days freak!

Why, he knows *nobody* else knows! So step up and talk to the Fool!'

He returned to morose silence. Of course nobody understood his strange Fool's tongue ... but it made Her furious.

Why must he use that name? She asked fiercely. *What's wrong with SHEM? Why is he like this? It's his daughter! If that meddling child and her Weak Ones attack again before he seeds Me I swear I'll ...*

Abruptly she caught Herself. *What's wrong with Me? Has Azazel found a new chink to exploit? CALM DOWN, Tiy, or You'll never find and make the elixir tonight. Then it's all lost! Now RELAX!*

Yet still She wanted to turn and scream at him.

No! She clenched Her fists. *He'll mock! I'll be shown up!*

Instead She studied Her people. *My Children! Look at you!* She told them silently, fondly anxious, eyeing their ruddy broad faces, their bodies spared all famine, their well-made clothing of linen and wool. *Boann places you so fussily along the way! You're so fine and healthy! Yes, so you're more varied than when I began you ... but that's good!*

For by no means were they all from Her pool now. Once She'd bred a specific type; tall and broad, the blood of life in them. Now some were fair – Halfers. Some were very dark and heavy with dreaming eyes. But others were scrawny and thin, prey to diseases of lung and chest. This last type worried Her. Many of them combined wise hands with a capacity for abstract thought. *Like Hoel,* She thought ... and then, catching the bold eyes of a man who dared to stare at Her, She forgot Herself. 'I know there are man-cults among you!' She cried at him. 'Well and good! – but *think* on what happened to Hoel, as *thinking* is what you new men like to do!'

The crowd rippled in amazement. The Fool laughed. It cut Her to the quick. *The bray of an ass!* She thought – and Azazel reared in Her mind the moment She thought it. '*Sweet sissster!*' brayed the Beast, leering at her so that She gasped and swayed violently. '*So glad you care, but I can't stay! I'm busy kicking your army! I'll visit you soon!*'

And as Her weight shifted one of the porters slipped.

The palanquin began to plunge to the wet grass of the avenue. There was a vast sigh, a frozen amount of public horror. Then with a jerk the falling corner was stopped and borne up on the level again. She looked down, the feathers of Her robe fluttering with Her violent breathing – and the Fool, pole safe on his shoulder, gave Her a wink and a nod.

'Worked in the trade, M'Lady!' he brayed through the rain. 'Gaffer's mate! Know what I mean?' and with a cheery wave at the crowd he passed the weight back to the porter. But three soldiers from the guard behind stopped him. One took the pole; the other two dragged away the disgraced wretch, who went limp as if unconscious, feet trailing.

'What ...?' The Fool turned loudly on Her. 'Hey! Going to let those gorillas do him over? One slip and he's dead? Jeeesus!'

'Be silent, Fool,' She said waving away men about to grab him too. 'To shout at Me is ...' She breathed deep – 'blasphemy!'

'Okay.' He shrugged. 'Just trying to help.'

Under Her mask She shut Her eyes. *No, Tiy!* She told Herself. *It's not an omen. Don't let Azazel upset You. Be calm!* And again She studied Her Children as She approached the Gardens. Ahead, flowersingers waited at the high-hedged Rose Arch – girls, greybeards, boys and old crones whose rheumy eyes held knowledge that She of the Long Life feared to know for Herself. Her golden mask smiled as they threw their flowers, sang welcomes, cheered. But their cheers were half-hearted, their eyes were veiled ... and as soon as She was past She knew how they looked up and glared at the Fool as he shambled along, picking his nose, pulling faces at Her back.

So distress still iced Her as She entered the Gardens under the arch of climbing rose. Like a thorn in the heart She felt the doubt and resentful fear in Her Children. Their whole attitude spoke of fear – of Azazel, of Her, of everything. *Poor stupids!* She thought. *You were starving when I found you again, you didn't know Me, you'd have stayed and died in that desert if I'd let you. Now you forget again. What can Lullu remember? You die so fast and young! How can I remember all your generations? How can one live long and remember in this world?* At this her heart hammered painfully; She thought: *I hate this world! It just gets thicker! I'm caged deeper the longer I live; My memory goes so fast now that I can't ...*

But again it escaped Her: She cursed silently. *Fear's eating Me away! I won't recover what the Elohim stole if I shake like ... like a frightened Lullu virgin!* And with a shock She realised: *This is their life! The poison cloak of fear: they're never without it! No wonder they're so slow!*

The crowd was left behind. Yet as she entered the Gardens She'd planted so long ago She felt weary. 'To the Emerald Bower,' She said, glancing into the ring ... but its depths were still cloudy as they came to the heart of the Gardens past mulberry bushes and flowering hawthorn, past willow and alder fringing lily-rich pools where trout slid through thick shadows ... and so to the Emerald Bower where, hidden at last from public view amid the wet greenery and vast dripping ferns, She gave way to sentiment. *The raindrops on those leaves! How the path curves past these beds ... !* Wetness ran down Her cheek; She brought Her hand to Her masked mouth and in bewilderment wondered: *What's happening to Me? I designed every twist and turn in these gardens; I planted every shrub and flower – but now I forget why I did it; I forget the meanings and weep like a Lullu!* Yet a spasm of hope had Her turning abruptly to Her Fool. *Just a few more hours!* She thought. *You'll drink elixir and seed Me, you'll not resist Me, you'll fire Me with the knowledge I need – then you'll persuade Azazel to ...*

But he grinned contempt and gestured back at Her Children; his thin lips twisted as he strode up alongside. 'Well, My Lady!' he muttered, torn between mockery and fear. 'They don't exactly love You, eh?'

She stiffened. His grin was fixed, the scars of Owl on his left cheek white against his sunburned face.

'Maybe I'm not Your bloke,' he went on. 'Maybe they'll pick up on it. Maybe they don't like what You did to Hoel and Ailma.'

'Fool!' She declared, but still he grinned as he scratched his shock of greying black hair. She looked into his eyes and saw a dancing confusion – an angry laughing wet-eyed rebellion. *Are you really the son of Shemyaza who served me before?* She wondered. *We agreed how to send you, so why this dreadful hate you bring back with you?* She meant to wither him, but heard Herself add placatingly: 'Times change. I must do things I don't like.' Behind Her mask She tried to smile. 'Soon you'll taste elixir!'

'Sounds great,' he said sarcastically. 'Do I get a choice?'

Why provoke Me? Her eyes asked ... and again they became wet and overflowed, and this time he must have seen it. She shook Her head and eyed him fiercely. He pulled a face. 'So you don't care!' She cried through the mask. 'But you're Shemyaza's son! Half Elohim! Yet if your mind's typical of the Last Days, how will we overcome the Shift? It's so unbalanced! You mock without cause, you look at Me like Azazel does. As if life's a bad joke! Must Darkness win? Are you the true final result of what we did when we bred with you stupid brutes? Maybe the El were right to condemn us. Maybe Azazel's right too: we Old Ones should perish, this world's damned and polluted, the Starchamber should stay closed.'

She slapped Her thigh angrily. But the Fool just grinned.

'I repeat,' she muttered in a low, disturbed voice, 'now I have to do things I don't like doing. Act in ways I wouldn't have chosen before.'

He eyed Her in astonishment. *But you were always cruel when it suited You!* said his look. *Don't you remember? Don't you know what I suffered when You sent me through the Gate! Now You expect me to love You?*

'Don't look at Me like that,' She snapped.

He shrugged. 'Should people love You when You don't defend them?'

'You're not here to criticise!' Anxiously She pointed up at the high bare hill looming above them through the rain-swept foliage. 'Do you remember the Whole Place, Shem? *Shem?* ... do you know who you are?'

The questions made him dizzy: he shut his eyes. Terrible dim memories racked him. 'Yes,' he cried, 'I remember it! But do You?'

'We built it,' She snapped. 'You and I! Of course I remember!'

'Maybe not,' he said angrily. 'Maybe now You need fools to tell You what You did – when You still shone!' But as he said this he thought: *Be careful! Don't make her too angry ...* And he seemed to hear a voice from faraway, a voice he clung to ... for he was afraid too, mortally afraid:

'*Dad? Remember me? Chrissa? Dad, it's not all lost! The Shining Ones will help, so don't let Her use you or fool you!*'

She felt it. Ignoring Boann waiting at the outer precinct gates now visible at the end of the path through the Gardens, She leaned over and seized his arm hard. 'So I've forgotten a lot,' She warned him in a hiss, 'But don't resist Me or taunt Me or think your silly child and her Weak Ones can stop Me! Don't think I'll let sentiment get in the way, because when you and I join in the Womb-hall ... – Suddenly She shook her head and turned away, gazing up into the wet grey sky, and rain ran down Her golden mask. Samjoyce stared. 'Come along now,' She went on in a dull flat voice, 'I don't blame you for being a Fool: you've brought Me what I need. There's no time to lose. My people fear Me though I'm as weak as a kitten – but that'll change! It'll all change when the ...'

Shaking Her head, She hurried him along to the gates of the temple at the base of the Whole Place. Spearmen shouldered arms; loud blasts sounded from ram's horns; Boann and everyone else threw themselves onto the sandy ground. Into the forecourt came the palanquin. But someone still stood.

This was a younger woman, black-haired and black-robed, her haughty face pale as if she'd undergone a trial. She did not prostrate herself with everyone else, but stood gazing at the Lady, her expression nervous yet somehow transfigured. Samjoyce eyed her with interest, and briefly she met his gaze: perhaps she coloured a little.

'Zoe!' Tiy felt fresh anxiety; a sense of pressure and weakness that

She could not understand. She sat up; Her voice harsh. 'It's done? The place is ready?'

'Yes, Lady!' Zoe was nervous. 'But … I … sensed something … odd.'

'Odd?' Tiy leaned forward, glaring. 'What do you mean?'

The young woman trembled visibly, but controlled herself.

'Lady, I could have sworn I was being watched!'

'In what way?' Tiy demanded in a freezing voice.

Azazel! She thought. *But no! That's not …*

'From the inner planes. From …'

'Impossible,' Tiy declared. 'The Womb-hall's protected; I make sure of that! I've told you to control your imagination. How can you serve Me if you're lost in fantasy?' Sharply She indicated the dishevelled Fool at Her side. 'Now take this … take *Shem* to the Baths; get him washed – properly! – and fed and relaxed, then bring him to Me before the darkest hours.'

The young woman bowed her head, said no more, and joined the others in averting her eyes as Her porters set the Lady down … for She shone in the rain, and the raindrops grew many colours as they fell about Her. Yet Zoe sensed something febrile in Her light as She looked down at the Fool. 'Do as Zoe says. Eat, rest, prepare yourself,' She said sharply.

Then without waiting for a reply She turned and was gone into the inner temple depths. Only then did Boann dare to grin at Zoe's humbling. There were other grins too, though not many. Ignoring them all, Zoe flicked a finger at the Fool. 'Come!' she said flatly … and to her relief the Fool shrugged and followed, a strange half-smile twisting his face. And only when the two of them had followed Her into the depths did the Children retreat from the rain, full of doubt and foreboding. Perhaps She had plans for Her Fool, plans to throw Azazel back … but nobody cared to know (all knew what had happened to Hoel) … and none of them wished to be in the Fool's shoes, no, not for one moment …

4.
Waters of Memory

Despite his bold front Sam Joyce was terrified as the curt young woman ushered him through the jagged, narrow First Arch to the depths under the Whole Place. To wake up and learn he'd spent five years as a drooling naked idiot in this lunatic world was bad enough. Worse still to recover his senses amid (or even because of?) that barbarity of murder and lust in the grove. Yet worst of all were his vague but awful memories of these depths. He made himself enter the dim passage without giving in to panic, but claustrophobia struck instantly; he wavered and stopped where the curve of the passage behind cut off the last grey evening light. Zoe, her eyes red in the torchlight, turned and impatiently beckoned him through a second arch: grotesque wooden heads grinned at the ragged man as he forced himself deeper into the place where, he was sure, he had died once already – long ago when his name was not Sam Joyce but Shem son of Shemyaza; whose bloody nightmare memories had helped to lure him here from 1980s London. 'I ought to have stayed in Crouch End!' he told himself with a shaky laugh, knowing he had no option but to obey Her – or at least play along with Her until he got a break. *A break!* Sweat broke out on his brow. *A break? Nice one, Sam! How about a crushed skull in the Womb-hall?* The name sounded bad enough; what made it worse was his far memory, Shem's memory, of descending this tunnel. *She had me gored to death!* he cried silently as Zoe swept past the first of several doors. *That bloody black bull! I chose it for the sake of Her plan? To open the Starchamber? But She doesn't remember! Now what's She up to? Elixir? I just don't see it! Chrissa . . .!*

Abruptly the woman Zoe stopped and opened a wooden door in the wall of the tunnel. A damp, pleasantly scented warmth wafted out, but he was so taken up by the fight with his memories that he was slow to stop.

'In here,' she said bluntly, moving sharply to avoid bodily contact. He gaped and she frowned, gesturing meanings for words which of course a Fool would not understand. 'The baths. First hot, then cold. Then the Waters of Forgetting and the Waters of Memory. The attendant will show you what to do.' Her troubled gaze briefly touched his face, then dropped to the skins he wore. They'd been clean three days earlier; now they were wet and travel-stained. 'Take off your clothes,' she gestured.

'You what?' At a loss, he played his Honest John bit. 'You mean, here? In front of you, like? You doing the same, then?'

But she didn't understand. *Anyway*, he thought, *I've been running round starkers since I got here.* Scowling with effort he ignored her and tried to recall his dreaming state of mind as the innocent, ignorant Fool in the grove, all memory wiped clean by the shock of the Gate. But it was gone. Memory? Even to think was hard. *But I am awake again!* he insisted fiercely. *This is me! I'm here! Samuel David Joyce of 15 Berkeley Road, N8, and my wife's called Diane, and my daughter . . .*

Again he had to bite back a surge of panic and bile.

Zoe threw up her arms at his dithering. 'Are Last Days men ashamed of their bodies? I'll look away if you want! You *are* a Fool, aren't you?'

'You and whose army?' he muttered, stepping out of the skins. He stood shivering, slapping arms round wiry brown shoulders. She gave him a long cool eye. 'Okay,' he said. 'So I'm music to your eyes. Now what?'

She pointed him through the door to an elderly white-robed man, bald and plump with severe, distant eyes, who stood waiting with towels.

'Fiachnu,' she said crisply, and indicated that she'd be back.

So Sam Joyce had his first hot bath since leaving the twentieth century.

In the Warm Bath he hallucinated that he was five, playing with his toy boats and plastic ducks in the bath of their house on Ravelston Dykes in Edinburgh; solid worlds of solid walls on every side,

Mummy not sick and Daddy not angry ... but before he got too relaxed Fiachnu coaxed him out of the basalt tub onto red earthenware tiles and through a white-painted arch into the next room. He felt dazed, but sensed something odd about Fiachnu who, though he steered the Fool with respect, kept eyeing Sam's privates in a deprecating, rather pitying way. 'Look,' Sam said resignedly as the cold air hit him and he confronted the Cold Bath, 'I went through this lot when I was ten. Spartans, sadists, goolie-grabbers, you name it ... so watch it!' and he growled in mock-warning, but at Fiachnu's pale, remote smile he threw up his hands. 'So it's the Cold Bath! So let's get on with it.'

The freezing water was stern. He cursed and tried to climb out as soon as knee-deep, but Fiachnu pushed, submerging him so that his mind awoke and shrieked: WHAT AM I DOING HERE? He gasped, spluttered, his lips drew back from his teeth; he exploded out of the ice with new energy. 'JESUS H!' he screeched at Fiachnu who – totally unperturbed – slung towels round him and moved him along a narrow passage to a room pearly with coiling steam, warm and drowsily perfumed. 'Who are you anyway?' he raved on, yawning, losing the edge of his outrage as Fiachnu brought him to the sweet-scented tub. Roses floated on the water; jasmined candles flickered in wall-niches beteen carved stone panels. Sam took a closer look at the carvings, and whistled. 'Oy! What's this? *Up Pompeii?* Hey!' – for Fiachnu had turned to a table in a corner and was paying no attention. 'What's the use?' Sam complained. 'Don't sprechen sie Anglais, do ya? Suppose I have to pick up Q-Celtic or whatever you bunch are. Who do *you* think you are?' he prattled on. 'The Beaker Bunch? Bulgars? Brahmins? One of those exotic Irish ...'

'Fool!' Fiachnu turned to reprove him in an arch, high-pitched voice, so that Sam, shocked on two counts, began to get the picture. 'We know who we are!' he said in plain English as Sam stood gaping. 'We are Children of the Lady.' He ticked off items on his fingers. 'This is the Second Arch of the Inner Precinct of Her Whole Place. I, Fiachnu, administer the Waters of Forgetting and Memory. This allows me ...'

'But,' said Sam mildly, 'you're ...'

'... This allows me,' Fiachnu went on, 'to meet many fools, all wanting advice. But advice is not cheap here. They pay in corn and oil; they must purify themselves by continual prayer, sacrifice, fasting, days and nights alone in darkness. Then the scourging to drive out ill thoughts.' Fiachnu eyed Sam. 'A hard business, but as you're the biggest Fool you must be the luckiest too! The Lady excuses you from purification. All She asks is that you smell nice when you go to Her.' And Fiachnu, nodding severely, turned from the table with an obsidian cup. Chased round the rim with a fleur-de-lys design, it held what looked like cold fruit punch. 'She calls many, but favours few. Don't complain! Drink this, then enter the Waters of Forgetting. You'll find them kind and soothing, and ...'

'But,' said Sam mildly, ignoring the cup, 'you're speaking English.' He'd been trying to make this point for some time. 'Am I right? It's not just something in the air?' He stared hard at the old man. 'You *are* speaking what they used to call King's English, aren't you?'

'There's only one language here,' said Fiachnu gently, and again offered the cup. 'You could call it something in the air, yes. Now ...'

Sam felt dreamlike. *Well, why not?* he asked himself. *But don't get suckered!* And he eyed the drink suspiciously. 'What is it?'

'It will help you to relax and float deep ... very deep ...'

'No thanks.' And Sam had a horrible thought. *Speaking in tongues is one thing, but* ... 'Tell me ... Did She take you as Her lover?'

With a serene smile the old man nodded. 'Once ... long ago ...'

'And after that ...' – Sam gestured at the attendant's groin: no bulge showed through his robe – '... you were ...' He couldn't say it.

Matter-of-factly Fiachnu lifted his garment. Sam choked, and looked away. 'Did ... did *She* do that to you?' he cried out in revulsion.

The eunuch seemed insulted. 'Of course not! We take the sickle to ourselves. It's a great honour ...' – briefly the memory of agony touched his face – '... and a greater honour to be allowed to survive the act.'

His features were placid again ... but Sam's were not.

'But why?' he demanded in horror. 'What for? Do you sing?'

'Crucifying the flesh brings freedom.' Fiachnu smiled. 'I did it to become more like Her, and to prove my love which She graciously fulfilled during one long, ardent night. To ask for more, or to have sought ecstacy with other women, would not only have been base ingratitude, but spiritual suicide too. So! – I curbed the body to feed the soul.'

'You're nuts!' Sam, aghast, felt Shem rear. 'Am I expected to ...'

'You are a Fool, and Fools are expected to follow their own nature,' said Fiachnu with crisp disapproval, 'no matter how peculiar others find it. You are expected only to be true to yourself. Now – the Bath!'

'Thank God for that!' Shaking his head, Sam climbed cautiously into the fuming Waters of Forgetting, resisting the urge to cling to his fear-shrivelled scrotum. Yet in the fumes now shrouding him there must have been an opiate, for soon a pleasant drowsiness stole through him; Fiachnu's face wavered and grew indistinct above him as he lay in the warmly oiled water. 'Different strokes, eh?' he murmured, grinning as Faichnu deftly put the black goblet in his hand. 'You're a cut above the rest, Faichnu me old chum! Cheers!' And with a flourish and a smack of the lips he drank down the long, cool, spicy draught ... and without realising it began to drift through a world of rich colour and shifting form. During this drift he saw many things ... none of which quite made sense. But none of them threatened; there was nothing ugly; he was comforted as if all his wars were over. He could have stayed in the Waters of Forgetting forever.

But hands were shaking his shoulders, drawing him back.

'You've had enough,' came a voice. 'Time to get out.'

Dazed, yawning, utterly relaxed, Sam did not resist as he was helped through a door into a lemon-bright oval room, where, in a sparkling white tub, the Waters of Memory awaited him. His nostrils flared at the sharp, astringent and bracing scent that awoke a trembling at the back of his head. Eagerly he slid into the cool clear liquid, and felt his mind grow as crystal-clear and quicksilver-fast as the bath in which he lay.

'THE WATERS OF MEMORY!' The voice reverberated in him like cathedral bells at close quarters. 'THE WATERS OF MEMORYEMORYEMORYORYOREEEE ...'

Then sharp knives of vision slice him; his nostrils flare, his body arches, he grips the sides of the bath and sits up urgently, gazing up at a giant orange eye in the white ceiling above; an eye with serpent brow and abyssal pupil that seizes him and whirls him into his past!

He's off to work in London, trudging to GRYP with a day's caseload of blank, messed-up kids ahead. He's scolding Chrissa at home for playing her stereo loud: wide-eyed she hides from him a sketch of the burning man who plagues her sleep. Now he's in the attic, rediscovering the emerald ring, and from its depths She calls him to Scotland, to the moors above Gairloch, above Tir Nan Og where his grandfather once gave him the ring. Now here's the place the ring likes! Amid a stone circle he stands, in the Gate! The whirling fire dissolves him! Yet even as he plunges into the abyss, from these Waters of Memory he sees Chrissa follow him: he sees Diane alone in the circle, screaming as she hurls the ring into a heart-shaped loch where it vanished even as

Chrissa vanishes, as he vanishes ... into nothing.

Then She's there! A column of blazing fire towering from lost heights down to these crushing depths, and She seizes him into this ...

NO, not into THIS world! NO, someone else calls him somewhere else!

Abruptly he sees Chrissa! Pale, blank, near death! Two men carry her from the depths of a mountain – depths like these! On mule-back they take her by night, wading a freezing river past torch-waving soldiers, climbing through a blizzard to a castle on a huge crag! Now he sees her on a cot in a tiny slit-windowed cell between stone walls. Furs cover her, her eyes are still shut, and by her kneels a tiny old woman dressed in black, wrinkled left hand on Chrissa's face. The old woman serves him turns and whispers to him:

'So you're her father! So the Old One got you! Fool! Don't resist Her. Don't help Her. Find your own way. But beware of Azazel!' The old woman's face wrinkles in disgust, and in the bed Chrissa moans. 'Yes! That Beast nearly seized this child when she sought you in the glade. Watch him! Don't let his false shapes fool you! Don't lose hope or worry about your child! We have her safe here at Montségur: there's purpose to this: even the Old One chaining you serves it, though She doesn't remember! Look!'

She lifts a stone disc on a silver chain. An equal-armed cross is inscribed in it. Set in the middle of the cross is a small cut emerald ... at the sight of which he spins into ...

'SHEM!' cries an agonised voice, echoing from a gulf beyond vision. 'MY SON, WHY SERVE HER? DON'T YOU REMEMBER? WE CONTAMINATED OUR BLOOD WITH THE FLESH OF LULLU; WE ABUSED THE LAW, AND FOR THIS I'M LOCKED IN THE HIDDEN PLACE, AND FOR SERVING HER YOU'VE DIED ONCE AND YOU'LL DIE AGAIN!'

Worlds of pain erupt in him: vistas of memory too great to grasp; shining faces plunging through eternal night as if the universe itself is a screaming mouth ... and for a moment in terror he teeters, he looks, he ...

'YOU FOOL!' an angry voice cried as a dense black shadow swept through him - the wing of a vengeful predator, occluding the vastness, blotting out his memory. 'YOU'VE SEEN ENOUGH! COME BACK BEFORE YOU GO TOO FAR!'

In vain, furious without knowing it, he fought ... and fell like lead from the vortex, fell with only the fading image of a cold green star hanging before him amid the dying vapours of the Waters of Memory ...

5.

Dion's Challenge

Elsewhere in Alba an owl shrieked through the wild black night. From the invisible willows overhanging the matted vegetation of the fen came a rustling, almost inaudible through the pattering of the rain. But Dion heard it, Camped without fire or light amid a thicket of thorn on higher, drier ground, the curly-haired traveller smiled grimly to himself, took his lyre, uncrossed his legs, crawled from the shelter he'd made from bracken, ash-withes, and sods of turf, and stood, hands cupped to his mouth.

'Come out, you women of the night!' he bawled. 'I know you're there, I know who you serve, and I know this is your sanctuary! Yes, and I know how you deal with those who trespass uninvited – quite right too! – and I've heard how you dealt with that fool of a man who tried to kill Her Fool the other day! Did the tossing of his bones tell of good luck? Was the marrow to your liking? Did he taste good ... or was he just a little too salty?'

For a while it seemed as if the night itself had been shocked into silence by this lunatic challenge, for briefly the wind dropped and the rain faded. But then from behind the stranger where he stood there came a shrill laugh followed by a cracked, high-pitched voice:

'Tasty? Yes, Hoel was very tasty! But tell me – O Man who must die for coming here uninvited – how did you guess at the saltiness?'

Without looking round Dion returned the laugh. 'O Woman who does not yet understand that I am not to be torn to pieces for your pot, I heard it from your sisters in my native land that of late the meat of men has grown salty and strange to the taste. It's a matter of curiosity to me – no more – to know if this is true everywhere. If so, how do you explain it?'

'Sisters of ours?' cried another voice from a different direction through the darkness. 'What were you doing talking to sisters of ours?'

'Asking where I might find you and She whom you serve.'

'And why did our sisters in your native land not rip you up and put you in their pot?' came a third voice from yet another direction.

'At first they thought they would.' Dion laughed again, and in his voice was that pure joy, that sublime confidence, which had arrested the drinkers in that tavern across the Narrow Sea. 'But I gave them cause to think again, so instead they told me how to find you.'

'What cause was that?' came the first cracked voice, now closer behind him. But the uncertainty in it made Dion smile, and had it been day those circling him would have seen the twinkling in his deep blue eyes, and they'd have been even more taken aback, being unused to men who did not fear them. 'Why should we not do what they failed to do?'

'Let's just say,' said Dion craftily, 'that She whom you serve will be exceedingly displeased if you touch so much as a hair of my head. I'm not here to provide your supper, but so that you may have the honour of guiding me to Her. Do this, and She will know that you serve Her truly, in spirit, and not merely for the sake of your wizened old man-hungry bellies!'

'The honour!' Carrion breath hissed into his face from a mouth only feet away. 'O Man, you must do more than boast before you convince us of this! Speak quickly! Who do we serve? Why should She want you alive?'

'She once of neither sex who is now of one sex,' said Dion. 'She who was double-sexed with the womb of the moon and the horns of the great black bull. She from the stars who goes underground to find what She lost. But She'll remember nothing without my help, and without me Her Fool cannot help Her ... and if She fails, then you are dead ... for the time that comes is the time of hard and stringy men like the one you just ate! I know,' he went on gently amid the rustling of bracken as they closed in on him, 'that however well you boiled and seasoned Hoel's flesh, still you found it tough and unfriendly, so that it gave you a pain in the gut. Then, as I also know, you scanned his liver and cast his bones ... and what you read from that foretelling gave you a pain in the head much worse that the one in the gut – a burning pain. Is this not so?'

There was a silence. He could sense them all about him, their bloody long nails itching to rip and slice and tear, just as they'd done in the Fool's grove only days earlier. But he could also sense their doubt.

'It is so,' admitted the cracked voice behind him. 'But how do you know, and what does it mean?'

'There comes a time,' Dion said softly – and now there was a lilt in his voice, the cadence of a song beginning to well as, moving carefully in the darkness, he took up his lyre and found the strings – 'There comes a time,' he repeated, and struck a warning chord, 'when hard men like the one you tried to eat will curse you and trample you, and call your taste evil. Calling in iron voices on the name of Love they'll light blazing fires and burn you women by the thousands until you bow down at their feet.' He struck another chord. 'Their god will be invisible, high up in the sky! It won't do you any good to start asking them why they're doing this, for by then they'll have forgotten everything – including how to cry.'

And now a quick succession of chords, jangling, bringing gasps of fear from the darkness as his voice grew ever more sombre and sweet. 'You see, my dears, it's fear that blinds us all. We're vexed by the flesh; we make use of false charms and spells that wreck our hopes of better days. We can't go on in ignorant trance like this without losing our memory. Now She you serve can see all this! She knows She's lost Her memory! She hopes to get it back again, but knows it's useless ... unless ...' And here Dion played, with tears running down his cheeks, a long slow elegy on his lyre that had the Wild Women reaching tenderly to touch him, their claws caressing this stranger in the night, their own tears running down their grimy cheeks as their beasts – panthers and wolves and bears – prowled disconsolately outside this unprecendented circle; and inarticulate cries rose up into the wet sad night as Dion played the tender melancholy of his vision. '... Unless,' he continued, his voice a softness in the rain that fell like dark soft flowers, 'She can greet her brother as She greets a sister.' Suddenly he cried out: 'Azazel won't leave these lands or let go man's minds so long as She regards him as an enemy! Nor will he let go so long as She refuses! He seeks death and She seeks life: they're brother and sister, each defined by the other – without purpose save through the other! She knows that – he does not – have you not just eaten man-flesh that turned your guts to jelly? How can Light be without Dark? or Man and Woman without each other? How can Up and Down find the in-between of existence without each other? And how', he cried wildly, striking a series of notes that dizzied the minds of the women who listened, 'can I get to where I must be without your help? Myself I'm nothing – but now you know I bring something! Will you help me?' And calmly he awaited their reply ...

6.
Elixir

Tiy had gone quickly down to the depths, racked by anxieties that fed on themselves. As She reached the unlit zones beyond Third Arch and went on down to the River, She felt weaker and more nervous than ever She'd been in all the endless centuries since, hopelessly trapped in the dense body, Her friends at Kharsag had released Her from the Valleys of Fire. Yet now not even that terrible time was clear, She realised sadly as She activated the Quiet Door and took the steps bypassing the drop through Fifth Arch. All Her centuries, all Her experiences and plans were now a broken jigsaw of faded, dislocated pieces – flashes here, scenes there, but nothing clear any more. Her past had become an obscurity more dreadful than the darkness shrouding Her now as She came down to Sixth Arch and the River.

Can I be sure of even these last few days? She worried as She called the Ferryman, paid the coin and took Her seat in the black boat, ducking under the rough low roof that in places nearly kissed the unseen water. And as the hooded old man silently backed water and started across, She scolded Herself obsessively. *I'm too anxious. The elixir won't distil if I can't relax. Then Shem won't remember his part. He'll remain a slave who hates Me. He'll never fire Me! I won't remember either! What's gone wrong? He's awake, but he's not Shem enough! This Samjoyce creature and his daughter! Between them they're ruining Me. How did it happen? Did Azazel infect him in the Last Days? Wretch! Mocking Me all the way here! I think he kicked that bearer into dropping Me so he could snatch Me up – save Me – and make a fool of Me to match himself. In front of everyone! It's his passion for ... What did he call it? Equality? No – Democracy, that's it! Last Days nonsense and delusion!*

There was a cough. A voice interrupted Her thoughts.

'I'm glad of the coin, My Lady,' wheezed the Ferryman – for the boat had put in at the Womb-hall pier, 'but have ye a bone for the dog too?'

Yet again, nerves singing with tension, She caught Herself.

'You've been Charon here for a long time, haven't you?' she asked as She stepped ashore and tossed scraps to the drowsy hound.

'You know how long, My Lady.' The old man was grim, and in a fresh surge of cloudy panic She thought: *No, I don't know!*

She said, 'Do you want to see the sun again?'

'No, My Lady.' The reply was prompt.

'Oh?' She paused. 'Why not?'

'How would I see it now, My Lady?' said the Charon so bitterly that again She was struck by the sensation of having done things – committed crimes? – that She'd forgotten. *Did I blind this man?* She wondered.

'What do you want to do?' She asked.

'*Want?* Lady, I am the Ferryman!'

'Yes. Of course.' And for a moment as She turned away towards the Womb-hall Her heart and mind convulsed with cramp. *I'm strangling!* She thought dully, forgetting Zoe's warning of an inner-plane spy as She came by narrow ways to the anterooms of the Womb-hall and entered a candle-lit cave where a spring bubbled up from the world's warm heart. She sighed, shrugged off the soaked Gown-of-the-Feathers-of-many-bright-Birds, removed the golden mask with equal relief, yawned, stretched, and then bathed deep in the fuming bath prepared by Fiachnu and Zoe. Later, calmer, She went to the Dry Room and donned a green robe laid out by Zoe. Then She went past the Womb-hall and in darkness paced the 180 steps down to the Room of the Rose.

This tiny pentagonal chamber marked the deepest point of the Whole Place system – the Seventh Arch. In its geometry, symbols and measurements lay codes to open the higher mind. *I made it long ago*, she told Herself, entering dubiously. *I made it when ... what was it? When I knew I was ... ?* And fear caught Her again. Now Her former brighter Self seemed a fantasy, a painted dream of chimerical history. *I no longer fit My own skin!* She thought, horrified. *My shape's fixed! I forget My own heights!* Then She breathed deep. *But that's why I made it! A message to Myself!*

So She approached the white crystal cube at the centre. She lit the five candles on their sticks of brass that occupied each point of the pentagon, then knelt at the cube and focussed on the wide-petalled red rose and other symbols carved and coloured into it. But instead of oceanic calm She felt only dullness as She eyed them. 'Yes,' She whispered, 'there's the 8, the 18, the 360, and the 1080 – and the Fool brings the 666, for he's both of the Elohim and the Lullu we changed – but if I can't make the elixir we won't even light the fire!' Trembling, She shut her eyes and tried ... but it was no use! She was possessed by a sense of looming peril; as soon as She spurned the imps of anxiety they flooded back in new forms. First she saw Azazel: Azazel with his cockerel head – his new Lullu-scaring prank – leering and crowing at Her. '*Well, sweet sissster! Here we are again. I've got something to ssshow you!*' And then as if She were there Herself She saw the Eagle Regiment in flight through the storm; saw the cream of Her army slaughtering each other and cursing Her name as they died. With an angry shout She threw the Beast out ... but immediately saw Hoel, glaring at Her from the flayed mess of his face as the Wild Women tore at him. Worse, through his mad eyes She saw Herself as he saw Her: a huge red bird of prey, Her talons dripping blood! And Ailma too, wailing at the sight of Her, hiding in Shem's arms ... And then it struck Her.

Shem! Where is he? Something's wrong!

She searched for the scent of him. She realised: *He's in the Waters of Memory. But ... what's going on? Weak Ones! They've got him again. Hoel, I swear you'll kill them for me!* And in a fury She went after him. The emerald depths seemed clear again: through them into the subtle world she followed him to a cell at the top of that castle the Weak Ones called Montségur. And she saw: *That Child! His daughter! She's sick! I did hurt her! But who's that old woman? She has a green stone! What's she saying? SHEM, DON'T LISTEN! DON'T LOOK!*

Too late! She shuddered as his memory awoke to shining fields beyond his capacity to contain, and to darknesses ... to the Hidden Place, to ...

'*SHEM! MY SON, WHY SERVE HER? DON'T YOU REMEMBER ...?*'

Shemyaza! Panic swept Her: She stretched dizzily into the abyss, into the Hidden Place: quickly she snatched Shem up and swept him back. 'YOU FOOL! YOU'VE SEEN ENOUGH! COME BACK BEFORE YOU GO TOO FAR!' And in the same deft way – applying old skills, in Her fury not considering Her new weaknesses at all – She caught his roaming mind and pulled it triumphantly back, back, back to Fiachnu's bath . . .

'There! That's that!' She cried, Her face glowing with fervent fire. 'I'm not so weak yet, you know!' It was only then She sighed with relief. Another narrow escape. Much too close. But She'd caught him back!

The elixir, She told Herself. *It's now or never.*

Again She tried. She calmed herself. She dwelt on the meaning of the symbols carved in the cube. She relaxed her breathing. Her heart stopped thumping. Her mind grew still and clear. Then (though clouds lingered) She began the soft chant of the sounds in a rhythm and at a pitch, which, resonating in Her with the power of the newborn moon, the Horned One, set hypothalamus and pituitary gland to work.

The red rose expands. It leaps into Her blood, into Her brain. And suddenly She catches light: chemical messengers course through her from head to toe, spreading the word: PREPARE THE WAY!

BUT WHERE IS THE ESSENCE WE NEED? demand envoys from every region of Her, and She replies: I GO FOR IT NOW!

Then softly the memories burst in Her: veils of weight and form fall from Her; the signing fire lifts Her on wings She'd forgotten, and over the vital, elixirous ocean of Her chemical mind She flies to a jagged, ragged, smoking black isle. Here, torrents of water cascade from recently elevated mountaintops and every gleaming slate-flat surface glows a royal violet that sings: 8 AND 18 IN 1080, BUT WHERE'S THE MUSTARD-SEED?

And the fieriness of Her is a furnace that roars:

666 WILL DO THE TRICK!

A spear of light bursts rock. Heavy fragments explode and vanish: a ravening sphere of violet light rapidly brightens and passes beyond sight, snatching Her with it through a vortex to set Her down in a shining vast hall where all is curve and pulsation; where a jackal-headed dwarf in a stained smock toils over bubbling vats.

I MUST HAVE THE ESSENCE OF THE ELIXIR! She cries.

But as She made her demand there was a shift, a change in Her view of things, as if suddenly She was very small.

'Don't should like that!' barked the dwarf without turning from his work. 'Who do you think you are? Have you forgotten good manners along with everything else? How dare you burst in here and make demands?'

'I've come for the brew that enlightens the Lullu,' She said humbly.

'Why, when you haven't come in so long?' With a cross look the dwarf at

last turned to Her, wiping his hands as he did. 'So you know the code, but you can't just turn up telling me to do as you want.'

'The need's absolute,' She protested. 'I've crossed the sea, but there's a wider sea to travel.'

'We thought you'd forgotten that too.'

'I have. I'm ill. I must remember. Please help!'

The dwarf grunted sceptically. 'Why do you need the brew?'

'To help one who fell to rise again.' She declared.

The jackal eyes burned on Her. 'In whose name?'

'In the name of the Shining Ones.'

'I've had no new instructions about you,' he said suspiciously.

'Is it not the Law that all who seek must be helped to find?'

'I'm not a lawyer,' grunted the dwarf, scratching his snout with a huge hairy hand. He eyed her. 'But I see you haven't lost all your wits. The Beast hasn't got you yet. So – what are the numbers?'

'The 1080,' She said firmly. Then less firmly: 'And ... the 666.'

'What, again? Isn't that what got you into trouble the last time?'

'No!' She snapped. 'Azazel broke that law, not I! But now what other way is there? Didn't the Elohim plan it like that? Is there any option?'

'I'm no philosopher either.' The dwarf shrugged, and without warning transformed into a blazing ball of flame within Her. 'IT'S DONE!' a huge voice roared; violet light seared Her as the jackal-dwarf ruling Her glands fired the process. Her mind erupted; She gasped and opened Her eyes to see the rose on fire as fire ran through Her, striking veils apart and in that moment reuniting Her with ... with ... still She could not quite ...

But it was done. She knew it was done. She could feel it, born and brewed in Her brain, descending to the birth-hall in Her. Yet She could hardly bear the pain of it, and as She withdrew from the work and came shakily to Her feet, a hot and greedy sensation poured through Her ... a gloating lust that made Her shudder. But in Her weakness She failed to sense in this anything other than an unpleasant by-product of the process She'd invoked in her body – the manufacture of the elixir, the Lily of the Valley which soon her Fool would drink. Yet as She left the Room of the Rose to await Shem in the Womb-hall She was not as alone as She thought.

7. *Remembering*

'Fool, where are you? Aren't you hungry?'

He floated in a daze, staring blankly at the orange eye in the white ceiling above. Until Zoe's voice broke into his stupor he was unaware of anything but the sense of being ripped violently from . . . from . . .

My Father? He felt doubting horror. *Was that . . . Shemyaza . . .?*

'Fool!' Zoe demanded again. 'Aren't you hungry?'

This time he heard. Opening his eyes he saw Zoe and Fiachnu nearby. He saw Zoe rub her stomach and smack her lips, presumably for his benefit.

'Aren't you hungry, Fool?' she repeated. 'Chop-chop, eh?'

Hungry? he wondered, eyeing the wiry brown body that lay in the waters. *Body-hungry? Whose body is this? Who am I? What happened? I saw Chrissa! At Montségur! So her burning man's real! They have her safe! Then . . .*

'Fool, stop dreaming!' Zoe snapped. 'Get out, get dried, get dressed!'

Her tone was plain. He heaved himself slowly out of the Waters of Memory, feeling dizzy and strange. Yet as he took a towel from Fiachnu he felt suddenly full of energy, and towelled himself so briskly that soon he tingled in a tumult of awakened appetites. The sense of his flesh blooming reminded him of an LSD trip. Zoe's dark eyes fixed on him with a brooding, dissatisfied look. 'Still shopping?' he demanded with a leer. 'Sorry, my love, I'm booked.' Yet as

Fiachnu gave him clothes – red wool leggings, a loose white smock, flat leather shoes – he felt haunted by some terrible event approaching; he felt the old woman warning him from that castle of Montségur where she laid healing hands on Chrissa ... Montségur where the Cathars barricaded themselves against Church and State, faraway upwhen in the thirteenth century after Christ. Upwhen? And the dizziness seized him.

Yet he grinned at the eunuch. 'These my gladrags? Listen, Fiachnu, old mate, you parlez anglais, so ask her for me, what's on the agenda?'

Fiachnu gave him a remote look and said nothing. 'Okay, be like that,' said Sam. When he was dressed he gave Zoe a grin and slapped his belly. 'Where's the grub, then?' Zoe frowned and beckoned, but before he followed her he clapped Fiachnu on the back. 'See you,' he said with a smile as grim as he felt. 'Thanks for the bath. Don't do anything I wouldn't, eh?'

But the eunuch only smiled obscurely, so that Sam's fears blossomed again as he followed Zoe deeper, down towards the River of the Dead, down towards the Womb-hall where She waited and where Shem had died.

For Shem was awakening. Sam could feel him stirring ...

Past Third Arch into unlit darkness, down spiral steps to Fourth Arch, and with every step Sam's sense of threatened identity grew stronger. For Shem was awakening. To Sam it felt like some long-dormant stratum of his being turning over, yawning, stretching and opening its eyes. It was and wasn't himself: its personality was vaster than his, and brought with it a huge, melancholy perspective; another realm of experience infiltrating his world-view. Yet he felt no panic. This rise of Shem's urges and memories seemed natural and inevitable. They'd always been there in him, and since his plunge through the Gate he had in any case been wiped clean of Sam's past. Though still aping Sam Joyce of London in 1985 he was utterly changed already, and this flood of new sensation was emotionally neutral, indwelling and not alien, an increase, not otherwise. Despite everything he felt good – energetic, alert and oddly relaxed, even optimistic. *It's probably the baths,* he acknowledged. *Or maybe I'm starting to face facts at last.* And as Zoe with her torch flickering down the passage ahead reached Fifth Arch he recalled what the old Cathar woman had told him:

'*Find your own way.*'

Zoe turned and eyed him.

She gestured at the Cervix.

He eyed the dark hole doubtfully.

'What's down there?' he said. But he knew.

'Let yourself drop.' Zoe's whisper echoed, and her shadow swooped on the wall behind as she mimed the act.

'What's this? Death and Rebirth Express?' joked Sam, his legs dangling. Then he let himself drop – and for a terrifying instant which in its endlessness replayed his deepest horror he was falling, falling forever from – and then he crashed, scrambling, onto the sandy floor. '... But isn't this carrying things to extremes?' he ended breathlessly as above him Zoe hissed at him to get out of the way. And she too dropped the ten feet down to join him, and was immediately on her feet, tugging at his sleeve.

He looked round, but saw no ladder or way back up.

'Of course,' Shem murmured. 'The Quiet Door.'

'What's that?' asked Sam, surprised by the voice from himself.

'Fool!' said Zoe. 'Stop babbling to yourself and come along.'

But he had no more jokes as they descended to the River where Zoe paid the Charon two coins for the double load, for now he felt his divided heart freeze even as it hammered harder; and on the crossing his teeth and fists were clenched, for he smelled blood. Shem's blood. His blood. Gored by the mad black bull! Buried in the soft red earth of the Womb-hall floor, up to the neck, helpless, and She laughs as She watches! She laughs!

I'm here again! I'm here again! I ...

'Fool!' He shook. They'd landed. 'Let the hound sniff you.'

And from the shadows before him a growling, a snuffling, a shaking of chain, the breath of a beast, *and again he sees the bull, the mad black bull.* 'It's the only way,' he muttered, confused in time and identity. 'I must go to the Last Days, and this is the way! She's right! That's where we'll find the answer to the Shift! There I'll find a host who'll ...'

Nervously Zoe pulled him past the chained mastiff. It snuffled without interest. She was trembling too. She felt the Fool changing with every deeper step he took. She felt a sombre new potency emanate from him. *Now I begin to see why she wants him!* she thought, eyeing him almost piteously she brought him through winding passages to a rich-draped antechamber of the Womb-hall.

Here a table for two was spread with fruit and honeycakes, with red wine in a silver pitcher that shone in the glow of candles set all about. With her hands now shaking visibly and a desirous awe on her face Zoe nervously patted and pointed the Fool to one of the chairs. 'Sit down, eat!' she blurted, ' and I will tell Her that you ...'

'Zoe, you may go now!'

The voice, from behind them, was very soft and low, but in it was power that persuaded Zoe, for once, to bow very low indeed, her eyes fixed on the ground, shielded from Her shining glory as she backed out and left Her with Her Fool ... with Shem, returned from his mission to the Last Days ...

'Eat!' She said brightly, and if there was doubt or sense of danger in Her She did not show it. 'Drink! And then ...'

ShemSam ate with a will. Like two riders of one horse they shared the man's body seated at that table, and opposite them She watched in loving hope and expectation, Her eyes bright with fire that kindled a responding fire in them, so that fear of bull and blood faded before the certainty that what lay ahead was a different, finer death. For there She sat, Her black hair free, Her face unmasked, Her eyes like twin dark gems to match the brightness of the emerald ring on Her finger, Her body a ready furnace under veils of shimmering silk that trembled like banners in the mild cool draught moving through this place. And though Samjoyce had nearly escaped Her while in the Waters of Memory it was Shem alone She saw now, Shem She invoked with Her eyes and the languid motions of Her body; and it was Shem who responded as one who'd known Her well. Yet Sam, though usurped, still felt no panic; rather he rested like a torpid passenger in dreamy awe of the vast gloomy nature that Shem in his awakening manifested. For both were now united in an erotic pulse that grew every moment. With relish they bit the juicy fruit and drank the tangy wine; with looks increasingly hot and confident they met Her blazing hungry gaze, and in their face now She saw Her Shem returning to shine again as the poor weak Samjoyce faded. 'I knew it would be all right!' She cried happily, feeling the subtle rosy distillation of elixir firing Her as She sat there. 'Soon you'll have the finest wine of all to drink, for I've been to the isle where the vine is steeped in the fields of light, and I've brought it back for you!' And at the slow broad smile that lit up Shem's dark face She clapped Her hands in a spontaneous joy She had not known in so very long!

'Yet still She ignored that hot, greedy taste that lingered inside Her. *No*, She assured Herself. *Nothing will spoil this! It will be done right!*

When he was done eating Her eagerness overflowed; She took him by the hand (the bronze band of the emerald ring dug hard into his fingers) and led him through sinuous passages to the Womb-hall. The very shadows seemed to Her to pulse with their own rich light! Yet then Shem grew pale and She felt his confidence falter as he entered the great hall. 'Look at Me!' She insisted, and he did. Small, wiry, ruddy; he looked up at the shining face of this woman a head and shoulders taller than himself, and sensed a sad humour that said: *Shem, Shem, why did you lose so many inches? Couldn't you take a taller form? I hate looking down on men all the time!* But that was quickly gone, replaced by a smile of such radiance, such hope and love, that almost all his doubts and dark memories were lost in the flood of Her fiery light. 'Do you see Me, Shem? Do you know yourself? Do you remember how you built the great gates for Me, and the zodiacs in the land? Do you remember how we constructed the circles and the places of power?

'I do,' said the Fool, though the images in him were vague, disturbed by Shem's huge and mournful desolation of soul, and even as he tried to think back other images from Samjoyces's mind disrupted him.

('Chrissa!' cries a silent voice unheard.)

('... YOU'VE DIED ONCE AND YOU'LL DIE AGAIN!' cries another.)

'Do you forgive Me,' She asked, 'for what I had to do?'

'Yes,' he said slowly, eyeing the emerald ring in a troubled way. 'But it's hard to remember ... there's so much that ...'

'That's right! And there's more to remember now.' Tension crept into Her grip on his hand. 'Come now, Shem.'

So with a whirling sensation in him he re-entered the place where many generations earlier he'd been buried up to his neck, where the mad black bull had been set on him to smash out his life and hurl him to the Last Days. All about them, as they advanced under the unseen roof's high curve, shadows vied with the flaring light of torches sconced on the smooth black oval walls; light which glowed soft on the raked red earth of the floor and died in the narrow, fuming fissure that divided the place, wall to wall.

Also it fell on the bed – *a bed and not a bull this time!*

The bed, wide and soft and low, stood across the fissure, and by it, also astride the fissure, stood a gleaming brass tripod. On this sat a carved wooden box. And the Fool's eyes widened when he saw this box.

'The bells,' he breathed, and She smiled brilliantly. 'So you do remember! Yes, I still have the bells. And do you remember this too?' She gave him a silver key. 'Open it! Let them ring!' She insisted. 'Let us begin! The elixir's ready and we have a long way to go!'

And he opened the box; he lifted out the tiny set of seven silver bells which, just as he knew they would, chimed as he lifted them, chimed with a music so sweet that he wept, and She wept, for all that they'd forgotten.

Then they took each other in that place of singing black rock, that place so full of the fuming hot scent of the earth, and began reawakening each other. They touched, they kissed, they played; they hit each other lightly, they painted signs and symbols upon each other's bodies; they oiled and stroked each other; they looked together into the depths of the emerald ring She wore and rang the silver bells above each other until the surge roared through Her and She knew the time was right.

Then tenderly She offered him the Lily of the Valley, the wine of the vine that grows in the fields of light, and he drank from Her – drank with gentleness, and slowly, for there was not a drop to be spilled.

And it tasted sweet with a faint clear chime like the music of the bells; yet the fire of it took him by surprise; it raced through him and he reared up with a gasp, his body suddenly as hard and bright as burnished brass; and every part of him – every nerve and sinew, every ounce of his flesh and blood – grew taut with an upward straining desire, and he felt the walls of his skull exploding in a dizzy expansion; so that he lifted his head and bellowed aloud in terror and ecstacy; he bellowed as the mad black bull had done, and then, with a sense of many dams bursting one after another under the weight of an unstoppable flood of memory – all his years, all his lives and deaths and journeys – he put his body on Her body and so they rode together from the blood-red room deep in the Hidden World to the heights that lay beyond ... and She cried, She bucked, She took his weight, his knowledge, Shem and Samjoyce, First Days and Last, and She broke the shackles on Her mind as the silver bells rang in a frenzy of remembrance, as over his shoulder She gazed into the swirling, vision-rich depths of the emerald set in the ring ... and never realized that they were being watched as She soared at last, soared to the memory of – how She had fallen ...

8.
Mission

… for long ago, before taking on Lullu flesh, Tiy in hir subtle body with two hundred other chosen ones swims the ever-veiled ocean world of the Elohim circling the Emme Ya star in the system where Three-in-One dance in glory. There, in a deep coral hall, like tongues of flame the two hundred dance before the Stone, the great emerald … in the depths of which floats the Hidden World. Clenched like a dark fist against the light, it calls them with its mad attraction which already they feel and fear … for soon these servants of the Elohim will enter the Gate of Inside-Out and descend the Sinking Ways that curve from these fields of light down to darkness; soon they'll enter the terrible thickness of time and matter, bringing wisdom to the fast-breeding Lullu of the Hidden World where wisdom has often been undone; where many of their predecessors lie trapped. And with hir fine flame vibrating through them all their leader, Shemyaza tells them:

'Yes! We agree the danger's great, but before the Elohim came to us weren't each of us like the Lullu ourselves, caught in time and weight on our different worlds? Weren't we gifted the long life of energy-bodies by the Wise Ones? The Elohim seeded us and brought us light. Now it's our turn to help others less fortunate than ourselves. We agree on this.

'Yet before we enter the Sinking Ways we must admit the painful history and peculiar difficulties of the Hidden World! We know how even some high Elohim – before the Shift that destroyed the last seeding, and more lately by seduction of the Lullu woman Chawwah – have fallen to its temptations and perverted the Light! Even for those with the long life and the subtle body this is a hard world to endure, as soon you'll learn for yourselves!

'But in twenty short generations since these new Lullu were bred, the tribes have done better than expected. They now require further education. Until now they've remained blind to their nature; they have few skills and their consciousness is undeveloped. The Council has concluded that some are now ready for new input. This is where we come in. Presently there are too few workers in the Hidden World to perform this delicate task, so we have been trained to undertake it. It cannot be emphasised enough how crucial is our complete dedication, and how carefully we must work! It's our job to guide the Lullu GENTLY! – to awaken them without alienating them from nature. Too much too fast will pervert them. The catastrophe of the last Shift and the failure of that mission arose because we moved too fast. Having bred this Lullu-hybrid we expected too much of it. The consequences of elevating intelligence too rapidly from its natural state are insanity and destruction. We can afford no more failures!

'Now your training is complete. You've been selected not only for the skills you'll teach, but also for moral strength. We're about to descend the Sinking Ways to the Hidden World where we'll adopt the dense body and go out among them. We have a brief, but we have to interpret it, and under extreme conditions. Soon you'll know what I mean: I repeat: many of our finest spirits have been lost there! We'll be far from our own kind and, though we must assume Lullu form to work among them – including the male and female genders – we are forbidden any bodily relations with them.'

'Why?' demands Azazel who, as the -el suffix and hir blazing scarlet flame indicates, has recently been elevated to the status of second-in-command, and this despite lack of experience of the Hidden World.

'Maintenance of a specific genetic balance is crucial,' Shemyaza explains. 'The Lullu are hybrids developed to precise specifications by the skills of An and El. Uncontrolled cohabitation would be disastrous. As I said, too much new blood too soon would drive them mad – apart from spawning monsters – and we'd be back where we started.'

'Then why not wait until the new way is confirmed in them?' asks Tiy, hir flame burning alongside that of Azazel. They're both from the same recently liberated, Shift-conquering world. 'What's the hurry?'

'We can't wait.' Shemyaza's light is that of a Lord of Flame, shining from gold to beyond violet. 'Once we start enlightening a world a tension is created. Darkness and ignorance are recalcitrant and blind in opposing change … and light-bringers descending to darkness risk seizure and defeat by the Enemy. It's war, which on this world has not gone well. Many say we should leave the Hidden World to its own misfortune. But that could be fatal. If we fail, we alert evil to our weakness. Now we've started, we can't stop. Even so, Council has decided that, if we fail, this will be the final mission. If we cannot raise up the Lullu but instead degenerate ourselves, the Hidden World will be closed and left to decide its own fate when the Shift next comes. And we'll be condemned for our failure in this! Yes, we'll be punished – severely! So you must understand how hard you'll find this. Of all the worlds that we An and El have tried to enlighten – including your own, whichever you come from – this Hidden World is the most problematic. So if any of you doubt, now is the time to step aside.'

And Shemyaza touches each and every one of them with hir brightness, including Tiy, including Azazel – but their flame of commitment burns pure and high. What finer task can there be than the enlightenment of a sad benighted world? So, led by Leapers who know the Sinking Ways, the two hundred chosen ones pour into the dance: on the vibration of the Song they stream like comets through the Emerald Gate and into the Sinking Ways – roads of probability curving from the subtle fields down to the darkness of matter and gravity. Like sinuous burning arrows they ripple down through interstellar canyons towards the singularity of the Hidden World. Into ever-increasing weight they flow, these Messengers of An and El, bringing light to realms where light is trapped in matter. Soon they come pouring past a yellow-bright sun towards the cloudy orb of the Hidden World, the pain of its jangled harmonic already pulling them, and Tiy, hir pure flame shivering at the first greedy suck of matter, feels mounting anxiety at the prospect of assuming the Lullu body. Since hirself gaining the subtle body with its long life there has been no desire in hir to return to the prison of fixed form. Yet Azazel volunteered for this and persuaded hir to do so too. 'It's our duty to the Light, Tiy – and if An and El reward our work, so much the better for us!' Perhaps. After all, both have served with distinction on other such missions: many worlds with emergent life-forms are in need of a helping hand. But the Hidden World … how will they bear it? For the Hidden World's unique. It fuels gravity so dense that the Stumpies and Bonies (Azazel's names for life-forms there, names banned by Shemyaza, who insists on the term *Lullu* for the Bonies) maintain form only by virtue of a rigid skeleton which typically – such is the huge strain on it – lasts only one Emme Ya cycle before decaying totally! Incredible!

Of course, in the Hidden World oceans live cousins of the Elohim – but the main work is with the land-based, two-legged mammals. These forms are so dense that their soul-sparks frequently drown in them, falling so far from the Light that they lose all sense of origin. The poor souls don't even always know how much they suffer! *Yet*, thinks Tiy amid hir dizzy downward whirl, *we'll teach them what they forgot! But first we must put on flesh and blood and bone; endure tides that tore apart other missions! We must resist* – like a chant it bells through hir, through the two hundred – *the pride that plagues us here! Fail, and the Hidden World's lost!*

So hir spirit shudders: terror grips hir as the Hidden World reaches greedily up at hir, a howling storm tearing hir body of light with sharp claws. *It's worse than Shemyaza said! It's … it's … it's … oh, I can't …*

But then Shemyaza behind the Leapers sends into them, veterans and novices alike, hir calm advice:

We're entering the dark sphere! Can you feel the pulse, the wobble, of its axial movement? That's a result of the last Shift. And the pain and wildness of its song! From now on we toil in agony! Now you know why our previous missions have been difficult! Your light is dimmed, you feel the heavy attraction of matter. Not easy, but this darkness plays its part. From what did we ourselves arise? Now! Soon we'll join the Lullu, to take their form and awaken them. But first we have to get used to this weight. This we'll do in easy stages. To go all the way down at once would tear us apart. In any case, the direct link we maintained before the last Shift was abused and has been closed by Council order. So we make our first stop at the high station where the weight is not so great; there we'll take on the dense bodies and practise using them, for they're difficult garments to wear, and we must grow used to the demands they make – demands which we'll have to master and, if need be, resist!

But even as this call goes out Tiy senses Azazel, hir humour quite unmistakable – sardonic, wry, some might say ambitious:

Shemyaza's worried!

So they descend through darkness to the Gate at the high station in orbit above the plains where the Lullu live … the place where heaven and earth meet, the place much later remembered as the Whirling Castle …

The weight! Tiy groans now to experience again those first dreadful moments in hir dense new gender-ridden Lullu body – HER body. So thick and slow, like a shroud on the spirit, enveloping hir subtle body and drowning the free high senses! For one by one during this orientation phase each of the two hundred new arrivals are fused and fitted with garments of flesh cultured and grown for them in the laboratories of the medical elite specialising in Hidden World biology. Most of these world-weary technicians have done long tours of duty both in this high station and down at the Elohim base in the highlands overlooking the plains where the brief generations of Lullu live and breed and die. They too wear the adapted mammal bodies prepared for the new worker corps. 'You shouldn't think,' the doctor called Ninkharsag explains crisply to a groaning Tiy during Tiy's first hours of unpleasant subordination to the flesh, 'that we don't know what you're suffering. It's a trial we all have to endure. Existence in these depths imposes unfortunate conditions.' And Ninkharsag smiles tightly as Tiy, still unco-ordinated, attempts to walk but stumbles and falls yet again to the solid laboratory floor. Lending a hand to help her up, Ninkharsag goes on: 'You'll never appreciate the difficulties of the Lullu unless you share them. Now come on! Try again!'

So Tiy tries again and again, but like all the rest of the two hundred she feels utterly isolated in the – in HER body. The inevitability of this isolation is clarified at seminars held for the new arrivals. 'Now you can see,' they're told, by verbal speech, as they sit in glum rows, 'how these bodies make sensitive communication difficult. This is due not only to the limiting senses which you now use, but also to the spiritual isolation that results from being caged in flesh. Many of you say you feel separated not only from one another but also from yourselves. Be warned! This sense of separation is one of the chief perils of the Hidden World. It is exactly this which has led to the downfall of so many of us already. Recognise it for what it is! Do not give in to it! If you do, you'll fall!'

So they practise using their bodies, uneasily focussing on each other through their limited new senses, their perceptions bizarre and estranged as they learn how to wear clothes, co-ordinate limbs, eat solid food, speak with Lullu tongue. The sole relief is that they're spared the strange and terrifying need of the Lullu for the regular little death called 'sleep' – but there's no avoiding the fifty-fifty division between male and female; and division it is, with separate instruction for each sex. Uneasy tides are immediately apparent – dark desires and painful urges arising directly out of the responses of the bodies to the currents that surge in and about the Hidden World. Tiy and others in female form are instructed about the Hidden World's moon and its effect on them; Azazel and those in masculine form are told how to control the aggressive urges to which male Lullu are subject. Amid all this, though so slowly – everything connected with the bodies seems desperately slow – they learn to recognise each other not by flash of spirit but by shape of body, expression of face, idiosyncrasy of gesture. They learn to imbue their new forms with typical characteristics. Shemyaza, tall, slow, dark, deliberate, often frowning with concentration. Azazel, with ruddy flaming hair and eager eyes that quickly grow impatient as time passes and still they're not sent down to the highland base. Tiy, tall and graceful with jet-black hair and remote expression. And also they begin 'turning their hand' to the particular disciplines that each will be teaching the Lullu – agriculture, medicine, astronomy and the rest. They are told what they can and cannot teach.

At last, the hour of their descent to the Hidden World ... descent which, now that they're embodied, is conducted in an odd solid-skinned craft that keeps out the vaccum which would destroy these weak bodies they now wear. With an unaccustomed sense of vulnerability these heirs of the long life are lowered to the surface of the Hidden World. Down on the final stage of their journey they come, using their new apparatus of eyes, ears, nose and mouth to interpret to themselves and each other the arid hard landscape below as bare sun-bleached mountains rise to meet them and the weight, the intolerable weight, grows ever more intense. Now, rapidly approaching, growing larger, they see below them a green oasis with low white buildings set beneath a large reservoir of – what is it? – That's water! And then, with a scarcely perceptible jolt, they land on the surface of the world whose inhabitants they come to enlighten ...

9.
The Daughters of Men

So Tiy comes to Kharsag, the Elohim base in the arid mountains of that land once called Sumeria, its white buildings set about the Great House and the House of Knowledge; its stables, sheepfolds, cattlepens and orchards, cornfields and plantations all watered by channels from the reservoir that lies in a fold of the mountains above. Over six centuries the Elohim have developed this centre to uplift the descendants of those Lullu who survived the last Shift four millennia ago; many teams have come and gone on their tours of duty, but those at Kharsag now feel understaffed, overworked, and forgotten by the Council. For decades they've overseen the development of Lullu tribes on the plains; for years they've been petitioning the Council to send teams to do the fieldwork they don't have time to do themselves.

So when at last, dazed by weight and by bodies and by the turbulent song of this sphere, the new arrivals stumble out of their ship into the harsh sunlight they find themselves joyously greeted. Bemused, Tiy stands for the first time on the hard, dusty surface of the Hidden World as out of fields, laboratories, libraries and workshops the excited scientists and technicians pour with waving arms, pumping legs, shouting voices, bright eyes ... and with her own eyes, her own face, she frowns at Azazel beside her, for the emotional atmosphere is disturbing. 'Are these our people?' her voice asks, her tongue and lips shaping the words with difficulty. 'Is this what happens to Elohim here? Will we all go mad like this?'

But Azazel grins and points in another direction.

'Look!' he says. 'Over in those ... fields. Those are Lullu!'

Sensing the oddness of his mood, she follows his finger as his grin broadens; she squints into the sun ... and for the first time sets eyes upon the Lullu. Painfully, resisting the weight, she stares at the bent, fur-clad, black-haired creatures cowering against the green growing crops.

'Those? Those are Lullu? But they're so ... stunted. And dull!'

'They won't be dull when we've finished with them,' says Azazel.

'Rest,' Shemyaza tells the two hundred at a preliminary meeting in the quarters set aside for them. 'Relax and get used to this world before you try anything else. Walk about. Use your eyes and other senses. Taste the fruit of the trees and the water of the streams; learn how day gives way to night and night to day; speak to our people here and learn what they say about the discipline you'll be teaching and what the Lullu know already. But don't approach the Lullu yet. They're primitive and easily disturbed, even those who work here, and our arrival has frightened them. They think us gods: these bodies which seem clumsy and dull to us are giant to them, and in their eyes we shine like fire so they can hardly face us without being blinded. We'll win their confidence slowly and with care ... and we'll not go out among them until the Lord Arbiter here gives the word.'

But after several days of inaction Azazel and others grow impatient and bored of behaving like tourists. One afternoon with Sariel the astronomer, Kashdejan the embryologist and Penemue who will teach writing, Azazel walks in a field of growing corn and chances on a Lullu woman. Bare to the waist in the burning heat, with painful slowness she uses a clumsy wooden hoe to weed thistles from the corn ... but at the approach of the four Shining Ones she drops to her knees and ducks her head.

Azazel grins, his eyes on her breasts.

'Don't you feel what I feel, O comrades who now wear the bodies of men?' he asks in a jesting voice. 'Do you not feel desire?'

'What?' says Penemue. 'For that poor creature?'

Sariel and Kashdejan simply eye each other and shrug ... but all three are shocked when impulsively Azazel bends and takes her by the arm. She gasps as if burned, and Penemue cries: 'We're forbidden to ...' But Azazel ignores him. 'Easy!' Azazel murmurs, smiling at the terrified Lullu woman. 'I won't hurt you. But wouldn't it be so much easier if you had a hoe made of metal instead of wood? That's what I'm here to teach, you see. New ways of doing things, to make life easier for you.' And in a friendly, pleading voice he adds: 'You mustn't be scared of me. I won't eat you! In fact, I think you could be beautiful. Look at me!'

'Beautiful?' the woman whispers fearfully. 'What's that?' She eyes him timidly – then with a cry drops her hoe, jumps up, and flees the field.

Azazel laughs at his shocked companions.

'We're going to be here a long time, friends, and the Council is a long way away!' He nods thoughtfully. 'She could be ... attractive ... if ...'

'You let matter's tides disrupt you already!' Sariel says grimly. But he and Kashdejan both eye the fleeing woman. Only Penemue shakes his head and instead faces the high blue sky. And from a hilltop above Tiy sees it all. Later she asks Azazel why he touched the Lullu woman. He shrugs 'No harm was done,' he says cajolingly. 'I was just curious to see if the poor creature could respond intelligently.' Upset without knowing why, Tiy cries: 'But you're second-in-command! You should support Shemyaza.'

But neither she nor the others mentioned this event to Shemyaza. Already separation and mutual doubt grow in them – even in this protected oasis ...

In time they're ready. Divided into twenty squads, each with a leader, they complete their own preparation by training selected high-potential Lullu recruited and brought too Kharsag to be trained as assistants. Some of the Lullu thus trained are sent out in advance to prepare the way.

On the day they leave, Ugmash the Arbiter harangues them in the hall of the Great House, warning of backsliding but promising Kharsag's support for their work. 'We await results!' he declares. Then Shemyaza thanks Ugmash and others there for their help ... but Tiy, looking at Azazel, who has been quiet these past weeks, notes his hot, cynical eye, and feels apprehensive.

So they leave Kharsag and travel south-east to a fertile valley at the head of a great, winding brown river – the Jordan – on the lower banks of which Lullu tribes flourish. Here in this valley they establish their centre; one by one the squads set out to work in different regions with different tribes – some north to Ur, others south to Khem, and others even further afield. And for many years the work goes well. The Lullu learn crafts approved by the Elohim: agriculture, astronomy, medicine, surveying, building, weaving and writing: they leave hide tents for houses of brick; they tame the wild ass to draw wheeled carts; they domesticate wild barley to fill their granaries; they grow numerous and healthy and tall; the men handsome, the women beautiful ... and Shemyaza's teams grow deeply involved in the lives of these quick-learning, attractive people. Yet throughout these years they maintain their discipline, even Azazel, who teaches the Lullu how to mine, smelt, and work metals to makes ploughs and suchlike, while Tiy, working with Kashdejan, also travels widely, explaining causes of sickness and diseases of the womb.

Naturally, success is greatest in specific regions: the Lullu leaders in a land called Khem, at the south-east corner of the sea to the west, are first to understand that their radiant helpers come from a world circling the fixed star they call Sothis, brightest in their sky, the annual rising of which presages the fertilising flood of the great river flowing through their land. Shemyaza, working chiefly in Khem, attends a great ceremony there: one marking not only the political uniting of the tribes under one king, but also the foundation of a new city on the bones of one much older, and of a new calendar marking the New Year by the annual rising of Sothis. At it the priests of Khem confer on him the title of 'Amen', and call him a 'God' – a title leading to talk behind his back and teasing to his face.

So his reports to Kharsag – and thence up the Sinking Ways to the Emme Ya world – glow with accomplishment. Yet nothing is heard in return.

And as time goes by, the weight of the Hidden World makes increasing demands. Their subtle bodies and the world of spirit become ever more a distant memory. Discipline begins to fail as, spending years in distant lands, living among the Lullu, the squads grow independent. Here and there rules are bent by this worker or that, forbidden things begin to be taught – the making of knives and ornaments, how to prepare cosmetics. And the Lullu clamour for more. They begin to offer their hearts, minds and bodies to their lonely benefactors in exchange for knowledge of these things that excite their senses ... a bargain that grows ever more tempting.

So one day Tiy returns from a long journey to Ur to find the valley in uproar ... caused by Azazel. He has taken a Lullu wife, and with impetuous arrogance brought the poor, painted, fearful girl with him to the valley. In direct challenge to Shemyaza he's exhorting the others to solve their loneliness and the pains of their flesh by doing likewise. And many … now dressing and even looking like the sun-burned Lullu they teach – hear him with enthusiasm. It's a madness; a feverish excitement in them as at last – willingly and with huge relief – they decide to bow to the stresses of the Hidden World. Yet Tiy, though acknowledging the desires that flood her too – the yearning that seizes her nightly under the big yellow moon in the camps and growing towns of the Lullu – disapproves. 'It's wrong!' she tells herself, at first silently, seeing Azazel take open, defiant pleasure in his 'wife'. For before everyone – just as if demonstrating metalworking technique – he ogles and touches and strokes the terrified woman, advising everyone else to do the same. 'Why not?' he cries in his passionate heat, red hair flaming and eyes alight. 'The Elohim abandoned us! They sent us here to do this work and expect us to act as if we're still in the subtle body! We're not! We're creatures of flesh and blood; we've been here for years and this is our world now! You should do as I do! Take mates from these Lullu, join with them and have children by them! Accept this delight the denial of which racks and torments us! How can you know if it's right or wrong if you won't try it – though I know very well that many of you *have* tried it! I know by the way you won't meet my eyes! Are you all scared like old Shemyaza here, who sucks up to the Lullu and behaves like an old woman and only says what you're not allowed to do?'

And with a sad, weary look, knowing that most of those under him agree with Azazel, Shemyaza (his hands brown and calloused from years of work in the fields) stands to remind them of their vows and scold them for their weakness, but they shout him down.

'Wives!' they cry, and 'Husbands! Let us be open about it and not be cowards any more. Here we are, and here we live! This is our world!'

'Then take pleasure among yourselves,' he cries fiercely, 'but leave the Lullu alone! You know it's forbidden to touch them.'

But they laugh at him. 'Hail, you God! Hail, Amen!'

And Tiy's shocked to hear herself shouting with the rest of them.

Shemyaza sighs in distress, then bellows back at Azazel.

'Do this,' he shouts, 'and it'll doom this world. Have you forgotten? Breed with the Lullu and the balance will be upset: we'll create monsters! Mad monsters! Kashdejan, tell them! Don't you see? Our flesh is manufactured; we're not compatible! And when the Elohim learn about it they'll close the entire mission down … and I will be held responsible!'

'It's hard being a God!' Azazel sneers. 'But don't worry. We'll take that load off your back. We'll bind ourselves by mutual vows to do this, then you'll not be blamed ... not that An and El will ever find out about it, since they never show interest in our work anyway. As for incompatibility, maybe that was true when we began, but not now. We're more like the Lullu, and they're more like us. I say we do it! Why not?'

Tiy, Penemue and others stir themselves to protest, but they too are shouted down: the rebels cheer as Azazel, grinning hugely, canters about with his blushing bride on his shoulders, just as if he were an ass.

And Shemyaza walks away, shaking his head.

So the end begins. Soon most of Those-Who-Do-Not-Sleep, or Watchers (as the Lullu call them) follow Azazel in taking Lullu partners. They mate with them and teach them forbidden things, so that men's arguments become falsely sophisticated and women's faces cunningly attractive. And Azazel, secretly doubting, encourages them to more serious violations to provide cover for his sin. At first they're tentative but, when Shemyaza takes no action to stop them or report them, many enter a phase of wild abandonment to the Hidden World's temptations, assuaging their guilt by carrying it to extremes, making a virtue of whatever's forbidden. Some take power in new cities and teach their Lullu techniques of war as the priority; they argue aggressively against each other; they encourage illusion and the greedy collection of precious things ... and soon the first children are born.

As feared, the uncontrolled mix of Elohim and Lullu produces giantism and abnormality. The monstrous children develop monstrous minds but the parents fondly excuse them, calling monstrosity progress. So the spoiled, monstrous children get out of hand. Without rein or authority they do as they want, turning to cruelty when they fail to get their way. Many, as Shemyaza warned, are mad, filled with hate for life ... and soon they turn against it. From the casual slaughter of birds and beasts they turn to the casual slaughter of people and each other. Soon the lands are blighted by war, plague, famine and fear. And Tiy, who has held off taking a Lullu lover, sees the work fall to pieces. Shemyaza sulks impotently while at Kharsag Ugmash refuses to tell the Elohim what's happening, fearing that Council's judgement (they don't understand the pressures here) will be too harsh, ending the mission (and his career) once and for all.

At length a Lullu delegation protests to Tiy and Penemue, and Tiy goes to Azazel in the city called Jericho where he rules. 'Stop this madness,' she says. 'Have you forgotten everything? Look at you!' For by now his physical features have taken on the fat, slovenly, cruel imprint of his new Hidden World nature. But he laughs in her face.

'Oh, poor Tiy! Still clinging to dead ideals?'

'We came from the same world,' she reminds him. 'Once we too needed disinterested help. Is this what you offer the Lullu?'

Azazel only jeers. Furious, she goes to Shemyaza, demanding: 'Use your authority and stop this now.' But Shemyaza just shrugs. 'Madness is the way here,' he mumbles. 'My appointment wasn't promotion. Don't you see it? The Council want to be rid of this world. They're looking for reasons to close it down. Just keep quiet, Tiy. Hope it blows over.'

Of her own accord she goes to Kharsag. Still Ugmash tries to play it down. 'We've had no complaints from the Lullu,' he says carefully.

'If I produce a witness,' she demands, 'will you listen?'

'Very well,' Ugmash agrees reluctantly.

Returning to the lowlands, Tiy consults with Penemue and those Lullu willing to stand up against the evil. From them Penemue the writer chooses his favourite student. Enoch the son of Jared is already fluent not only in Lullu tongues but in Kharsag's speech too ... and unimpressed by Azazel's threats against him. Risking assassination, he records complaints against the Watchers and their monstrous children; Tiy and Penemue bring him to Ugmash at Kharsag. 'Enoch bears witness to the evils we told you about!' they insist. 'We demand you put these complaints before the Council.'

Ugmash, a career bureaucrat, puts a report through, but still plays it down. In time a Council Inspector arrives. Reluctant to endure the dense body too long, the Inspector lets Ugmash fool hir, observing the letter but not the spirit of the law. The Kharsag law-enforcers, called *satans*, are forbidden by Ugmash to denounce Azazel and his confederates: the false game is played: the Inspector departs shaking hands all round.

But matters get worse until finally Ugmash realises the crisis can't be hidden any more. If he doesn't act now he'll be fatally compromised. At last, as if he has only just discovered the corruption, with righteous fury he appeals direct to the Council. 'You see everything! You must know what is happening here! Why then don't you tell me what to do about it?'

And so the axe falls. Tiy, Penemue and Enoch are called to testify in person. So again Tiy and Penemue and for the first time Enoch take on the subtle body and ascend the Sinking Ways. For Enoch the experience is a dream-vision: lightning-flashes impel him up and a wind directs his flight to heaven, through a crystal wall surrounded by vibrating flame, striking him with terror as he passes through it. So through the Emerald Gate he enters the ocean depths of the Emme Ya world, and there about him, like a blaze of fire, through subtle eyes the transformed, terrified Lullu man sees the Elohim in their great dance, in their thousands of thousands and myriads of myriads. Yet once he overcomes his terror he wishes only to stay in this world – a wish granted him, once he completes his mission.

But no mercy is shown to Tiy or Penemue, nor to any of the two hundred all of whom are judged with harsh finality, as is the Hidden World itself.

For when they've made their report, Tiy and Penemue anxiously see the speaker of the Council turn to Enoch and tell him: 'Enoch, go back and tell the Watchers who have given up spirit for flesh: "*You have caused disaster! You cannot be forgiven! You'll see the death of the children you love and you'll weep for them, but you'll never know mercy or peace. Instead you'll be jailed in the Hidden World, and there you'll stay until the Shift brings you the death you have earned!*" And more in this vein until at last the Speaker faces Tiy and Penemue. 'And you Watchers who have done nothing wrong, you too must be imprisoned with the rest, for we cannot let the contagion escape. Go now, and abandon the subtle body forever!'

'Is this how you reward those who serve best?' cries Tiy in a fury.

'To speak of reward is proof the disease has infected you! We have done what we can, but the Hidden World turns the best of us to bad. We can no longer escape the need for quarantine. Now go!'

So they do. So they did. And somewhere sounded mocking laughter ...

10.
Judgement

Subliminal, it whispered through the Womb-hall, teasing torch-flame, raising Her short hairs. At last Tiy heard it and with a thrill of fury knew they were spied upon as She rocked with Shemyaza's son, Her nails raking his shoulders, Her back arched, Her eyes wide in the green depths of the emerald ring. Yet She ignored it. The moment was crucial. With each of Shem's thrusts she was rising higher on waves of recovered memory to the terror of Her rejection by the Elohim. She knew who it was, but refused to see as She groaned in that deep, blood-red place. And above Her Shem, his body arched like a bow, groaned too. Yet something was wrong with him! His motion was too hard, too mechanical: a new fear seized Her. 'Do you remember?' She cried, fixing dilated eyes on his scarred, darkly gleaming face; 'Do you remember, Fool?' But in his face She saw how the fire that roared through him left no room for understanding yet; his features were a sweat-slick, shining mask. And in a passionate rant She poured out Her memory even as he rode Her, striving to awaken him to face the menace!

'No, you can't remember! You weren't alive! Not then! But the seed of Shemyaza is in you! You must know! The Elohim were cruel! They never meant us to succeed. All but a few wanted to close the Hidden World; now they hope the Lullu will stay too ignorant to gain their better nature and overcome the Shift when it strikes again. Yet you're from the Last Days and what can we hope for? I did no wrong! But they condemned me! They offered no hope, no apologies. Why? Because they encourage the Beast!'

Again that haunting laugh: a vague shape glimmered and danced at the edge of Her sight, yet still She ignored it, for still Shem's face remained mask-like, lost in the elixirous flood. Giddy, She brought Her left hand before his eyes. His face shone in the emerald light of the ring: briefly the bronze sigil of moon and horns set in it alerted him.

'Yes!' She cried in relief. 'You know this! Through it you've come back to Me! A fragment of the Stone! It was given to Me; these too ...' – She rang the silver bells – '... by friends on the Council I must not name! They gave Me these even as Penemue and I were banished! "*Use them well!*" they said. "*And don't forget we're with you!*" Now see again!'

And in a daze he sees how down they go again, down the Sinking Ways to the Hidden World, Tiy and Penemue, Enoch too, and Tiy and Penemue in despair at being driven back into the same dense bodies, back to the heartache of the divided, thickened condition ... back to the horror of imprisonment.

From the Whirling Castle they descend to Kharsag. Ugmash is careful to offer them neither hope nor sympathy.

'Then ...' – Tiy's face twisted as the brief light in Shem's eyes faded. *Is the elixir too strong?* She feared, shaking him as he rode Her, rushing on – '... Enoch was sent with us to the others to deliver the judgement. Shem, wake up!' Groaning anxiously She pulled back, but still he moved in Her like an automaton. 'The Council told Ugmash, "*Lock Shemyaza and Azazel in the Hidden Place of the land drowned by the last Shift! Lock them where the Starchamber lies shut in the deep; leave them there until the Hidden World is seared again by fire and cleansed by flood! Only then let their long lives end in death.*" That's what they told him!' She cried hotly, glaring up into Shem's uncomprehending face.

'When Azazel heard this ...' – Tiy jeered at the phantom at the edge of Her vision – '... he looked like a Lullu boy caught stealing apples! His fat face went purple with rage, then – ah! Shem! stop! – white with fear. I didn't pity him. Not after his crimes! He brought us disaster. He's got worse since then. I'm not proud I'm from the same world. Then *noble* Enoch told us we were to be shut in the Valley of Fire, and in ... ah! ... in our fear we begged him to plead for us! Penemue and I did not beg! Off goes *noble* Enoch, and in his dream Council tells him to scold us again! You should have heard him! SHEM!' Slapping him, she cried breathlessly: 'Like a judge he told us: "*You Watchers should help men, not men you. You were spiritual, with the long life for all your time on earth. But now you deny the spirit and take wives among the Lullu. Now you breed monsters and teach evil. Never again will you know peace!*" OH, SHEM! WILL YOU STOP?'

At last Shem stopped moving in Her. With a sigh She went on rapidly:

'Shemyaza just hung his head (he loved his own guilt) but Azazel began organising resistance, which might have succeeded, who knows? – except that Ugmash was ready, of course he was, because he was in trouble himself if he didn't round us up. He had a squad of satans on the spot already. They grabbed Azazel and the rest before they could move. Azazel and Shemyaza were taken away that night, to the western ocean, to be buried alive – and that would have been it so far as you're concerned, but ...' – with twisted mouth She remembered, She looked aside – '... I knew what was coming, and I thought: *Tiy, you're condemned for doing nothing wrong; maybe you'll never escape the Valleys of Fire, but in case you do, and in case the Elohim abandon this world and leave us to it, you should prepare for the future.*'

Shem's eyes slowly focussed. In a drugged voice he asked: 'What ... what did you do?' But it was an effort, the light in his eyes was faint.

Still Tiy ignored the phantom form, the subliminal, now-angry laughter, yet Her voice took on a shrill, bantering note that dared denial:

'The night Enoch dreamed I acted. You're the result!' She smiled brilliantly. Shem lay back with a slack, exhausted look. Her smile faded. She made a face. 'I went to Shemyaza where he lay moping, and ... got him to give me his seed. It wasn't the most pleasant hour I've ever spent with a man. He wasn't like you, Shem, he wasn't ... he didn't ... anyway, Kashdejan had taught me ways to preserve seed. From what you've said these ways are known in the Last Days too. So next day, when the satans seized Shemyaza and that beast Azazel ...' – Her voice was vicious: She glared at shadows, then silken-soft She eyed Shem's puzzled face – '... I literally held you in My hands. As for the womb that bore you, well, that comes much later.'

Suddenly She flinched, as if unexpectedly gripped by an invisible hand; the torches flickered in a sudden draught: Shem shivered with cold.

'Much later?' he mumbled, obscurely recalling that cry from Shemyaza he'd heard while in the Waters of Memory. 'How much later?'

'More than many centuries,' said Tiy grimly. 'Be glad you know none of it. We didn't escape until the Elohim gave up. After what some call *The Year of Light.* Something unexpected. About two thousand years ago, or six thousand years before your Last Days. A star in the southern hemisphere ...' – She examined his memory, but found no name – '... blew up. The energy from it reached this world so strongly that it dissolved the atmospheric layer that protects against the wasting disease. Many creatures that stayed out in daylight died – but there was worse. The heat of the sunburst melted the ice accumulated at the south pole. There was a global flood.'

She smiled up at him.

'That was it for the Elohim. A blessing in disguise. Their own clean-up had failed. They'd tried to undo Azazel's work too late. The Lullu had learned too much; they'd become aware again, as we'd stopped, but breeding with us tormented them. Yes,' She went on, sardonically eyeing him, 'the poor creatures became self-conscious, but madly so, tortured by perpetual headache, by guilt and fear and loss. The problem was they couldn't face the fear of their past; the fear of Shifts which had destroyed them before. Individuals who faced this amnesiac fear and dared speak of it were torn to pieces by their fellows. More and more this inner war, with different parts of the brain fighting each other, led to a mad race – always fighting for personal advantage. The balance of their development was destroyed by us, just as Shemyaza feared ... and just as happened before the last Shift! In short, disaster again. So ...' – She shrugged wearily – '... the Elohim lost control. Then – the arrival of the explosion from this star I speak of. Of course Council had foreseen it, but internal politics ensured that those who wished to end the Hidden World project won the day. The warning wasn't sent until too late. The mission was told to get out, quick. But I must say this for Ugmash: he did his best; or so I gather, because I wasn't around to have a say. He warned the Lullu ... some of them ...'

'Noah,' muttered Shem in a drowned voice.

'What? Who?' She swept his comment aside. 'When it was clear what was about to happen, and with the withdrawal order already through – this was after our imprisonment: we had no part in this – he sent out teams to as many lands as he could, to warn the Lullu of the fire approaching. But by the time it fell he and the rest of the Elohim had gone. *All* the Elohim left this world – except for us!' And She seized his shoulder, making him look at Her, but his eyes remained dazed and blank. 'When the Flood struck we were rotting in the Valleys of Fire – all two hundred of us, except for Shemyaza and Azazel, who were buried much deeper elsewhere. And at least we were buried higher than the Flood! Shem, do you know about the Valleys of Fire?' She demanded, 'Volcanic ravines above Kharsag? Long before our mission the Elohim had dug underground hell-holes to lock up any of their servants, like us, who didn't live up to their *sublime* moral standards.' She shuddered. 'Shem, I was shut in a hole for *centuries, awake all the time!* Long Life in the dense body! I starved without food and thirsted without drink; I went blind without light, my ears rang with the groans of the world – but I had Long Life and couldn't sleep, far less die!'

She squeezed his limp hot hand. 'Shem! My flesh feels like ordinary human flesh, doesn't it! But it's not! The DNA's modified. The cells are self-renewing, self-sustaining. The irony's dreadful! Look Me in the eye: see Me!' And he did, but his look was blank. She raised Herself up on her elbows and continued sadly, flicking glances at the shadows. 'Do you think you've endured the worst this world can offer?' She demanded, 'Why do you think I forget so much? Could *you* bear such memory? Listen! In knowledge of all I am and was and might be I lay in a hole no bigger than this bed! On My back. I couldn't even stand! My muscles grew slack, My face fell, I hurt perpetually; I had to breathe, yes, and so in their *mercy* the Council had built vents to let in air that stank of sulphur and burned the lungs with each gasp! Shem, how often would you gasp for breath in the course of hundreds of years? Thirty times a minute, thirty-four and a half thousand times a day, twelve and a half million times a year, and a thousand years – it gives you time, Shem, it gives you time to think, with the mind always racing, filling the blackness with phantoms, without sensation save for the subtle currents of the world-field flowing through the rock!

'You think this is a dreadful place even for an hour, don't you? Then try to imagine a thousand years on your back in utter darkness in a trapped body that refuses to let the spirit go free! Try to imagine that!'

But still Shem gaped emptily at Her, and She laughed.

'Fool! Understand! I knew only despair and a mad hope rooted in hate – and hate is what I clung to, for better or worse! I avoided madness by going mad! Don't you think I know that?' She demanded fiercely, and leaned over him to shake him. 'I'd be in that place still if not for the bells and the stone in this ring! Look in it,

Shem, look! For the music of the bells kept memory awake and what I saw in the stone gave Me more to look at and think about than the blackness alone. And there was the phial in which I had the seed – Shemyaza's seed, your seed! And after the Flood some who had disagreed with Council descended the Sinking Ways again and – at great risk to themselves – released Me, and Penemue, and ... they released others too. I've never understood why! I was still sane, but some of the rest – Oh, they survive, like shadows, vegetables – or beasts!' Again She looked aside, and She laughed pointedly. 'I survived with My wit not only because of the bells and the stone but because of My purpose! But when they – they never showed Me their faces – let Me out I could barely think. I was free only in the dense body, I was still mired deep in time; many years passed before I had any sense of who I am and what I must do, for they let Me out only to face the terror of this flooded world they'd abandoned.

'I lived through it. So did others. Some Lullu survived too, warned by Kharsag – descendants of *noble* Enoch among them. I have no clear memory of it. Shem, the world was devastated. Mud and ash covered everything. Nothing grew. For years the sun didn't show its face. Men hunted and ate each other like wolves. It's amazing anything lived! I wandered for years until I was far from Kharsag in a vast open land. It was cold, and snow lay thick – but the clouds of poison ash were clearing at last and the sun had begun to show again, though vague and pale and weak. And there I met a struggling band of Lullu, hunting the huge woolly beasts called mammoths. They dimly remembered the Elohim and the world before the disaster; in fear they'd taken to human sacrifice to appease the angry Elohim. So when I met them they thought I'd come to destroy them; they threw themselves on their faces; they grovelled and apologised miserably for daring to be alive when obviously the Shining Ones wished them dead. Yes, Shem! They thought life itself a crime! And before I'd even opened My mouth they were binding up their virgins and offering them to Me with knives at the throats of the poor terrified children. Well, I put a stop to that! I told them I and My kind were to blame for their misfortunes, but they took that as a sign of My greatness, not My guilt, and insisted on worshipping Me as a goddess!

'I wasn't alone in this predicament. Other Watchers found themselves started on similar careers as gods and goddesses. The worst of it was we had no option. With the Shining Ones gone and Kharsag closed down we were on our own. I did my best. I took these wretches as My people; I taught them arts they'd forgotten; I led them to warmer lands with good hunting; I took the best of their men and bore children to strengthen them ... and in time we came to these western lands closest to the drowned continent where Azazel and Shemyaza were imprisoned. I didn't know that Azazel had already escaped, leaving Shemyaza behind. And here, Shem, I chose a womb and used Ninkharsag's art to plant Shemyaza's seed in her, and so you were born!'

Hopefully She looked at him. She sighed.

'I raised you Myself. I taught you all I knew. And here we built this place and its gate – and here I set My plan in motion.' Again She fixed Her gaze on him; Her voice grew more intense. 'You must try! We'll stop the Shift the next time – this world will live! We'll open the Starchamber again! Azazel could have done it when he broke out of the Hidden Place and left your father stranded – but he didn't care! Instead,' She snapped in a voice so angry that Shem was alerted, 'he attacked us! The first I knew about his escape was when he invaded this land with the brood he reared on the shores of the continent across the sea. I went to meet him, but he'd gone mad; all he cared about was power and lust and death. "*So I hear you want to regain what's lost, little sister!*" he sneered, "*Well, you must reckon with me first, for I'm Lord of this World of Darkness, and I'll not give up my grip on Death! I'll win it all – starting with you!*" And he nearly had us! Shem, I got you away to the Last Days just in time. Don't you see why the black bull was necessary?' She shook him, but still his eyes seemed blank. 'It was urgent; I had to get you away! When you were gone he drove us out of this isle; we were scattered to the south. I built more gates and signs in the land – I was desperate too; I could feel My memory going. It was so long before I gathered the people again and we came back here – and now you're back too, with the knowledge we need. It's somewhere inside you! Shem! Shem, wake up! We can free Shemyaza – though he's an idiot, like you – and travel the Sinking Ways, and we'll face those criminals. They owe us an explanation! And as for that Beast ...!'

Then at last She faced the flickering shadows directly.

'As for you, Azazel, you'll help us,' She cried, pointing a shaking finger. 'You can show yourself now! I know you're here! You lurker! You spy! You voyeur! Kneeling, She cupped Her breasts and thrust out Her hips and Her tongue. 'Not seen enough?' She jeered. 'Want to see more?'

11.
Spies

Shem gaped at Her, and followed Her glare. He saw nothing. He turned this way and that, but nothing showed itself. Nothing stirred or moved but torch-flame flickering in the draught, and shadows, creeping in the furrows of the raked earth floor and dancing along slick black walls, and the fumes that coiled so lazily up from the cleft dividing the Womb-hall. Yet as he gaped he felt the increase in him of that heavy dismay which had held him since his groggy emergence from lovemaking. Her tale made no more sense to him than his own vague memories of … of *what*? Remotely he felt some essential part of him had been dead too long to return to life: he felt like a heavy sleeper reluctant to wake; he could not; did not want to, make the leap to full consciousness. Now this new distraction, and with it in him a sudden huge wish to die, to rest forever, so that whatever he was trying to grasp receded still further, and Samjoyce began to stir again as on the bed beside him Tiy sat up, Her body gleaming, Her eyes blazing.

'Who are you talking to?' he mumbled. 'What …?'

'So Zoe was right!' With fists clenched She ignored him: She cried in fury at something or someone he could neither sense nor see, 'You've been spying!' Very clever! I didn't know you had the talent. I underestimated you because I despise you, and I despise you because you're rotten, but as you're here you'll help us – because you can't resist a challenge; because you know where Shemyaza's locked and where the Starchamber lies, and also because despite your miserable vices you still have a spark of light in you; you'll still choose life if given a chance – and now I challenge you to take it! So stop hiding! Show yourself!'

Then boyish laughter broke out, peal upon peal of it, high-pitched and highly amused, and at the sound of it Shem groaned with a deep despair as the urge to die grew stronger: not knowing what to do he shook his head and clenched his teeth as the laughter rang about them from a dozen points of the dark hall; as a coiling shape took smoky form amid the fumes sliding up from the cleft in the floor that ran under the bed. Then he started with fright, for from the fumes now giggled a voice. 'Sweet sisster!' it lisped in a piping, derisive alto. 'Thanks for this offer of ssalvation! Even though you desspise me? So self-deluding! Very well, I'll show myself!'

And there at the foot of the bed the fumes writhed into the shape of a smiling youth, fair-skinned, flaxen-haired, seeming solid, as naked as the two of them, wearing only his smile ... but this smile was a cold, artificial thing, a parody of good humour ... and as it fixed on Shem, Shem withdrew in horror, and Sam found himself again. Amazed, unsure where he was, he eyed Tiy, but She was glaring at ... Sam whispered it silently ... *Azazel!*

The beautiful youth bowed to him with good-humoured mockery.

'Correct! So you're Shemyaza's brat!' Azazel bowed again. 'All the way from Last Days, eh? *Shem*, is it?' And sharp blue eyes pierced him like icy drills, ransacking him, making him gasp – then Azazel's gaze grew as soft as air. 'No! Not Shem! Mr – what is it? – *Samjoyce*, of ... let me see ... *15 Berkeley Road, London N8*? Correct? I *am* pleased to meet you, and I'm *so* glad you know my name!' he purred. 'But do you like being victim of Tiy's self-righteous lust?' The beautiful youth tut-tutted sadly at Tiy who, still glaring at him, seemed speechless. 'She was always like that,' Azazel went on easily. 'Thinks herself a cut above the resst of us, and *so* hard done by? Fasscinating, her version of our hisstory! Tiy, you should be ashamed! Missleading this poor boy with your lusst and your lies!'

'You hideous hypocrite!' hissed Tiy, 'You ... monster!'

'Monster, is it?' And Sam flinched, for suddenly Azazel shifted shape into a grotesque blue giant, taloned and hairless with a cockerel's head. 'Oh, ssweet sisster!' he crowed, looming over them, scarlet comb erect and beady black eyes burning down like angry coals, 'Is thiss how you see me? You're so predictable! So we can escape? Do tell us how your lusst that got us into trouble can get us out again! How will riding Shemyaza's little bastard open any gates other than the one between your legs?' He turned his shrivelling look on Sam. 'Just as well you're not really Shem. Didn't She tell you? Shem was born from Her own ssweet flesh!'

Thunderstruck, Sam stared at Tiy. Her face was dark with rage.

'Don't listen!' She hissed. 'He's lying, as usual!'

'Am I?' Azazel leered at the horrified man. 'If you were really Shem, wouldn't you know your own dear mum? No? Oh, tut! Still, it's all in the interests of ... what would you call it? – Science? Elixirous alchemy and Hunt-The-Stone? Enlightenment? Oh, please ...' – and again Azazel shifted into the beautiful youth, lissome before them, raising a slender hand in a self-deprecating gesture –' ... don't be surprised! I do keep up with the news – and do you know,' he went on airily, 'that I've just had the great joy of meeting Mr Samjoyce's beautiful golden-haired daughter? Look!'

And suddenly, horrified, Sam sees Chrissa helpless on her back in the grove where he's lived his life as the Fool, terror in her blue eyes as Azazel advances on her, cold blue erection throbbing, scarlet cock's comb wagging, horny talons digging into the sweet green turf. There's a red rose in her hand, and "Dad!" she screams ... then she's gone.'

'And that sweet child's given you trouble?' he asked Tiy innocently. 'And her pacifist friends? The Weak Ones? I hear they got him away from poor Hoel. What's his name there? *Brother Jean*? Didn't do his job, did he? But I've helped you out!' And he smacked his lips as She glared in speechless fury. 'She was tasty. So vital. I feel so refresshed!'

'Liar!' Sam shouted, almost fooled, just in time recalling the Waters of Memory. Chrissa at Montségur! The little old woman in black telling him: '*Yes! That beast nearly seized this child when she sought you in the glade where you were! Watch him! Don't let his false shapes fool you!*' Now, trembling, he stood and eyed both Tiy and Azazel with loathing. 'She got away from both of you!' he cried, 'You're both as bad as each other!'

Azazel pulled a face at this. Tiy shut Her eyes and reared stiffly up as if demanding strength. 'Fool, he's trying to divide us!' She hissed, 'You know he's a liar! It's true I've had to fight your daughter, but that's because she persists in resisting Me and seeing Me as ...'

'... the liar and thief you are!' crowed Azazel, cockerel again. 'You stole this place from me, but soon I'll have it back. Don't you know what happened to your army today? Has your Long Sight been … a little cloudy?'

'Stop!' Tiy shouted. 'We must find agreement and open the Starchamber. You know how to find it, and the codes to open it. We can …'

'Live forever?' asked Azazel, grinning madly, preening himself as Sam gaped. 'Why? Life's over-rated; it exissts only to feed Death, which is the climax of all dessire, and it's Death I seek – so why stop the Shift? Let Fire and Flood come! Yesss, and so say the Lullu of Mr Samjoyce's Last Days! They know it's all a lie – riches, pleasure, life itsself!' He eyed Sam with real admiration, then crowed: 'Their beautiful madness; the lovely weapons they make: far beyond the simple designs I sowed! They don't need us – they've outstripped us. Of course we do our best, and their disbelief in us makes our tassk much easier. Oh, their lovely wars! So tassty!

'But,' he added magnanimously, 'Samjoyce has come so far for so little, and I *do* love challenge and competition because – *truth*, Tiy! – I'm bored; and it hardly matters. Whatever happens, the Lasst Days are mine! Then I possess everyone, and … BOOM!' He flicked out his tongue and rolled his beady eye at Her. 'As for you, sssweet Tiy, I'll have you soon. The man-time you hate is near! – though first there'll be a Feast of Light. Do you know what I mean?' His eyes rolled up in ecstasy. 'I see it now! Forests torn up, the sea sick, the green places black! So, send Mr Samjoyce to me! If he can defeat me on my terms, then maybe I'll agree to help you. *Maybe*! But I don't think he'll defeat me. Who ever defeats Death in this world?'

Abruptly he was fading, his voice a whisper as he turned to Sam. 'I'll look forward to meeting you, Mr Samjoyce … in the flesh, as it were. It'll put a little spice into life. Ask for me at the Panting Cliff. Everyone knows where it is. Bring friends, if you like, but watch out for the Feast of Light, and don't bring Tiy, or I won't agree to anything – I find her so hypocritical.' And he heaved a wondering sigh. 'Why can't she be honest and admit that her true lover is Death? But you don't want to listen to me moralising, and I must go now, I must meet my sons and congratulate them on their victory.' He wagged a ghostly finger. 'Your Eagle Regiment, Tiy! Such a pity! So many fine, tasty men!'

Azazel laughed … and then he was gone.

So Tiy and Sam were left facing each other, nakedly alone together in the depths of the night, in the depths of the Womb-hall, elixirous ecstasy of far memory fled, and hate in Sam's heart that he could not hide as he glared at Her beautiful, furious face. And in his mask-like expression She saw nothing of Shem. Her heart sank: silently She raged at Azazel. *He fooled Me! How long has he spied? How much does he know? He stopped Shem waking up ... but he didn't stop Me remembering. He won't get away with it!*

Yet when Sam opened his mouth She knew She had to get the first word in. She threw up Her arms and cried in a dull rapid voice: 'Shem, wake up! See how he's trying to divide us with his jabber about death, and owning the Last Days. Don't you see? He fears you! He knows with your help I'll beat him! He knows I mean to send you against him; he's trying to stop that with an invitation you'll refuse, and ...'

'So You're Shem's mother,' Sam interrupted with flat distaste.

She glared at him then, turning wearily from the bed, reached for the full, opaque green robe that Zoe had laid out for Her.

'Shem,' She said, pulling it over Her head, 'you can't ...'

'I'm not Shem!' Sam cried harshly. 'I'm Sam Joyce! You sent Shem looking for a sucker like me as host, and yes, he *is* in me – but I'm Sam Joyce! It doesn't matter if You *are* his mother ... but if I *were* him I'd feel pretty sick right now! And as She moved towards him he shouted: 'DON'T COME NEAR ME!'

She gasped angrily and began pacing round the Womb-hall, Her bare feet leaving deep prints in the raked red earth. Every time She looked at him he was gazing straight back at Her with hate in his eyes.

'Shem,' She said carefully, 'I am NOT your mother, and ...'

'Who cares?' He snatched at his tunic. 'Though from Shem's point of view it's preferable, as it makes him a pure-bred ex-Elohim pervert with no dirty Lullu blood in him.' And savagely he dressed.

'Listen!' She insisted, 'I'll tell you how together we built the ...'

'No!' he snapped. 'I've heard enough! You've used Shem, You've used me, You tried to kill my daughter – but the *Weak Ones* protect her; they've beaten You once and they'll beat You again!'

'Azazel lied about your daughter!' She cried. 'Why can't ...'

'What's the odds?' Thought of Chrissa infuriated him. 'You may mean well, but if half Your story's true no wonder You're mad!'

At this She seized his shoulders. 'DON'T – BE – FOOLED!' She hissed, emphasising each word with a shake. 'THIS – IS – WHAT – HE – WANTS!'

Without warning She stopped. She reared back, gasping. Something – what? – She felt most peculiar – torn and divided inside!

And even as She stopped shaking him Sam seemed to hear the old Cathar woman who'd spoken to him from the Waters of Memory. '*Shut your eyes! Look now!*'

He did . . . and in a blaze of emerald light before him saw not Tiy but a blue-eyed young woman, tall and striking with waves of yellow hair. She looked at him anxiously, for at first he didn't know her . . . then it began to dawn on him. '*Yes, Dad,*' she said urgently, and, amazed, he heard her. '*It's me, Chrissa! Yes, years have passed, but there's still a chance – if you can defeat Azazel. But you'll need the ring. Remember Old Davey's tale!*'

Tiy shuddered, utterly bemused by the invasion. She felt some fresh bright younger self using Her eyes, speaking with Her voice! It was quite intolerable! So bright! How old and dark She'd grown! *Weak Ones!* She cried silently, turning on Herself in angry panic. *Hoel! Destroy them!*

As abruptly as it had come the brilliant, fearful presence left her. Sam opened his eyes as, panting with relief, She let him go.

'Don't worry, Lady.' Shocked himself, he turned away, thinking fast. *Don't let Her know!* 'I'll go to Azazel,' he said rapidly. 'Why not? I've got nothing to lose.' He glanced at Her left hand. 'But I must have that ring.'

'What?' She clutched at it. 'Why do you want it?'

'Because I need it,' he said, straight-faced, 'and it's mine.'

'*Yours*?' Angrily She thrust it at his face: he stared past moon and horns into the depths. 'I'd give it to *Shem*,' She hissed, 'but you say you're *Samjoyce*! How can you justify a claim to it? Tell Me that!'

'My grandfather gave it to me,' he said. 'He got it from his father, who got it off a corpse who wore a birdfeather robe – like Yours.' At her expression he showed his teeth in a humourless grin. 'Want to hear more?'

She stared at him. 'Go on,' She said slowly, Her heart beating hard as the sense of invasion gradually receded. Yet She felt confused.

'The corpse was one of three, all in those robes.' He met Her gaze. 'Two men, one woman. He found them in a room in the rock of a volcanic isle that came from the sea. It looks to me,' he went on boldly, now with Her uncertain attention, 'that You and me and that overgrown rooster already got to the Starchamber and left this world for good!' He faced Her obstinately. 'You mean You don't know any of this?'

'My memory's been poor,' She cried. 'You know that.'

She's not sure! I've got Her! 'I don't buy predestination,' he said, grinning harshly, 'but it looks as if we'll get there, whether I like it or not. If we can't get there without his help, then plainly I'm going to get him to give it.' His grin faded. 'So I'll go. But I need the ring. And good guides.' He waited … but at Her doubting look exploded in calculated outburst. 'For Christ's sake,' he yelled, 'is that too much to ask?'

'Christ?' She whispered, caught by unformed fears. 'Who's that?'

'Doesn't matter!' he snapped. 'I'm just using his name in vain. I'm fed up. Why should I trust You if You don't trust me?' And with an angry gesture he turned away, but She grabbed his arm.

'WHO – IS – CHRIST?' She blazed at him. 'I must know! Is he a Weak One? A friend of your daughter? Does he plan to help you escape Me?'

Sam laughed out loud. 'My Lady, he won't be around for – I don't even know when we are – two thousand years? And he'd be Your friend, in fact I think it might have been You,' he went on, 'that the hard men were about to kill for Your sins, but he said: *Let him who is without sin cast the first stone.* So they killed him instead, stole his message of love, and for twenty centuries they've been telling suckers his murder redeems mankind of its sins, and killing anyone who disagrees.'

'Hard … men …?' She asked, utterly perplexed.

'Like Hoel,' he said acidly. 'Christ's message was stolen by women-haters of the man-time run by men like Hoel. You wouldn't like them.'

'And you?' She asked, wondering: *Is this Christ of the Elohim? What if they haven't abandoned this world?* 'Did you … like them?'

'Nope.' He shrugged. 'Though maybe *You'd* get along with them.' Again his disturbing grin. 'So they'll wipe out all memory of You, but they'll wipe out the Weak Ones too.' He eyed her impatiently. 'So how about it? The ring. And good guides. Then I'll go.'

'I'll think about it,' She said wearily, feeling a headache coming on.

'Suits me,' said Sam Joyce as silently She called Zoe. He whistled a Madonna hit until She cried at him to shut up. 'Fine,' he said. 'But I want the ring. And guides.'

And as Azazel emerged from his bath atop the Panting Cliff to greet (in the guise of venerable grey-bearded king) the conquering heroes of his army; as Deru miserably awaited death and the Wild Women led Dion through dark woods to the Whole Place; as Zoe, alerted from sleep in her cell by Her call, struggled with ideas she dared not admit: so, faraway in a man-time, Brother Jean d'Aubigny the Dominican friar, now *vicaire* to the Prior of the Diocesan Chapter at Carcassonne in the Aude, resisted sleep for fear of the nightmare that often seized him and prepared the trial of three heretics taken in a raid on the Cathar convent at Fanjeaux. And at Montségur, high on its crag in the Pyrenean wilderness, the goodmen watched and waited in the knowledge that the strands of a great scheme were now beginning to knit together even as they seemed to be falling apart ...

Nervously entering the Womb-hall Zoe found the Lady distracted and the Fool grim. 'Take him to the room I told you to prepare,' Tiy said, not meeting the eyes either of Zoe or the Fool as Zoe led him away.

At last alone again Tiy groaned, rubbed Her head, and went to the Room of the Rose. There She lit the five candles, knelt before the crystal cube, and wept freely. She remembered enough now to make Her wish She'd remembered nothing. But too late now. Rage replaced Her tears. To think of Azazel's spying, of this boorish Samjoyce creature who'd supplanted Shem! And Shem, proving so weak and letting it happen!

Worse still, that alarming invasion!

Was that Samjoyce's daughter? Does he want the ring to bring her here and supplant Me? But ... it seemed like Myself ... only brighter ...

But worrying about it did no good.

There was a lot to decide, quickly.

'What's gone wrong?' She asked the emerald depths. 'It was Shem I sent to the Last Days. I prepared him as carefully as if he were my own ...' – Her mind clouded; She had to shut Her eyes and clench Her fists before going on – 'I explained it all! He couldn't fail; he hasn't; he's back, but ... he's not Shem any more!' And She looked into the ring, wondering if Samjoyce's tale of his ancestor finding it was a lie. 'It foxes Me,' She declared angrily. 'Who *is* Samjoyce? How can I send him against the Beast when Beast-projection's enough to turn him against Me? If I give him the ring he'll use it against Me, but what else can I do? I'll have to chance it. At least he's willing to go! But why? Does he think once he's out of My sight he'll escape Me? Maybe he thinks the Weak Ones will save him, or this Christ, or his daughter, or … who knows? I'll send Zoe to watch him. And guides … yes …'

In time She was calm enough to try Long Sight through the emerald. And discovered that the fog on Her vision had lifted. Weakly She took wing; west through the wild wet moonless night She glided over forests and plains to black gloomy hills where rivers rushed. So She came to the ford where the Eagle Regiment had been massacred by the death-wish weapon. So She confirmed that not everything Azazel had told Her that evening was false. The Ass had kicked Her army. The Regiment was destroyed.

Grimly from the scene of the slaughter She came to the base-camp of Her army. Like a great invisible owl She swooped over the sodden plains to the low hill on which the camp stood within its palisades. There She inspected the confusion, the sleepless fear that gripped the men. She came to a tent in which lay the officer who'd condemned Deru and a dozen others to death at dawn: the man was tossing and turning, and he shivered as a cold wind swept through him … and from him She learned about Deru.

She found the miserable half-free in the trench where he lay. *Hmm,* She thought, inspecting the wretch's subtle knowledge, *perhaps … but I must move fast, or the Beast'll be all over us.*

And Deru groaned, held in a nightmare of a great bloody bird that tore his mind apart … then the terror was gone.

Back to the Whole Place She winged, now more settled in mind despite the disasters of the night. And so later a message was sent.

And by dawn, more directly, She learned about Dion …

12.

Out of the Frying-Pan . . .

For at first light three of the Wild Women came to the Whole Place, to the outer precinct of the temple. 'Gatekeeper, open up!' they cried, so when he peered through the spyhole in the gate and saw them waiting on the road in their rain-soaked rags, mud-caked ropes of filthy hair hanging over their faces and sharp blood-encrusted nails raised, he hurried to let them in. He kept his eyes averted as he did, for it was man-lore that to meet the gaze of these crones was to risk being turned to stone. Superstition apart, it was well known how they'd dealt with Hoel a few days previously.

The gatekeeper ran to find Boann, and Boann went to find Zoe, whose subtle hearing had already alerted her.

'What is it, Mothers?' Zoe asked them respectfully.

'A word for the Lady's ear,' one of them whispered.

'Of a stranger with sweet music,' hissed the second.

'Even now our sisters bring him,' the third said grimly.

So down to the depths Zoe brought them, past the cell where the Fool was held under lock and key, and over the River to the door of the room near the Womb-hall where Tiy was resting after the night's exertions. Into Her presence they went, and down on their hands and knees, and at the sight of them Tiy felt a fresh premonition, a new fear.

'What is it?' She asked.

'A man came to us last night,' said the first.

'A strange man who knows Your secret name,' said the second.

'A beautiful man who is not like other men,' said the third.

'He knows what we foresaw in Hoel's boiled bones,' said the first.

'He makes music so sweet we could not kill him for invading our secret place,' said the second.

'He says You would be angry if we touched a hair of his head,' said the third,' and that neither You nor Your Fool will succeed without his help.'

'Our sisters bring him to You now,' added the first.

They fell silent, and in silence Tiy regarded them. At length, with a troubled face, She made a gesture, and they left Her.

Meanwhile on the palisaded hill amid steady drizzle Her army assembled to witness the execution of those wretches condemned to death the night before. Thirteen stakes of ash, sharpened both ends, were set upright in a circle on open ground at the shallow, grassy summit of the hill. Ladders stood against them, and as the thirteen victims were brought out to die a buzz of expectation ran through the ranks: men muttered grimly how these bastard traitors deserved to die; skins of hard liquor went round with sergeants turning a blind eye. And Deru, still gagged, his arms bound behind his back, saw how crows squabbled expectantly in the branches of a nearby tree ... and his heart beat, horribly alive, as the first man in line was seized and dragged, kicking and struggling, up the rough-made ladder, to be planted squarely on the stake and ...

At the back of the line he shut his eyes.

He had been put at the back of the thirteen, the last to die, very deliberately ... for the message from the Whole Place had been received.

One by one the victims ahead of him were dragged to their slow, hideous death. They made no sound. Like Deru, they were all gagged. Deru kept his eyes shut: his mind was frozen and he knew nothing but an overwhelming sense of his own stupidity as those ahead of him were impaled. He tried not to listen, yet could not help but hear (and count) the roar from the assembled ranks that greeted the horrible piercing of each of them.

... nine ... ten ... eleven ... twelve ...

A hand shoved him in the back; other hands grabbed him. 'Your turn, mate!' a harsh voice jeered. His legs failed him; he wet himself as he stumbled and fell. His eyes opened at last, and what he saw before him ...

Delirious with terror he was dragged forward ... and he had been forced halfway up the ladder when a voice cried out:

'No! Not that one! Take him down! The Lady wants him alive!'

The last he heard before he passed out were the boos and the huge groan of disappointment that rose from the ranks of Her army.

An hour later, barely conscious, he was on his way to the Whole Place.

At noon sunshine broke through the clouds: at last the rain stopped as Dion was brought to the Gardens round the Whole Place. No crowds gathered for the arrival of the curly-haired, blue-eyed man; in fact people were conspicuous by their absence from the Serpent-Way, for word had spread concerning the approach of the Wild Women with a stranger. Those who did dare to look from a safe distance noted the confident walk and easy disposition of this second stranger to arrive at the Whole Place within two days . . . and also saw how the terrifying crones surrounding him fawned on him, and left him with reluctance when, at the Rose Arch, Zoe met and politely dismissed them.

'The Lady asks me to greet you, Old Mothers, and does not forget how you serve Her, and asks me to lead this man to Her in the Emerald Bower.'

So, keeping her thoughts and eyes strictly to herself, Zoe led this new arrival to the sparkling ferns and shrubs of the Emerald Bower.

'The Lady will be here shortly,' said Zoe, and left him there.

In fact Tiy, masked and robed in green, was hiding behind a mulberry bush. She wanted a good look at this new man who'd entranced Wild Women not noted for their love of men. So She was intrigued to see how, when Zoe left him, he smiled a secret smile, sat down on a bench, and from the pack on his back took out his lyre. Gently at first, then with mounting fire he improvised a wordless song of sustained harmonies that made Her shiver and set Her blood pulsing. For his music was resonant of events She'd recalled during Her firing by the Fool the night before; events of the heights from which She'd been banished. And as She listened a hope stirred in her; a hope She hardly dared admit . . . but as the song winged higher Her hope grew stronger so that, still not showing Herself, She eyed the stranger more intently and Her breathing came faster.

At length She lifted the emerald ring, and past moon and horns looked into its depths. Her eyes widened at what She saw.

'*Use them well*,' She murmured, as if repeating someone else's words, '*And don't forget we're with you?* But can it really be?'

She sighed, and with the diffidence of a shy girl stepped out from Her hiding-place and showed Herself. Dion, still with that quiet secret smile on his face, finished his song and laid down the lyre. He turned, and stood and bowed, but very slightly, as an equal to an equal, and his bright blue eyes did not leave Her masked face.

'In what land did you learn to play like that?' asked Tiy, voice harsh with poorly-suppressed emotion.

'In the land of the asphodel, Lady,' he said quietly, 'and recently in Khem, where much is known ... including your name and original nature.'

'And what is My ... original nature?'

'Once of neither sex, now of one sex,' chanted Dion; 'once of subtle flesh, now of dense! Once timeless, now thick in time. Once like the wind, now like the earth. Once like the stars ... now like the dust.'

She stared at him in silence, and he met Her masked gaze.

'Once high in the sky beyond the Whirling Castle,' he went on, 'now gone underground to find what you lost. Once double-sexed with the womb of the moon and the horns of the great black bull ... and now with a Fool who does not know what to do, nor how to do it. But with my music' – he shrugged – 'perhaps the Fool may overcome even the Beast.'

Still speechless with hope, She stared at him.

'Lady,' he said, no longer smiling, 'you don't need the mask to protect me from your brilliance. I have looked upon the Shining Ones, and it cannot be said that I am blind.'

'My brilliance isn't what it was.' She was surprised to hear Herself say it. Slowly She removed the mask, and at his steady gaze Her shoulders slumped a little, as if in relief. Then, biting Her lip, She showed him the ring on Her finger. The emerald sparkled in the sunlight.

'And ... the original nature of this?' She asked.

Dion smiled. 'The same as that of the bells you have.'

She found it hard to contain herself. 'And who gave them to Me?'

'Must you test me like this?' he asked. 'Didn't we say we were with you still? Isn't it enough that I'm here when you and your Fool need me?' He eyed Her gravely. 'You fear your plan's undone, that Shem's lost, and that your Last Days man is a poor substitute. But Samjoyce has a daughter, and perhaps you're wrong to resist her ...

for it may be that her nature is not so dissimilar to yours, and that the goal is the same in either case … and that *your* plan runs wider and deeper than you thought.'

Her head was whirling. 'What are you saying?'

'Tiy, Tiy,' the man called Dion reproved Her, 'you've remembered some things, but there's much more to come before the Beast's defeated, so the sooner we set about it the better. Also,' he said without any change of emphasis, 'I've come a long way, by roads not much used in recent years. I'm hungry, and I could do with a bath and a rest.'

Again She felt tears welling in Her eyes, and did not try to hide them from him as She looked up into the blue, blue sky, trying to see something invisible to Her now-too-human eyes.

'Do … our kind still maintain the Whirling Castle?' She heard Herself ask. 'Is that the way you came … or is there … is there another …?'

'You don't need to ask,' said Dion gently. 'Besides, you have other business to deal with while I rest. The man you reprieved this morning is here now, awaiting your order to guide the three of us through the mountains to confront the Beast …'

'The three of you?' She asked sharply.

'Your Fool, myself, and your servant who brought me here.'

Convinced now, She gazed at him with a lightness in Her heart which She could not recall from all Her time in this world. Then She felt green fire leap from the emerald in the ring; the ring that …

'That too,' agreed Dion.

'What?' She was startled again.

He nodded. 'Trust him with it,' Dion said, 'and maybe you'll find he's not such a fool.' And as he started towards the temple, he added: 'But be ready for sacrifice, Tiy.' His eyes lingered thoughtfully on Her. 'You won't find any of this easy. If you truly wish to overcome the Beast and see this Hidden World open itself up to the Light, you may have to give up more than you know, or choose, or want! So be ready!'

Faint with hope and amazement She led him out of the Gardens.

Masked again She came with Dion to the outer precinct courtyard, where Boann, on hands and knees and apparently overwhelmed, stuttered that Deru the half-free had arrived and was in a cell. 'Oh?' She asked with a sharp eye on Dion, who remained quiet and calm. And with Her mind in a whirl Tiy saw Zoe there too, and told her:

'Take this man to Fiachnu; alert the kitchen to his needs; prepare a room. Then meet me in the Emerald Bower. I want a word with you.' Too preoccupied to note the fear in Zoe's eyes, She turned to Boann. 'I'll see the half-free later,' She said … and then strode back to the Gardens, unaware that She shone much more brightly than usual.

Zoe, in fear She'd read her secret thoughts at last (for Her eyes had blazed), mutely led the fascinating new stranger to Fiachnu, then returned to the Emerald Bower where the birds sang, where sun sparkled on wet leaves and where the Lady Tiy, deep in thought, was pacing slowly up and down.

Trembling in her subtle senses, Zoe waited until She turned.

'Zoe,' She said quietly, 'would you die for Me, if I asked you?'

Zoe breathed sharply. *So this is it!* she thought. *She knows!*

'Die for You, Lady? Yes, but … what … have I …?'

'You're one of the few I can trust,' Tiy went on, and Her voice held a note of exaltation and hope Zoe had not heard before, 'and I have a task for you. A dangerous task. You must go into the heart of Azazel's realm with the Fool and the two strangers who arrived here today. Now come here!' She commanded, crooking a finger. 'Don't be afraid! See this?' And She showed Zoe the emerald ring, and if She noted how wild were Zoe's eyes and how fast came her breath, She made no comment. 'I will be giving this ring to the Fool,' She said, and only then realised that Dion *had* convinced Her. Yet still She felt a wrench in Her heart, and sighed before going on. 'It contains power; it's valuable to Me, but the task will be hard, and he may need it. But,' She said, choosing words with care, 'I'm not wholly sure he can be trusted: I Myself cannot go on this mission; I need eyes and ears – you will be those eyes and ears!' Her eyes flashed through the mask, and as they fixed on her Zoe felt briefly paralysed. 'I repeat: this journey will be dangerous. Will you do it … for Me?'

Whether She suspects or not, Zoe knew in horror, *She has me!*

'Yes, Lady.' In a dream, or maybe a nightmare, she bowed, and as she did nervously she fingered the bronze figurine of the Lady that clasped her long black hair. 'For You, My Lady, I'll do it,' she heard herself say.

'Good,' said Tiy, remotely pleased. 'I'll instruct you after I've seen the half-free. Now. You'll bring him to Me beyond Sixth Gate, where I must impress certain facts on him. But on the way, test his subtle senses on the Quiet Door.' She laughed, short and sharp. 'He won't be much use as your guide if he can't pick *that* up!'

Then, leaving Zoe standing, She swept away … but as She went She was turning the emerald ring round Her finger, still plagued by doubt…

Deru, no longer sure of anything, grew even less sure when the black-robed young woman came and haughtily indicated that he should follow her. He was still shaken and bruised by the mad ride from the camp. After his unexpected reprieve he had been slung over a horse like a bag of corn; the escort taking him to the Whole Place had ridden hard all morning, without pause save twice to change horses, until the high crag loomed ahead as the rain at last faded and the sun came out. Still bound hand and foot, with no explanation offered – far less food and drink – he had been dragged to a cell in the outer precinct (with a few kicks and insults for good measure) and left on a damp earth floor to consider his sins and likely fate. He decided numbly that he'd been saved from impalement for a death even worse – no doubt after torture to drag from him information he did not have. So when at last the door opened and the young woman appeared with a soldier who cut the rope round his ankles (but left his wrists bound) he was sure only that the torment was about to begin. 'You were right, Mother,' he muttered bitterly as he was pushed past gaping onlookers to the downward passage beyond the jagged slash of First Arch. 'I should have settled down! I've thrown Long Life away. Deru is a fool who deserves the worse!'

So daylight was left behind. Soon, despite his dullness of mind and body, his pricking skin told him what kind of place this was; and he knew his capacity for terror was not yet fully tested, for the deeper they went the more acutely he felt the violent dragon-tides jarring his bones and turning his blood to water. It was no consolation to smell the fear of the soldier shoving him along behind the haughty priestess as they passed under the grotesque carvings of Second Arch and beyond Third Arch into the utter darkness where Zoe turned and dismissed the man. 'I'll take care of this creature now,' she said coldly. 'He's no danger. You can go.'

With the relieved man gone at a near-run back to the light, Zoe raised a torch to eye the trembling, ugly half-free with distaste. 'You're a spy,' she said contemptuously, her voice echoing – yet as she spoke he sensed she too was afraid, and he wondered why. 'But if you prove useful you may live – for a while. Now. Tell me what you sense about this place?'

'The d-d-dragons,' he stuttered.

'Come along!' She seized his bound arm. 'We go deeper.'

So past Fourth to Fifth Arch they came. Zoe held up the torch to show the hole in the floor at their feet. 'There!' she snapped. 'Jump!'

'Jump?' he asked, his teeth chattering as he looked down.

'Yes! Jump! Now! It's the only way!'

And Deru, faint of heart, his body on fire with the dragon-war, was about to jump ... but then intuition bade him pause. Frowning, he drew back.

'What's keeping you?' the woman demanded, tension in her voice.

'Are you testing me?' asked Deru strangely. 'Give me a minute!'

And when with a sigh she stood aside he knew he was right. He shut his eyes and quietly felt the warring currents, calming himself until a subtle map of what lay about formed in his mind, the hot and cold, the solid and hollow of it ... and at length he walked to the blank smooth wall, laid his head against a particular point, and said:

'Here. A door. Stairs beyond. But my hands ...'

'... Stay tied,' she said, but sounded relieved as she found and pushed the node that opened the Quiet Door. *I could almost believe*, thought Deru, *that she wanted me to succeed!* And he began to wonder about his chances of staying alive long enough to see daylight again ... but Zoe moved him down the steps bypassing Fifth Arch. Along the steep, narrow, sandy-floored passage they went, at one point passing several heavy wooden doors set in the rocky wall. From behind one of them (though they passed with hardly a sound) there came a sudden rattling, and the muffled sound of a furious voice. Deru jumped in alarm. 'What's that?' he cried – but Zoe pushed him on. 'Just a Fool like you!' she said roughly.

So they came to the River of Death, the focus of the dragon-currents, where Deru felt drowned in a huge mournfulness. It took an effort to stop himself weeping as the Charon rowed them to the jetty where the drowsy hound mumbled at the scraps which Zoe threw it. And at the entrance to the winding passage beyond he was seized by such a primal flood of dark images that his legs jellified and he could not move at all.

'You're right to be afraid,' whispered Zoe grimly when at last she got him to move along. 'Do you know where you are? Do you know Whose place this is?' But he kept quiet. Grimly, unable to hide the tremor in her own voice, she hissed. 'The Lady Whose army you betrayed.'

But Deru kept quiet as he was brought to Tiy in the Womb-hall ... yet when he entered that dim, terrible place, and saw the great looming figure of the Red Lady of War before him, awesome with blood apparently dripping from Her, his control snapped and he wailed aloud.

'Come here,' murmured Tiy.

Gripping the terrified half-free with Her eye, Tiy told him what he had to do and what would happen if he failed or tried to betray Her. 'Do you think,' She asked, eyes blazing in his face, 'the fate you've escaped is the worst? Try to trick Me and you'll find there's much worse!' And his misshapen face twisted in agony as Her eyes burned him: he cowered as She laughed. 'Free Men! So sensitive!' She said acidly, 'But as it's your sensitivity I need, I won't complain. Guide My Fool safely by the subtle ways and dragon-paths to Azazel, and I'll forget your other treacheries.'

'But ... but what protection is there against Azazel?' Deru cried out.

'Protection? Keep moaning and you'll find that stake up your arse!'

Then, dismissing Zoe with the cringing half-free, She said:

'We'll meet at sunset on the height. I'll bring the Fool. You see to this creature and ... the other one. Go and make your preparations.'

Alone again she brooded on Dion's advice about sacrifice, Samjoyce's daughter ... and the ring. Particularly the ring. Tight-lipped She went to the Room of the Rose where She knelt, turning the emerald ring round Her finger, filled with doubt and worrying about the blue-eyed stranger.

'He's from the Elohim,' She muttered, 'How else would he know all this? But he asks too much! I've lost so much already! I must get rid of that child! I can't give Samjoyce the ring with her still free. Hoel failed Me once ... but he can try again!'

She donned the birdfeather robe and began the chant; through emerald depths She flew far upwhen, at last to find her prey. She smiled to see the pathetic creature, rocking and moaning in a cell in a tower of stone, far from the green woods.

I sent you to the man-time to do My work, Hoel,' she sang, invading his mind with her chant –

... and as She chants She sees Hoel rape and possess a red-haired woman in Her name; She sees Samjoyce's blue-eyed daughter and this red-haired woman in conflict; She sees a house burning; She sees the hateful child in chains, rotting

in a cell; She sees fire bloom and cries triumphantly:

'BURN, CHILD! BURN! –

And She was about to leave the emerald connection when ...

'What?' She flinched. 'What's this?'

For someone touched Her! A mind on the green ray of Long Sight!

She looked ... and saw that tiny old woman; that tiny old woman with the green stone from the castle of the Weak Ones! Staring at Her!

'You Weak One!' She cried, and in fury struck, hurling her opponent into darkness which surely she'd never escape. 'I'm amazed at your folly! Did you think you'd invade Me like this? It was you here last night, wasn't it? And that child! So you caught Me unawares once, but not ...'

Then something utterly unexpected happened.

A brilliant flare of light burst through Her.

It blinded Her, hurling Her from the emerald depths so that She lost Her grip on the old woman; it came and went in an instant, but in that instant terrible visions of failure flashed in her like suns exploding.

Then it was gone, leaving her in darkness, leaving no clue as to its origin. It was a time before She stood, dazed and grim, changed in a way She could not identify as, slowly removing the ring from Her finger, She left the Womb-hall, crossed the River, and came to the Fool.

'Let me out, damn you!' Sam shouted furiously.

But the feet receded. With a groan he stopped rattling the door of the cell and sank back to the cot. How many hours since he'd awoken, he had no idea, any more than he knew how long he'd slept. The cell was cold but at least the cot was warm, piled high with furs. Beside him in the darkness he'd found a loaf of bread, a jug of wine, and an empty wooden bucket.

His memory of events in the Womb-hall was vague and fantastic. As in a dream he recalled Shem surfacing in him, the elixir, the lovemaking, Tiy's tale of the Fall, Azazel's challenge, and his own ultimatum to Tiy – but he was not sure any of it had really happened. He had no memory of entering this cell. Did it matter? He'd slept dreamlessly. Now he was awake. For what? Deeply depressed he lay down and pulled the furs over him. Soon he slept again, and dreamed ... and Azazel, the beautiful youth, came prancing before him like some absurd catamite.

'*Well, Mr. Samjoyce! So you're coming my way, eh? Soon we'll see how you tassste! Don't expect to win; the Elohim don't care about this world, they know it's mine – and so does Tiy. Poor Tiy! She's so dessperate! Clutching at falssse hope! And you too, thinking your sssweet daughter can save you. But she's lossst too! Hoel's got her at lassst. Look!*'

And images form –

And here's Hoel – *Hoel, cut to pieces before his eyes only days ago. Did it really happen?* – Hoel, wearing a friar's black robe, grinning madly at him through the bars of a window high in a tower!

'*Fool!*' Hoel cries, '*At dawn Christ triumphs and Ailma's mine! Too bad, you can't stop me now! Nor can She! She's dead!*'

And now he plunges, into a dark cell, and in it he sees, chained to the wall, the little old Cathar woman he saw from the Waters of Memory, tending Chrissa in the castle. With a fateful calm that bodes no good she meets his eyes. Then in another cell he sees an old man he doesn't know, and –

Chrissa!

In a third cell, curled up on her side.

Chrissa!

The same tall, thin, adult Chrissa who (did it happen?) came to him in the Womb-hall, who gave him advice and hope. But that Chrissa was strong and bright, and now – in his dream he shakes his head in dismay, for with utter clarity he sees her, shut up like himself, but in much worse shape. Unlike the other two she isn't chained, but her face! So gaunt and disfigured by sores, unkempt long hair lank from lack of sun, only her eyes still bright, given an ageless look by pain.

Yet she sees him. Her eyes light up in desperate hope.

'*Dad! You're still there! You are, aren't you?*'

Then the flash of brilliant light leapt through him.

It blinded him and tore him out of his dream. It was as if the blazing sun had leapt into this cell, dispelling every shadow.

As suddenly as it came it was gone, leaving him dazed in darkness that seemed deeper than before, clutching his head as he sat up.

'Chrissa!' he muttered over and over again in his horror and grief.

Time passed. At length the door grated open, and a lesser light shone.

Slowly he got to his feet and saw Tiy standing there, holding a lamp in one hand, regal in birdfeather robe, fully masked. And in Her other hand –

She was holding out the emerald ring!

'Take it, Fool,' She said in a freezing whisper, 'I'm persuaded you'll need it. But be warned! Misuse it, or use it against Me, or to contact your daughter, and I'll know at once! Now put it on!'

Tentatively, in shock, he did so ... and gasped as the green fire of its power flooded his blood and brain, so that wild light surged in him again amid a welter of visions he could not catch. Dizzy, he would have fallen, but She caught him by the shoulder, and Her smile fearful and ironic.

'Now follow Me, you brave strong man! You're about to meet the guides you asked for. Three of them! Tonight you leave ... to confront Azazel!'

So Sam Joyce followed Her ... up ... towards the light again, at last.

13.
. . . Into the Fire

That hot September night of 1240 was still. The waning moon had not yet risen: the sky above the besieged city, though cloudless, was dense with haze pierced only by the brightest stars. Earlier, from the courtyard of the Citadel, itself newly walled within the great curtain walls of the city, hammering had been heard, but that (to the relief of all who knew what it meant) had ceased. Now a fearful hush lay not only on Carcassonne, high on its scarp above the rebuilt suburb of St Vincent and the marshes of the Aude, but also on the camp of the besieging army on the river's west bank. Indeed, the silence was such that guards on the ramparts and towers of the outer walls, alert for any sound of enemy sappers, could hear frogs croaking in the marshes, and see the fires of the enemy army; but if they looked inward they heard nothing and saw only a few dim lights shining in the winding, narrow streets inside the walls: there was neither sound nor sign of activity in Carcassonne that night.

Yet behind shut doors the event scheduled for dawn was causing fury. In a rich apartment high in the Citadel, Guillaume d'Ormes the seneschal of Carcassonne stood glaring at the bleak thin cleric who perched on a stool like a scrawny bird, fists clenched into his lap. 'You're the *Prior!*' the French commander cried, 'Locking up that lunatic wasn't enough! Couldn't you find a *formula* to prevent this disaster.

'God isn't a juggler.' Ricard de Capdenier didn't blink; his voice was harsh and uncompromising. 'She condemned herself. There was no option!'

'No option?' The seneschal eyed the Prior in amazement. 'What do you mean? We're besieged; relief is weeks away; the countryside's up in arms and the suburbs are unreliable; yet you say there's *no option!* It's pure provocation – didn't I *beg* you to control your *vicaire* and hold off?'

'You did,' agreed the Prior acidly, 'but we can't compromise where heresy's concerned. I did all I could; I took over the case myself, but she wouldn't recant! Don't you see that God's will is being done?'

'I've no doubt God is wonderfully pleased,' the seneschal snapped. 'But it's what men think and do that concerns me here!'

'Take care, my lord,' the Prior warned, primly furious. 'You risk forgetting that this war's fought for the soul, not the flesh.'

With a cry of disgust the seneschal threw up his hands and strode to an open window where, tall and moody, he brooded on the dark silhouette of the Great Tower in which the condemned lay fettered, awaiting their fate.

I hate priests! he told himself. *And I'm sick of this land!*

Behind him, the Prior fumed too. *How did I get caught in this web? Worldly needs don't marry the soul's – they're distinct and apart, and . . .*

Suddenly realising the heresy of his thought, he paled and stood.

'Have I your leave to go?' he demanded.

'Is there no hope of stopping this?' the seneschal asked bleakly.

'None whatever. God's will must be done!'

'Then in *God's* name get out of here!' barked the seneschal.

'Will you be present at the relaxation?'

'No! I will not! It is your act, not mine!'

'It is God's act,' said the Prior coldly as he withdrew, leaving Guillaume d'Ormes with a knotted brow and a headache which would not go away, not even after a flagon of Burgundian wine and a visit to his wife

Meanwhile, via many whisperings and knockings at doors, the news reached the world at large. First out with it was a clerk of the tribunal at which that afternoon the Prior had pronounced sentence. By sunset this clerk was in bed with his mistress, the wife of a baker out after grain smuggled in via the Porte St Nazaire the night before. 'They burn at dawn,' the clerk told her. 'Hear that hammering? Behind the walls because the seneschal fears riot! That's why he was down in St Vincent last night, getting folk to swear on the Gospels they're loyal to the King!' So the *vicaire* raves in his cell, but he still got Capdenier to do his dirty work, and on the word of a madwoman! If Trencavel gets us now … I hope that bastard rots!'

By the time the baker returned his wife had told her friends, even as a soldier of the escort which had taken the maid back to her cell stumbled into an inn by the city's heavily guarded main well. 'She was fainting; we had to help her walk,' said this broad simple man, his hands shaking and spilling wine from the cup he held. But however much he spilled, other hands refilled his cup until he'd told it all. 'She's not like any of the others!' he insisted; 'She has a strange, holy light; her death's a crime that could happen only in Satan's world! I don't care who hears me!' He glared challenge. 'Go out, denounce me now, I don't care! I helped to hold her, and …' – tears formed in his eyes – '… she thanked me! *Me!* I know I'm a foreigner, serving France and His Holiness, but …' – in distress he shook his head, and his listeners sighed in sympathy – '… I've never seen anything like it! It makes me think things that could …'

And though then he clamped his drunken tongue, all those who heard him knew exactly what he'd been about to say:

'… bring me to the stake myself!'

So the news spread, first through the higgledly-piggledy streets of the old town then later, by various means and messengers, through narrow gates in the walls to the older, well-protected suburbs hugging the city – the Bourg to the north, the Castellare to the south. From these still-secure environs it came, carried by folk slipping through the hazy hot night, to the reckless streets of St Vincent – streets razed by de Montfort in 1209 and now rebuilt. Here, in humid taverns and heretic households, it caused such fury that those few Catholic clerics and other lovers of the French who'd not yet fled this threatened suburb crossed themselves as they shut their windows and dragged heavy chests across already double-locked doors.

Later a rider broke past weak defences and clattered over the narrow wooden bridge that spanned the Aude. He burst past watch-fires into the Trencavel camp. Challenged, he dismounted, gasped out his news, and was taken to the tent of Raymond Trencavel, who with his lieutenants was dining on roast partridge, pheasant, quail, and the wine of the Corbières.

Trencavel was still young, his hard brown face dominated by a Roman nose, his grey eyes determined. Even now at table he wore a long tunic of scarred black leather, stitched all over with iron studs. Thirty years since the French crusaders, having sacked Béziers, had marched on and taken Carcassonne! His father Viscount Raymond-

Roger, giving himself up to save the people, had died in jail. *Dysentery*, said the crusaders; *poison*, said the Carcassonnais as they fled and as the infant boy was smuggled over the Pyrenees into Aragon. Briefly in 1223 he'd retaken the city, only to be excommunicated and driven out again. Now he was back in the land of his fathers. In a month his army, marching north, had seized all the land between Roussillon and the Aude: now, his force swelled by local support, he sat at the very gates of his father's city which the French still held.

He knew his chances were slim. The Count of Toulouse had refused help; Carcassonne couldn't be taken by direct assault; his only hope was that French relief would come too late to prevent surrender through lack of water – the city's main weakness. Success or failure lay in the balance.

In the meantime, the messenger had brought him another matter, one directly concerning two of his companions at the table in his tent.

'Yes,' he said, speaking Occitan to the messenger. 'Speak!'

'My lord, bad news,' the man said rapidly. 'Three stakes are up in the Citadel. For dawn.' He paused grimly. 'One for the goodman Bernard de Laurac. Another for the goodwoman Fabrisse de Montréal. The third ...' – he cleared his throat, grimacing as he did – '... is for the maid Joana ...'

There was a grim silence. Eyes met.

'You're sure?' Trencavel demanded.

The messenger shrugged. 'Everyone knows it.'

'That damned friar!' snapped a gaunt dark-haired man who wore not military gear but shepherd's garb – hooded woollen smock over jerkin and strapped leggings – 'The little shit thinks he's won, does he?'

'Yes and no.' The messenger sneered. 'The cretin's shut in his room. A devil took his mind during the trial: he's been raving ever since. Prior Capdenier gave the verdict – though it's said he tried to avoid it.'

'*Tried to avoid it!* cried Pierre Belot the shepherd.

'It's said she condemned herself out of her own mouth.'

'She would!' Pierre's shoulders slumped. 'She would.'

'And the other two?' asked Trencavel, with a careful eye on the slim fair man seated to his right who, though perfectly still, was breathing with harsh emotion, the knuckles of both hands white as he clenched the samite-draped edge of the trestle table. 'They refused to recant?'

'My father and mother recant?' burst out the slim fair man, furious colour mottling his cheeks. 'Of course they wouldn't!'

'Easy!' Trencavel gripped his arm, and Roland de Laurac, gritting his teeth, fell silent. 'Go on,' Trencavel told the messenger, 'what else?'

'That's it, my lord.' With grim sympathy the messenger eyed Roland de Laurac. 'As you say, your folks won't recant. They die at dawn unless ...'

And he shrugged, and folded his arms.

Trencavel nodded. Nobody spoke. The messenger added:

'Have you any encouragement for me to carry back ... my lord?'

Trencavel gave the shepherd Pierre Belot a sharp look. 'We expected this,' he said. 'Wait outside. We'll let you know ... in a few minutes.'

The messenger bowed and withdrew from Trencavel's tent ... yet even as he did, a distant yet terrible sound stopped him in his tracks.

A scream. From the walls of the besieged city.

It might have been the shriek of a screech owl, yet all who heard it knew it was nothing so natural or ferally innocent.

It was the scream of a tormented soul; a drawn-out wail of despair; a terrible sound that set all who heard it shuddering ... all, from Trencavel's tent to the streets of St Vincent, to the Bourg, the Castellare, and the old city where it burst from a shuttered window high in the tower hard by the Great Tower – the ancient tower built eight hundred years ago by the Visigoths whom the Trencavels had driven from this land. And in the smoky guardroom of the Great Tower the men on duty, dicing away the night, heard it and eyed each other grimly. They knew who screamed, and thought they knew why. They were hard men, but tonight the hardest of them felt soiled by association with what they all agreed was an evil act reflecting no credit on anyone – least of all on Brother Jean the *vicaire*, whose cries now split the night and their heads. And one of them, a grizzled old man, spat in disgust and commented between the screams.

'At least that evil shit has a conscience!'

But others knew better. In a hovel in the walls, a red-haired woman with wet mad eyes heard the screams and laughed. Soon after she got up and went out towards the tower at the top of which Brother Jean lay.

And in their cells in the Great Tower, those due to die at dawn sensed it was not Christian conscience which had set the black friar sceaming, but the terror of a man trapped in dreams of the Old One.

But Brother Jean didn't know this – not consciously.

In his sleep he screamed as the nightmare rode him.

For Ailma's betrayed him and broken taboo! There! Bucking two-backed on the sweet green grass with the Fool! 'Father, give me strength to aim true!' he howls as with a wild cry he charges and strikes at them … as his spear turns into a serpent that writhes and bites him; as the Wild Women converge and swarm over him; his screams start as they begin tearing with their teeth and nails, wailing their work-song and ripping him until he's a flayed, dying mess – then SHE comes! Through bloody veils of pain he looks up with his one eye left to see a great red bird of prey, Her unmasked eyes glaring triumphantly down as he gapes and falls, screaming, into the void!

With a violent jolt he awoke still screaming, sweat-drenched, lashing out at an unseen enemy, seized by guilt which even in his madness he never escaped … and with both hands began tearing furiously at his own body, for under his habit was a hair shirt which had not been removed in six years, not since the events of a certain winter day on a road south of Tarascon-sur-Ariège. Now it was infested by a crawling mass of worms and lice. *Eat me!* he begged them, shuddering so hard that he fell off the cot to the bare flagstones of the cell. *Keep me from all soft ways!* There, crying out, he rocked back and forth, rubbing his fleshless cheeks against the cold hard comfort of the stone until he came up against the locked door … and despite the horror of the nightmare (already vague in him, for he could not, would not grasp it) his eyes gleamed to know that the souls of three sinners were at last close to salvation in the bosom and burning love of the Lord.

At last! Six years since Bernard de Laurac and the shepherd Belot had escaped him, carrying the succubus Joana to the safety of Montségur! His failure had nearly ruined him; instead he'd ensured the ruin of others – many others, for after that setback he'd launched persecution throughout the region. Many had died. God had been served. But the flames had not reached Montségur, high on its crag in the hills near Lavelanet. Bernard de Laurac had not been seized, nor Pierre Belot, far less the girl they'd spirited out of the caves at Ussat. Yet the friar's zeal had brought him a summons to papal audiences in Rome, and he'd gone eagerly, for though Pope Gregory IX was now over ninety he had proved energetic, burning heretics, canonising the blessed Dominic and establishing an Inquisition at Toulouse. And so that summer of 1234 Brother Jean had hurried to the Vatican in high hopes that His Holiness would bless the increase of his good work. But Gregory (doctors and fat cardinals hovering) had been unimpressed. 'You must dampen your fervour,' he'd ordered the outraged friar. 'There are riots against Us. Heretics have been seized from Us in Narbonne. The Count in Toulouse complains about Our court there on grounds of illegal procedure, and also he complains about your work in ... where is it?'

'The Ariège, Your Holiness,' Brother Jean had said, coldly formal.

'Yes. The Ariège. The Count of Toulouse, my son, is a tender young plant. We must water him with care and nourish him with the milk of the Church. Therefore we are transferring you to ...'

'Holy Father!' Brother Jean had forgotten himself. 'Fear of God is all these heretics understand! Cease our work now and they'll take it as a weakness, and surface with their damnable ravings again. Forgive me, but immediate steps must be taken to reduce the dragon's head – Montségur!'

'Montségur?' The grim old man had beckoned one of the cardinals, who whispered in his ear. 'Ah. The last redoubt. Patience! In time We'll have it ... but We have other work for you now. You're appointed *vicaire* to the Prior in ...' – irritation wrinkled the aged papal features – '*where?*'

'Carcassonne, your Eminence,' murmured another cardinal.

'Yes, Carcassonne. Brother Jean, you will ...'

'But I have not finished God's work in the Ariège!'

'That is not for you to decide!' Gregory had cried in a sudden rage so violent he'd turned purple, bringing doctors anxiously to him and alerting the fat, smooth, hungry-eyed cardinals. 'Do you deny Our authority?

But once in Carcassonne Brother Jean's depression had lifted, for Prior Capdenier agreed that Rome did not understand local needs; that rules were made to be bent and sometimes broken; and that illegal procedures was not illegal when dealing with pride-puffed heretics. What could one do but fight fire with fire? Why show Satan mercy? Soon between them they'd turned Carassonne into a potent bastion of the Faith; the Great Tower was filled with heretics; the fires blazed so often that people cursed them.

How can such men exist? folk asked. *Their mother's milk was sour! They credit lies; they torture for confessions and murder men who speak against them; they burn folk to save them? Devils! And they sleep well!*

But Brother Jean never slept well. This wasn't due to bad conscience. He never slept well because he feared and hated sleep. Sleep brought the nightmare which had tormented him since childhood. Now as he writhed and scratched he was glad of the agony of worms, distracting him from the evil images ... but not from Her voice that suddenly came hissing in him:

'*I sent you to the man-time to do My work, Hoel! Now you strut about attacking women; you think you serve your mad man-god – but you serve Me! Poor Hoel! You think you fight Me, but what's thought? You're so bound by thought you can't even admit me! You call Me succubus, and pray to God to save you! Yet you serve Me, and at last you've got that child where I want her – and you think it's all for your invisible god! Stupid Hoel!*'

Screaming, the friar leapt to his feet and rushed to the window where, beating his head with his fists, he glared through a slit in the heavy oak shutters at the silhouette of the Great Tower. Again he screamed to drive Her out, and as he did he seemed to see the blue-eyed golden-haired face of Ailma who'd refused him; Ailma who, now calling herself Joana the heretic maid, had tortured him during her trial with terrors of memory he could not and would not now recall! There she was, her beautiful face a huge smiling mask suspended in the night, mocking him! *But now I have her!* He grinned madly, and as he did he saw too the scarred face of the Fool who'd bested him, and he cried out: 'Fool! At dawn Christ triumphs and Ailma's mine! Too bad, you can't stop me now! Nor can She! She's dead!'

He didn't know what he shouted, but Prior Capdenier, on his knees in the cathedral of St Nazaire, heard it and prayed for him. The seneschal, deep in his cups, heard it and cursed. Pierre Belot heard it in the tent, and vowed to kill the vermin with his own bare hands. The warders in the Great Tower heard it, and spat in disgust. And the three condemned to die at dawn heard it, and they alone knew what it meant; they alone knew that the friar was wrong, quite wrong, at least in his final claim ...

Yet Dame Fabrisse feared that the Old One had won.

All day and night she'd been preparing for reunion with the Light, praying, back erect despite her weariness and pain, eyes open not to the damp invisible vault of her cell but to whatever freedom lay beyond the flaming door she'd enter at dawn. And she had to admit she was afraid.

Not for herself. Not for Bernard. The old woman knew he was

no more impressed than she was by this evil world they'd leave so soon. Its joys had worn thin over so many years of war, murder and death. The horror of the stake would be brief compared with so many painful years. They'd lived long lives; they were ready to follow their many brothers and sisters who'd already gone down this fiery road in witness to the faith.

It was for Joana-called-Chrissa she sorrowed and feared.

Six years we've fought the Old One for her soul! she'd told herself. *She's made such great strides! But she's not ready for this. It doesn't fit the visions that brought her to us. She has more to learn before she can take on the Old One – not to mention that Beast! And it's odd – very odd! But her dreams and Bernard's say Bernard joins the Feast of Light only when Montségur falls; and there's no sign of that. Montségur isn't even under siege! So are their dreams false? Or has the Old One and Her creatures changed the patterns of fate that brought her here? It looks like it. But it isn't over yet! The Shining Ones will not abandon us!*

She had to admit she felt little hope.

Yet she was still praying for a last-minute deliverance when she heard Joana returned from the court and knew that the worst had happened.

She heard the door slamming. A key grating in a lock.

Then silence – until the black friar began screaming.

The clamour didn't affect her. That weak man feared to live more than she feared to die. Yet as the screams grew more frenzied she heard, by way of the drainage duct connecting their two cells, Joana beginning to cry and moan and argue with herself in her Chrissa-tongue. The sound distressed her. Coughing, dragging her chains, she crawled to the wall separating them. When her outstretched fingers met it she sighed and sank back.

'Joana,' she called, 'can you hear me?'

At first Joana paid no heed to the screams.

The storm in her own mind wailed much louder.

Her faith had failed. This, the last night of her life?

She'd been left unchained, but it made no odds: she lay curled up as usual on the mouldy straw in the damp dark cell, tall and thin, covered in sores, her head in the hollow worn in the wall by many other heads, unsure who or where she was or how long it was since the night the soldiers had descended on Fanjeaux, the black frair and poor mad Sybille at their head.

She couldn't grasp what was happening ... and when at last the cries from the nearby tower, piercing the tiny barred street-level window high above her head, did penetrate her mind, she could only think in terror: *Had the Enemy won after all?* Then she grew confused, caught in visions without any rhyme or reason to them, wishing herself at Fanjeaux – but no, she was shut in this cell, gaunt and fearing death; a terrible voice screaming nearby, the sound of it piercing her skull as the soldiers rode her down, burning brands in their hands. They were led by the bloodily flayed friar, one eyeball dangling useless on his cheek as he howled … then something in her JUMPED: now she tossed feverishly in a cabin on a ship moored off a black isle risen smoking from the depths of the sea. A voice in her cried: 'At the Sometimes Isle we'll recall it all!' Then that was gone: instead she was running down a hard black road; roaring metal beasts stinking of burning flashed by her. 'What's this?' cried another voice, 'More of Satan's tricks?' – but a third voice immediately answered: 'Silly! It's London, for heaven's sake! It's me, Chrissa, coming home from school!' – and images of her other life flooded her: Dad, and Mum – yes, Mum! – and the emerald ring, and going to Scotland, plunging through the gate after Dad, and … then another scream: she's torn apart by a giant force, plunged through a crushing implosion; she swoops through a huge night into sudden blinding light – through lightnings, through a shining emerald mist – and into the ecstatic peace of a deep calm ocean where the great grey ones swim in their eternal dance. 'FOUND US AGAIN, HAVE YOU, CHILD?' asks a grave kind voice from the heart of the dance. 'BUT YOU CAN'T STAY HERE TILL THE JOB'S DONE!' And as her ecstasy dies she looks down, down from the heart of the ocean through the green mists to see, so dark and far below, the perplexed sad Hidden World wrapped tight in its maze of pain, pleasure, time and sensation. 'No, I won't go!' she cries, but it tugs inexorably at her … and down she falls, wrenched to a woodland grove; she smells blood, she sees a man torn apart by nine wailing hags, she sees the Enemy in Her gorgeous robe standing over a couple on the grass – a girl alseep, a thin man with a scarred, confused face, and at the sight of him she cries: 'Dad? Remember me? Chrissa! It's not all lost!' And angry wings beat her away but then she's back in that grove, holding a red rose as a giant blue beast with a cockerel head attacks her, terrifying her until a soft voice says:

'A good spirit guards you. Find the Song!'

'Mother Fabrisse,' she murmured, thinking the voice a production of her memory, not realising it came from the neighbouring cell … then the scream tore the night again: with a start she jerked upright and stared into the darkness. *I'm going to die!* she realized, and in terror felt her body. So thin, so sore! *This is Joana's body. They're going to burn it! A woman's body. I don't even know how I got it! Where did I come from? Who am I?*

'Chrissa,' she said aloud in English. 'I'm Chrissa, of course.'

She stared wildly round, seeking the source of the voice.

'Is that you, Satan?' she cried in Occitan. 'Still at me? But I won't recant! No I won't. I meant what I said and I'd say it again.'

'Rubbish!' she shouted angrily in English. 'Stop this! We've been through it all before! Wake up! There's no time left!'

Another scream caught her; she sees a gaping red face, its mouth looming open, yawning wider round her as fire gouted from it and engulfed her: she sees Father Bernard writhing before her in the smoke and flame, his face a peeling ruin, his eyelids burned off – and Mother Fabrisse is there too, dying in the flames – AND HERSELF! – yet Bernard's singing; he's singing to her as she writhes in her bed … her bed at 15 Berkeley Road in London:

Quant lo bouié ben de laura
Planto soun agulhado
AEIOU

With a jolt she was back in the cell, sitting up in the darkness as seconds, minutes, hours went by towards dawn; her mind split by fear and confusion. 'This world's a bridge; we shouldn't build on it!' she cried in Occitan, then in English she groaned: 'What are you saying?' – and again in Occitan cried fiercely: 'Blood! I see blood here, and the fire as well!' – and she shrank back, for here's the Enemy again, grinning, Her body blood-drenched, Her eyes like empty zeroes … but then in her death-cell Joana's eyes widened and she gasped, for suddenly she saw Sam!

'Dad!' she whispered in English.

For there he stood like a ghost before her, glowing green, eyeing her with horror. He was no longer naked, no longer in the grove. He had a sharp, determined look, and when she saw him her eyes lit up with hope and she struggled half to her feet. 'Dad!' she cried, 'You're still there! You are, aren't you?' For a moment longer he gazed at her, then – even as the black friar screamed again – a brilliant flare of light, shockingly sudden, exploded in her. Even as it burst she knew it from another time, she knew where it came from, who sent it … *and in that instant she soars, she sees, she knows great joy, for all theese trials are worthwhile after all! 'YES, CHILD!' cries a great voice from the heart of the shining light, 'THE WORLD BELONGS TO YOU ALL – BUT ONLY IF YOU REMEMBER! WHY ARE YOU HERE? HOW IS THE SHIFT AVOIDED? HOW IS THE STARCHAMBER OPENED?'*

But then, as quickly as it had come, it was gone.

Only an instant it lasted, and her insight faded with it as darkness returned and she realised amid her daze that Sam was gone too.

'Why did it happen?' she wailed, cast into a deeper despair and sense of loss, her hands clawing at the air as if she could pull him back, and the light back too. 'It's the black friar, isn't it? He's the one She had torn to pieces when you were with that girl in the grove. Dad, where have the Shining Ones gone? Dad, all that burning I saw before we went through the gate ... it's ME! But it shouldn't happen yet! It's too soon!'

She began laughing hopelessly. Only after a while did she realise how, in the cells on either side, both Dame Fabrisse and the goodman Bernard were trying to reach and encourage her.

14.
The Healer

'Joana. Can you hear me?' But there was no answer.

Grim in her weakness (she'd been ill before the arrest; now she was so sick she knew the end of her life was near whatever happened), Fabrisse lifted up the stone disc that hung on a silver chain inside the neck of her filthy black robe. Set in the equal-armed cross inscribed on this disc was a small emerald which, now laid against her brow, brought cool clarity to her mind and some strength to her body. Then, sending her vision out along the green ray, she sensed Joana curled against the wall, hopelessly lost in the confusion of her other, Last Days Chrissa-self. *Oh child, haven't we been through this before?* she thought, mentally reaching out... and she murmured: 'A good spirit guards you. Find the Song!'

But still no response. And as she knelt there six years fell away.

She found herself again in that room in the keep at Montségur that wild winter night, watching the pale strange girl Bernard and Pierre Belot had found at the Gate of the Stone deep in the caverns near Tarascon, her right hand on the girl's solar plexus, left on her brow, murmuring as Joana fought the Beast for her life: '*Can you hear me, child? Can you feel my touch? Take my love. Take my strength...*'– until at last near dawn those blue eyes had opened ... blank with shock and terror.

Then that visitation by the child's father. That confused watching mind, drawn by love from the Old One's realm to Montségur, present long enough for the goodwoman to warn him against the Beast, against Her. But then She'd found him and snatched him furiously back to Her own world.

But the child had been saved. Even as Joana opened her blank eyes old Esclarmonde de Foix had come to say that Bernard showed signs of returning from the abyssal edge he'd walked ever since fighting the Old One for the child's soul. So she'd left Joana; gone to the room by the North Door where Bernard lay, there to meet Bishop Guilhabert de Castres and the shepherd Pierre Belot, without whose wit neither Bernard nor the girl would have lived. Yet with very mixed feelings that freezing night six years ago she'd gazed at the skeletal face of the man to whom she'd born three sons, the gentle poet with whom she'd fallen in love one night at the court of Lombez long ago before the war began – the man she hadn't seen in all the years since they'd both been baptised in the spirit.

For, with shutters banging in the howling mountain wind, Bernard had awoken that night at Montségur with a sad, unguarded look that plainly expressed his desire never to wake up in this world again.

But those baptised in the spirit could not give way to earthly desire, not even the desire to leave the earth. For desire was desire.

Yet wake up he had, to tell his tale of how after the capture and death of his companion Gaillard he'd gone into exile south of the mountains to Puigcerda, where nightly in dreams the golden-haired child who claimed to serve the Shining Ones had cried out from a dark place for his help, until at length he knew where that dark place was, and sought out Pierre Belot to lead him over the snowbound passes to the Gate of the Stone.

He'd told them how in dreams he'd entered the future age from which the child came, had alerted her in her dreams as she alerted him in his, and how in her dreams he burned in a mass pyre at Montségur. And how in that future age he'd seen her and her father enter a gate in a moorland place; her father to be seized by the Old One, and herself to be taken to the world of the aeons, where her purpose and mission were explained.

In her cell Fabrisse remembered how at the point of his narrative his weakness had left him, he'd sat eagerly up, his face joyously transformed:

'*In my dream I went with her!*' he'd cried, '*I was caught up into the highest heavens where Three-in-One dance in eternal delight, and I heard what the Shining Ones said! "THIS IS THE DANCE OF OUR HOME IN THE SUNS BEHIND THE SUN THAT RULES THE DARK WORLD OF TIME AND SHIFT AND SEPARATION! CHILDREN, HERE IS OUR TRUE HOME! REMEMBER THIS WHEN YOU RETURN!" Then lost in the Light we plunged to bright depths where great grey ones like Leviathan's glide! There in a wall is fixed the Lost Stone – and there they told us that this world is not fatally damned! The World can be overcome, and the torment mitigated by self-redeeming human action!'*

Yes. She remembered it still. A joyous moment of truth.

Then he'd told how the child had been sent back to this Hidden World; how he and Pierre had reached the Gate of the Stone in time to wrest her from the Old One. The fight had nearly killed him; the Old One would have won but for Pierre's disobedience. At which point from Bernard's bedside Pierre had asked:

'*But who or what is this Old One we fought?*'

And Bishop Guilhabert, the wisest among them, had said:

'*One of those who fell from the aeons to be caught in time and matter, so that Her dark side prevailed over the bright. It's said once in these parts when She still had human form She built the Gate of the Stone in an effort to regain Her lost realm. Now She's formless; few believe in Her, and She has a seat in our hidden minds. And She's not alone. Others fell with Her. Worse is that Beast who so nearly got this child. By comparison She's only forgetful, maddened by sadness at Her loss. But the Beast longs for the extinction of the human mind – for only through that extinction may he die himself, and end his imprisonment in this world.*'

'*But,*' Fabrisse had quietly interjected, '*She can still be redeemed, for Her darkness is the sorrow of the world.*'

'*This child,*' Esclarmonde de Foix had asked, '*How do we help her?*'

'*By helping her recall her true nature,*' Bernard had said. '*Or the darkness of the Old One in her will destroy her. Yet maybe in the search for her father she'll find the Old One and bring Her to the Light again.*'

'*Can the Old One harm her here?*' Esclarmonde de Foix had asked.

And Fabrisse had said: '*Not if we love and protect her.*'

And Guilhabert had turned to her: '*Dame Fabrisse, you've brought her back, so you may be the one to direct her recovery and growth.*'

Now, with all three of them awaiting death, Fabrisse groaned. Her words that night so long ago now returned to mock her cruelly:

'*I'll take her to safety near Fanjeaux,*' she'd said. '*These heights aren't yet for her. She needs the healing woods.*' And – Good Spirit save her! – she'd smiled. '*Her body's ripe, but her eyes are blank. She's like an infant again. This is no place for infants. She needs the woods.*'

So it had been decided. Next day with her companion Braida she had left Montségur and taken the child whom already they called Joana to Fanjeaux.

That cold morning the child's eyes were still blank.

Now, hearing empty laughter from the next cell, she knew those bright eyes were blank again, and blamed herself.

Why did I bring her to Fanjeaux? Why didn't I guess the Old One was watching? I've been a fool all along!' The child's right not to hear me!

She called out again, but there was no response.

Fabrisse felt confused, sad, useless, doomed, spiritually dead.

Then she sensed a presence watching her. It seemed familiar. It . . .

Without warning that tremendous flare of light burst in her: a fire making all her worries small, bringing hope even as it stunned her.

For she knew it! It had happened to her before. The Shining Ones! *We're not abandoned!* she knew gladly as darkness returned. She realised that the watching mind was gone. Her nerves quivered to Joana's broken laughter as she sensed Bernard's silent question: *Who was that?*

She wasted no energy replying. Again she set the emerald to her brow. It was like moving from fog into icy sunlight . . . and then she had it! That sense of familiarity . . . she knew who that had been! *Joana's father! And on the green ray! He must have the ring!* Again she tried to contact the young woman. *Joana!* she cried silently. *It's not over yet! Remember that light from the last time? Will you abandon all your training? Don't let your mind split again! So you're Chrissa, and Joana – yet both those faces are no more than part of a greater, shining face! And that light is its face!*

At last Joana heard Fabrisse's voice. She breathed deep. The quiet voice, seeming to speak an inch from her ear, made her ashamed of giving in to despair. *Mother Fabrisse*, she answered, *I saw my father. He was here!*

I know! So don't give up hope! Perhaps he finds strength to help you as you helped him. Her dark side won't prevail . . . unless we let it. So!

She reached out, mentally grasping Joana's hand. As she did she sensed Bernard, invigorated by the light, casting out – and making contact with a friendly mind. She sensed the shepherd Pierre Belot nearby . . . and someone else with him. She saw a face she hadn't seen in a very long time.

'Roland?' she murmured, amazed. 'You're here too?' And at this image of her third son she hadn't met in years her heart quailed: terror struck her. But, controlling herself, she turned to her task.

Do you remember Bérenger and Alais? she asked, breathing hard.

Joana, sensing the old woman's distress, thought herself to blame.

'Of course I do!' she said aloud. 'You brought me to them!'

Do you remember your first days with them? Fabrisse persisted.

Wrinkling her brow, Joana thought, then shook her head.

'No,' she murmured in wonderment. 'Not that far back. I was a baby again. I wasn't Chrissa any more. I was lost!'

Then look! urged Fabrisse. *Come on! Remember how you became Joana!*

15.
Childhood

Then, amid a whirl of dreamy wonderment, Joana sees herself stumbling through bare wet woods, her hand held by Fabrisse. She's tall, yet hardly knows how to walk; her blue eyes gape blank at a cold sky. 'Come along,' Fabrisse murmurs, 'they'll welcome you, and don't worry, I'll come often.'

The old woman's words are meaningless but comforting. So in time they come to a wooden hut in a clearing. In front of it an old man saws wood; from it emerges a thin woman with tired eyes, tugging and scolding a goat. Chrissa stares as the surprised old couple bow the knee to the goodwoman.

At first Bérenger and Alais were utterly taken aback by the child's blank blue eyes, by her aura of witless oddity, by the regularity of her so-white teeth and the softness of her skin. It took a lot of coaxing to persuade them to take her in. 'She's seen things,' Fabrisse told them, 'so foul that her mind and memory have fled. God willing, we'll get her healthy again, for she's important to us. The need is great! Take her in, bear with her – but don't spoil her, and don't worry if in her sleep she speaks an unknown tongue. Tell nobody about her. I'll come when I can.'

At last the old woodcutter Bérenger grumpily gestured the child into their hut. It was just a leaky room with wattle-and-daub walls, its thatch roof open at the ridge to let out smoke from the little fire at the middle of the earth floor. Such a tiny fire . . . yet the girl gawked fearfully at it . . . until she felt the old woman touch her arm and guide her in. 'This is your home,' Fabrisse whispered, 'and from now on we three are your family.'

* * *

So bare branches bud; the wood greens, summer heat comes, leaves fall: the world grows grey, bare branches bud again. For an entire year Joana's a trial to them. It's months before she responds to the name Joana: longer before she speaks... but only as a two- or three-year-old would. Her mind's in a daze; things loom large and empty; she's fretful, self-destructive, ruled by unconscious habit from her lost world. *Where's the toothbrush? Where's my nice clean bed? Where's the car, the cornflakes, the central heating?* Consciously she misses none of these things ... but in that filthy hut she acts like a princess with a pea under her mattress: her moods anger Bérenger more every day. She's gangly, gawky, pubescent; she should help Alais with the chores and be dreaming of love, but she can't be left alone a minute without disaster – spilling curds, tripping over a stool, cutting, burning, grazing, hurting herself and sending the birds hurtling from the trees with the violence of her wails. She has to be shown everything, even how to use her thumb to crush lice – no wonder the old couple get tired of it. And it's worse at night. Sleeping on the floor by the little fire she thrashes in her dreams, shrieks her unknown tongue until, red-eyed with no sleep, they lose their temper. Once, after a year, the world budding and her sap rising too, she screams all night and Bérenger, at his wit's end, thrashes her 'to get Satan out'. Next day Fabrisse asks about the bruises.

'Lady, you mean well,' Alais exploded, 'and so do we, but we get no sleep, we have to watch her every minute! Lady, you take her off my hands when you're here and I'm glad, but she likes you, she never shrieks at you. You don't see her like we do! How is she important to the faith? She's so strange! Whoever saw a baby so tall? I leave her for an instant and she cuts herself, or falls over. It's as if she hurts herself deliberately!'

'She does,' said Fabrisse. 'The clumsiness, the self-hate, the dreams – these are an Old One's darkness in her. Look! I mean this one!' Checking Bérenger wasn't about, she sketched a sign. Alais paled. 'Men call Her evil,' Fabrisse went on, 'because they see only one of Her faces. I see Her others too ... and it's our task to awaken this child. So be patient!'

Alais never complained again. After all, the goodwoman brought more food and clothing – even wine for Bérenger – than they'd seen in years.

So seasons come and go, and Joana walks with Fabrisse, and sees Crocus bloom from Snow, Sun breaks out from scudding Cloud, Fox grinning as he pads away from her noisy human feet ... and her blue eyes brighten, gain focus and vivacity; her face tans; her skin grows clear and her gold hair long; her body buds and blooms; she begins to speak in Occitan. The accidents cease; her sleep grows peaceful; she helps Alais without being asked, and Fabrisse is tempted to hint about her past and the outer world. But not yet. First Joana must ask the right questions. So she hears nothing of the war; of the two hundred burned at Moissac nearby; of how the black friar Brother Jean d'Aubigny seeks her. Nor does she know she's growing: to her things just happen, Fabrisse just comes to spend time with her in quiet places, touching her, knitting together her fractured soul. She doesn't know how Fabrisse exhausts herself in this work; or realise how slowly each time the old woman returns to the house an hour away through the woods, or know how the women of the house wonder where Dame Fabrisse has been going so often these last two years. There are rumours, but nobody speaks, not yet. So it's a huge relief when – at last, long last! – comes the bright spring day they sit in the woods on a carpet of bluebells and the girl laughs, points out a rabbit timidly watching them, and says: 'Rabbit! That's rabbit, Mother! Friend me!' – and Fabrisse hugs her with vast delight.

Yet still she hasn't asked about her past or spoken Bernard's name (though sometimes muttering a name that sounds like *Sam*) . . . and whenever Bernard makes the arduous journey from Montségur (since that ordeal he's weaker, and very lame) she doesn't know him, though she's disturbed by his face, and Alais tells how her dreams again grow violent after the goodman's visits; how she stares fearfully at the fire, sometimes humming the refrain of that song the goodman once found; the song of her namesake, Joana. So it's decided Bernard should stay away until she's ready, until she asks.

A third hot summer parches the woods: now she cooks, she chops wood, and though there's little warmth between them, sometimes Bérenger will show her a carving he's made or chuckle at her laughter, and Alais, hearing her sing happily, smiles with a sense of night beaten back. So things improve: Fabrisse begins teaching her the natural lore of birds, beasts, trees and plants; how to identify and use roots and herbs. Soon it's clear she has the Touch. Her fingers are deft; she can mend a broken wing; treat wounds with cobwebs (to staunch bleeding) and moulds (to fight infection). When Bérenger sprains his ankle she chooses the herbs, makes the poultice and applies the paste . . . and when the swelling goes down his attitude changes; he softens, and thereafter doesn't object even when she drives them mad again by taming wild creatures and bringing them into the hut. Peire the

Rabbit, a grumpy hedgehog, an oriole with a broken wing. By then she's asking questions they can't answer; which later she asks Fabrisse:

'Mother, why do toadstools grow in rings?'

'Mother, why is it best to plant when the moon's waxing?'

'Mother, is it true that the rennet of hare stops you having babies?'

One hot afternoon, the whole world drowsing as Fabrisse tells her a tale about the moon, suddenly she protests. 'Why tell me silly stories?' she complains, 'The moon's not like that! Nobody lives on it; it's a ...'

She stops, frowning, puzzled by herself, and drops it.

Eyeing her, Fabrisse asks: 'Tell me, do you dream at night?'

'Have Bérenger or Alais said?' Joana asks back warily.

'I want to hear it from you.'

'Yes,' Joana admits, her face clouding. 'I do. But ...'

Again she shuts her mouth. But on another hot day soon after they're out looking for mandrake when the girl, finding a root, flinches as if it bit her, and turns to demand directly: 'Who is my father? Where is he?'

Those blue eyes! Looking into them Fabrisse feels dizzy, for now there are depths there, no longer the glassy sheen of nobody-at-home. *At last!*

Sucking in her breath she asks quietly: 'What does he look like?'

'He's old.' Joana eyes Fabrisse intently, examining, at last aware of herself as One and Fabrisse as Other. '... I've been dreaming ... I think his name's ... Bernard? Mother, there's a song ...'

Then, in an unsure but sweet clear voice, she sings:

Quant lo bouié ben de laura
Planto soun agulhado
AEIOU!

Fabrisse shivers ... then plucks a wild red rose from a bush nearby.

'Look into it.' She gives it to Joana. 'Breathe it. Then close your eyes and see what you see. Invite it, let it come by itself.'

Deep into the delicate mystery Joana gazes, breathing its scent: she shuts her eyes, and the bees drone as Fabrisse watches the confusion on her face. At last she opens her eyes, her shining-wet, brilliant blue eyes ...

'Mother, what's my name?' she asks, her voice trembling.

'Joana, of course,' Fabrisse answers, as calmly as she can.

'Yes, I know, but ...' Joana shakes her head angrily.

'Easy!' advises Fabrisse. 'Let it come in its own time.'

But that night she sent word to Bernard de Laurac at Montségur. THE STONY GROUND IS CLEARED. THE FIELD IS RIPE FOR SOWING.

16.
Childhood's End

A week later Joana sat on a log by the hut making candles, frowning as she dipped the tapers into a tub of wax and laid them up to dry. Again in her dreams of last night she'd heard herself talking in that other tongue. 'Was I at it again?' she'd asked. Alais had shrugged it off. 'Oh, you were muttering away, girl, but nothing like as bad as when you came here.'

Bérenger was away in the forest, cutting wood. Alais was baking in the hut. Now, peering out at Joana, she shivered. The morning was bright, but she felt a dark shadow hover over her.

How much longer? she wondered. *I've come to love her as if she were my own. But she doesn't belong to me. She never did, and it's three days since the Lady Fabrisse last came. I fear the worst, but why?*

Soon she found out. For soon, with Bérenger still away, Lady Fabrisse came again. But this time she was not alone. There were three others with her. Beside her walked another black-robed lady, stout and red-faced, and also two goodmen – one thin, dark and saturnine, and the other . . .

Alais recognised that white-haired, hobbling figure in an instant, and came swiftly out of the hut, gesturing at Joana as she did.

'Girl! Bend the knee!' she whispered.

But Joana did not. She'd heard feet behind her, had turned to greet Fabrisse. But at the sight of the others, particularly the thin old man with the stick, her mouth fell open; she let the tapers drop.

Her startled gaze fell on the goodman Bernard.

'Joana!' Alais caught at her elbow. 'Remember yourself, girl!'

'Remember myself?' she asked in confusion – and, like Fabrisse before him, Bernard was struck by the clarity of her gaze. It was like looking into the sun: he drew sharp breath, and Fabrisse knew he'd seen as, fearing the ground might open up and swallow her, Joana took a puzzled step towards him, then another, and another, until she reached Fabrisse. 'What is it, Mother?' she asked, troubled, not taking her eyes from him. 'I know him, but ...' – she darted Fabrisse a quick look, but she had to look at Bernard: her eyes returned to him – '... I mean, I do know him, but I feel so ...'

'Do you know me, Joana?' asked Bernard, his voice unsteady.

For a while, her lips moving slightly, she stared at him in silence. At last, in a halting but eager voice she said:

'You *are* him, aren't you? I *do* know you? I don't know how, but I do! *You* sang the song and called me from the ... from the ...'

Without warning she stiffened; her breath hissed out and she shook in a terror so great that her eyeballs rolled up until the whites showed; her fists, clenched tight, shuddered up to her face to cover her eyes.

Fabrisse was aghast. It wasn't just that there had been nothing like this before. Fabrisse was exhausted. In response to her call Bernard had come the night before with his travelling companion Imbert to a house of believers in the hamlet of Villasavery: after holding a service there he'd slipped into the woods to meet her and Braida – the only other woman in the house who knew about Joana. Half the night she'd spent persuading him that it was time to take Joana out of the woods. 'We can't forever treat her like a delicate vase that'll break if dropped! We must take the risk, or she'll remember nothing!' At length he'd agreed. The other half of the night had been spent getting here. Now, with the child in a fit, Bernard too failed to move at once, while both Braida and Imbert eyed each other in mutual bafflement. It was Alais who, with a strident fearful oath, got off her knees, and seized Joana by the shoulders from the back.

'Control youself, girl!' she said. 'Bow to the good people!'

Joana shuddered. In her other tongue she cried at Bernard: 'Who are you? Is it you I came to find? Weak Ones! Cathars!' She fought her fear. 'I read books,' she whispered, 'about the war, about Montségur and how ...' Abruptly she paled. She shut her mouth. She tore her eyes from Bernard and stared instead at the ground.

'What is it?' asked Bernard quietly.

I saw you on fire, Father Bernard!

She didn't say it. She swayed. Blades of grass before her eyes were alternately blurring and coming into sharp focus. Fabrisse met Bernard's eye, then motioned the others to leave them as Joana retched and ran for cover. Doubled up amid the willows, she seemed to fall into a bloody darkness. Amid it she saw a thin naked man staring a her.

He had a shock of grey-streaked black hair, his cheek was scarred, his expression sorrowing and desperate – pleading, maybe calling for help ...

Her stomach heaved again; the vision vanished amid fresh nausea.

At last, wet-eyed, she turned to see Fabrisse and the old man talking. Gulping air she studied him – his dark blue robes, his horny sandalled feet, the pouch at his waist on an leather belt with an odd buckle, his thinning hair and bony face. *You're Father Bernard, but not my real father!* she thought, bewildered, and the heaves seized her once more, for suddenly she saw fire enveloping him again, and again began to choke.

'The rose!' Fabrisse said quickly. 'Find it!'

She did. Afterwards she turned to Bernard. 'I know you're not my *real* father,' she said wildly. 'But when I cried out you heard me. And ...'

Suddenly, with no warning, the abyss again seized her. She saw the Enemy, mocking black eyes sucking her in, and on Her finger that emerald ring. 'SOON YOU'LL GO UP IN SMOKE AND STOP INTERFERING!' the Enemy cried. With a wail she fell to her knees at Bernard's feet, hiding her face.

The rose! she thought frantically. *See the rose!*

Slowly the vision faded. Bathed in sweat she looked up.

'Was that the Enemy?' Fabrisse asked gently.

The girl sighed and said nothing.

'Did you see her?' the old woman demanded. 'What does she look like?'

'I've seen Her often,' said Bernard casually. 'since I fought Her at the Gate. She hasn't forgotten us, for in my dreams She glares furiously – though Her robe,' he went on hurriedly, for Joana's face was twisting in fear again, 'is very colourful and hints at brighter possibilities ...'

'Goodman, that's enough!' said Fabrisse sharply.

But Joana, her face white, asked: 'Her robe?'

Bernard smiled. 'What's it made of, child?'

'Feathers!' she cried. 'Father, do you see it too? It's not just me? For I see Her as you say, but blood drips from Her; She hates us and ...'

'Do you see nothing of yourself in Her?' asked Fabrisse mildly.

'What?' Joana stared at her without comprehension.

'Do you see Her only as darkness?'

Joana burst out: 'She stole my father. She tried to kill me! She's where ... *Sam* is! I'll go there ... when I'm ready!' Her gaze darted between them. 'What's my *real* name? What are you hiding from me?'

Eyeing Bernard briefly, Fabrisse raised Joana to her feet.

'You were hiding from yourself, child. Now you're ready to leave here and live in my house.'

Joana stared, not understanding.

Soon afterwards the four *parfaits* took their leave.

Bérenger returned later. Alais wept as she told him what Fabrisse had said to her. 'She's to be taken away from us. Soon.'

Bérenger's lips tightened. He said nothing about it, then or later.

The last days were hard. Joana was both terrified and exhilarated. She felt like a butterfly about to burst from its chrysalis into a raging sky, full of unknowns. One night she awoke to find Bérenger and Alais sitting up in bed, gazing fearfully at her. 'I've been so ungrateful!' she cried, and across the hut she rushed to hug them both. 'I won't forget,' she went on, like Alais weeping, 'I'll come back often, I promise!'

So arrived the day when Fabrisse came for her. 'I'll be back,' she swore, and in her eyes they saw their future: silent and stiff they held each other as they saw her go, as dry leaves whirled in the wind of early fall.

The wind that day had many voices and fingers, taunting and slapping and tugging at Joana's mind. As they started through the wood to Fanjeaux it skirled so wild round her, whipping her hair and seeming to cry: YOU'LL NEVER RETURN, that her excitement at leaving turned to doubt and sorrow. Reluctantly she followed Fabrisse past favourite places where she'd spent happy hours, troubled by more than the wind and her leaving, for there was also the gown the goodwoman had brought her to wear – a plain black ankle-length gown, hooded and sleeved and cinched at the waist by a linen strip knotted over the left hip. 'It's the gown of an aspirant,'

Fabrissa had told her, adding severely: 'You won't wear it in towns. There we disguise ourselves. There's no merit in embracing the stake while we still have work to do. Now put it on, for today you join the House.'

So, with the wind and the knot at her hip both making her anxious with their unknown meanings, she followed dazed. It wasn't until Fabrisse led her from her known world that she began to note the broken up-and-down tract of gnarly oak-wood they'd entered. Fabrisse at last turned.

'Do you remember this wind from last year?' she asked.

'Yes! It brings the bad dreams, and ... the things that happened,' Joana said falteringly, 'but it blows them out as soon as it blows them in!'

'Then we'll turn our minds from it,' said Fabrisse. 'See that?' She pointed ahead at a tall, large-leaved plant lurking in the shade by the path. 'Tell me: what's that plant? What are its properties?'

Joana laughed jaggedly. 'Alais calls it Devil's rhubarb. She says poor fools eat its berries and die; rich ladies get a juice from it to widen their eyes so that men'll fall into them!' And with another laugh she ran pell-mell forward in such a way that Fabrisse's heart leapt.

'Child! Don't touch it!'

'I wasn't going to.' Joana whirled round, hair skirling in the wind, a giddy look in her eyes as Fabrisse hastened up.

'Joana,' she said gently, 'beware the wind on days like this, for it's the breath of the Beast, and before you know what it'll have you embracing folly! Nobody can chain your spirit; you must rein it and purify yourself. Now!' She turned to the belladonna's glossy black berries and dark purple flower. 'See this Old One? Yes, dark and deadly, if that's all you see. She makes the heart race, the pulse grow weak, the eyes grow wide. Misuse Her, She'll kill you! Respect Her, She'll help! This ...' – Fabrisse's eyes flashed with a power Joana hadn't met before – '... proves there's good even in darkness, if only enough to let us seek light. Now come along, child! We have a way to go yet, and this wind makes me scratchy too!'

Soon the trees thinned out. They emerged onto the bare brow of a high limestone bluff even as the wind, after delivering a final series of cruel buffets, died away as if losing interest in them.

Fabrisse stepped onto the bluff and stood within feet of the fall to a mottled canopy of a sun-browned foliage below. The sight made

Joana dizzy; she breathed deep before joining the old woman. No trees! Nothing but the baked, hazy blue sky and the drop to the forest below. With a shudder she gazed east to hazy hill-horizons beyond a vast plain on which vineyard and forest alternated. Southward rolled the hills of the Razès: rising in the middle distance she saw a walled town on a broad summit. 'Fanjeaux?' she asked, and Fabrisse nodded: as she stared at this a sudden fright of double vision took her. For a giddy instant she felt like someone else somewhere else ... then sought and found the stabilising image of the rose.

'What do you see below us?' Fabrisse asked, as if nothing had happened.

Cautiously Joana looked down to see a stream sparkling in the sun. It bubbled along the foot of the bluff before vanishing into the forest.

'A stream running into the wood,' she said.

'Look again.'

This time, squinting into the light of the trees below, she made out a too-straight line, then a segment of rose-tiled roof ... and suddenly saw the rambling house hidden in the wood with its gardens, hen-runs and outhouses; she saw steep pasture where goats and sheep gazed, and the narrow millet strip that ran up to the bluff. 'You could be feet away and not see it!' she cried, and then: 'Do they know about me? Have you told them?'

'Everyone knows they have a new sister today,' said Fabrisse.

Joana eyed her anxiously. 'What did you say?'

'I told them you're an orphan from the north where blue eyes and fair hair are common. A weaver from Flanders brought you here. He was seized and burned for spreading the Poplicani faith. You saw him die and fled into the woods where I found you. So if folk think you odd or hear you cry out, they'll put it down to your ordeal.' Smiling sadly, she added: 'You'll find you're not the only one with bad dreams.'

'But if I speak my ... other tongue, will they think ...'

'I said your mother-tongue's a dialect of Saxon, unknown to us. Don't worry! Watch, listen, and wait! Braida and I know about you, the ladies Alice and Gaia know a little; the rest know only rumours. Go to Braida if you can't see me ... but take care! I can't favour you. There are dangers. This is a house of refuge. Only four of us are baptised in the spirit. The rest are here through accident of war. There are twenty women, mostly widows, and a dozen orphaned girls. You'll live with them. They're not all balanced in mind. Take care! The Enemy takes many forms! But if you're to grow, you must face these dangers.'

'What are the rumours, Mother?'

'It's said some years ago a spirit in the form of a girl was sent by the aeons to aid us against Satan,' Fabrisse said carefully. 'It seems she came through the Gate of the Stone; that her hair is golden, her eyes sky-blue. It's said Bernard brought about this miracle – so it's best that few know of his visits to you … or they might start believing this … mad tale!'

'And her name, Mother?' asked Joana.

'Joana.' Fabrisse grimaced. 'A common name: we won't confuse you by changing it. Just remember: this is a house of work and prayer, then more prayer and more work! So watch, listen, wait, work and pray!'

'Will I learn about my father through this work and prayer?' Joana asked. Her tone was flippant but her eyes were startling and icy.

'Come along now!' said Fabrisse sharply. 'It's nearly suppertime.'

They followed a goat-track down to the trees; past the millet strip to gardens where women worked, and so to the house, its low wings rambling between the trees, and Joana wondered nervously: *Where is the Enemy here?*

It was a time before she found out.

17.
Fanjeaux

Once through the iron-studded door Fabrisse's demeanour changed. In a stern voice she told Joana: 'As a novice you will observe absolute silence for forty-eight hours unless asked to speak. I advise you to spend tonight and the next on your knees in prayer.' Then she turned her over to the old dame in charge of the kitchens and left her on her knees, scrubbing flagstones.

Communal supper of grains, berries, bread and water was eaten in the whitewashed stone hall. In their dark robes the women came in silence from their work and prayer. The *parfaite* Dame Gaia broke and blessed the bread. 'Benedicite,' murmured the women. 'Deus vos benedicat,' Dame Gaia replied. There was no talk as night darkened the trees outside. Afterwards Fabrisse knelt on the dais to receive the kiss of peace from the virgins (a formal term: some had been raped). Joana, told to follow the others, approached mutely, her hair now bound in a net, her gaze low as she waited in line then bent to kiss the goodwoman's brow. *You'll do!* Fabrisse thought as she went to perform her part of the ceremony. The older women knelt at their places by the trestle tables, and as she kissed each of them on the brow Fabrisse assessed their feelings; their tension or ease. *Will they accept her?* she wondered, and afterwards said to Braida, to Dame Alice and Dame Gaia: 'Join me at the first sleep.'

Before this meeting Fabrisse prayed in her cell. She knew the risk of bringing Joana here, especially with that friar sniffing around like a dog in heat. Persecution had been slack since the deaths at Moissac, but three decades of war since de Montfort's northern horde had descended to sack the south had not left her sanguine. The sun still shone but the land groaned, the faith was wounded. How many dead? How many protectors made to kneel? The lords of Cabaret, Foix, Béziers, Carcassonne, Toulouse and many another place had forfeited their castles and bowed the knee; or were excommunicate in exile, or had died at Puivert, Termes, Minervet, Muret and Lastours; or were rotting in gaol ... they were all beaten. *It's only a matter of time*, she knew as she went to meet the other dames. *But that was plain when I came here. How long is it?* And realised with shock as she trod the dark passages that the answer was: ten years. Since she and Bernard had been baptised in the spirit by Bertrand d'En Marti; since she and he had parted. *Ten years of war*, she thought. *They must think I'm mad to bring her here.*

They did. They were polite about it, but they did.

The four goodwomen met in a cool bare room kept for meetings like this. The waxing moon threw silver light onto the flagstones between them where they sat. To Alice and Gaia, Fabrisse described the history which so far she'd kept to Braida and herself. 'Now she needs wider experience,' she said, 'but care is still needed. Thus the false tale of her background.'

Dame Alice's black eyebrows shot up in amazement.

'You ask us to break our vows by conniving at untruth?'

'Any blame is on me. The alternative is to kill her ourselves. That friar won't linger if he learns that the child who escaped him is here.'

'Then send her to Montségur!' Dame Gaia was disturbed. Tall, frail now, she had owned this house before gifting it to the faith.

'Yes, she'd be much safer there,' Braida agreed.

'We can't cocoon her.' But Fabrisse felt a sudden sense of doom, of unavoidable fate. 'How can she learn from Montségur without first knowing the outside world?' She stared through the window up at the pale sad moon. 'Though God knows we're hardly "outside world" here! She won't find the strength she needs if we plan only for her safety – or our own!'

She didn't tell them Bernard's dream that sooner or later Montségur too would fall; that the faith would be destroyed. Satan would not let them live.

'But the risk!' Alice – big and often cantankerous – was appalled. 'Sister, here among us are disturbed children who might run to the Enemy; and for all your tales, someone's sure to note her blue eyes, her golden hair, remember another tale ... and talk! And if that happens ...'

Alice spread her red, work-worn hands in dismay.

'We're precarious enough as it is,' Braida agreed. But when Fabrisse gave her a steady look she shrugged. 'Well,' she admitted grudgingly, 'if Bishop Guilhabert approves of this ... I'll put my doubts aside ...'

Alice and Gaia eyed each other in silence.

'I beg you all,' Fabrisse said quietly, 'help this child; keep in mind that she's been where we only hope to go. She's sent to us, and her task is one nobody should envy! She's only a child; what she went through to reach us almost destroyed her. Sisters, she's the soul of our struggle! So pray that the good spirit will help us to help her!'

And for many months, until after Christmas, it seemed that it did.

Work and prayer. Soon Joana had neither time nor energy to worry about her dreams or how others saw her. Soon she had no idea if bending in the gardens was harder than scrubbing the kitchens, or if daily Gospel lessons were more boring than prayer-meetings from dawn to dusk, nor if the task of keeping her mouth shut, curbing her spirit, and getting along with other troubled girls was worse than a diet which not only allowed no meat – ('for meat,' Dame Alice told her one day with an utterly disapproving look, 'is full of earthbound soul; by eating it we become more earthbound ourselves') – but which often went no further than bread, berries and water.

Fabrisse wasn't harsh for the sake of harshness. Her rule was designed to lift the spirit and help war-shattered women. Many there, silent by day as by night, had been terribly violated. Some had seen their men tortured and killed. Others had had their children snatched from them. Their souls had been screaming: through the comradeship of work and prayer they began to heal, to rise above horror. Silence, though encouraged and respected, was not a rule. Yet it *was* a rule that nobody should pry into another's background or business without being asked. So, inside the house and for the time being, Joana found herself safe. Outside? They were hidden from the road, but many potential enemies knew about them: the French fort at Montréal wasn't far off. To date nobody had bothered them, but that was no guarantee of safety. Fabrisse could only hope, and watch out for trouble.

Joana's early days in the house were a bewilderment of new faces, voices and ways. She kept quiet and went about with modest gaze, fearing what Dame Fabrisse had said about the Enemy being everywhere. She made herself inconspicuous, full of worry that she'd betray herself by some loose word, or by screaming in her sleep. At first she avoided sleep as much as she could, praying all night ... yet sleep and dreams would not be jilted forever. Often when she dreamed it was of lost woodland freedoms: of running through sunlit glades; of how Alais had wept at her leaving; of Bérenger's rheumy disgruntled face ... but some nights her other self burst out, waking the dormitory. Yet she wasn't the only one with nightmares that woke everyone up. Nor, she soon knew, would the other girls make any trouble. Poor, pale creatures, most of them. But it disturbed her to wake up raving in that Other tongue. 'A Big Mac, a Mars Bar, please oh please!' she cried one night, waking as this mad gibberish burst from her mouth. And at dark Tierce prayers she'd sense the fear of skinny Adala beside her, and Arsen and Blanche at neighbouring beds. 'Was I making a fuss again?' she'd ask Adala in a hiss loud enough to be heard by the others. 'I'm sorry I woke you, but my dreams were unhappy.'

Thus she mollified the other girls (who'd heard only the tale of her northern origin, and who in her blue eyes saw mysteries no worse than the mystery of their own existence) – and also fell prey to an increased sense of her own separation. *I tell lies and they believe them!* she told herself fiercely one windy day on the eve of All Saints as she plucked berries in the gardens with such angry speed that Braida, watching her, intervened.

'You pick so fast, and on your own,' said the goodwoman.

Joana barely turned round. 'I pick as I pick!' she said.

After scolding her for this rudeness Braida told Fabrisse, who laughed. 'Look at her!' Fabrisse pointed out of the window. 'She was shy. Now she buzzes like a queen bee! But I hope she learns proportion!'

Later, before supper, Fabrisse sent for her.

'Child, you're too proud,' she said crisply. 'You have a long way to go yet. And it's time you paid a visit to the old couple.' And at Joana's expression she said: 'You did promise them. Don't you want to go?'

Joana pouted. 'Mother, I don't know the way there.'

'Rubbish, child. If tomorrow's fine, you'll go.' Fabrisse hid her doubts at this course. 'Take them a basket of bread and a skin of wine.'

That night of All Saints storm descended on the land, battering the house of women as in their dormitory the girls whispered tales

– tales of black Pyrenean fairies; of the queen of the night-hags, Diana Nocticula, leading her covens to sabbats where children were slain in fields of wild flax then eaten raw, regurgitated, and put back in their cradles. From this they went on to talk about the black friar, that mysterious ogre Brother Jean d'Aubigny ... and when next morning Joana, carrying a basket of bread and a skin of wine from the Corbières, pressed into the windy, no-longer-friendly woods, she couldn't get that name off her mind.

Brother Jean d'Aubigny! The name alone conjured up her vision of the grove where her lost father – that scarred, naked man! – was kept by the Enemy, and where the Beast had attacked her. Her heart beat harder as she went deeper into the bare woods. And as she went on a foul vision of a man being torn to pieces by nine naked hags seized her: he was screaming at her as if she'd done it! She focussed on the rose, but saw instead the Enemy's beautiful, terrible face watching her ... and she froze with the fear that something feral crept up on her – a wolf, or bear, or, worse, a French patrol from Montréal. And as she shivered there she imagined she heard a horn-blast through the wind: into her mind came the sharp, terrifying image of a company of men riding her down. They all held burning brands, and they were led by the man who was torn to pieces – and torn to pieces he rode, his body flayed and bloody under the black friar's robe, an eyeball dangling on one cheek, the other eye glaring at her as he rode her down, as the soldiers tossed the torches at her. '*BURN, CHILD, BURN!*' the Enemy cried as the fire roared up round her ... and time passed before she swam out of that horror, found herself standing alone, trembling in the wild wood ...

When she reached the hut it was hard to hide her fear and her sense of claustrophobia. The moment she entered she felt caught in a mire. The hut was so tiny, so dark ... and it smelled of sickness. She saw Bérenger and said shakily: 'I've brought you sloes in wine ...' – but at the sight of her he grunted and went out, limping. 'He had a bad accident,' mumbled Alais, who looked exhausted, 'with the axe. The bone's broken. I told him you or Dame Fabrisse can set it, but ...' She shrugged ... and what that '*but*' meant she wouldn't say, and Joana couldn't get it out of her.

Heavy-hearted she returned through the misty twilit woods. All the way back she fought the phantoms of her father, of Brother Jean d'Aubigny, of the Enemy ... and of her own other self. She sensed the Enemy hovering a hair's-breadth away over the line of her sanity; the woods grew vague and insubstantial to her save when she blundered into a tree, or thorn-thicket. Once, seeming to hear a warning voice, she found in her hand the deadly black berries she'd been picking from Lady Belladonna that Fabrisse had showed her. With a cry she flung them away, and in the echo of her cry she heard an answering wail of rage and disappointment.

'You don't get me so easily!' she shouted back, and stamped her foot when the echo mocked her ... then, catching herself, applied the exercises she'd been taught and kept at them all the way back to the house. When she returned Fabrisse saw that something had happened, but Joana only said: 'They aren't well. I'm scared. Bérenger's broken his foot but won't ask for you, wouldn't even let me look at it. They don't want me there now.'

'Nothing else happened to you? Did you meet anyone, or ...?'

'Not really,' said Joana dismissively. 'I just imagined I did.'

During the month of fast Fabrisse saw how hard she was thinking, yet left her until one day Joana came and said: 'Mother, I must go again!' But then the snow came. Wind shrieked off the mountains. For days the storm continued, making travel impossible. At last after Christmas the melt came and Fabrisse said: 'We'll go tomorrow.' So they struggled through the woods to find Bérenger and Alais in their hut, in their bunk, in each other's arms, eyes closed, faces at rest, their bodies frozen solid.

'But they died without being consoled!' Joana whispered.

'They consoled each other, child,' Fabrisse said gently. 'Didn't you know who they were? Never mind. They're at peace now.'

Yet on the way back through the frozen woods Fabrisse suddenly stopped and turned, fixing Joana with her eye.

'You're going to have to confront all this, child! Too much caution is as bad as too little! Remember, you have a task!'

But Joana was evasive and, though she learned more all the time, there were things she would not face. Instead she earthed herself prosaically, hiding from the terrors which had convulsed her that day Father Bernard came to the hut and she knew him.

She's putting up walls to hide behind! Fabrisse knew, but could find no way to break them down.

Until Sybille came, and trouble with her.

18.
Sybille

One cold evening before Candlemas a tall, lank, red-haired young woman turned up, begging aid in a loud harsh voice. She was barefoot and ragged, with wet wandering green eyes set wide in a filthy face; her nails were bitten to the quick and her legs were covered in scabs and bruises.

Fabrisse always saw chance arrivals immediately. So the poor soul was brought to her by Dame Jacotte, who withdrew with a significant shake of the head. And rightaway Fabrisse felt a chill. *Joana*, she wondered, *how will you deal with this one? I can't turn her away. Yet can bread and work and prayer alone cure her? Her wits are scrambled … but by what?*

'Sit down, child,' she said gently. 'What's your name?'

'S-S-Sybille,' the young woman stuttered, flinching at the goodwoman's voice. 'I'm – I'm – Sy-Sy-Sybille!'

'Where are you from, Sybille?'

She bared her teeth in an awful grin. 'Li-Li-Limoux!' she cried, with every stuttered syllable wringing her hands together so tight the knuckles gleamed white. 'On the Au-Au-Aude near Car-Carcass-Carcass …'

'I know where it is. How did you find us here?'

'A man in the vi-vi-village.' Sybille swallowed nervously. 'He t-told me … g-good ladies here … give me f-food and a place to … to …'

'Child, sit down, relax!' Fabrisse tried her most imperious voice.

It often worked with people whose minds were so broken they'd respond only to orders. In this case it didn't. Sybille went on standing, trembling, her mad gaze jumping about. 'We won't hurt you,' Fabrisse said, smiling as she stood, took the girl's arm, and moved her gently to a stool. 'You have food and a bed tonight ... but you must tell me who you are and what brings you here. It'll go no further – but you must tell me if you want my help.'

Sybille began laughing and hiccuping, her eyes bulging. Fabrisse put one hand on her hot, grimy brow, the other over her solar plexus ... and felt energy drain out as if sucked by a vacuum. Pale, the goodwoman stood back and listened as Sybille gasped her story, in a daze thinking: *The Old One possesses this child! I must turn her away for the good of everyone here!*

But after the girl was taken away for a bath and a good night's sleep, Fabrisse thought again, and told Braida bleakly: 'We must care for her, though she's like a mad storm, and no wonder, if half her tale is true.'

For haltingly Sybille had told how a week ago before dawn Brother Jean d'Aubigny and his bullies, the bailiff of Limoux with them, had knocked, and when her father (a leatherworker of the faith) had opened up, they'd marched in and dragged her mother and her brothers and herself from bed. *Heresy! Secret denunciation! You're all arrested!* Not even a formal summons! Then the friar, the bailiffs and the soldiers went to it; and when those stinking French pigs started pawing her mother and herself, her older brother had broken free, stabbed one of the soldiers, and ...

'She says,' Fabrisse concluded wearily, 'when they were done she was the only one left alive, and only because they thought her dead. *Blood!* she cried in my face, *Everything covered in blood!*'

'How did she get here?' Braida asked grimly.

'She doesn't remember.' Fabrisse sighed.

'Oh. You mean, just like Joana?'

Fabrisse inclined her head at the accuracy of this sarcasm.

'Do you believe her?' Braida persisted anxiously.

'The tale's true.' Fabrisse shivered. 'But her madness – Braida, when I laid on hands it was as if some black mouth opened and tried to gulp me whole! She's sent to try us ... or Joana.'

'Then turn her away!' argued Braida. 'She makes us too precarious.'

'No.' Fabrisse stared through the tiny panels of the window. The world beyond was a blur. *I wish*, she thought, *the future was as invisible.*

'We can't run,' she said. 'Dark tests light. Light enters dark to be weighed, measured, and set in form. Light sacrifices itself to seed darkness.'

Her voice was lyrical. Inwardly Braida groaned.

Oh no! she thought, *Something's got into her.*

'But light must remember itself to renew itself,' Fabrisse rushed on strangely. 'Or dark absorbs it and breeds ever thicker night, so that a world and all souls in it grow heavy and collapse. If light remembers itself, then dark grows brighter until it rediscovers the Light!'

And she nodded in obstinate agreement with herself.

'Will you tell the goodman Bernard about this?' Braida demanded.

'There's no need!' Fabrisse said sharply. 'He's an old man, it's a long way, and Joana's disturbed by him.'

'Will Joana be less disturbed by this poor mad child? I think you're taking her in not for *her* sake but to stimulate Joana. But what if it's the wrong kind of stimulation? And what about everyone else?'

Fabrisse eyed her old friend with respect. 'Yes,' she admitted. 'They'll clash. But perhaps in striking sparks they'll find light.'

'And if the sparks lead to a conflagration in which we all burn?'

'I am not turning the girl away,' said Fabrisse in her softest, most undeniable voice. 'I cannot. I must not!'

Braida groaned. 'You wouldn't!' she said.

From the start there was ill feeling between them. Next morning Sybille descended on the dormitory during Gospel-study. 'Joana,' Dame Alice was asking, parchment open on her lap, the girls in a circle on the floor around her as Dame Gaia appeared at the door with the new arrival, 'Corinthians I, chapter 15, verse 45. Tell us about it!'

'*The first Adam was made a living soul, the last Adam was made a quickening spirit*,' said Joana promptly. 'In this the teacher tells us that the life of the spirit on earth is meant for growth; that it's the life of light in darkness that leads us to our freedom from ...'

'B-B-BLOOD!' cried Sybille from the doorway, her eyes dancing with mockery, for she'd slept and awoken safely; she'd eaten again and now here she stood in a clean black gown ... and rightaway her gaze fell on a golden-haired girl who was talking, the startling blue of whose eyes she hated instantly, without reason. The mere sight of

Joana made Sybille's gut twist: caught her back into visions of murder and rape. Throwing Dame Gaia's hand off her arm she burst out in a sweat and cried: 'BLOOD! WE'RE F-F-FREED FROM THE B-B-BODY THAT'S FULL OF BLOOD!'

Silence. Mouths fell open. One girl giggled, then shut her mouth as Sybille eyed her … and both *parfaites* saw how Joana glared, and how Sybille sneered back with her wet green eyes. 'This is Sybille,' Dame Gaia managed to tell Dame Alice. 'She has lost her family … but she has found us.'

'Sybille, sit down with us,' Dame Alice said forcefully, 'and don't forget again: you observe silence for your first two days and nights here.'

Sybille bit her lip fearfully. Like a clumsy stork she collapsed her limbs to sit heavily down. For the rest of the hour she neither moved nor spoke; she stared at the floor and Joana ignored her. But Dame Alice felt the ugliness between them, and wondered why Fabrisse had done it …

Joana knew. The moment she looked into Sybille's eyes she knew. In them she saw everything she'd tried to forget … everything Fabrisse wanted her to remember. So her peace of mind vanished.

There was no open clash. They avoided each other. After that first outburst, Sybille brooded in silence for weeks, doing as she was told in a surly, distracted way, speaking only when spoken to, stuttering when she did. Nobody made fun of her for that. The older women knew better; the younger were scared of her. Her wandering eye and stink of fear were bad enough. Her dreams were worse! Nightly for a week in bed by the dormitory door she relived her pain, crying out the name of Brother Jean d'Aubigny as she was attacked, beaten, raped and left for dead in her sleep. And at the far end of the room Joana, rigid on her knees, desperately clung to the image of the red rose, torn by her own terrors as the burning man and dark watching faces prowled in her; as her own mad voices wailed. *Who am I?* they sobbed. *Why am I here? I don't belong, I'm tired of it, I'll run away! Stop crawking, you mad red crow! So your mother and father were cut in pieces and thrown on the dungheap: why should I care? What about MY mother and father? My REAL mother and father! No, Joana, no! Get out, Satan! There's no salvation in that! Just burning, burning, that's all! Why must I remember it? Stop shrieking, Sybille! SYBILLE!*

At last one night Joana could take no more. As Sybille panted and shrieked she was seized by foul vision of a man who was not a man but a blue giant, hairless, with an impossible cockerel head. The Beast hissed and lurched and tried to seize her until, unable to bear it any longer, she ran down the dormitory aisle and shook Sybille. 'Stop it,' she cried. 'Stop it!' And before Sybille was awake (though the others all heard it) Joana was outside, and spent the rest of the night crying in the gardens.

Nothing was said of it. Sybille did not remember. Yet next day Dame Fabrisse called Sybille and laid on hands. Again the energy drained out of her. But she persisted until Sybille grew more calm by night and relaxed by day. Yet she never smiled, she could not concentrate, and the look in her eyes made Fabrisse think dully of frantic birds beating at a window.

And as Sybille grew stronger her war with Joana also grew. They never spoke. But they watched each other. In the gardens, at table, at study, in the dormitory – each glance was a blow in the silent war which Sybille began to win. For Joana grew depressed. A darkness entered her face; she stalked about as if everyone insulted her, and became haughty with the older women, who began muttering. *Who does this child think she is? She acts like a queen we should obey; she turns those blue eyes on you and they pierce you through!* Sybille they pitied; the poor girl was understandably mad, but Joana ...! And though nobody mentioned the rumours, they stared at her with increasing suspicion. So her depression deepened, she felt afraid and threatened, and grew bossy with Adala and the other girls, until one bleak day near Easter Dame Fabrisse called her. She came and she faced the old goodwoman, and Fabrisse hid her alarm, her mounting sense of error.

'Child, you act like a prig!' Fabrisse said sadly, assessing the young woman – tall, thin, face sharp, bright eyes remote, hair severe in a net. 'It's not good enough! Sybille needs help, not your contempt.'

'Yes, Mother,' Joana agreed tersely. 'I see that. But ...'

'Until you love what hates you,' said Fabrisse, locking eyes with her, 'you are nothing and you will do nothing. Do you understand me?'

'Yes, Mother,' said Joana quietly enough, but her eyes flashed.

'Then,' said Fabrisse, 'spend a night or so considering it.

'I will do that, Mother,' said Joana.

'So you will.' Fabrisse paused. She had a headache. 'But ... have you *seen* or *remembered* nothing? Have you had no visions or dreams?'

'*Visions*, Mother?' asked Joana, her face as blank as could be.

Fabrisse sighed. 'Never mind,' she said. 'I only asked.'

'Yes, Mother,' said Joana, and left abruptly. And Fabrisse thought wearily: *Child, you're letting this attack overcome you. What do we do?*

That same night the three other *parfaites* came and protested.

'This war between Joana and Sybille,' Dame Alice insisted, 'It's ...'

'What war?' demanded Fabrisse, full of pain as she heard this denial come out of her mouth. 'There's no war! We must help Sybille all we can, and as for Joana, she must learn humility. I've talked to her, and we'll have no more about it – they must sort it out themselves!'

'So the house is to be poisoned by hate?' Dame Gaia demanded with a passion she hadn't shown in years. "Fabrisse, what has got into you?'

'More,' said Fabrisse in an iron voice, 'than I can say now!'

When Alice and Gaia were gone, both visibly upset, Braida said: 'You must stop this. I'll speak my mind! There's evil in that child, though it's not her fault – and not only is it getting into your precious Joana, *and* into you, but into all of us. My friend, don't you see how ...'

'It must come to a head,' said Fabrisse. 'If we can't deal with darkness in our midst, then we deserve to be swept away.'

'You've never spoken like this before,' said Braida. 'That child has sucked spirit out of you. I beg you, look deep tonight – for all of us!'

She's right, Fabrisse admitted that sad night as she knelt in her cell, her breath labouring. *The Enemy infests us; I'm not myself since I laid hands on that girl. Stupid! I'm letting Joana down! Sybille's driving her to darkness, not memory or self-recognition. Child, you're so sullen now – it's my mistake! But so sly, to attack us through a poor mad girl we have to help. Joana, I'll fight back against Her! Now!*

From a drawer in the oak chest by her cot she took out her pendant. The emerald set in the stone disc flashed in the candlelight as, not really pausing to think or relax, she placed it against her brow. The cool green fire flowered in her temple ... yet she felt so dull as she sought her inner vision. Over and over she murmured the Lord's Prayer, but the first signs of far sight when they came were not encouraging: the flashing lights appeared amid a swirling mist shot through with bloody, sombre hues; the ringing in her ears, too high and painful, turned into a harsh croaking ... and through the mists she saw, watching her as it winged in such slow, deliberate circles above, a great black crow that dripped with blood, its eyes gleaming pits that sucked and tore at her. '*Weak One!*' she heard Sybille screech – yet it was not Sybille, she knew that, but the Old One!

Then a huge inner jolt made her gasp; she found her gaze locked with an immensely tall, masked woman who, wearing a robe of bright feathers, stood in an underground place the colours of blood and night, a flashing emerald ring on one finger. '*You Weak One!*' She cried as a storm of unseen wings spun Fabrisse into ever-deeper darkness. '*I'm amazed at your folly! Did you think you'd invade Me like this? It was you here last night, wasn't it? And that child! So you caught Me unawares once, but not ...*'

What did She mean, 'last night'? It didn't matter. Fabrisse knew she was lost. Then something extraodinary happened.

For without any warning a dazzling flash of light exploded through her, enveloping her, sweeping her out of the Old One's presence. It came like a mighty wind, and amid it she saw faces sweep past in a rapid blur. Some she knew, others not. There was a man with a lean brown face, his left cheek scarred; he had a sharp, determined look ... yet sharper was the deep blue eye (deeper than the blue of Joana's eye) of another man who walked with him, seemingly through a shining mountain day. These two saw her and somehow steadied her – and then, amid the burning blur (and perhaps she'd called out to him) she saw Bernard before her at Montségur.

'*What is it?*' he asked, and she cried, '*Come quickly: the Enemy has a foothold here, the child's in danger, you're needed.*'

Then the roaring fire of this dissonant vision overwhelmed her: she found herself in a stinking cell and moaned involuntarily with insight.

I let pride trick me into this! Please God it's not too late!

She fell back on the cot; all night she lay unconscious until at dawn she was found by Braida. It took her all day and another night to recover her wits ... even as the crisis broke.

19.

Benedicite

Tiy was alarmed. She'd been priming Hoel in his man-time when the Weak One came – on the green ray! And almost She'd had her! Then that flash of awful light, snatching the Weak One away! What? Who? Dion? She didn't know: in confusion She went to give Samjoyce the ring and send him on his way to Azazel, not at all sure why She did so.

Only later did She learn the where and when of that great light.

It rippled through many times, many places, a multiple echo of the same aeonic event, and many sensed it more than once, then and later.

It hit them then; it hit them later; it was a single event.

Diane Joyce in Last Days Edinburgh gasped in her sleep.

Samjoyce in his Whole Place cell was torn from vision.

Zoe, preparing for the journey with the Fool, shuddered.

The stranger Dion nodded quietly to himself where he sat.

Deru moaned in his sleep and thought himself speared through.

The Beast Azazel sensed it, and licked his icy lips and laughed, but shivered too, for there was something in it he did not like.

The goodman Bernard in his hut outside the walls of Monségur sensed it, and sat up from his contemplation of the starry night, and he rose and called for Imbert when he heard Fabrisse's desperate cry.

In his cabane on a high pasture Pierre Belot awoke in a sweat, fearing for the strange child he'd carried from the Gate of the Stone, and told himself grimly: 'There'll be more for me to do before this is all over.'

Brother Jean was on his knees on the cold stone floor of his cell when it happened; it was a terror but a relief too: he'd been fighting nightmare commands which (like a soft female song) had been infecting him even though he was wide awake. When the light flashed he cried out; his heart racing at the dreadful vision it brought, for he saw a golden-haired head, a blue-eyed face, and he bared his teeth in a rage he did not understand. 'I'll bring that girl to God yet!' he promised himself, scratching furiously.

Sybille sensed it too. It seared through the dream that tormented her with the inadmissable memory of how the black friar had raped her that horrible night her family had died. Raped her physically and mentally. His stinking worm-eaten body ... she remembered the other rapes, the bulging eyes and organs of the soldiers ... but this she had driven from mind just as Brother Jean had driven from mind his origin as Hoel. So both were slaves. How could they fight what they did not remember or see in themselves?

Yet when the light flared in her, her dream shifted to a worse horror: the sight of a furious woman who sat in a pot of bubbling, boiling blood, a pot with fire blazing under it ... and the lady was Joana, her blue eyes like spears, her golden hair a nimbus of light. And Sybille screamed in rage.

Joana passed that dark night on her knees in the herb garden, fighting not to take to her heels and flee. She was angry: at herself, at Mother Fabrisse; at the house; at the endless work and prayer and suspicion: she was sick of the furies Mother Fabrisse wanted her to confront. So stupid! Before Sybille had come it had been all right! Since then – no peace. Sybille's mad wet eyes! *Even Mother Fabrisse gets at me now!* she thought. *What can I do? Why must I remember my past? What does it matter? Why can't I be like everyone else? – ignorant, stupid and ...?*

Stupid yourself! she knew. *She scolded you because you're scared!*

And as she thought this the blinding light flashed in her: she choked in shock as she heard Sybille wail; she seemed to expand to impossible size as she looked down on the dark hidden world and saw ... and saw ... but no. She couldn't grasp it. All she knew, as night returned and she choked on her knees, was that it could not go on like this. Something had to break!

It already had.

Next day the Cerce blew from the east, irritating everyone with its mischievous tugs and buffets, and Mother Fabrisse was not seen. The other *parfaites* were grim. The mood in the house was nervous.

At work Joana suffered Sybille's hate. Under greening plane trees she planted thyme cuttings with Adala. Sybille was sowing millet in the strip higher up the hill, watching her, hissing like the mad wind. Joana didn't look up, but she became dizzily sure that the slaps of the wind were Sybille's blows. Enemy blows. She resisted her own tension by chattering loudly to Adala about anything at all, until Dame Braida, supervising them, told her sharply: 'Girl, you talk too much. Eight-day silence, starting now!'

Joana straightened with a gasp. Blood roared through her head. She stiffened, nodded angrily – then controlled herself and went on working.

Braida, iron hair wind-tugged, had reacted thoughtlessly. *I blame her for Dame Fabrisse,* she realised. *Wrong. But I can't retract now. She'll have to live with it. So will I. May God save us all from this evil!*

Soon everyone knew about this humiliation, knew Dame Fabrisse was ill. Gossip began. All day Joana endured it. All day the Cerce blew, leeching colour from the land and sense from the mind. But it was fear of a fight with Sybille that made Joana abscond from supper that night, from the Kiss of Peace. Afterwards Dame Alice found her in the gardens and said, as sharply as Braida, 'Where were you? Who do you think you are?' And in the dark hours she nearly did run away. Yet even as she quivered with the need to bolt, she found strength. NO! IF I RUN NOW I'll NEVER STOP!

All next day she worked silently in the garden, not looking up even when, with Sybille nearby, a giddy heat and constriction of breath seized her. Her meekness averted crisis till later. For, though Sybille was in distress, outwardly her mood seemed normal and went unremarked. With the entire house upset the *parfaites* had no wish to look deeper into the mire which (as Gaia and Alice thought) was caused by Mother Fabrisse's obsession with Joana. It was Joana they blamed for the confusion in their once-quiet community. They blamed her for her mystery, her very existence, and agreed with Braida's action. None of them saw how close Sybille was to the edge.

All it awaited was a clash of eyes.

Since her dream of Joana glaring at her from a pot of blood Sybille had suffered a high singing wail in her head. An evil connection was made in her imagination. She knew now that Joana had caused all the pain that had befallen her and her family. Joana was responsible for the torture and murder! Joana had raped her body and soul so now all she saw was blood!

But Joana didn't know this. Still she refused to face her fear. She wanted nothing to do with any of it; she refused even to meet Sybille's eye over two whole days ... until supper on the second day.

Though hardly recovered, Fabrisse was there, and just as well.

Something – that brilliant light? – had affected her eyes: everything was a blur to her; she was giddy and after two days and a night her ears still rang. *Yet I saw Her and survived*, she assured herself. *I was saved by those wiser than I!* Even so, she felt danger shrouding the house, and that second afternoon she insisted weakly: 'I'll sit at supper tonight.'

Her sight of Dame Gaia, in front of her, was still vague.

'Are you sure that's wise?' Dame Gaia asked dubiously.

'I'll be there,' she said, and so she was when, that evening, Sybille pushed Adala out of her place beside Joana. She took it herself, elbowed Joana fiercely, and hissed: 'I'll n-n-not let you g-g-get away with it!'

'What's that?' Fabrisse asked sharply, sensing the unease in the hall, yet unable to see the cause of it.

Braida told her.

'Does Joana react?'

'No. She sits like a statue, looking into her bowl.'

'Be ready to lead me down,' Fabrisse said. 'Don't delay when I say.'

'Do you know what you're doing?' Braida demanded.

'Better than I did two nights ago. Be ready.'

After the Benedicite Joana sat, apparently ignoring Sybille completely. But as she spooned her broth Sybille continued whispering from the corner of her mouth. All the girls at the table saw it, and watched Joana's face.

They couldn't hear what Sybille said. But Joana could.

'D-D-Do you know what I see?' Sybille stuttered with dark glee. 'I see b-blood hissing and p-popping in a fire! I see you being k-killed by the righteous! Yes, you bitch! I see you will die in b-b-blood and F-F-FIRE!'

On and on she went, and though nobody but Joana could hear her, all sensed the atmosphere; they saw how Joana shivered as Sybille went on ...

'... And after you d-die your master'll come and make you kiss his ice-cold shitty bum and you'll have to suck his c-c-cock just like the f-f-f-friar made me do, except forever! Forever! Do you know B-Brother Jean? D-D-Do you know what he d-did? He f-fucked me, he c-c-cut my mother as he f-f-fucked me ... and it's your fault, b-b-bitch Joana! And you won't ...'

Then without warning Joana's brittle mind broke in the heat of the vision that roared to her as Sybille ranted quietly on. With no change of expression she stood and began to shriek at the vision she saw, the vision of fire and death, the vision of this house on fire, of herself on fire, of Mother Fabrisse and Father Bernard on fire, of the whole world on fire.

'Now!' said Fabrisse sharply, and Braida took her arm and led her, but nobody noticed, for there stood Joana, her blue eyes staring at nothing as she shrieked ... for only she saw the other worlds, the images too great and too many to absorb. All they saw, agape with fear, was how suddenly she stiffened, stopped shrieking ... and with a different face altogether turned to point a rigid finger at Sybille, who grinned in mocking delight.

'You're mad! You're a total nutter!' Joana cried.

In English. In the language of her other voice, her other mind.

And briefly Chrissa stirs from the amnesia which has blanked her since she came through the Gate after Sam. She hears her London accent; in huge confusion finds herself staring, first at her own unfamiliar hands, then at the mad unhappy face of the red-haired woman laughing up at her, then at the many blurred half-known faces all about her ...

'Peace!' said Fabrisse, catching clumsily ar her arm.

'What?' asks Chrissa dazed. *It's a dream! I'm at home! In bed! At Berkeley Road!* 'Who ...? Where ...? Are you ... are you Cathars?'

'Do you hear?' Sybille ranted to all the hall. 'She speaks the devil's tongue! She's sent to destroy us, to ...'

'Be quiet!' Braida's voice was like a bull-roar when she wished, which was now. 'Both of you, be quiet!'

And Joana (*or is it Chrissa?*) stared, not knowing herself at all now as Fabrisse at last found her deep sight, catching the girl's distracted gaze with her own ... even as with a wild laugh Sybille stood and stumbled away, laughing as she did: 'B-Blood!' she screamed. 'I see blood here, and f-f-fire as well! Wait for blood! It will come!'

Then as the women stared in fear at her she fled the hall and the house, crying madly as she ran into the woods, into the night ... and it was a long time before she was seen again ... before her prophecy came true ...

20.
Journeys

In the woods again. *Who am I? Where?* Lost in a storm. In the woods, babbling. Shut in a stinking cell, stupefied on a pile of foul straw with terrible screams piercing her skull as men ride her down, burning brands in their hands, led by the flayed black friar, eyeball dangling on his cheek as he screams … then Sybille's mouth yawning round her; fire gouting from it: Father Bernard writhing in the smoke and flame, face a ruin, eyelids burned off; Mother Fabrisse there too, dying in the flames; and the goodman singing as she writhes in the flame in her bed at 15 Berkeley Road …

That night she was sedated. Next day she still slept. That night when Braida and Alice came she didn't know them. They took her to Fabrisse, who blessed her. She didn't know it. Through the woods they coaxed her as she babbled. They reached the hut where Bernard waited. When she saw him she shrieked and went into a fit. When she awoke it was clear she'd regressed again, for her blue eyes were as blank as they'd been when she'd first come to this age. Then Bernard signed and said to Braida: 'She can't come with me; she can't stay in the house. Ladies, you must find her a safe refuge.'

Braida and Alice eyed each other in shock.

'But we can't leave either,' said Braida.

'What about that shepherd?' asked Alice.

'What shepherd?' said Bernard blankly.

'The one who helped you deliver her into this world,' said Dame

Alice with a trace of sarcasm. 'Can't he give her shelter for a while?'

Bernard shrugged. 'Who knows where he is? We must act now. She must recover her health – and will, if we don't lose heart!'

Braida conferred with Alice, then sourly faced the goodman and said: 'We know a place. But only until the storm blows over, or until Dame Fabrisse is well again ... or until she stops wailing at the sight of you!'

'That day will come,' said Bernard, grimly optimistic.

So it did. But not for months. The two *parfaites* took Joana to a safe house remote on the high Plateau of Sault. It was empty, in easy reach of Montségur, its only neighbours tight-lipped believers. Alice went back to Fanjeaux, but Braida stayed, and all summer found herself nursing a body which seemed to house at least three separate people. By turns Joana was Joana, cowed and only half-alive; or someone calling herself Chrissa, who had a wilful and aggressive nature; or an infantile, giggling creature who sucked her thumb and gazed at the world through guileless blue eyes. There were other personalities too, more disturbing by far, both dark and bright. Braida was glad they appeared only occasionally and briefly, for she didn't feel equipped for this task: her talents were practical ... and the way she dealt with the girl was practical. All summer no matter what the shifts in name or nature, Braida called her Joana, acting as if nothing was odd. 'Milk the goat, Joana!' or 'Fetch water, Joana!' or 'What do you mean, you refuse? Very well! But don't expect to eat!' And by fall Alice, who came and went, was able to report to Fabrisse: 'She's waking up!' For gradually Joana swam out of her daze; her scattered mind knit again as day succeeded day in calm rhythm and her fears receded. And this time her recovery was firm and sound; her face, healthy again, took on a purposive, contemplative look; she was silent for days on end, and Braida (who perhaps still felt guilty at her earlier harsh treatment of the girl) saw how for hours she'd sit on a log, gazing out over the mountains. So the goodwoman was glad when at last one quiet night as they sat at the hearth, after she'd broken bread and they'd said the Lord's Prayer together, Joana said:

'I've been thinking.' And her eyes were steady and bright.

'I know,' said Braida with quiet humour. 'I've never seen anyone think so much. Are you better for it?'

'I am,' said Joana. 'How is Mother Fabrisse?'

'Well, and waiting to hear from you soon.'

'And ... the house? Is all well at Fanjeaux?'

'No trouble ... though some sisters left.'

'What ... happened to that girl ... Sybille?'

'Nobody knows, child. What's happened to you?'

Biting her lip doubtfully, Joana asked:

'Braida, have I been a great trial to everyone?'

'Child, you have undergone a great trial.'

'I know,' said Joana sadly, 'and there's worse ahead. Have I ...' – she stared so hard that Braida felt pierced through – '... talked in my other tongue? In my sleep? Yes, I know I have,' she went on before Braida could answer. Longingly she eyed blue mounains sharp against the sunset. 'It's English,' she said, barely audible. 'An English that won't be spoken for hundreds of years.' Her eyes filled with tears. 'Braida,' she cried, 'I'm so far from home, and I'll never get back, and I'm so confused, because I'm Joana now, but I was Chrissa once, and now in a way I'm both, and ...'

Then she broke down, but Braida felt relief, for her sorrow was open, with nothing hidden. At last Braida asked:

'Could you meet the goodman Bernard again now, without ...'

She turned down the corners of her mouth. Joana understood her.

'Braida, I'm sorry,' she said, wiping her eyes, 'but when I see him I'm reminded of ... oh!' She stood up against the sunset; her long golden hair caught its fire. Braida held her breath. Then Joana said: 'Yes! I can see him now. I've got a lot to learn, and there's so little time!' She laughed oddly. 'Sybille helped me. If not for her I'd still be hiding like a mouse. And you too, dear Braida,' she hastened to add. 'Without you ... and Mother Fabrisse ... oh, I do want to see her again!'

'No doubt it can be arranged,' said Braida drily.

Before Christmas both Bernard and Fabrisse came to visit. Bernard arrived first, with Imbert, and was overjoyed to find how at last Joana now accepted her name as a gift, not a curse. One frosty day as they walked in the pinewoods near the castle of Roquefeuil he told her how he'd found it in a song, *the* song, and she nodded slowly. 'It's a sad song, Father,' she commented, 'but there's hope in it. I'm still Chrissa, but the name *Joana* points me to my goal.'

Then he told her how he'd heard her cry for help in his dreams; how in those dreams she'd led him to the aeonic world; how he and Pierre Belot had invaded the Gate of the Stone to fight the Old One and pluck her from the depths. 'Without Pierre,' he ended, 'we wouldn't be here now.'

'When will I meet him?' she asked.

'Who can say?' Bernard shrugged.

'Does he have a home?' she heard herself ask. 'Has he a wife?'

'He's a shepherd!' said Bernard, as if that explained it. 'Now. Tell me: when you look at me, what do you see that you fear so much?'

At last, haltingly, she told him about the fire, and the song.

'I know all that,' he said calmly. 'It was made plain when you came to my dreams. Now forget it. We have work to do.' Ignoring her look he went on: 'When Fabrisse gets here, we'll discuss the Old One. One day you'll face Her, as you've begun to face yourself.' And he smiled thinly.

'Listen,' said Fabrisse the next night as the six of them – Dame Alice had come with her, leaving Gaia in charge at Fanjeaux – sat round the fire. 'An old tale about Her tells how when the first thought of the Aeon leapt from the unmanifest, many Shining Ones poured out of that thought, and some of them fell into this forming earth ... and She was among them! Listen!'

Fabrisse was weak. The past few months had been hard on her. Nothing had been heard of Sybille but fear that she would betray them had led nine women to depart. No attack had come; she felt able to leave matters in Gaia's hands. But the journey had been hard; she was weary as she told the ancient Gnostic tale of how:

She descended to the lower regions.
She generated angels and powers, by whom this world was made.
But after she generated them, she was held captive by them.
She suffered every disgrace from them,
So that she could not return to her Father,
She was even imprisoned in a human body,
And through all ages passed as from vessel to vessel,
Into one female body after another ...
Last of all she was manifest in a prostitute;
This is the lost sheep.

After a silence Fabrisse smiled gently.

'Joana. Do you understand?'

'Madame Pédauque,' Joana murmured, remembering another time, another tale, and then lifted her head. 'Sybille?' she asked.

'Yes,' agreed Fabrisse. 'And you, child.'

Joana stared at her. 'But ...' she said.

'Have you not been warring with yourself?'

Joana said nothing, just looked at Fabrisse, who knew her weariness was seen by those sharp eyes. Then Joana stood and went out into the night.

'She's ready to learn,' Fabrisse told Bernard. 'But can we teach?'

Soon after Joana went with Braida to Montségur. She first saw the castle as they passed through Bélesta. There! Distant on its bald high dome, the vast white ridges of Tabor behind! And a rush of fearful images made her gasp. 'What is it?' Braida asked sharply. Bernard had warned her this might happen. But Joana, white-faced, shook her head.

'I don't know,' she said, and pressed on up the trail.

But she did know, and when later that day they reached the foot of the pog and began climbing through the scrub and pine to the walls floating amid the mists, she found it hard to stay calm and not to keep turning to eye a grassy area below, *for she sees her friends chained and driven down to the stockade by French soldiers ... and then the flames, crackling and roaring* ... and when they entered the castle through the great South Door, vision seized her again, *of siege, of rocks flying over these walls, of men with crushed bodies in a covered place by the keep* that now she saw before her ... with difficulty she held her peace.

And the date that a voice kept chanting in her mind.

16th March 1244. 16th March 1244. 16th March 1244.

That evening in Bernard's hut – one of many on the narrow terraces hugging the castle's north wall, built only feet from the vertical drop to the valley below – she gazed over the rolling northlands and asked:

'Father Bernard, what's the number of this year? Twelve-what?'

'1239,' he told her, and saw how her lips tightened.

'Is there long to go?' he asked her quietly.

'Long enough!' she said harshly. 'Long enough to learn!'

They said no more ... and soon she grew to love Montségur, for the air here brought her a sense of freedom; the calm of her teachers strengthened her as much as the energy of the place itself. So she began to learn about what Esclarmonde de Foix called: 'The secret of Reunion with the Light.'

Later that year (hooded to hide her golden hair, for tales about her were growing) she went with Braida, Bernard and Imbert to the

Corbières, where amid steep valleys and on high crags Bernard told her of mysteries coded into this rugged land by ancient builders who'd served the Old One.

'The tale goes,' he told her one blazing day, his voice dull, for he had a headache, 'that She stopped here with Her people whom later She took to England. Worried by failing memory, She carved into the land knowledge She feared to lose. But look, child. What can you see?'

Joana looked hard from the sun-baked bluff where they stood. She saw heat-hazed hills, dusty forests and plunging valleys ... but no sign of any hidden knowledge did she see. Unless ... looking north she found herself gazing at a long, winding ridge of red rock, and in a trance she said:

'Father, there? That looks like ... like a snake?'

Bernard smiled. 'The Red Serpent. Here we're on the Black Rock. Line it up ...' – he pointed north-west – '... with Blanchefort, then ...' – stiffly he pointed south of east – '... you come to Rennes-les-Bains, where we're going. It's the centre of that circle of churches we've visited – Bugarach and Serres and the rest. They've been built to mark the image of the greater figure measuring out the deeper knowledge She feared we'd lose – pentagram and hexagram united, man united with woman, and the speed of the light that leaps from their union – as in the Gate She also built!'

Joana stared. 'I still don't see it,' she admitted.

'Maybe that's why She's angry with you,' he said, 'and why you're angry with yourself. For it's there inside us to start with ... but we're asleep.'

Joana eyed him thoughtfully. 'Father,' she said, 'I'm awake enough to know you've got a headache. Let me lay on my hands and I'll take it away.'

'No,' said Bernard. 'Thank you, but no.'

'Oh,' said Joana, a sudden painful heat in her, 'because you're *parfait* and can't let a woman touch you? But that's nonsense!'

'This is Chrissa speaking,' said the goodman.

She glared at him. 'Father, I know you think relations between men and women evil because it propagates sorrow in Satan's world, but didn't you just speak of the knowledge that leaps from such union?'

'Think for yourself,' he said calmly. 'As for me, I took a vow, and if you think it foolish, please respect it – as Satan's church does not!'

She stared at him some time before nodding in silence. But that night before she fell asleep she found herself wondering about Pierre Belot.

Never then did she meet Pierre, but he heard tales about her. Some came from women who'd left Fanjeaux: these told of her war with Sybille. Others came from folk who'd seen her about the land. He heard she was of spirit-origin, that she had the healing touch, that she spoke with the aeons, would save the faith, and so on. Yet he heard these tales only from believers. He heard other tales too as a new year came. He heard that the house of women was still safe, but that Dame Fabrisse was ill … and that hot summer of 1240 he heard how Trencavel's invasion to reclaim Carcassonne was at last under way, his army surging north from Roussillon through a land again alive with hope. Yet also he heard that Friar d'Aubigny was in Toulouse to argue Count Raymond out of supporting Trencavel … and as the liberating army came ever closer and the French mobilised to meet it with the folk of the Sault Razès hastening to join the standard of the faith, there came a day when he heard a new tale, a terrible tale, a tale that led him to leave his flocks with friends and go straight to Montségur …

21.
The Black Virgin

For two years Sybille wandered, always muttering a hated name. From summer to fall she drifted in the Dordogne, living rough, always moving on, for her mad eye and talk of blood alarmed whoever heard it. Yet something protected her: when leaves fell and berries were gone she came to Gascony, where King Henry's army of English Goddams gave her work on her back.

The career of camp-whore didn't last. Too many who rode her afterwards found their dreams violent with vision of hags who tore men into pieces. The whisper of '*witch!*' soon followed her; she was beaten often; at last she fled for her life . . . and one hot summer day of 1240 she limped into Toulouse, still mumbling the hated name; still mumbling about blood . . . but it was not revenge that took her along the Garonne to the walls. She came because she was pregnant after an encounter with a foul man in a hamlet in Aquitaine. She'd sought only shelter, but the brute had kicked her out as soon as he was done. Now, grimacing at the blister on her heel, this ragged red crow-like woman came gaunt and wary into the Bourg. 'La Daurade?' she cried, hobbling through crowded narrow streets of tanning workshops and shady houses with rose-tiled roofs, 'Where is La Daurade?' But few paused to help this gravid ghost; the sight of her alone unsettled the gut; the directions she did get confused her. So, lost in a maze of narrow streets, she came to the rich quarter round St Sernin. There a watchman about to arrest her for vagrancy took pity on her. 'La Daurade?' he barked. 'Not round here. By the Pont Neuf. And don't come back here!'

In a daze she wandered down to the river, and in time came to Nôtre Dame de la Daurade and entered the vast gloomy interior.

The church seemed deserted as she hobbled up the aisle under the high round arches. She made straight for the Lady Chapel in the southern apse. There, in a niche on the wall above candles lit by others in pregnancy, all gilt and gold save for Her midnight face and hands, the Black Virgin of La Daurade gazed down, impassive and calm ... and Sybille wept as with immense relief she sank to her knees, still with no clear idea who or what had brought her here, nor whose image it was now she begged for help.

'Oh Lady, Great Mother,' she began in a hoarse mumble, 'help me b-bear this child without too much blood; protect me from my enemies ... and may that golden-haired one burn as she deserves, for what she did, for ...'

It was then Brother Jean d'Aubigny, seated in shadow, heard her.

He was in Toulouse to dissuade the Count from aiding Trencavel's army. A delicate situation. Five years ago the Toulouse consuls had expelled the Dominicans. Two years ago the Pope had suspended the Toulouse Inquisition. But now Gregory was dying, armies were on the move, the heretics were on the run ... and lately Brother Jean had felt an excited sense of imminent triumph; and in his hate for his enemies he'd become such an over-zealous nuisance that Prior Capdenier (in the name of their absentee Bishop) had been glad to get the man off his back by sending him on this mission.

But after a week of waiting all day every day to dispute with the Count he was sick of it, sick of being shut up in the Château Narbonnais, an old Roman fort beyond the walls – the only safe place in Toulouse for black friars. And the Count! Slithering apostate! He was disgusted, exhausted. So last night, weary with politics, he'd drunk wine and ... fallen asleep.

And dreamed, awaking in dead of night, dripping with sweat, perhaps not fully awake at all, perhaps in nightmare still ... nightmare that told him what to do. 'How can Satan call me to a church?' he'd muttered fearfully, scratching his lice-ridden armpits. 'It was the Blessed Virgin! I'll go!'

When day came he hid his intention. 'I'm going out,' he'd told his secretary, Brother Pons, 'to see if the heretics dare insult God's servants in broad day.'

Brother Pons was shocked. 'You'll be lynched!' he'd cried.

Brother Jean had smiled tightly. 'God protects his own,' he'd said.

So into the City he'd stalked, and sure enough, he'd had to run from a gang of layabouts. 'You black pig!' they'd howled, hurling stones as he took to his heels ... but they'd soon given up on him. Now here he was.

In the Church of La Daurade. In the Lady Chapel.

Hidden in shadow near the black virgin, breathing hard with excitement and self-doubt even before he heard the pregnant woman address the image.

For long before he'd joined Dominic's new order, when nightmares first troubled him as a thin nervous boy growing up in Paris, he'd found peace only in the city's oldest church, St Germain-des-Prés, and there only in a side-chapel where the thin, tall, flimsily clad black icon of the Virgin had drawn him, soothing his fears. Gazing at that serene dark face he'd put aside the weak, tortured nature of Jean, son of the merchant Claude, for a sweeter world where he was a stronger man. Yet increasingly in that dark face he'd sensed mockery; had felt himself drained by that image. In the meantime his nightmare of being torn to shreds by wild women had got worse. So his doubts grew, until, the day he was ten, he'd learned that this black image was not an image of the Virgin at all, but of the pagan Isis, after whom Paris was named. Then in horror he'd rejected her, concluding he'd been tricked by Satan. He had never gone back.

Now here he was again before a black virgin, in Toulouse, the city of La Reine Pédauque, the Goose-Foot Queen, as pagan as could be, the stuff of his nightmares ... and his heart beat hard as he gazed at the image, for mad shrieks echoed in him, he felt pressure in his groin, he knew he was close to the Pit, trapped in perversion ... and when the gaunt red-haired woman approached the image at first he noticed her no more than she noticed him.

Then she started her hoarse, half-mad mumbling.

'Oh Lady, Great Mother, help me b-bear this child without too much blood; protect me from my enemies ... and may that golden-haired one burn as she deserves for what she did, for ...'

Brother Jean started. *Golden-haired one?* He looked up as she mumbled on, and though he did not know her, her voice alerted an image that lay deep in his mind. *A shining, glaring face, a blood-red bird ...*

Something stood him up. Something moved him to the woman, and when he interrupted her his voice was so gentle he did not know it as his own.

'Sister,' he said, 'do you need help?'

She spun round, startled, and in the gloom stared up at the hooded face of the black friar above her ... and then suddenly she twisted away in panic, raising her arms to defend herself as she began to sob and wail.

'You!' she screeched. 'Oh God in Heaven, protect me!'

'What?' he demanded edgily, looking around … but they were alone, and at his feet he saw nobody he knew, just a mad wretch. Yet as he looked up to the carved image above, a violence disturbed his brain, a half-memory. He gripped her. 'I won't hurt you,' he said. 'Why flinch? Now …'

'Won't hurt me?' Sybille babbled, shivering. 'No, how can you hurt me now? You did it then, so why again? B-but you might hurt my child, who'll soon be born into a world awash with blood and fire and cruel men who …'

'What did you say?' He tightened his grip on her.

'Father!' she cried suddenly. 'I have a c-c-confession to make! I have been with heretics … but I escaped them! I can l-l-lead you to them!'

His heart hammered. His head roared. *Now I know why I had to come here!* he marvelled amid the storm in him. *I am led by … by …*

Fearfully he looked up at the image of the black virgin.

'Heretics?' he asked carefully. 'What kind of heretics?'

'Oh Father!' Sybille wailed, throwing her arms round his legs. 'I know I've sinned. but I'm no heretic, I worship Christ our Lord, and …'

'God will forgive you if you tell me everything,' he said. 'Start with this *golden-haired one* I heard you mention …'

Mad eyes bored into him. Again he was struck by an uneasy sense of half-memory. 'Yes!' she babbled: 'But I must have f-food for my b-baby! Do as you l-like with me! Everyone does! You all laugh at poor S-Sybille! Especially J-J-Jo-Joana, with her g-g-golden hair and her b-b-blue …'

'What?' The friar jumped. 'Who did you say? *Joana?* Yes?'

Then joyfully he turned, ran to the high altar, and threw himself down on his knees. 'Praise God!' he cried. 'You brought me here to find this poor lost lamb who has strayed into evil, to lead her straight and true …'

He went on like this for some time until he realised that the pregnant woman stood by him, staring with hot wet eyes.

'She *will* b-burn, my lord?' she asked, trembling hard. 'You *will* get them, won't you … if I tell you where? And you *will* … protect my child?'

'God loves the truth!' Sharply he rose, angry at her effort to bargain with the Almighty. He beckoned, avoiding contact. 'Now come with me!'

Later, well-fed, Sybille told him all she knew.

That night he dreamed of a golden girl writhing in the flames.

'Hoel!' he murmured in his sleep. 'Oh, Hoel, we have her at last!'

22.
The Ray and the Raid

'You're sure you know what to do, Joana?' Fabrisse asked severely, her face white in the candlelight flickering from the top of the chest by the cot in which, shrunken and tiny, she lay. 'If you have doubts we'll put it off. The last time I tried this myself...' And the rest she left unsaid.

Joana breathed deep. She eyed first Fabrisse, then Bernard and Braida. They all looked tired. *It's hard on them*, she knew. *Sometimes I feel like a monster. Mother Fabrisse has spent all her energy on me, and this search drains them all. And the risk of coming here. Is it worth it?*

But over the last year they'd worked so hard for this particular night. Of course it was worth it! Besides, with Fabrisse so ill, they had no real alternative but to come to Fanjeaux for the operation itself. Esclarmonde de Foix at Montségur had taught her a lot, but nobody knew the green ray like Fabrisse. Often these past few months she'd come with Father Bernard to the hut in the woods to meet Fabrisse for the necessary deeper training. But since Whitsun the old woman had grown too weak to travel any distance, though her eyes blazed as bright as ever. And with Trencavel's invasion the risk of visiting Fanjeaux was minimal. The land was in uproar all the way from Perpignan to Foix: the garrison at Montréal was away patrolling the Fenouillèdes to the east; the black friar was said to be in Toulouse. A raid seemed unlikely. 'Anyway,' Joana had broodingly assured Bernard, 'it's not *that* time yet.' No. It was time instead for Joana herself to make a raid – into the world where her father was held by the Old One.

'I'm as ready as I'll ever be,' she said.

'Very well.' Fabrisse nodded. 'Braida, please?'

Putting the candle carefully aside, Braida opened the chest and took out the emerald pendant. Bernard, watching Joana's eyes, saw how the gem sparkled in the depths of her widening pupils.

'Give it to her, Braida.'

But for all her self-control Joana's heart pounded as she bent her head for Braida to slip the pendant round her neck. *The ring*! she thought in English, reminded of the day she'd followed Sam through the gate; of her last moments as Chrissa ... and at the memory there was a beating of wings in her mind, the sense of huge rushing flight, of dizzy waves that ...

'Careful!' said Fabrisse. 'Control memory, don't lose yourself in it! This stone is a guiding light. It lacks the power of that fragment of the Lost Stone which brought you here in the flesh, but if you let your imagination loose it will all too easily overwhelm you.'

Again Joana breathed deep, and steadily she cleared her head.

'Yes,' she said. 'I hear you. I'm ready now.'

And by the cot they knelt in a circle, Fabrisse the fourth quadrant as Bernard began saying the Lord's Prayer. '*Our Father, which art in heaven, hallowed be thy name. Thy kingdom come, bringing the salvation of Christ to the pure ones.*' And Joana, intoning these words subvocally, began to relax on their tide as with each successive trigger-phrase she deepened her self-induced trance. '*Thy will be fulfilled on earth in the Christ, for he said: I am come to do the will of my Father.*' Now, lifting the pendant to her brow, she imaged from its green, shifting depths a brilliant red rose that glowed against a golden, equal-armed cross. '*Give us this day our supersubstantial bread through which this earth takes daily shape and form,*' Bernard intoned, his voice now swirling, fading into the shining green distance like smoke down a tunnel as, from the heart of the rose, she drew out successive veils of perfumed light to envelop her, each pulsing with the colour of its sphere — the muted earthy mix of daily thought, the moony, rippling silver of dream, and blazing sun of clear insight, and so on to a shimmering violet phasing high beyond sight as the whispering in her — '*And forgive us our sins as we forgive those that sin against us ...*' — became a ringing, blazing sound that curved high with the light and drew her to the shining ways — '*FOR THINE IS THE KINGDOM, THE POWER AND THE GLORY, AND CHRIST THE BREAD AND WINE OF IT, FOREVER AND EVER, AMEN*!'

And as this AMEN rang out she steadied and paused and found herself far above the Hidden World, looking down the Sinking Ways in search of her path even as she heard a voice from far below. '*Good, child! Now go, find your father, but don't forget that your mind is your servant, not your master*!'

Then, calling up the green ray, she cloaked herself in it, and drew on her Chrissa-memory to find Sam's face. When she had it she set it firmly before her like a membrane over the shifting world below, so that it filled her vision. Now she brought the fire of will to bear, and as she began her descent she cried his name over and over again as the light grew thick and the dense waves of the Hidden World's passion hit her. '*Sam*!' she cried, homing in on his face. '*Dad! Where are you? This is Chrissa*!' And down, down, down she went until she saw an island below like a shadow floating within her image of Sam's face; she recognised the shape of England and Wales; she sank lower through the clouds, she saw rolling forested plains with mountains in the west where armies clashed; she saw flaring beams of light and bright horrified faces gaping in agony up at the heavens from which she'd plunged. She felt the lustful triumph of the victors; the last fading wisps of mind of those slain. She fled through ravines and over high pastures. She felt a pull. She felt a lusting mind she knew.

It belonged to the one who'd almost caught her before.

Over the brow of a vast crag she soared, and there! there below her! his vast, monstrous body stretched out apparently asleep and submerged in a cold tarn high on the bare mountainside she saw Azazel! The Beast!

She knew him immediately, though he was not cockerel-headed, but a vast pallid cyclops. And his one eye was shut, for he was dreaming. He was dreaming of the death his armies inflicted on the Eagle Regiment, he was dreaming of death through the ages, he was dreaming of death and evil, of stupidity, entropy, division and desire and disease. He was dreaming of the failure of the human race, of the triumph of darkness in the Last Days, of the Shift that would destroy the Hidden World ... and himself, at last.

And even as she saw him and knew him she faltered. Then that cold and deadly eye opened on her like a door to the grave.

For a moment she wavered. Panic almost owned her then.

But this time she was stronger. Or perhaps she was helped. For even as his freezing gaze struck her she felt a fire blaze out of her heart; she found the subtle light of the veiled Emme Ya star; she found the depths where the great grey ones glide, where the Lost Stone is found; she found the Song, and her own eyes opened wide and so did her lungs; she met the Beast's challenge with the Light that poured through her. '*AEIOU!*' she cried, as she'd done once before, in Berkeley Road – and the blackness of his eyes was suddenly a crumbling door through which light poured.

She saw many things in that instant he tried to grab her.

She saw connections. She saw the importance of the emerald ring. She saw Azazel's fear, and his desire for death. She saw the Sometimes Isle in the depths of the ocean, and the three figures in their feathered robes in that chamber Captain Davey had found. In the light. *IN THE LIGHT*! And ...

She saw the Whole Place where Tiy was ... and Sam. And Sam.

Then Azazel hissed in fury and lost her, for she was quicksilver-fast as to the Whole Place she flew, to the great rock, to the depths where ...

Without warning a force seized and upset her, a spiral of unseen fire spun out of those depths and shook her like a leaf. She steadied herself.

'*Dad!*' she cried, hunting, '*Where are you?*'

She sees his face. She follows it. Down dark tunnels to a blood-red hall she plunges. And there he is! On the bed! And she! Her! The Old One! The Enemy! In a fury, shaking him, shouting at him, the emerald ring blazing on one of Her fingers. She doesn't know I'm here! She ...

Then it happens. Somehow she enters the Old One's heart and mind, bringing light to that vast, gloomy, ancient nature. Gasping, Tiy rears back, face twisting in ... pain? pleasure? And Sam's eyes are shut ... yet he sees her, at first doesn't know her ... then (she feels so torn by the Old One's sadness!) it dawns on him! 'Yes, Dad, it's me, Chrissa!' she cries with Her voice as She, enraged, hunts the source of the bright invasion. 'Yes, years have passed, but there's still a chance – if you can defeat Azazel. But you'll need the ring. Remember Old Davey's tale!'

Then she's thrown into confusion and horror, for She turns in an angry panic, silently crying what sounds like: 'HOEL! DESTROY THEM!'

Then in a dizzy spin as Chrissa was hurled from the depths and heights she saw the flayed black friar leading the dark horsemen with the burning brands, his bloody one-eyed gaze on her, closing in, crying out a name that sounded like 'Ailma!' Flung with a huge jolt she was suddenly back in her body at Fanjeaux, drenched in sweat, opening her eyes to see Bernard and Braida on their feet, staring through the window into the night – the night split by flaming torches, by war cries and screams.

'So you found Her,' said Fabrisse drily, 'but She's found us too.'

With Brother Jean at their head they burst from the misty pre-dawn woods, hard men armed to the teeth, scarlet cross of crusade on their white surcoats. They didn't take chances even with a house of women. Trencavel was near: why risk ambush by some band of heretic knights? All night from Carcassonne they'd ridden, picking up more men at Montréal, and if any were shamed by attacking women, none had protested to the friar. He was clearly mad. Who crosses a madman in power? As for the gaunt, terrified, pregnant red-head who'd denounced the women, he was merciless, urging her on as hard as the rest of them, though her belly was huge. She'd lose her child on this ride. Three men had bets on it. So what? Who cared? Brother Jean? Hardly! 'He can't get it up. He wants to see them burn' they'd muttered to each other when given their orders – but orders are orders. The bitches are heretics, aren't they? Denying Cross, Virgin Birth, Resurrection and Life Hereafter! Worse, calling both His Holiness *and* King Louis Antichrist! Heretics! Never learn, do they?

At last they dismounted and led their horses quietly to a wooded gully within arrow-range of the silent dark house where the women slept.

'Be thorough!' the friar urged, shivering with anticipation which had grown steadily since meeting Sybille. Now at last it went well! Only hours ago his spies had reported the arrival of his prey, while his success in warning Count Raymond off helping Trencavel had so raised his prestige that neither the prior nor the seneschal had dared deny his demand.

'There are three I must have alive,' he gasped, out of breath. 'You know their names. If in doubt, bring them here …' – he indicated Sybille who, moaning in agony, slid off her horse – '… and God's holy witness here will identify them. Now! In the Name of Christ! Go to it!'

They did. They were professionals. A foul job was still a job. They dismounted, divided into four squads of fifteen, and surrounded the house. An owl-hoot was answered. They lit brands. They joked. Then, howling, they charged; with torch and sword they burst through doors and windows and went about their business. Soon the dark night was bright with flame, bloody with death. Pale half-naked bodies ran choking through acrid smoke quickly thick enough to hide whatever was done in it.

In the virgins' dormitory Adala rose with shock from her prayers as three men with drawn swords ran in to the middle of the floor. She'd been preparing to receive the *consolamentum.* Since Joana's departure she had dedicated herself to the spirit.

'Out! Out!' one of them bawled in French. 'All of you, out!'

'Pretty girls like you shouldn't rot in a dump like this!' bellowed the second, and laughed. 'Don't be scared! We're just poor soldiers!'

'Shuddup, you two!' roared the third, looking about. 'Joana de Laurac. Which one of you is Joana de Laurac?'

'She went away two years ago,' Adala heard herself cry – and then, with smoke curling into the room as the others ran screaming – she found herself surrounded by the raised swords of huge brutes who stank of leather, wine and onions. And they breathed death on her. (Elsewhen, Azazel dreamed.)

'Whaddidya say?' the sergeant demanded, peering down at her.

'She's not here,' said Adala clearly, and with her hands clasped before her began to sink to her knees ... but the other two grabbed her.

'No tits,' said the first, the son of a forgotten mother.

'Not much else either.' The second felt no rise in his root.

'Are you a heretic, girl?' asked the sergeant, a concerned man.

'I believe in God!' cried Adala, and to her shame wept helplessly.

'We'll save you the pain,' said the sergeant sadly, and gestured. The first knife went into her back. The second into her stomach. She fell in the smoke, choking in utter bewilderment: 'But ... how can you ... how ...?'

They were already gone at a run. She died without an answer.

Into another room in the west wing a squad of soldiers ran and found four people – an old woman in bed, an old man beside her, a thickset woman with a red face who stood up grimly, and a younger woman who, though she was kneeling, gave them such a fierce glare they skidded to a halt.

'You stupid, ignorant prats!' cried Joana witheringly, but in English, and as the rest of the men eyed her with lustful fear, one of the soldiers (his father had broken skulls here under de Montfort) turned and shouted:

'Sarge, we've got them here!'

At a run through the smoke and screams the sergeant who'd just – as he thought mercifully – ordered Adala's death came as fast as he could.

Outside Brother Jean licked his lips and tried to curb his distaste as flame caught the summer-dry timbers of the house, leaping up from the hall as women ran screaming into the woods, chased by men who, despite their armour and the cross and the smoke, were after them like mad billy goats.

'Is this good?' he burst out at Sybille who crouched, clenching herself against the pain of a sudden contraction. 'Why are soldiers so brutal?'

Part of him was genuinely shocked. It was the same each time he caused such mayhem. Giving orders was easy. Witnessing their execution was not. *Never before*, he thought, shivering as he watched a screaming woman leap from a blazing upper window, *have I bathed in such horror*!

Yet as the woman fell in a broken-boned heap and he saw a soldier hack casually at her, splitting her skull as he ran by, the friar ran forward at the burning house, frantically wondering: *Where is she? Where's the girl? I must have her! She's the heart of it. Without her this is nothing*!

'You're sure you'll know her?' he cried back over his shoulder.

Behind him, on the ground, Sybille had started to writhe.

He shut his eyes. He stopped where he was. 'I hurt!' Sybille cried, rocking in agony. 'It's coming. You promised!' He didn't hear. Heat and ash in his face, heat and ash in his soul. The house boomed like a bright blazing flower. A terrified half-naked girl, running blindly, crashed into him and he drew back with a shudder, flapping at her with his hand as the soldier after her bellowed at him to get out of the bloody way. Something in him screamed. He went forward again. *I must have her! Where is she*?

He didn't know it, but his final madness had begun.

Meanwhile the sergeant thrust his way through the smoke into Fabrisse's room. His eyes touched on each of them. He nodded with a humourless grin. "Fabrisse de Montréal?' he said at Fabrisse where she lay, and when she met his gaze he nodded and turned to Bernard. 'And you. Number two. Bernard de Laurac, right?' The goodman opened his mouth but the sergeant, already eyeing Joana, said glumly: 'Don't tell me. Who's this?'

'The one we want, sarge,' said the man who'd called.

'I think you're right, son. You! You Joana de Laurac?'

'Yes, I am,' said Joana. Then Braida pushed in front. 'Get out of here, you brutes!' she cried. 'Leave us alone! What have we done?'

'Wrong place, lady.' The sergeant raised a finger. 'Wrong time.'

A soldier stepped forward and knocked out Braida with a single blow. 'Mm!' the sergeant grunted, his gaze on Joana, and without looking round told Fabrisse: 'Stay there, old woman. We've no order to protect her; she's safer asleep with my boys getting so hot.' To Joana he said: 'You and these two here are denounced as heretics; you're coming with us. To the Bishop's Court in Carcassonne.' He spoke in a routine way, the smoke was choking now; Bernard fainted and slumped where Braida lay. 'You're in custody of Holy Mother Church,' the sergeant told the three of them, 'so don't worry about getting roughed up or nothing like that. Now let's get out of here. Take 'em, boys.'

So they were dragged out with the whole house now firmly on fire, Joana struggling furiously, shrieking at the men to bring Braida too, which they would not. 'Damn you!' she cried, clinging to the doorpost. 'Save her!'

'She'd only burn later!' shouted one of the men, beating at her hands. 'Come on, bitch, stop making a fuss!'

Outside Brother Jean had retreated from the heat.

'You're sure you'll know them?' he cried again at Sybille.

'I'm hurting!' she moaned, rocking back and forth. 'The r-ride ...'

'Yes! You'll lie in comfort later. First you must identify them!'

'Yes! Yes!' With a shaking finger she pointed. 'There they are!'

Fabrisse and Bernard were the first to be brought before him. Bernard was unconscious, but Fabrisse, smoke-blackened and frail, was calm. She met the friar straight in the eye. "So this is your church of love!' she said. 'Killing and raping innocents!'

'Innocents?' Brother Jean laughed, his gaze so bright as he recognised the old man as the goodman who'd escaped him on the road south of Tarascon six years earlier. 'Their innocence is doubtful, though of course Mother Church deplores unnecessary brutality.'

'Poor baby!' cried Fabrisse witheringly. 'What did women do to you to make you hate us so?'

Then the men holding her saw her turn pale and look away, his eyes widening as if he saw something invisible to them all. But soon he was controlled again, though his voice trembled as he turned to Sybille.

'Woman, is this old lady one of those you denounce?'

'Yes,' Sybille said through clenched teeth, her eyes shut.

'At least look her in the face!' the friar snapped. 'How can you denounce her as a heretic without even looking at her?'

'She's in great pain, you brute,' Fabrisse said evenly.

With an effort Sybille met Fabrisse's sad, wizened face.

'She's Mother at this house,' Sybille croaked, and turned to Bernard, who was stirring. 'But him … I d-don't know …'

'I do!' declared Brother Jean with great satisfaction. 'I've waited a long time to see this old …'

Then from the flaming house he saw three soldiers dragging towards him a kicking, struggling, cursing young woman whose hair shone like burnished gold against the leaping fire, and at the sight of her his mouth fell open; he felt a hand squeeze his heart, and a torrent of violent dream-emotions poured through him, turning his limbs to water even as Sybille beside him suddenly giggled madly … for through the haze of pain she saw Joana too. 'Blood!' she cried in a dragging voice, her eyes suddenly wide and gleaming, mouth gaping. 'Is this what y-y-you want, friar? Blood! Blood b-b-bubbling and boiling, bubbling and boiling in Her p-pot! Is that what you want?' she screeched. 'Your golden g-g-girl, full of b-blood that'll b-b-bubble in the fire at the s-s-stake!'

Brother Jean eyed Sybille in horror, for her agonised mockery conjured up images which he felt as nails and teeth tearing at him, and when he met her eyes he saw a hate so deep he could not touch its source; he felt the giant black wings beat in his skull, and in haste he turned away from her mad red face … and instead met the eyes of Joana as she was brought before him by the three soldiers who seemed in awe of her, for they handled her reluctantly. On the way out one of them had thrust his hand up her gown, grabbing at her nest even as the smoke and flame swirled round them … but she'd given him such a piercing look that not only had he withdrawn his hand instantly, he'd actually heard himself apologise, though he couldn't remember ever in his life before apologising to a woman. Now, as they brought her before the friar, with a sudden furious gesture she threw off their hands and with shamefaced looks they let her stand alone. And as she stared at the black-robed man before her she saw the flayed and bloody creature with the eyeball dangling on its cheek, and she laughed too as the force of her gaze exploded in him. He flinched visibly, and for a moment seemed about to collapse in a fit, for his face grew purple with congested blood and he gagged for breath. And all the soldiers saw it.

Breathing hard, she saw Sybille, whose wet eyes had no focus. She opened her mouth to say something, then decided against it. Behind them, the house roared, flames reaching to the tree-tops as the light increased and the sun began to hint its approach through the mists that wrapped the trees and the despoiled gardens.

'Braida ...' Joana said to Fabrisse. 'They wouldn't ...'

'Remember the Song, child,' Bernard whispered. 'This is not the end.'

'But I've seen all this so often,' said Joana, bewilderment overcoming her fury. Fearfully she eyed Father Bernard. The burning? Now? *But it can't be*! she thought. *It's not the right year! What if I got it wrong*?

And full of doubt she gazed again at the black friar.

Then Fabrisse, still supported by the hands of the men who held her and who heard all this, laid a gentle hand on Joana's arm.

'He's dead, child. He lost his mama and never found his love. Try not to hate him. That'll only distract you from ...'

'Blood!' screamed Sybille, making everyone jump as she half-rose to her feet, clutching her distended belly, and in her agony she squinted at Joana with a mad look, and in that gaze Joana saw She who shook her father in that deep underground place ... and for a moment there was perfect knowledge between them as the house blazed and thundered in its death-throes. '*For I am the whore and the holy one*!' She shrieked through Sybille as the black friar moaned and the soldiers stared. '*Don't pretend you don't know who I am! You scattered Me, but now I've gathered you in! You fools*!'

Then she wailed, and her wail became a long shriek as her fruitless labour began, as flame roared merrily through the house of women and the sun, a giant bloody disc, rose through the mists that ghosted the woods.

By noon the house was burnt out and nobody was left there alive.

23.
Trial

Chrissa stood in a torchlit hall, ragged nails biting into her palms. Through watering eyes she made out a black crucifix on a white wall. The three men before her were a blur. One sat on a high-backed chair, black cloak over white habit. The second, on a stool below him, was likewise dressed. The third, also on a stool, but in brown, sat at a desk, quill expectantly poised. Through high windows, black night.

I'm dreaming, she told herself, swaying slightly on her feet, hardly aware of the hacking cough that racked her. Her body was a mass of scabs and sores. The bailiff's escort had come for her after the bells had rung prime. The door banging open. The blinding light of a candle after long night. A key scraping in the lock of the manacles chaining her to a ring in the damp stone wall. The agonising bloom of pins and needles as they'd walked her up and down. The gruff voice of the old guard, friendlier than the others. 'It won't be so bad if you repent. He's got no evidence but the word of a madwoman. Answer him quiet and he can't do nothing. He's been at the others already. They said nothing against you.' She'd got the feeling they were on her side. They'd helped her out of the cell, out of the tower, up a narrow, twisting cobbled street where all was confusion. Soldiers running this way and that. Carpenters hammering by torchlight, building what vaguely she knew to be giant catapults. A sudden silence as she was hurried by. Eyes on her. A rough man defiantly removing his cap as she passed. Then under a barbican and into this hall. But none of it was real. It couldn't be. *I'm not really here at all*, she thought. *I'm at home in bed. I am. I'm asleep. Soon I'll wake up and go downstairs. Mum'll tell me I was playing Wham too loud last night. I'll go to school, and Miss Misery'll tell me to pull my socks up or I'll never get on ...*

It took her time to realise that the man in the high-backed chair was speaking to her, that he was the crazed friar who'd arrested them. However long ago. At Fanjeaux. *What's his name*? she wondered vaguely. *I suppose I ought to know. Brother something.*

In a slow, pedantic voice, speaking a rough Provençal laced with Latin legalisms, the friar told her she'd been denounced as a heretic and found in a house full of heretics; that she appeared before this court not to be punished but to be scrubbed clean of all sin; and that Holy Mother Church wished only to see her repentant and saved. The evidence against her had been recorded; there was no need for counsel or witnesses; she was here only to answer truthfully the questions put to her. His voice trembled slightly as he asked if she understood. She nodded vaguely, not yet aware of his nervousness. *Yes*, she told herself, scratching her lice-ridden head, *I know what happened. They burned the house down. They killed everyone but us. Why not us too*?

An oath was sworn on the Gospels. The questions began. The scribe began scribbling. She wished she could sit. Hard to stand after weeks spent chained flat on your back in filthy stinking straw in the darkness. *Murus strictus*, she knew it was called. Solitary confinement. No news, no visitors, no light. Only black bread and stale water. She wondered how Father Bernard and Mother Fabrisse were doing. Dully she realised: *I'm on trial for my life. They want to burn me.*

'Your name is Joana?' Brother Jean asked harshly, finding it hard to face this tall, bony, cell-grimed young woman. Her gaze was as lacklustre as her lank long hair, but still it stimulated unpleasant images in him. *Take care*! he warned himself, aware he walked a dangerous path. For the case was a scandal! Murder, rape, three seized for trial on a lunatic's word. No formal denunciation, no chance to recant. And this girl said to be a holy virgin in face of whose contempt he, Brother Jean d'Aubigny, had shown fear. he knew folk openly said he was driven not by holy zeal but by lust. Especially after Trencavel had taken Montréal and sent the garrison commander's head to Guillaume d'Ormes with a message. SOME OF THE DOGS WHO KILL WOMEN HAVE BEEN DEALT WITH. CROWS PECK THEIR BALLS. SURRENDER THE FRIAR AND THE OTHER GUILTY ONES BEFORE WE RECLAIM OUR INHERITANCE. And now the siege had begun. For the first time in years the French in Carcassonne were threatened. The pennants of Trencavel's army fluttered on the north bank of the Aude. Already refugees were scurrying from St Vincent to the walled safety of the told town. 'People turn to the enemy because of this business at Fanjeaux,' they were saying. 'They call the maid holy and the *vicaire* a beast!' Even the Prior had tried to make him drop the case.

'We may have to release them,' Capdenier had said. 'Political need.'

'Satan's need!' Brother Jean had snapped. 'They're heretics!'

Three among many. Why are they important to you?'

'We have a witness! We must proceed!'

'Everyone knows that poor wretch is mad,' the Prior had said coldly. 'Again I ask: what have you got against this maid?'

'I told you!' The friar had glared. 'She's the one they say was found in the caves of the Ariège. Joana! The soul of their damned faith! We can strike a blow against the heart of the heresy! Back off now and it'll be seen as weakness! We must proceed! God wills it!'

'God's will? Or your own?' But Capdenier had failed to outstare his *vicaire*. 'Very well,' he'd said grudgingly. 'The more we delay the more it looks as if they were seized illegally. So go ahead. But no torture. And the maid must not go to the stake. Find a formula.'

The friar had gone ahead. First Bernard de Laurac. He denied nothing. Then Fabrisse de Montréal, a sick old woman who had to be carried into court. She too refused to recant. Both unrepentent heretics who'd burn. They didn't touch his nightmare. They didn't disturb his prayers.

But Joana was different. Now, facing her, his heart beat too hard. He knew both the scribe and Brother Paul the court assessor were angry to be roused at night. But what do they know ? a voice in him whispered. *Night's the time for this; the sun shouldn't see it at all* !

For a moment he seemed to be not in this hall, but in some warm green place where the sun beat down on spilled blood – *his* blood!

And this wreck of a girl before him ...

No pity ! he thought. *Be like iron, brother* !

'Your name is Joana?' he repeated. 'Answer!'

And was taken aback, for without warning her eyes flashed.

'Yes,' she said clearly. 'Joana's a good name! So's Chrissa!'

For amid her fog she'd suddenly realised: *I've got nothing to lose. I've been through worse than this.* And her head began to clear.

'What?' He stared at her. She said no more. 'Record her name as

Joana,' he told the scribe, and demanded: 'Where were you born?'

'Out of a woman's womb.' She smiled. 'Like you, I hope.'

He thought he saw a smile flickering briefly on Brother Paul's lips. His face darkened. 'I ask you again: where were you born?'

'A house called Nantgewydd,' she said strangely, and began coughing, then laughed. 'In the land of the Cymri, which the English call Wales.'

He stared at her, flummoxed as much by the tongue-twisting sound as by her incomprehensibly carefree mood. 'Nant ... *what*? Where?'

'Nantgewydd! *Cewydd's brook*. He was a saint a long time ago,' she went on with a Welsh lilt, 'though I don't suppose you've heard of him.'

She's playing with me! A chill ran through him; the sense that he too teetered on an edge. 'How did you come to this land?' he demanded.

She shrugged. 'I don't know. I can't remember.'

'I suppose Satan materialised you,' he said sarcastically.

She met his eyes without flinching. 'I have no clear memory.'

So it began. What was her relationship with Bernard de Laurac, with Fabrisse de Montréal? Did she know they were already condemned as heretics and that they'd denounced her? Admit it, child, you hold the false beliefs of the sect called Cathars! Then, if not, do you accept the true teachings of God's Church? What are these teachings? Surely you know! Daughter, your soul's in great danger! And so on until her head swam. But she kept answering with spirit, with questions of her own, meeting the pale angry man in the eye. Scowling, his heart pounding, he tried again and again to bludgeon her into admissions she would not make.

'Do you claim that this world was made not by the good God but by Satan; and that Evil is co-equal with Good through all eternity?'

'I claim nothing!' Now with each exchange she saw him more clearly. She felt faint; her head was singing, but the light in her was growing; she felt she floated high in the hall, high above her own weak body ... and her gaze secretly terrified him. *You poor man*! her look told him. *You serve Her and don't know it*! 'But if this world belongs to the good God,' she heard herself ask, 'why do men like you rape and murder in his name?'

Brother Jean saw the light blaze in her face. Below him Brother Paul saw it too, and thought on rumours that this girl was from a spirit-realm – meaning owned by Satan, and the quicker to the stake the better.

'Let's be clear.' The *vicaire* tried again, shutting his eyes to deny the frightful images that she awoke in him – *a green glade, a golden-haired girl, nine naked hags who* ... 'You say the life God gave you is evil, that this world is hell, made by Satan?' he demanded in a choked voice. 'Yes?'

She shrugged. 'Just tell me what to say.'

'Don't let pride delude you into thinking me your enemy!' he shouted.

'Oh! You burned down the house and killed all those women just to help me?' she asked quietly. 'Well, thanks! You're a real friend!'

'I wish to save you from error.' He realised he was standing. With an effort he sank giddily back; the hall about him a blur, only her eyes clear before him, and in them he saw blue sky, he saw grass and trees, he smelled the perfume of roses ... remotely he heard his voice trembling. 'Don't you see the evil of this faith the heretics make you accept? Why cut yourself off from Christ? A beautiful ...' – he licked his lips, his voice rising, for she would not smile on him as he lay flayed, dying on the bloody turf – yet despite the sweat of fear drenching him he went on – "... a woman like you should be married to a good Christian, bearing children to the glory of God, not hugging this sad, cheerless belief that damns procreation.'

'Sad? Cheerless?' She laughed, light blazing from her as she looked down on this city, this court, this sad man who didn't know himself ... and as she looked she felt the Old One's power. '*You* don't look so happy or cheerful, brother! Does the black pot contain only blackness? Maybe you think a woman like me should be married to a *good Christian* like you!'

'This talk will bring you to the stake!' he cried. 'Take care!'

'It doesn't matter.' Her eyes flashed; she drew herself up, and a terrifying sensation seized him, that he was looking up at Her, towering above him, Her face unmasked, merciless in revenge. '*Poor Hoel*!' She cried; and fearfully he told himself it was illusion; she was a starved prisoner on trial, no more. Yet as she went on he couldn't interrupt her, and both Brother Paul and the scribe (who'd forgotten to take notes) stared in amazement at the transformation in the dirty, ragged young woman. 'You poor man!' She laughed angrily at him. 'Miserable as sin yet calling others cheerless! Why let Sybille lose her child? Why kill innocence? Is that serving the God of Love? You're the sad one, scaring folk so they'll dance to your tune! Why use death as a threat? I've been through that already! So have you!

But you know nothing about it, because ...' – she pointed at him, her face on fire, seized by the vision she'd had during translation from the Last Days to this age, her vision of the glade; of that thin dark man – Sam, her father – loving a golden-haired girl on the grass (and at the sight of that girl she was jolted by sudden recognition of the multiplicity and unity of identity) even as the hags flayed the man who'd tried to kill them as they loved ... and as she saw that shrieking man she knew his name; she laughed triumphantly; her pointing finger stabbed him deep – '... because you're lost! You don't know why you hate and kill us, do you? You've forgotten! They killed you because you tried to kill love!' And at his open horror she groaned, seeing how his tragedy was the common tragedy, of forgetfulness and division. Her tragedy too! Tears came to her eyes as she cried: 'Do you dream, brother? Good dreams? Or nightmares? Are you too scared to sleep? Do vipers crawl in your dreams? Do you know your name, Hoel? *Hoel? HOEL! DO YOU THINK I'M THE ONE WHO WOULDN'T LOVE YOU, WHO LOVED MY FATHER INSTEAD? HOEL, DO YOU KNOW ME*?'

But she'd exhausted herself; a fit of coughing doubled her up so that she couldn't go on; the light left her face as she sank to the floor.

Silence. The *vicaire* said nothing. Brother Paul looked up and saw how rigid he sat, his face beaded with sweat, his eyes unfocussed, his mouth half open, his fists clenched before him as if to ward her off.

'Brother?' asked the court's assessor uncertainly, 'surely she has condemned herself out of her own mouth?'

Brother Jean looked round wildly. He shuddered. And his face was no longer that of the *vicaire* of Carcassonne, but of a lost soul.

During the last nights her trial was conducted by the Prior.

Soon everyone knew how she'd caught the *vicaire* with his own devils. He'd gone raving to Capdenier, who'd confined him to his tower-top cell, where now he wept and prayed all night and day long.

The Prior was more subtle. 'I only want to help you,' he said urgently on the fourth or maybe fifth night. 'Daughter, I don't want your death. Let's go over it again! Of course false beliefs can't be rooted out in a day; they run deep. So our Church is a Church of fear? Daughter, beliefs that may lead you to death *must* be false! Help me to help you!'

Her resistance began to fail. Exhausted, she began to believe he spoke the truth, he really cared, he didn't want her to die like

Mother Fabrisse and Father Bernard must do. Sometimes she wept, for he was a consoling father, not a fearful judge. Soon she was ready to give in and say what he wanted ... and the Prior thought himself home and dry. The other two, of course, were obdurate. No option but to burn them. Too bad. But Joana was a different matter. And that last night he had her weeping with remorse, ready to say anything – when, without warning, that wild spirit in her suddenly blazed up out of nowhere! It brought her to her feet, her eyes too bright to face. He was astounded, utterly taken aback.

'You pretend kindness to get me to agree with lies!' she cried. 'But why bow to the Lie that condemns us to this world? I recant nothing!'

And that was that. He argued, he tried, but ... that was that. She would not back down. She sealed her own fate.

So it was the Prior who heard himself pronounce sentence, naming her as apostate and heretic, and abandoned to the secular arm with recommendation that she be spared mutilation of the limbs or death – meaningless, as all knew. She'd burn at dawn with the other two.

How did I let myself get caught in this web? he fumed in silence later when the seneschal, in a fury, summoned him.

There was no easy answer. Not even she understood. And as the escort returned her for the last time to the Great Tower she felt no triumph, only fear so crushing she could hardly walk. *What possessed me? I mustn't die yet! It's not time*! she cried silently as the warders, often brutal with those too proud or stupid to recant, helped her gently, casting troubled looks at her closed eyes, her sallow face, her thin, dirty, unsexed body. 'Recant,' they told her anxiously, 'save yourself!' But she didn't seem to hear, not even when the hammering began inside the Citadel, and they helped her with quiet reverence, as if handling the bones of a saint long dead.

Then night fell, and Brother Jean began to scream ...

24.
The Shepherd's Journey

Yet despite the screaming it was soon clear to Pierre Belot that few of Trencavel's lieutenants wished to mount a rescue. They believed the news of the burnings at dawn a diversion. They spoke of *strategy* and *military necessity*, reminding each other that the French had not only strengthened Carcassonne's walls but built an outer wall too. 'You can't just walk up and knock!' grumbled Olivier de Termes, a grizzled old *seigneur*, shrugging at Roland de Laurac. 'And if she's so popular, would they anger folk by killing her now? I say it's a trap, to draw us into a foolish attack.'

Then Pierre knew he was about to burst with the rage which had been growing since his futile visit to Montségur a week ago. In the last hour he'd tried to contain it, telling himself these men were professionals – but as he heard them argue on without deciding anything his heart sank.

Their war first. Everything else second, he thought, meeting Roland de Laurac's equally angry gaze. *They fight for land, not faith! They think the tales about Joana old wives' stuff! If not for Messir Roland and me they'd not bother at all! What's three more at the stake to men who live and die in war? More martyrs to get folk to join the cause, that's all!*

But Trencavel's grim face told him this was unfair. On taking Montréal the man had certainly dealt with those involved in sacking the convent. No quarter for those who'd given none. Rough justice for the rough. And how could you ask men so long in exile to risk not only their lives but their lord's reconquest of his city just for an old man, an old woman and a girl? Their caution made sense; he had to admit his fury at Montségur's apathy had carried him here with demands which most generals would have dismissed out of hand. Except, of course, that in this case two of those about to die were the parents of one of Trencavel's closest friends.

Yet even you don't know, he thought, eyeing Roland. *You haven't seen your folk in years, and your talk about Father Bernard shows you never knew him like I do. I see you're a bold man: you'll go with me if I stand up, because it's a matter of family honour to you, which is fine, but ...*

'Your thoughts, shepherd?' Trencavel asked suddenly, seeing how Roland met the gaunt man's stare so whitely. 'Anything we need to hear?'

'No, my lord,' Pierre muttered, squinting through the door of the tent at the night outside. '... Just that dawn still lacks four hours.'

Trencavel sighed. 'I can't hold back the dawn.'

'My lord, nobody's asking you to,' Pierre retorted.

'So tell us how we get in,' demanded Roland de Laurac, and the heat of his voice said he resented the looks the shepherd kept giving him.

Pierre's jaw jutted. 'If you mean to act, why talk? But don't worry about me! I'll just twiddle my thumbs while you talk!'

Trencavel shrugged. And as they talked about gates and guards, Pierre thought back six years to that dreadful journey he'd made with the goodman Bernard. Over snowbound mountains to the depths of the caves near Tarascon. Seeking the goodman's dream-child! *I didn't believe it until we were there*! He clenched his teeth. The horror was with him still. Often at night he awoke in a sweat, back in the maze, following the goodman to the Gate of the Stone and the Old One's teeth. He'd nearly gone mad, yet he'd passed that deadly barrier to find Bernard and his dreamchild – real, in the flesh, come from nowhere! – curled up by the black pool, both near death. Somehow he'd got them back to the sweet outside world, evading the black friar to get them up the blizzarding slopes of Tabor until, with the child still unconscious and Bernard fading, he'd killed a mule, slit its belly, and thrust them in against its gut-warmth, protecting them from the storm with his own body until – miracle! – a party from Montségur had found them. So they'd reached safety; the healers had taken over: Dame Fabrisse had drawn the girl back from the abyss. He could have left then, gone back to his winter pasture ... but he'd stayed until both Bernard and Joana were awake. Joana! He couldn't forget her lips on his neck as he'd carried her out of the caves! An odd one, and himself only a shepherd; yet even dogs may dream, so he'd lingered at Montségur, not finding it easy to leave the rare, holy atmosphere of the place – especially not after a journey which had touched on so many truths and terrors beyond normal experience.

But that was six years ago.

How different this time! he thought savagely. *I couldn't wait to get away! Even Bishop Guilhabert! What's the matter with them*?

For as soon as he'd heard of the sack at Fanjeaux he'd left his flocks and gone straight to Montségur ... to find a most worldly mood of military crisis. The garrison – fifteen knights, ninety men-at-arms – was at work. Men were out collecting food and money; others were deepening the cisterns, reinforcing the keep's west wall, building huts for the swelling flood of refugees on the terraces above the fall to the valley below. Even *parfaits* and believers had foregone prayer for picks and spades. They expected trouble, and though he couldn't see any army ever taking the place, he'd joined in with a will while awaiting audience with Bishop Guilhabert.

The Bishop's attitude had shocked him.

'My friend,' Guilhabert had said, 'don't judge events by their outer face. It may seem a disaster, but I assure you, the processes involved go far beyond our own short lives here. We cannot act as the world requires.'

'You mean you'll leave them to burn?'

'They're in the hands of that Shining Light which we all serve.'

'Then why,' cried the shepherd, 'all this building of walls here? Why not just invite Satan in and offer yourselves up to this glorious Light?'

But the bishop was firm. No action. So in a fury Pierre had come to Trencavel, seeking men who'd act and not talk. Now here he was, listening to them jabber as fatal hours flowed by and the black friar screamed, even as a gruff voice said: 'And if she's so popular, would they anger folk by killing her now? I say it's a trap, to draw us into a foolish attack.'

His rage flooded over. He stood so violently that his stool fell over behind him. He slapped the samite-draped table hard. 'Listen!' he cried in their faces. 'Doesn't that screaming chill you? When the goodman and I found the maid I was more than chilled! I didn't endure all that to see her die now.' He eyed Trencavel coldly. 'My lord, there must be a way to get them out, and it can't be half as bad as what we endured to get her out of the caves! If you'd been through that you wouldn't sit here, you'd be doing whatever's needed to save them. For if they die, then our faith dies, and we might as well give up to Antichrist and the King of France!'

Flushed, he glared at them. Roland de Laurac nodded harshly.

'Shepherd, we know many think the girl's life vital to the faith. But miracles can't be drawn from nothing like water from a well.'

'No!' Pierre, beside himself, felt fiery wings beat in his head. He bared his teeth in a savage grin. 'Not if you don't try!'

'Then tell us how,' cried Roland de Laurac in despair.

'Very well,' Pierre distantly heard himself say. He felt that his head was about to explode. Suddenly weak, he raised a hand, and –

It was then the blinding light burst in him.

It was the same light that rippled through many times and minds; which burst in Joana, Fabrisse and Bernard; which had awoken Pierre from sleep on high pastures two years earlier. But this time it blazed so bright it woke in him a sense of vastness, immortality. He lurched like a drunk, mouthing stupidly. Round the table Trencavel and his men eyed each other, but spoke not a word. For though that fire did not touch them directly (save Roland, who gasped as in a flash he saw a pale, sick old woman in a cell, and knew: *That's my mother*!) they felt it, so that suddenly all they saw – the pewter dishes and flagons of wine on the table, the striped tent walls, the known and unknown faces around them – became insubstantial, meaningless. Briefly they fell into an awful novelty of feeling upon which no familiar thought or experience had any bearing … and knew they'd been taken from the normal orbit of war and love and existence. Yet, seeing the shepherd, they knew their experience was only a shadow of whatever had seized this gaunt man who'd been scolding them; who now stood shaking, his gaze fixed elsewhere.

For amid this blaze of light Pierre felt a force seize him and bear him up. He felt a war in his limbs; he felt his body falling away in clots and fragments and thought: *I'm dead*! even as he saw these bits of himself spin away into green smoke. And he was amazed to know: *I'm not scared! I feel fine*! – as amid the light the figures of two men took form, attracting his wonder. Calm, they floated by him. One was gangling and tall with a grey-streaked shock of black hair and a scarred left cheek; the other was short, wiry and dark with blues eyes of such depth that Pierre fell into them with a sensation of grace and self-surrender.

'*No*!' cried a voice from one, or the other, or maybe both. '*That's not what we ask you to do! Look down and see the world!*'

Reluctantly (for who'd want to go back to the world?) he did as he was told. He looked down and saw an isle in springtime, green from shore to shore save in the west where bald hills rose, and he saw war on that isle: he saw monstrous sleepers heaped on hillsides, shield and axe beside them.

'*You see? Do you see, shepherd? Do you know what you have to do and what you must become to save us all from the Shift? No? So look closer!*'

And he looked and saw the most monstrous slumberer of them all, asleep in a pool of freezing water, and round this sleeper ranged dripping heights that flickered, at one moment seeming like natural crags, mossy black, down which turbulent waterfalls streamed to woods below ... and next instead he saw the pillars of a vast palace, its dimensions greater than anything he'd ever seen; greater even than St Sernin in Toulouse, for its roof was the sky and its cellars the heart of the earth, and its rooms were each of them a country wide, and each of those rooms was decorated in ways that ...

'*No! That's Azazel's illusion! The Beast we must overcome! Face him, or you'll never do what's needed to help my daughter through to us! Look closely, shepherd! Start to see and play your part in this!*'

Despite his terror he faced the cockerel-headed sleeper: saw the fear and sadness there, shook with the sense of his soul invaded by dreams born in evil, and heard his own father's voice from long ago at the start of the war against the faith: '*Now Satan will not rest until he has destroyed us all, for he can't bear to see free folk.*' And looking down on that sleeper he knew he saw the Enemy, but the Enemy was ... in himself.

'*You begin to see it, shepherd. That's not all of it, but it'll do for now,*' said the voice. '*Now look to your own world again.*'

Vertiginously he fell, and dizzily back above the city of Carcassonne found himself floating, as if held in a sustaining bubble of light. There below him it all lay, his gaze penetrating through the walls of rooms and skulls as into the Great Tower itself he seemed to swoop. And he came to three cells, side by side. In them lay Bernard, Joana and Fabrisse. And he looked down on Bernard's face as the goodman, pale and thin, stirred and looked up, smiling faintly. Then he heard Bernard's voice in his mind, and even as he felt the weight of his body in Trencavel's tent pulling him back he knew the goodman had called him. 'Very well,' he heard himself telling Roland de Laurac through the roaring in his ears as he returned to the tent with an idea bursting in him, 'I ... have a plan ...'

25.

Commotion

It was dead of night. Three stakes, dry wood piled round them, stood waiting in the Citadel as the besieged city dreamed uneasily under a hazy, hollow moon. Behind tight-shuttered windows most folk, disturbed by the screaming, could not sleep. The screams had ceased even as many sensed a blazing light burst in them. Now those who *were* asleep dreamed of demons passing through the air; of damned souls pouring along the roads to hell. An owl screeched from the river: insomniacs crossed themselves against the lamia and other monsters; guards on the ramparts peered into the night, fearing the hoot was a signal for sneak attack. But nothing moved.

Perhaps only mad Sybille, rocking on her heels and crooning to herself in shadow below the Visigoth Tower, heard how Brother Jean, gripping the bars of his window and staring at the cold moon, now moaned in the night.

'*Percurrimus foedus cum morte et cum inferno fecimus pactum*!' he was muttering. '*We have made a covenant with death, and with hell are we at agreement*!' She giggled at his terror. In some dim corner of her broken mind she saw everything. The light had torn her back to Fanjeaux where it had struck her last, tormenting her then with the image of Joana in a pot of bubbling, boiling blood, her eyes like spears, her hair a fiery halo. Now she struggled for courage to obey the orders which had come to her in delirium earlier as she lay in the hovel where Brother Jean had put her. A mere hole in the wall, she'd lain babbling in it for weeks, more dead than alive, unharmed, for folk said that even to lay eyes on her would bring luck as bad as she'd brought on the three who'd die in a few short hours.

Yet it was barely before the commotion began that she mastered her fear and limped up the steps to the battlements ... to his guarded door.

Meanwhile Bernard lay hopeful in his cell.

Though nothing seemed to move he could feel the currents stir.

In that instant when the light flared he'd soared high, as high as he'd soared years ago when Joana had called him. Far above the city he'd found himself ... and there was Pierre Belot too, with two Shining Ones. Seizing his chance Bernard had drawn him down, into the Great Tower, through barred gates and past guards, along dark corridors ... to these three doors.

Do you see, shepherd? Quickly, now!

Also, as the darkness returned, he'd sensed Fabrisse on the green ray, contacting ... *Is that Roland*? And drawing Joana out of her terror. Now, no sound from Joana in the next cell, but he felt she was calm. At last! He knew something was about to happen. After all, Joana's dreams – and his! – said their fate wasn't due until Montségur fell, and there, not here.

The Old One thinks She has us, but it's not over yet!

So when sounds of commotion penetrated the tiny window high above his head, he sighed and waited for whatever might happen next.

Seconds before this the guard on the battlements at Brother Jean's door had jumped with shock, levelling his spear as Sybille appeared in the moonlight. 'Who goes there!'

'Good sir,' she whined, holding out a leaf-wrapped parcel, 'I heard the poor man cry out; I've prayed to the Blessed Virgin to show him mercy; and I've brought him honey-cakes which I beg you to give to him.'

Recognising her, the guard snarled and thrust at her with his spear.

'Get away! Go on! Get away!' he hissed. 'Shoo! Go away!'

Backing off, she dropped the parcel of honey-cakes at his feet.

'Please, sir! Please give them to him! Show mercy!'

'I'll show you mercy, witch!' he cried after her as she turned and ran down the steps. Cursing, he was about to kick the parcel after her when a loud shout erupted from the streets of St Vincent, down by the river.

'Trencavel's here! Let's get the priests!'

The honey-cakes were forgotten as the riot erupted.

Under that hazy hollow moon Trencavel crossed the Aude and came to a safe house in St Vincent, admitted by citizens who the night before had sworn on wafer, relics and Gospel that they were faithful to King Louis.

Loyalists spread the word. It was all the people needed. Into the streets they erupted, howling for vengeance. So riot burst the quiet of the night. From their battlements the French looked down to see torches weaving through the suburb as the mob broke down doors to get at priests who hadn't fled. Flame lit the darkness as Guillaume d'Ormes, awoken from stuporous sleep, came to the ramparts. Even as he did, more dim figures slipped unseen over the bridge from the enemy camp to mingle in the chaos. With Prior Capdenier hurrying out of the cathedral of St Nazaire, where he'd been praying for the condemned, many shadowy shapes were seen fleeing for dear life up the steep and high-walled approach to the Porte de l'Aude. 'Open up!' they cried, scarcely audible against the shrieks and uproar now rising from St. Vincent. 'Open up and let us in! They're killing us all!'

By the light of torches above and blazing houses below the seneschal saw no troops following these refugees. 'Let them in,' he ordered, 'but take care! Count them as they come! Watch for tricks!'

A grill in the latch-gate was opened. Light flared on desperate faces. Then the latch-gate itself, pikemen ready behind it, was opened just enough to let through one at a time ... but the refugees, many barefoot or in their nightgowns, tumbled through in such a panicky rush that accurate count was impossible: the soldiers backed off with their sergeant shouting futile orders as, below, houses blazed and the riot, like a bright short-lived firework, died. Peace returned. The latch-gate was shut. The soldiers stood down, relieved not to be sent out to deal with the rioters.

The refugees milled about like dazed sheep. It took time to gather them together in a hall of the Citadel, where they identified themselves to Guillaume d'Ormes. 'Fifty-three – is that all?' he asked the Sergeant of the Guard, and that poor man, who had no idea, assured him that it was ... an assurance that later cost him his life. For he was wrong.

It was dawn before anyone knew that.

Among those who came through the gate were eight men in priest's gear who'd come one by one, mixed up with the others. Once inside they used the confusion to avoid the soldiers, slipping into the narrow climbing alleys where, behind trees and in shadowed doorways, they hid until the commotion ended. With the coast clear they met behind a buttress of the cathedral.

Here they waited until near dawn. Then their leader removed his gown. Below it he wore the gear of a garrison soldier. The others were dressed likewise. He pulled them close.

'So far so good!' hissed Roland de Laurac. 'Move fast and we'll be in and out before they know it. Jourdain, Isarn, help me. Pierre, Jacques, deal with the maid. Imbert, Bernard, get the portcullis or we're all dead. Don't raise it too soon. You'll know when.' He paused grimly. 'If there's trouble, the girl comes first.' He looked at Pierre. 'You've got us this far. May God see us through the rest. You're sure you know the way?'

'Yes.' Pierre nodded. 'Don't ask me how, but I do.'

'He's right,' said young Jacques. 'I visited my brother here.'

There was a hint of light in the east.

'Good,' said Roland. 'Let's go.'

Five went to the Great Tower, three to the Porte de l'Aude. Sybille, still lurking by the Visigoth Tower, saw them pass, and laughed softly. Then she gazed up at the lopsided old moon. 'Oh, Great Lady!' she sighed.

Five came to the Great Tower, Citadel walls black above them. Nobody about. They eyed each other, loosened swords. Roland hammered the door.

'Bailiff's escort!' he cried in French. 'Come for the heretics.'

A spyhole opened. An irritated eye observed them.

'Bit early, aren't you?' grumbled the voice behind the door.

'Seneschal's orders. Trencavel agents got in with the rest from St Vincent. We have to do it now, quick, in case they try anything.'

Grumbling, the guard raised the bar. Roland and Jacques, shoulders to the door, burst in as soon as it opened. In seconds the guard was dead and the door again barred. Jacques led them to the guardroom. Four sleepy men found knives at their throats. 'Quick!' Roland demanded. 'The three you thought you'd burn. Bernard de Laurac. Fabrisse de Montréal. And the maid Joana. We want them now. Any tricks and you're dead.'

'Gladly,' croaked the grizzled old warder. The relief in his voice and on his leathery face seemed genuine. 'I'll take you.'

'So do it!' Roland jerked him to his feet. 'Now!'

Leaving Jacques, Jourdain and Isarn to cover them, Pierre took a torch and followed Roland. Along cold passages they prodded the warder. Doors opened off at intervals. At a fork the old man started right. 'No!' And Pierre pulled him up short. 'This isn't the way.'

'Who told you that?' The warder stared. 'Satan?'

'Who told you to murder innocents?' snapped Roland. 'Satan?'

'I don't like it.' The old man shrugged. 'But two wrongs don't . . .'

A shove in the back shut him up. along they went until Pierre stopped by three heavy doors. 'Here!' he said harshly. 'These! Open them!'

The old warder crossed himself. Roland jabbed him in the ribs.

'Open them. No!'

Chrissa was as ready as she'd ever be. Still she couldn't take it in. Her dreams, false? If so, the Enemy had won. Dazed, she lay on stinking straw, her head in the hollow worn in the wall by so many others who, like her, had awaited their last dawn here. That pale hint of light stealing through the tiny window high above her head. *Strange,* she told herself, *I'm not scared now. Maybe I'm too scared to feel scared. Maybe because nothing makes any sense. Life on this earth? It's the Beast's bad joke*!

Yet now she knew why she'd refused to recant. It wasn't just pride. For there was a chance – just a chance and no more – that by going through the fire she would indeed come to the realm of the Shining Ones.

'Is it likely,' she asked, 'that all this is only trickery?' *No,* she decided. *It can't be! The Enemy owns this world, but there are others. To fear for our flesh in this one is to lack faith. And that . . .*

She heard something! Footsteps in the passage outside. Then a key, grating in the lock of the cell next door! She began to shiver.

The key grated in her lock. The door opened, and her self-control fell apart. 'Oh, Dad!' she wailed, cringing from those dark faces behind the torch. 'Do something! You MUST do something! I don't want to . . .'

A hand touched her shoulder. 'Be calm!' The voice struck a faint chord of memory. She saw dark caves. She moaned. 'Can you stand? We're friends. We must get out of here quick before they realise what's up.'

So for the first time in six years she met Pierre Belot. Shivering in the dark cell, she gaped up without understanding.

'What?' she asked tremorously. 'You haven't come to ...'

'Joana!' It was Father Bernard! His voice so weak, yet alive with new hope! 'It's Pierre. The Shining Ones sent him. Come along!'

So she let Pierre lead her out to the passage where, barely able to stand, Bernard leaned against the wall. At the sight of him she groaned. He was skeletal ... but his eyes shone at the sight of her.

'You don't look any better yourself,' he said cheerfully.

As the third door was opened Pierre couldn't take his eyes off her. So tall and gaunt! She bore no resemblance to the child he'd rescued. He stared at her, entranced, as Roland entered the third cell.

Roland gasped. Fifteen years since he'd seen his mother; he knew she'd been here a month: he hadn't expected her healthy, but – 'Mother?' he asked, scarcely believing. For he remembered a robust woman. But before him he saw skin and bone. Only her eyes lived. 'Unlock her!' he told the warder. At his voice Fabrisse peered into the torchlight. 'It *is* you,' she whispered hoarsely. 'Roland! I thought so.' With slow, trembling, twig-like fingers as the warder unlocked her she lifted the emerald pendant from her neck. 'Here. It's Joana's. She's the one who has to live.' Her voice was barely audible. 'Her and your father have a fate.' She smiled. 'I'm past my time. But I thank God for letting me see my best son again.'

'What are you saying?' Weeping, Roland cradled her through the door. She weighed nothing. 'You won't die here.'

'I don't want to die here either,' the warder muttered. 'Take me with you. They'll flay me alive, and worse.'

'Then carry the goodman, and fight for us!' snapped Pierre, hoisting Joana onto his back, just as he'd done in the caves years ago. 'Now let's go!' And back to the guardroom they went as fast as they could, Roland carrying Fabrisse, the warder supporting Bernard ... and Pierre was consumed by rage and sadness as he carried Joana; rage at life, sadness at the loss of his simple life. *But I'm just me*! he cried silently. *What can I do*?

Jourdain, Isarn and Jacques had tied and gagged the other guards. The older warder put Bernard down. He faced Pierre without flinching.

'Kill me now,' he declared, 'or trust me and take me with you.'

Then from the door, a loud rapping. 'Bailiff's escort!'

Pierre eyed Roland de Laurac, whose shrug said: *You decide.*

'Deliver them to us,' he told the warder. 'Or die now.'

The warder eyed Joana and sighed. 'For her,' he said. 'Not for you.'

They left Chrissa and Fabrisse and Bernard with the helpless guards. Chrissa was confused. Roland had put the emerald pendant round her neck. Bernard and Fabrisse lay calmly. Heart in mouth, unable to find words, she listened. Behind the door six men waited, knives and swords drawn. The old guard unbarred the door. 'Got 'em for you,' he said. And the escort, numbering six, entered quickly in single file, not expecting trouble.

The fight was short and brutal. The first three died as they entered, the fourth and fifth, alerted, fought so hard that Isarn fell with a knife in the guts. The sixth almost escaped. He ran, howling 'Treason!' The old warder, drawing a knife, hurled it through the half-light and caught the man in the back. Down he went and died, gagging on his own blood.

Too late. A bell began to toll. Roland bent over Isarn. 'Get – out!' Isarn choked, his breath rattling. The others returned with Joana, Bernard and Fabrisse. 'Go on, get …' The rattle got louder. His eyes rolled up. His head fell back. It was the warder who pulled Roland away.

They ran down cobbled alleys to the Porte de l'Aude. The gatehouse loomed ahead, portcullis still shut. 'Now!' Pierre roared, knowing that if the other three hadn't taken the gatehouse they were lost. Voices shouted from the battlements; horses' hooves rang closer as at last the heavy iron gate began to creak up. From Pierre's shoulder Chrissa met Fabrisse's eyes and saw in them a knowledge that terrified her. She saw the knowledge and acceptance of death. Now that life was possible the threat of death was suddenly terrible. 'Mother,' she cried, 'I won't …'

Then all was confusion. She saw soldiers hurry down from the ramparts; horsemen on black destriers charging them; the portcullis coming up so slow as Pierre turned angrily, an arrow splintering off a wall by him. 'No!' cried Roland. 'Shepherd, run for it! We agreed!' She saw a young man, seizing a horse by the bridle, duck a blow from its rider as the old guard yanked his knife from a man he'd killed and used it again. 'Pierre!' cried Jacques, pulling the rider off. 'A horse!' Tripping a charging man, the shepherd heaved her over the horse even as the old guard fell with an arrow through the neck: again she met Fabrisse's calm gaze as her son, carrying her, spun and ducked a blow, as the other young man threw the horse's reins to Pierre and ran to Roland's aid: Pierre cried at Jourdain who heaved Father Bernard over the horse behind Chrissa, who automatically held him.

'Get out, shepherd!' Roland cried again.

Jourdain, bellowing as an arrow struck him, caught a soldier round the waist and flung him under a horse's hooves; the beast reared and threw its rider: Jourdain knifed him as Jacques faced another man; Roland grabbed the riderless horse as Pierre ran his burdened beast to the gate. 'Mother Fabrisse!' Chrissa cried as Pierre mounted precariously behind her and Bernard. And the last glimpse she got showed her Fabrisse smiling as a voice roared through the clanging bell: 'The gatehouse! Stop them!'

Then more soldiers were running at them, converging, swords pale in the dawn, Pierre kicking out at their faces as through the gate and down the steep cobbled slope beyond the walls he forced his way. A thrown lance caught the horse's flank; the beast bucked and nearly threw them and he cursed, grabbing hold of Bernard and Joana ... then they were sliding down towards the safety of St Vincent. A crossbow bolt hissed past his head, then another, clattering off the walls that hemmed this exit; he grunted and swayed as a third bolt struck his leg; for a moment thought he would faint. 'You cretins!' he screamed, fighting for control ... then at a gallop he carried them out of danger, into the streets of St Vincent.

There he collapsed, bleeding heavily. When a surgeon pulled out the bolt and cauterised the wound, he passed out.

Soon oily black smoke was seen rising from the Citadel. It was a hot, muggy morning. The stench of burning hung in the air for hours. Raymond Trencavel, suppressing his rage, briefed teams of sappers then met with local citizens. When Pierre came to that evening he learned that none of the others had escaped. Fabrisse and Roland were dead. Bernard de Laurac was awake but very sick. As for Joana, she was in a deep, opiated sleep.

But during that sleep Chrissa began dreaming about the journey Sam made with three others to overcome the Beast ... and about someone else.

She began dreaming about her mother again. About Diane.

Part Two

Feast of Light

'The spirit is something that no one destroys.'

– Traffic, *The Low Spark of High-Heeled Boys*,
Island Records, 1971

26.
Timewaves

In bed alone on a winter night in her rented flat on the third floor of a greystone tenement on Rankeillor Street in the Newington district of the Last Days City of Edinburgh in Scotland, a gaunt, fiftyish woman moans and shifts. Her eyes are open. Apparently she's looking through the wide high uncurtained sash window, her gaze fixed on a dazzling blue-white star that hangs low over opposite rooftops below and east of Orion's right foot.

In fact Diane Joyce is fast asleep and dreaming.

Fourteen years since her husband and daughter vanished, and nightly for years she dreamed, bittersweet, that she was still living in that little house on Berkeley Road with Sam and Chrissa, both still normal, life itself normal – unpaid mortage, street violence, backed-up drains and rising prices – only to awaken in a sweat, consternated by her appalling loss, and return to the bare wires of her tranquillised half-life alone in Edinburgh.

She was on antidepressants for years. Her dreams were dark, elusive, delusive. Cotton wool. No light or hope or communication.

Until that evening in August two months ago.

She was getting off the bus to change at Waverley, on her way 'home' after her usual Tuesday night at the Church of the Second Coming over in Portobello. She's never liked changing at Waverley since the night a year ago she got knocked over by a Knight of the Purple Heather, a brawny young man in tartan tatters. He'd burst out of the station, the police whistles blasting, a megaphone bellowing: 'GET DOWN! WE'RE ARMED!' – and cannoned into her, all doped-up adrenalin, then sprung away screaming, 'Free Scotland from

Norman Money!' He'd weaved away through dense Princes Street traffic. There were shots. The news that night said he'd tried to bust the Waverley Station money machine – with a defunct Access card. Crested party papers on his body identified him as Domhnall Conallach MacIain, sennachie to the Laird of MacIvor. The card identified him as Ian Sproat, 26, unemployed, of Saughton Mains Terrace, Corstorphine, E11.

Either way, he was as dead as could be, and after that Diane shook visibly every time she had to change at Waverley. She could have stayed in and not gone out at all . . . but the Church was her lifeline; a car or taxi was far beyond her wage. It was the bus or nothing. So that Tuesday night she was already trembling as she stepped off the bus when, with an utter clarity, she heard a once-familiar voice cry in her ear. 'Diane! Diane!'

SAM! She knew it! She swung round, her mouth opening . . . then confusion took her; she'd have fallen if not for the quick hand of a young man who caught her. She stumbled away in an utter daze. SAM! His voice so real, as if he'd been there beside her! And he had been! She'd felt it! She walked home all the way over the Bridges and up Nicolson Street, not once thinking of the risk. Nobody laid a finger on her. And, that night . . .

That night she had a new dream. A bright light filled her room and from it a great voice told her about the Shift; told her Sam and Chrissa still lived; told her to be ready. Next morning she threw away her antidepressants. Since then she's plumbed heights and depths that would once have had her at the shrink right away or, more recently, spilling the beans in the always-open ear of Gussie Farquhar, resident Church medium.

But she's kept it to herself.

She had enough of psychiatrists after Sam and Chrissa 'went'. They never took her story at face value. All of them rationalised it, explained it in terms of guilt, background, chemicals, her sex life . . . whatever.

She knows what she saw. She has no faith in psychiatry. She believes in survival of the spirit . . . though not in spirits of the sort fronted by Mrs Farquhar. But since August she's even stopped going to Portobello, despite the friends she's made there since old John died. He turned out as sour as Sam always said he was. At least his invalid demands kept her from her own problems . . . some of the time. Since then? Nine years alone! Determined to stay that way! Only at the Church, full of folk like himself seeking messages from lost loved ones, has she found the love and understanding she needed. But she can't go back there now. She can't just walk in one night and say: 'I know better! The spirit survives, but not how you think.'

She doesn't dream of telling them what's happened.

It's none of their business that Chrissa has been visiting her almost every night.

At first she didn't know it was Chrissa.

How could she? Her memory of Chrissa's been fixed for fourteen years. Bespectacled blonde bookish twelve-year-old who plays Wham and Prince too loud, average at school, stays out too late too often then sneers at motherly concern. Nothing strange, in fact quite normal – until Chrissa dreams of the burning man and Sam rediscovers the ring. Then everything goes mad. Literally. She'd gone mad too. And her image of Chrissa has been fixed ever since. Sweet and innocent, twelve years old. What else?

So she didn't know how to react when this tall and golden young woman, blue eyes bright in a sharp tanned face, emerald pendant round her neck, first appeared at the foot of her bed. Haloed in light. yes. Haloed!

'Mum? Mum? Can you see me? This is Chrissa!'

After that first visit her sensation on awakening was that she hadn't been asleep at all. It's so real! Of course it's impossible!

'Mum? Mum? Can you see me? This is Chrissa!'

To begin with she was bemused. First, Sam (nothing from him since: TYPICAL, now that she recalled how he really was) . . . and now Chrissa, sprung like a jack-in-a-box in her sleep. It was a shock at first. Since then she's grown used to it. it's like a nightly videophone call from a grown-up daughter working the other side of the world. Yet in daytime it's hard to accept. Chrissa's in the south of France? So she says – and it does explain the tan. But . . . 756 years ago? Calling from 1243? Diane shrugs now. If people can vanish into thin air, anything's possible. Why deny a dream that lets her awake happier than she's been in years? True, it's not so simple. Only the other night Chrissa showed her what's happening where she lives now – or then, depending. Showed her the siege. The siege of that castle, Montségur, which she was reading about before she disappeared.

Now Diane's reading about it too. About the Cathar war.

'Don't worry,' Chrissa insisted the night Diane admitted her fears. 'History books only tell you the outside. Honestly, it's all right, and so am I! Do you want to meet my friends? By the way, I'm called Joana now.'

'I call you Chrissa' Diane said firmly. 'Always did. Always will.'

'Okay, Mum,' said Chrissa. 'Fine by me.'

So Chrissa introduced her friends. They seemed very nice, all things considered. But even in a dream it was odd talking to people burned to death seven centuries ago, since (Chrissa freely admitted it) most of them would die soon. So they were 'passed on', as Mrs Farquhar always put it. Diane didn't really understand, though Chrissa tried to explain. Among them was an old man. Chrissa called him Father Bernard. He had a kind face, and in her dream Diane thanked him for looking after Chrissa, and said: 'I feel a lot happier knowing she fell into good hands.'

But at work next day she realised with a cold shock that this 'Father Bernard' must be Chrissa's Burning Man, responsible for her disappearance. That night she taxed Chrissa bitterly with this. 'Don't you even have a boyfriend?' she cried at her daughter. At which Chrissa's face fell.

'You don't understand!' she said, mouth tight, and Diane knew she was hiding something. 'This is so important. Father Bernard called me, and I called him, because the Shining Ones – oh, it's so hard to explain! Dad's doing something; he'll need help. If all goes well, then with luck . . .'

'You'll come back?' Diane asked anxiously.

'Don't think that,' Chrissa reproved her. 'You'll only make yourself unhappy. But I'm well. And I hope you are too, because soon there'll be something important for you to do.'

That was the strangest dream . . . until tonight.

For tonight she falls asleep, and in her dream she stares at the bright star Sirius, until out of that light Chrissa comes flowing . . . but tonight Chrissa's not her usual calm self at all.

'Diane! You must come with me! Dad needs your help!'

'Come with you? What do you mean?'

'Diane, you must come!' Chrissa demands, imperious. 'I've been trying to reach him but the Beast has me blocked out – but if you talk to him, then maybe it'll work, because Azazel doesn't know about you.'

Diane gapes. The talk about 'Azazel' goes over her head. SHE CALLED ME DIANE, NOT MUM! *'But how can I?' she objects, feebly affronted.*

'Easy,' says Chrissa. 'Give me your hand and I'll show you how.'

And the shining young woman comes and takes Diane by the hand. The touch tingles. Diane flinches. Chrissa smiles. Then, heart thumping, Diane lets herself be taken . . . away . . . and away, and . . .

After that the dream grows very strange indeed.

27.
Towards the Panting Cliff

The Beast dreams too.

He lies in his icy rock-pool above grey, spray-lashed cliffs – or is it in luxury in an elaborate palace? And his form? Cold blue cockerel-headed monstrosity? Beautiful androgynous youth? Austere king, sumptuously clad? Or crabby old man in goatherding rags? Which is true? That's his secret. His real shape, if any, lies hidden safe behind the screens of illusion and dream he weaves in the minds of others. More than Tiy or any other Watcher still surviving he's a mental chameleon, taking whatever the form in which people perceive him. As for his true form . . . if anyone should catch him out in it, then . . . but as he lies in his den he knows this is unlikely . . . and so there he lies, dreaming many things, dreaming of blood and lust, plague and war, dreaming that rain falls on the cold moors from dark cloud above – or maybe it's sparkling rose-water from shining crystal fountains.

Mostly he dreams of those who come against him now.

Samjoyce! He looks forward to the fight. He feels an anticipation he hasn't known since . . . who knows when! His war with Tiy bores him. He likes spying on her and teasing her, but she lacks all humour. So serious about reopening the Starchamber and saving the Hidden World from the final night he seeks! Yet she showed initiative, sending her Fool to the Last Days, to that mad, lovely age of mounting tension with the Shift already shivering in the wings. *And bringing him back to send against me*! He smiles. He knows Tiy's power is failing. *So she gives him that ring and hopes he'll do what she can't – but he's not her Shem at all; he's a wild card, a joker full of Last Days pride. Much more my man than hers*! the Beast assures himself. *When I take him I'll learn so much! And the emerald! I can use that! How convenient he's coming to me! And his tassty little daughter! She's bound to follow! I'll take his companions one by one. And then . . .*

Yet he's uneasy. What if it's not so simple? What about that light that flared through the inner planes? Yes, it deprived Tiy of one of those Weak Ones protecting Samjoyce's daughter – but they're his foes too. And that girl – she's escaped him twice! And Dion? *The Elohim are involved*, he realised. *What if Samjoyce wins and I have to . . . but it can't happen! No! I'll absorb them, then Tiy's mine! The Shift's assured!*

Night falls on the Panting Cliff. Dreaming he sees his armies thrust into Tiy's realm . . . sees the four who press deeper into the wild lands, and eagerly plans the game of illusion and death he's about to play with them.

It was their first night in enemy land, amid hills near the ford where the Eagle Regiment had fallen. For hours Deru had led them through a wood of wrinkled trees and strange cold sounds, along a trail only his subtle senses defined as such, and though they'd seen neither hide nor hair of Azazel's forces they were tired and scratched; Zoe moaning continually that Deru couldn't know where they were, warning the half-free that betrayal would bring his instant death. 'The Lady watches us!' she kept hissing at their guide, increasingly anxious as his confidence grew, so that several times as light faded and they pressed ever deeper into lands which he alone knew he turned, pulling his ugly face into uglier shapes for her benefit.

Dion walked alone behind, deep in thought, a stranger more enigmatic every hour. He'd said little, his lyre had stayed in his pack. But Sam, third in line and just as quiet (not least as he didn't know the language), knew he'd trust Dion before Deru or Zoe. Somehow the little blue-eyed man encouraged him. At camp last night as they'd lain down to sleep under the trees, Sam had gazed hard at Dion's prone silhouette before sneaking a look into the emerald ring . . . and in those clear depths he'd seen a bright double spiral of light, like the DNA helix, or the caduceus. It shimmered with serpentine energy. *Mercury-Hermes*, he'd thought. *The winged messenger.*

Whoever Dion was, Sam already thought of him as an ally.

Now, the moon rising as light faded, Deru entered a clearing high on the south slope of a long ridge. A stream gushed down the hillside and cascaded through dark rock-pools. Without looking round or speaking he gestured that here they'd stay the night. Zoe immediately shook her head. 'I'm not sleeping here on these rocks,' she said categorically, and turned for support to Dion and Sam, dark eyes flashing. But Deru, ignoring her, tore off pack and shirt and threw himself down by the water.

Then Sam, turning away from Zoe's histrionics, for the first time saw the tattoo on Deru's back – a maze of cupped spirals joined by curling lines. 'Cup-and-ring marks!' Sam said in English, wishing he was able to ask Deru what they meant. Deru, sensing his gaze, looked round at him and made a surly, contemptuous sign with his uplifted finger.

Sam suppressed anger. 'You don't have to be like that,' he said, aware of Dion and Zoe watching. He pointed at Deru's back, then up at the sky. The first stars were appearing. 'In my time,' he went on in a friendly voice, 'nobody knows what those marks mean. They're found on megalithic stones. Some think they're star-charts . . .' Again he indicated the sky. 'Others call them dowser maps of underground water.' He pointed down into the earth. But Deru only glared at him and spat. and suddenly Sam lost his temper. 'So treat me like a leper,' he said, 'but you're not so great yourself. Remember you'd be dead if not for me. With a stake up your arse, if I heard it right!'

He turned and stalked away, not looking back, crashing up the slope.

Dion stared after him. 'You half-bred cretin!' Zoe snapped at Deru who, yawning, rose, took a sling from his pack and began looking for suitable stones. 'You want to eat rabbit tonight, O Servant of the Lady,' he said curtly, 'then get some wood – dry wood, that won't smoke and give us away. Though Azazel's creatures won't come near this hill.'

'Why's that?' Dion asked.

'Those Elohim we Free Men call the Children of An were here once,' Deru muttered. 'Their influence lingers. Too bright for Azazel.'

Dion was interested. 'So, you know about that!'

But Deru, sling at the ready, was gone.

'Friendly, these Free Men,' Dion commented.

'He's not a Free Man, he's a half-breed!' Zoe said. 'The Free Men are even worse! Think they're better than everyone else.'

Dion eyed the slope. 'I'd better go after our friend.' His brilliant smile touched Zoe's heart. For a moment she felt she was falling into his blue eyes. 'My dear,' he said softly, 'we can't afford division. It's just what the Beast wants. Please stop taunting the half-free.'

Zoe stared after him as he went. Then, alone on the darkening slope, she sighed, sat on a rock, and massaged her aching feet until something made her look up. Above her in the twilight glided an owl. At the sight of it she shut her eyes, breathed deep, calmed her mind, and let pictures form – pictures that her Lady, far away in the Whole Place, awaited. But when she came out of her trance she felt confused. *What am I doing here*? she wondered. *What does She hope to gain? Why did She give the Fool Her ring*?

Shaking her head, she went looking for firewood – *dry* firewood.

Meanwhile Sam, having rapidly climbed some hundreds of feet, came to the treeline. Black, the hill continued up to a rocky crag that stood hard against the last light. A stiff wind moaned through wiry ankle-high grass. He continued climbing. As he did his anger at Deru faded.

Instead he found himself thinking about Chrissa ... and Diane.

Tears came to his eyes as he mourned his past. His past? The future too. A huge loneliness seized him. 'Diane,' he whispered, seeking some voice or sign, hearing nothing but the wind, 'what happened after we went? I'm so sorry. I hope you didn't do anything silly. I hope ...'

Then as he trudged over a sink of level boggy ground he came across a circle of cold stone men. Like black uneven teeth they stood before him in the strengthening moonlight. He stopped, hackles rising as he eyed the ring on his finger, for immediately the standing stones reminded him of the place the ring liked, on the moors above Gairloch. That awful gate where his trial began! Then abruptly as he looked into the emerald depths Shem came to life in him, surging up in an angry flood that made him stagger.

Yes! I built this place! Shem thundered mournfully in him. *Why won't you hear me? Our father in the Hidden Place cries out! How can we beat the Beast if you cling to Last Days pride and refuse to hear me? It's just what Azazel wants! At least learn the language, listen to the half-free and to Dion! They know things you've never even dreamed of! If you won't hear them – and me! – then the Beast will conquer and turn Her best intentions to evil! Now sit down and stop trying to THINK all the time*!

Sam grimaced. He sat on a mossy stump and stared at a rock in the pale moonlight. After a few seconds he saw how on it were incised cup-and-ring marks almost identical to the tattoo on Deru's back.

'Here they are again!' he cried. 'So what do they mean?'

And Shem, the voice of his blood, scolded him contemptuously:

Fool! There you are! That's why he doesn't like you! You see his tattoo and want to know what it MEANS. Why can't you see what it IS? You can't use logic or reason here! You're a thousand years before Akhenaton; two thousand before the Greeks! Reason's gone so far with you Last Days folk that you see nothing you can't snare in words. Beast-delusion! So you drive yourselves mad! Learn better! Didn't Heisenberg give you a new line on it! Feel these stones! See who I was and what I did before She made me get involved with you. Sit still and learn by keeping quiet for once instead of rushing about like a Last Days madman.

Sam was chastened. Even so he tried to argue. 'You'd never know about Heisenberg if you hadn't invaded me,' he grumbled. 'Now you drag me here. Why?' And he breathed deep, for the last few days had been hard on his precarious ego. It wasn't just Deru's contempt, but Zoe's hauteur too.

As for Dion ... for Dion he had no description.

Three days and nights, and still he had no line on Dion.

So try seeing yourself through their eyes! Shem advised.

He tried. And remembered the night they'd left the Whole Place.

They'd met on the summit, Dion and Deru and Zoe waiting until She came with her Fool in tow. Dion and Zoe both saw immediately that Samjoyce now wore the ring, but said nothing. They too had been struck by that flash of supernal light; they felt Her uncertainty, Her unstable mood. So did Deru. Still shocked by his encounter with Her, he hung back.

Through Her mask she saw packs on their backs, staffs in their hands.

'So,' She said to Zoe, Her voice painful, 'you're ready to go.'

'Yes, Lady,' Zoe said simply, bowing her head.

'And you!' – Her eye held Deru – 'You know what happens if you fail?'

'Yes, Lady,' Deru gasped, gaping at Samjoyce and sensing behind the Fool's grim face the terrifying aura of Last Days fire. 'Yes, Lady!'

'And your music!' – She turned to Dion, her voice softening scarcely at all – 'You know how to soothe the Beast? About the ... Forty-Nine Heads?'

Dion only nodded. She saw how Zoe looked at him and abruptly took Samjoyce by the arm. Over the forests She gazed to the dome-like hills in the west. A bloody light played on them. She sensed

Azazel's armies advancing.

'Now, Fool. Look in the stone. Tell Me what you see.'

Samjoyce felt giddy. It wasn't just his vision of Chrissa so weak in that cell, nor that light which had flared in him, nor the climb to these heights of the Whole Place, but the enormity of the trial ahead that made his mind spin. Reluctantly he gazed into the emerald depths, fearing he'd plunge into an abyss. He swayed. Her hand steadied him.

'You must do better than that if you're to use this power well and defeat the Beast,' She said. 'I've kept My side of the bargain – you have the ring, and your helpers – now tell Me what you see!'

He looked. His face grew pale. Stirring in the depths he saw shapes that terrified and perplexed him. He saw things he knew he couldn't tell Her. Speaking his tongue that only he and She (*and Dion*? She wondered) understood, he chose words with care. 'Blood!' he said harshly. 'and that black isle with the Starchamber. And You and me on a ship with the Beast.' He grimaced. Suddenly he broke free of Her grip and spun round with a wild look. He eyed first Zoe, then Deru, then Dion ... on whom his gaze lingered.

'Now can we go?' he demanded. 'I hate waiting!'

They stared at him in silence, taken aback, even Tiy. Impatiently he said 'So who's the guide?' His gaze moved from Dion to Deru. Suddenly he laughed. 'I see! *Two* guides! One to the land, one to the spirit!' And he went to meet them, clapping Deru on the back and shaking Dion's hand. 'It'll work out – and you!' He swung on Zoe. 'Don't glare at me like that. We're on the same side, right? So let's get on with it!'

Before they knew it he was shepherding them off the height. Even Zoe, despite her backwards look at the Lady, found herself on the move, helped along by Sam's half-push. Before Zoe could protest Sam turned and roared at the tall lonely figure left standing in Her mask and gorgeous robe.

'Don't worry, Lady! D'you want me weak, or d'you want me strong? I won't beat this Beast by hiding my light under a bushel, eh? So you've got me my team and now I'm going to lead them ... all the way to Azazel!'

She stood unmoving. He raised a hand in ironic salute. The sun's last rays flared on the emerald ring She'd given him. She felt smaller as She watched him go. She'd said not a word since he'd looked into the ring, since the change from servility to swagger had swept him. Now She simply stood and watched as he set out on the mission that would win Her a slim chance to find the Light again – or guarantee darkness.

And secretly, weakly, She wept.

But Sam sensed it. So did the others. And his first forced enthusiasm for command quickly faded as they came off the height and passed through the outer precinct to the shadowed world beyond. Only too clearly he felt the mute hostility of Her people watching the four of them as they left the now-threatened Whole Place; felt the falsity of his position. *I have the ring, yes, and I'm the mystery Fool, the focus of this journey*! he told himself savagely, eyeing his three guides as they entered the woods. *But I've got no skills that they lack. I need them to help me do what I can't. I can't even speak their language! So bide your time, Sam. Don't make enemies of them.* And he wondered what on earth She'd meant, asking Dion if he knew how to soothe the Beast . . . and about the Forty-Nine Heads.

All that night they'd walked the road through forest and field. Horses would attract more attention. So the Beast knew they were coming, but why make life easier for him? He couldn't see everything. So they'd started, so they went on. And during that night and the next two days a pattern of relationship had begun to form. Dion, silently self-contained. Zoe, at first haughty, acting as if this journey was below her proper station in life; but also (Sam sensed) secretly nervous not only about the war ahead but also about being among three men. This nervousness at first she'd taken out on Deru, who'd been quiet to start with.

Now back in his own wild lands, Deru no longer bothered to hide a resentment which not even Dion escaped.

And under the moonlight high on the hill Sam sat among the stone men with Shem energetically scolding him as the night grew darker.

Well? So now can you see it from their point of . . .

'My friend,' a quiet voice interrupted from the darkness beyond the stone men. It spoke in English. 'It's time we talked.'

28.
The Stranger

Sam didn't turn. He wasn't even surprised. As soon as he heard that voice he knew he'd been waiting for Dion. 'Who are you?' he asked with tight self-control. 'I know you're Dion, but … *who or what is Dion*?'

Dion shrugged. 'A stranger, like yourself.' Choosing his spot, the small dark man sat down opposite Sam, his back against a rugged menhir. He laid his pack beside him. He grinned. 'Tiy asked me the same thing.'

'Yes,' said Sam. 'But …' He paused. He didn't want any answers too deep to cope with – not yet. He looked at the emerald. It gleamed in the pale moonlight. He asked: 'What did She mean when She asked if you know how to "soothe the Beast"? What are the Forty-Nine Heads?'

'You'll find out.' said the stranger, 'if we get there.'

'Nice of you!' growled Sam. 'What about the ring? Did you …?'

'I suggested it,' said Dion easily. 'But you asked first. Why?' And he added: 'Don't you see you're as much a mystery to me as I am to you?'

'And to myself,' said Sam grimly, feeling Shem stirring in him.

'Oh?' Dion settled himself more comfortably. 'How's that?'

Sam glared at him. 'Why should I trust you?'

Dion laughed and pointed at the emerald ring.

'Do you know where that comes from and what it is?'

'Tiy told me all about it during our night together,' said Sam self-mockingly. 'She was given it by secret sympathisers on the Council of the Elohim after the condemnation and imprisonment of the Watchers.'

As he said this he stared hard at Dion.

'You don't believe it?' Dion asked.

'I don't know what to believe!' Sam threw up his hands, anger vying with self-pity. Suddenly he knew he had to spill out all his frustration. 'I have no terms of reference that make sense,' he complained. 'Some of the time I think it's all a mad dream. The rest of the time I sweat with fear. I mean ...' – he fumbled for words – '... here I sit on a prehistoric bloody hillside, hijacked by a twerp called Shem who lurks like some damned ancestral double in my subconscious and calls me a fool for trying to think things out. Maybe he's right! I mean, how can I?' And grabbing his head in both hands he continued in an angry rush that Dion did not interrupt. 'It's all very well, this magic lateral thinking bit, but I was taught to think in terms of cause and effect, this and that, subject and object. How can I make sense of this? I thought I was crazy even before I went through the Gate. She drove me nuts in my dreams every night – but that's nothing to what's happened since. I lose my mind, and next thing I'm playing Adam-Before-The-Fall in the Garden of Eden, and I don't know a damned thing till Ailma spreads her legs to wake me up, and that poor bastard Hoel gets torn to bits by the local female hit-squad. Then I remember I'm Sam Joyce of 15 Berkeley Road, London N8, but Tiy comes along and tells me that's not who I am at all. 'Oh no!' She says. 'You're Shem, and I sent you to the Last Days to learn how to defeat the Beast and open up the Starchamber, and when are you going to get it right, Fool?' So She drags me down to Her hole in the ground with Shem grumbling in me like a bad bellyache, and puts me through this pseudo-tantric bit, complete with kundalini and cut-price instant soul awakening like you can buy from any half-arsed fake eastern guru in London in 1985!' He laughed jaggedly. 'So we rock and roll all night long and She swamps me with a dream of world history consisting of Madame Blavatsky, Erich Von Daniken, and the Book of Enoch in equal measure. Then this spook Azazel turns up like an ectoplasmic voyeur, drooling challenges to come and meet him for fifteen rounds of heavyweight battle to decide the Fate of the Earth four thousand years from now!' He paused, glaring hotly at Dion's shadowy figure. 'And now I'm sitting on a hillside under the full moon in the middle of nowhere speaking twentieth-century English with you like you're some bloke I met in the pub down the road, for chrissakes!'

'What about your daughter?' asked Dion quietly. 'Chrissa. Or Joana, as the Cathars call her.'

Sam stared at him. Terror seized him.

'You still haven't told me who you are!' he whispered. 'How do you know about my daughter? What the hell's going on?'

'Ask the emerald,' suggested Dion. Reaching into his pack he brought out his lyre and plucked a chord that made Sam's head swim. The sound shimmered and rippled in his mind. He shivered. The moonlit landscape grew indistinct. 'Don't worry!' Dion's voice seemed to float from a far-off world. 'It's not so mad. As you say, the problem lies in terms of reference. This game runs deep! Look into the stone, hear my music, seek out Chrissa and her friends. We'll help them, and maybe they'll help us. The Beast can't be overcome by divided minds. Find your faith!'

Then Dion struck another note, and another. At first Sam spontaneously shut his eyes and resisted, but the third note was so plangent and sweet that he groaned and opened his eyes, and past moon and horns looked into the depths of the emerald. Swirling mists parted before him as if blown away by the breath of the music ... and then amid a flurry of notes the white light flared again, blinding, all-embracing, seizing him up to the heights of the night, of the Sinking Ways. Of a sudden he was united not only with Shem but Dion too: high above the Hidden World they winged. '*LOOK*!' cried the music, and dizzily, he looked – and saw below him a great walled city, a river flowing past it, and on the far bank the tents of an army. And from those tents he sensed another mind rising to join them – an honest mind with no cringing in it, only unconcealed amazement. The name *Pierre* came with the image of a tall grey-haired man whose weathered face looked used to high places. A simple mind too, one so overwhelmed by this vision in the light that it offered itself up in a mood of self-surrender.

But the voice of the music cried out:

'*No! That's not what we ask you to do! Look down and see the world*!'

And as Dion played on Sam forgot his arguments: in that high space he flew on a journey with a common goal: a journey west to the Land of Death where the Beast lay dreaming amid his realm of illusion, where the pillars of a titanic palace reached from earth to heaven. And the voice cried out:

'*No! That's Azazel's illusion! The Beast we must overcome! Face him, or you'll never do what's needed to help my daughter through to us! Look closely, shepherd! Start to see and play your part in this*!'

And more. Quick scenes like snapshots. The Beast snarling at the invasion of his dream as Pierre rides Chrissa and an old man to safety through a hail of arrows. Tiy, pacing in the Womb-hall as a tiny old woman's tied to a stake by unhappy men, but she's calm, and as the flames began to lick she looks up: and Sam sees the old woman who warned a Fool against the Beast during a bath in the Waters of Memory. And through her eyes then he sees the deep calm ocean where the great grey ones glide; where the Lost Stone glows in its coral wall.

There's a sudden jolt. Emerald fire. A scream. Then. ...

... He sees a middle-aged woman with a careworn look get off a yellow bus in the Last Days City! And he cries out: 'Diane! Diane!' The woman shudders, almost falls as she gets off: a man catches her arm; white-faced she thanks him. 'Anything the matter?' the man asks with what Sam knows is an Edinburgh accent, and Diane – yes, it's Diane, his wife, lost so long ago in his future past! – says, shaking violently: 'I just thought I heard someone I used to know. I must have been dreaming.'

Abruptly the music ceased ... and Sam fell back to himself from the heights. With fading echoes of vision he saw Deru in the woods below shrug as the music ended – then the half-free let fly with his sling and bowled over a rabbit in the night; he saw Zoe gathering firewood ... and with a jolt he was back in the moonlit stone circle with Dion opposite him and Shem inside sighing in deep relief. '*Now you see, don't you*?' Shem murmured. '*Can't depend on reason alone. Now we can move against the Beast.*'

And Sam flinched at his own voice, his own memories. Diane?

'But Azazel's alerted now,' said Dion gravely. He put away his lyre. 'Until now he thought it a game he's bound to win. Now he knows we're not easy meat. Now the true battle starts.'

Dion stood, and Sam joined him, puzzled. 'Were you speaking to me ... or Shem?' he asked suspiciously. Yet still his mind whirled with the image of Diane ...

'Two in one,' said Dion briskly. 'Let's get supper. Friend Deru'll have it on the spit soon. And I see ...' – he eyed Sam sharply – ... that from now on you'll have no trouble with language.'

They returned to the clearing. A fire blazed. Rabbit roasted. And Samshem found that now he knew the language like his own ... Shem's own.

For the first time that night they felt a unity together. They ate well, and did not argue ... and were not disturbed. The hill was safe. Soon they slept. But before he closed his eyes Sam found himself thinking not of the trial ahead but of Chrissa ... and that strange vision of Diane ...

29.
The Washerwoman

At dawn Zoe arose stiff and dew-soaked from her bed on the rocks. The day was dank, a heavy fog turning trees to ghosts. She saw Deru feeding the embers with the last of the wood she'd gathered, his face intent, as if relighting fires was a holy task. *So it is*, she thought, shivering and clearing her throat as she stood. Her dream … she sighed, automatically looking for Dion. But he was not to be seen.

'Up the hill.' Deru grunted, amused. 'He won't go without you!'

Remembering Dion's advice, she checked her retort and instead looked down at Samjoyce, buried asleep under a deerskin robe.

'Fool!' she said in a freezing early-morning voice.

'So give him a kick!' said Deru. 'Wake the idiot up!'

She almost did. Then she thought: *Why do as the half-free says*? And she recalled last night. Dion had returned from the hill with a Fool utterly changed, a Fool not only bubbling with life but speaking the pure tongue of the folk! She'd hidden her amazement, but now she told herself: *She sent me to look after him and report on him, not to abuse him! Yet …*

'Deru,' she said, speaking his name for the first time, and unsure as she said it, 'have I been … I mean … do you hate me?'

'You've served Her all your life,' the half-free poked hard at the fire, his voice guarded. 'You've known nothing else. Now you're in the middle of nowhere – where I've been all my life!' He looked up. The sudden grin on his ugly face said he accepted her half-apology. 'So stop worrying! She can't touch you here!'

Zoe doubted that. 'Did you dream?' she asked.

'I dream all the time.' The ugly man laughed grimly.

She approached him. 'I had a good dream.' Her voice was tentative. 'I'm sorry I snapped at you for choosing this place to stop. But how did you know about this hill? What stopped Azazel and his brutes troubling us here? I know you said it's the influence of An and El ... but *what* is that influence? I can feel a ... trembling in my bones, but ...'

Deru picked up a glittering lump of quartz and tossed it to her.

'That,' he said. 'That kind of stone puts out a power that obstructs the Beast's dreaming. Running water can do the same thing. That's how we Free ... how my people stay immune to his interference. We build our raths in places where the mineral spirits make it hard for him to affect us with his miseries. Here it's the same. So last night he couldn't hunt us in our sleep ... and his troops, being slaves to his dream, couldn't approach this hill, because he can't dream it! Easy!' He grinned, but his grin soon faded. 'There aren't many places like this. From now on it won't be easy.' He gestured at the sack of oatmeal. 'Now do me two favours. Make the porridge – then give that Fool a kick!'

Then Zoe laughed in a way she'd never heard herself laugh before.

And when Dion returned and Sam awoke their breakfast was ready.

With the sun hidden by the mists they left that hill and went deeper into Azazel's realm where only the Free men moved at will.

It was a war-ruined land. At first the mists were a mercy, hiding the evidence of horror past and present. But not everything was hidden. The track they followed took them through burned-out farms and over sad ruined pastures inherited by hawkweed and dandelion, yellow-bright in the gloom, a note of false spring cheer. For no cattle lowed. No sheep or goats were left; no songbirds flew, and if any humans remained in these parts, there was no sign of them. It was a land inherited by the raven and the carrion crow – by the dreaming of Azazel.

So their mood was grim when at last they came to a valley where a river rushed between hills through pastures thick with nettle and dock. The mist did not lift: the sun appeared faintly, a red eye in a dire shroud, only to be swallowed again. Trees loomed through the clammy mist; round their path stunted hawthorn and hazel bloomed, but nothing moved; there was no sound but for the harsh distant croaking of ravens on crags invisible above them. Deru still led, following signs invisible to the others, but soon called over his shoulder, a shiver in his voice: 'I know this land, but today it's strange! Take care! We're near a dreadful place!'

Silent, sensing disaster, they followed the river. It was rapid and brown. Bluebells at their feet were incongruous. Dion took out his lyre and plucked quiet notes to thrush and blackbird in the bushes, but there was no reply; the sense of threat mounted without any sign of its cause until Sam, scuffling through wet long grass, kicked into something rotten. Baring his teeth, he looked down to see a decayed human body. Empty eye-sockets stared up at him. He went on quickly without a word. Behind him Zoe gave a cry. Then he saw an abandoned breastplate, then through the fog another corpse. Subdued by horror they continued, their minds deadened by the mist. It was so dense they could hardly see their feet, let alone what lay about. And something was singing in their ears; something subliminal which the roar of the river all but drowned. They felt dazed, and though Deru in the lead trod ever more carefully (for he alone knew exactly where they were and what had happened here), his senses were numbed and he heard the muffled sound of clapping hands too late as, the mists briefly parting, he found himself facing the washerwoman. With a gasp he stopped dead.

She was tall, thin, dark-cloaked, grey-haired, white-bodied, her feet invisible in the swirling water. She sat on a tussock at the edge of the river, her head bent as she scrubbed bloody garments, clapping them with her gnarled hands in the water, and as she washed she sang in a slow thin high keen – that sound which had been whining in their ears.

'First torn breeks, then dirty socks,
Then caps that crowned those glory locks,
Then the shirts, all stained with blood,
Of a thousand men whose mouths eat . . .'

But at the sound of him she stopped and looked up with a snarl.

'Good Lady,' Deru exclaimed fearfully, 'we . . .'

'Don't "Good Lady" me!' she snapped. But a sly smile crossed her face at the sight of four healthy living bodies. She showed black teeth. 'More lambkins for the slaughter, eh? Come to feed your souls to his gut?'

'Aw hell!' exclaimed Sam, looking at Deru in fearful exasperation. 'You're supposed to keep us clear of this sort of nonsense! Who is she?'

'One who should serve the Lady but does not!' Zoe said.

Dion laid a hand on Sam's arm, and quietly pressed Zoe back.

'Woman,' he asked, 'whose clothes are you washing?'

The creature eyed him, then Deru, who stood shivering.

'The clothes of those led to death by this half-breed renegade!'

'That's not true!' Deru hissed, turning white with rage.

'Be calm!' Dion rebuked him. 'What does she mean?'

'Here the Eagle Regiment was wiped out.' Breathing hard, Deru glared at them. 'I led them here. Why not? It was a good site, well-protected, but the Beast used a coward's weapon and made them kill themselves.'

'Why didn't you die with the rest of them?' Zoe demanded.

'I went to visit my folk,' Deru admitted miserably. 'I returned too late.' He thrust out his jaw. 'I did my best! I led the survivors home. For that I was condemned. Nobody wanted to know what I saw! They just wanted scapegoats' Why should I be blamed?'

Dion quietened him with a look and turned again to the washer-woman.

'Who are you? Why do you meet us here?'

'Who am I?' She seemed amazed. 'I am the doleful one! I wash the clothes of brave men who die in war. Why waste good clothes?'

'She'll sell these corpse-clothes,' said Zoe with distaste.

'You judge me?' The old woman spat. 'What would you do if you lived here where beasts destroy everything?' Again her black teeth showed. 'Let me invite you to the green hill where I live! A pretty little cave!' And she stood and bowed with mocking politeness. 'Please! Come! Soon we'll all dwell in the land where those whose clothes I wash have gone. Let's join them, and end our misery! It's a fine land, a happy land, a land where …'

'… where the asphodel blooms,' said Dion sharply. 'Yes, old woman, I know! Where do you think I'm from? Tell me!' He widened his blue eyes on her. Into them she looked. Then, gasping with fear, she backed out of the water … and at the sight of her feet Sam choked. Her webbed feet! *Madame Pédauque*! he thought. *The Goose-Foot Queen*! In confusion he recalled the dreams by which Tiy had drawn him through the Gate, dreams in which She too had webbed feet like geese. Then slowly he nodded as Deru, barking with triumph, quickly stepped between the water and the washer-woman.

'Now grant my request!' he cried. 'Tell us: how will Azazel attack us?'

The old woman moaned and tried to regain the safety of the river, but Deru stood firm as Sam and Zoe eyed each other with mutual suspicion.

'Tell us!' said Deru again. 'Or I won't let you back to the water, and you'll die, which is what you deserve!'

Imploring, panting for breath, the old woman beseeched Dion.

'Good Master! Old One! Do you demand this too?'

Dion shrugged. He seemed amused. 'Deru knows the Law. You and I both know it prevails even where illusion appears to rule.'

She pulled a face. 'But this squint-eyed fool threatens me with death! How can death affect me in this land that's full of nothing else?'

Deru stepped forward. 'I'll wring your neck now if . . .'

She wailed. 'I'm just a poor old woman' But here's what I see!' And abruptly, closing her eyes, she pointed at Sam and started a keening chant:

'Beast hates Fool who sees him true!
Despises Fool whose mind is Two!
Kills a Sham who's not yet wise!
Fools a Fool still lost in lies!
But fears the Two who make a One
And groans at Moon who marries Sun!
For when Fool sees the shapes behind
Beastie dreams that kill the blind,
And when Goodman burns up in the fire
Then foolish mind will fly much higher!
Then the Daughter Beast tried to rape
Will show the Fool the Beast's true shape
Will fly to buried isle where Three
Seek the Song that makes all free;
Then Fool and Beast will make a One
And Three fly up to Hidden Sun!'

'And what's that true shape?' Sam demanded, shaking.

Opening her rheumy eyes, the old woman laughed angrily.

'You Fool! What's that on your finger? That ring!'

'What does that mean?' Sam asked.

'What does that mean?' she screeched. 'It means you're a Fool!

How can you be advised if you think advice enough? Why ask me when ...' – she looked at Dion with fear, respect and strange love – '... you're helped by one from the heights beyond the Whirling Castle? Can't you see who he is? Now let me go, for I've answered the question!'

'You've answered nothing!' said Deru – but Dion raised his hand.

'She has. Now let her be. Let's move on.'

So they went on through the mist, leaving the washerwoman ... yet as they left that place Sam looked back, for deep in his mind he heard a mocking laugh. It sounded like Her laugh. But, looking back, he saw no web-toed hag by the river, but another shape altogether, leaping away up the hill, lit by a shaft of sun that broke through the mists ... a red deer, winter-gaunt, spring-free ... and he shuddered with a sense of mysteries beyond his reason. And as that wild creature disappeared into the mists he stared bewildered at Dion before him. Shem in him chuckled bleakly.

I told you! said Shem. *Reason doesn't work here. When in the land of illusion, watch out! Can you explain it? Didn't you hear what she said? The Beast 'fears the Two who make a One,'* but '*despises Fool whose mind is Two.' Surely even you can understand that, Sam! So when are you going to wake up and realize what's going on? Only when it's too late*?

'Oh, be quiet!' Sam grumbled, loud enough for Zoe behind him to hear him ... and she saw how he glanced into the emerald ring on his finger; how troubled he looked as Deru, clambering up a bramble-choked gully, led them out of that valley of death. And as he climbed, seemingly unperturbed by the weird encounter, Deru told Dion about the death-wish weapon Azazel's army had used. But Sam didn't listen, and Zoe as she followed worked to form the Long Sight pictures as Lady Tiy had told her to do, for she was sure the Lady would want to know about the meeting with the washerwoman.

But Zoe was scared too, and as they went on her sense of danger made her look up to see, vague amid the swirling mists, the flock of wheeling ravens. And suddenly she stiffened and cried out:

'Look! Watch out! Beware above!'

30.
Illusions

The carrion birds had gathered even before the battle was over. Now, days later they still feasted on the corpses. Yet as the four strangers approached something made them stop squabbling and take silently to the air, a ragged flock soaring invisibly high in the mists until, as Deru left the gully for a bare ridge where no trees grew, they came together and in furious, screaming attack plummeted from the sky's wet grey shroud.

In a solid rush of beating black the ravens swooped so fast that Zoe barely had time to cry out before the leading bird, shaggy neck-feathers raised in rage, fell slashing at her eyes. She ducked, it struck her neck, tearing the skin as the rest of the maddened flock followed, ripping with beak and claw. Talons sank into Sam's neck: roaring with pain he tore the bird away and dashed it against a rock as two, then three more mobbed him; as Deru beside him stumbled and fell; as Dion cried: 'Back to the gully! To the bushes!' Tearing clawing birds from each other with bleeding hands they half-slid, half-ran down to the brambles where, days earlier, Deru had watched the slaughter. Gasping with relief they wriggled under the thick scratching briars as the ravens banked and hovered, croaking frustration, black wings beating at the tangled undergrowth in the fight to get at their prey. The four crouched back to back and slashed up at the demented flock with knives and broken branches until the ground about was littered with broken-winged bodies and their faces and arms ran red with blood.

'They'll pin us down until Azazel sends worse!' Deru cried.

Dion demanded: 'Can't Tiy help us? Sam, Zoe, reach Her, now!'

With aching arms protecting their eyes Sam and Zoe tried to reach Tiy, Sam gazing into the emerald depths until – there! he saw Her! 'Lady!' he cried as his right hand, beating away a bird, brushed the scars on his left cheek, and he remembered how, long ago in the future of the Last Days, her Owl had swooped on him in Highgate Cemetery, had marked him with Her mark. 'Lady!' he cried again as She eyed him from the depths, Her unmasked face tired. 'Send Owl to beat Raven off us!' And he saw Her grimace as she said from faraway: '*Fool! In trouble even with the ring and all your helpers? Stay there! Don't move! And don't ask again. You're in Azazel's domain. I can't help much.*'

Then She was gone, but still the attack went on, the ravens wheeling, plunging from the mists, beating through the briars at the contorted and bloody faces below … until through their harsh clamour sounded a hoarse, eerie, prolonged shriek. It came a second time, a third, then the din and confusion increased as hundreds of ghostly white heart-shaped faces plunged on the ravens, white on black. Croaking in fury the ravens left off their attack to meet the owls as Dion cried: 'Let's go! Run for it!'

They broke cover and fled up over the ridge, deafened by the squalling clamour as the birds beat and clawed at each other high in the mists. The few ravens that pursued were in turn chased by Her owls: soon the four were clear, stumbling down a boggy slope, the aerial pandemonium fading behind. Yet their ordeal wasn't over. As they stumbled away the mists grew colder and thicker, writhing about them, stinking of a decay that made them choke and cough as they ran. The breath of the Beast: a dirty yellow mud that oozed into their lungs and their minds, disorientating them so that Zoe, leaping over a tussock, screamed as she plunged straight into black mire. Through the gelid fog Sam heard her and in heart-grabbing flash-back saw that stormy day on the moor above Gairloch when Chrissa, tricked by Tiy, had fallen in a bog. Entranced, he'd almost failed to save her. But this was different. It was Azazel who attacked them now: Sam felt the Beast's greedy gaze as, grunting with effort, they heaved Zoe out. Reluctantly the mire gave her up. Shaking, slimed from head to foot, barely recognisable as the Lady's proud servant, she gasped thanks. They stood wearily, the foul yellow fog crawling on them like clammy custard as Deru, green cloak torn and blood-stained, swung this way and that, beaky nose sniffing out direction until with a maddened look he pointed. 'That way,' he gasped, 'we come to a lake. Across it we approach the raths of my people where the Beast can't touch us. And I sense the Singers, ready to help!'

But as they set out again Azazel tried something new. The yellow fog grew dense with wriggling worms of bloody, pulsing fire that whirled about them, stinging violently, invading them with chaotic thoughts. Roaring and yelping in pain they stumbled on, fighting the command to give up and die, beating off images of broken bodies, destroyed cities, the world exploding in fire and flood; of each other as shambling brutes with grinning, bestial faces. On they went, often falling, breathing harshly, beating their chill sodden bodies with bleeding hands, gasping talk at each other to hold the horror at bay. But with each step the red worms grew more active, whirling round them in the fog as if an unseen spider spun a web of stinging fire. They began to lose co-ordination; their steps became awkward, their sight more distorted; mad thoughts enraged them. 'How far to Azazel?' Sam cried at Deru, for now his feet seemed a million miles away; the washerwoman's prophecy rang in his mind like a cracked bell; Shem stirred in his depths like an all-engulfing mouth; visions of Chrissa burning to death racked him; and when he saw Deru through the fog he saw a capering, treacherous idiot. 'How much more of this must we bear?'

Deru giggled. 'Depends! On whose laws prevail!'

Sam scowled. 'What do you mean?' he demanded furiously.

Deru stared glassily at the Fool, at Dion, at Zoe trudging behind them. Tears streaked the mud caking her wild, bewildered face. *They all need me*, he told himself proudly, seized by contempt for them. *Even Dion! So what if he IS of An and El! They're as helpless in this lousy world as we are*!

CAREFUL, MY FRIEND! YOU'RE LETTING THE BEAST SEIZE YOUR MIND!

Deru gasped and nearly fell as the warning rang in him. He turned. The blue eyes of Dion were fixed on him, calm and clear amid the madness.

'I asked: what do you mean?' Sam said, enraged at Deru! *A turd who serves whoever pays most*! He spat. 'Answer me, you snivelling . . .'

Dion locked eyes with him. Sam glared, literally seeing red, longing to lash out at that calm, oh-so-superior face. *Who are you, you big shot*? his glare demanded. *You act as if this world's a lump of shit you dropped*!

IS THAT MY FRIEND SAMJOYCE'S THOUGHT? OR IS IT THE BEAST?

Sam flinched. The questioning blue eyes bored into him, as clear and cold and ice, and slowly he caught himself, biting his lip to find himself shaking with a rage that did not originate in his own mind. *You're right*! he thought, and stopped, staring in amazement through the malevolent fog at Dion. Then again he asked: 'Who are you? Why are you with us?'

'Where's the lake you promised?' Zoe wailed, pushing fearfully between them. 'I can't take any more of this! I ...'

'Don't worry!' And with a wild tenderness that amazed him more than anyone else Deru hugged her. Baffled, she stared at him with beseeching eyes. 'It's close!' he insisted. 'Fishermen lived on it until the Beast drove them out: we'll find a boat, and on the far side lies Free territory that the Beast can't dream! And I feel that Taishi's waiting to ...'

'Let's go!' said Dion sharply, for the red fire, driven back by his will, was at them again, though not as strongly as before. And soon, as they continued downhill over the boggy moor, it seemed Azazel had given up this particular attack, for the fiery worms and the yellow stench faded away. But the fog remained thick and clammy, chilling them to the bone as they went on, grimly putting one foot in front of the other, Deru helping Zoe, Sam watching Dion with a wondering eye.

But you don't need to ask! Shem whispered in him. *As soon as you decide to accept me as an equal you'll know all you need to know! If not, our fate'll be the same as that of our father Shemyaza, who ...*

'There!' cried Deru, pointing. 'Look!'

Only feet away, through a swirling break in the fog, they saw the moor end in a steep black bank of peat that fell to the lake. Below them, the placid grey water. There was no sound at all. Visibility was still no more than a few feet, though a mild breeze stirred fitfully along the water's edge ... and though there was no sign of a new attack, suddenly the day was oppressive again. West along the heathery banks they marched, Deru in the lead looking about with a wary eye, Zoe with him. Behind Dion Sam gazed into the ring. A mounting sense of fresh anger perplexed him. Half-glimpsed forms swirled in the depths; he imagined he heard mocking laughter even as, looming from the gradually-shredding mists, they saw before them the outline of a palisaded timber causeway – and then, perhaps fifty yards out in the water, the vague, massy shape of a lake-village. But there was no sight or sign or sound of life.

'I knew the folk who lived here,' said Deru. 'They fled when Azazel took the land. There may be a boat, or at least wood for a raft.'

Without more ado he ran forward and set foot on the causeway.

'Stop!' hissed Sam, his flesh crawling

'What is it?' Dion turned to him.

'I don't know! Listen!'

They did. They heard only the breeze. Through breaks in the mist they peered over grey waters past the empty lake-village to a vague tree-lined ridge on the far shore; then back up the slope they'd descended. But only the mist moved, veiling the heights, coiling like smoke on the breeze-blown lake. Deru laughed and beckoned to Zoe. 'You're imagining it! Come on!'

Dazed, she joined him. Only last night she'd cursed him, now ...? He slapped her thigh. He gestured impatiently. 'Come on!'

Dion shrugged and followed, leaving Sam no option. Looking back, he was last to step on the causeway.

Twin palisades of ash piles had been driven into the lake-bed; the space between was filled by rock and peat. In one place was a defensive gap too wide to jump. It was bridged by a single plank, left by those who'd fled. After crossing it Sam heaved it after him, breaking connection with the land. Dion came back to help. They said not a word, but Sam briefly met Dion's blue eyes and again wondered. '*One from the heights beyond the Whirling Castle?*' But there was no time now. They hurried on into the deserted village. It was small, a dozen circular wooden huts on a timber platform firmly anchored by piles to the lake-bed. The huts were empty. Nothing in them but a few fish-hooks and discarded lines. Yet on the lakeward side, where they met Deru and Zoe, there was a jetty ... and, tied to a post, a flimsy birchbark coracle.

There was no paddle in sight ... but Deru was jubilant.

'You see? I told you!' Running from one hut to the next, he soon returned with two slats of wood. 'Let's get going! We ...'

He saw Sam was staring over the water, into the mists.

'Now what is it, Fool?' he demanded. 'We can't ...'

But Dion and Zoe were staring too. He followed their gaze and saw what they saw. His jaw dropped. 'Oh,' he said flatly.

For some seconds none of them spoke or moved.

There was only a slight breeze. But the fleet of white ships steadily approached them over the lake. Lining their bulwarks stood armed warriors, naked, giant, their bodies the colour of wet clay; their faces oddly vague.

Yet there was nothing vague about the way that shafts of eerie light, emanating apparently from the timbers of the ships themselves, flickered on drawn swords, on the blades of bright huge axes.

As he stared Sam heard Shem cry in him. '*Wake up, Fool! Look behind the face of things!*' And he heard the washerwoman's keening rhyme:

... For when Fool sees the shapes behind
Beastie dreams that kill the blind ...

But the ships were closing in, approaching in a wide arc, their milky glow hypnotic, and there was no more time, for now the four on the jetty could make out the blank dead eyes, the slack open mouths of the giant warriors. Uncertainly Sam looked into the emerald, but Deru grabbed his arm. 'Come on, Fool!' Sam let the half-free pull him away. They fled back to the causeway ... but were brought up short by the gap, the gap no longer spanned by the heavy plank which Sam and Dion had pulled over.

Deru cursed. Zoe, hand to mouth, looked back. The fleet was drifting ever closer. Again they stared, caught.

'*Wake up!*' Shem kept muttering in Sam. '*Look again!*'

But even as Sam again eyed the emerald something flashed past and buried itself with a *thud* in the wall of a hut behind.

They stared at the quivering arrow ... then turned and saw, charging out of the mists at them, a mob of small swarthy men, armoured in iron-studded leather, waving swords and howling as they came, the archers behind them.

Deru jumped round, poised on his left leg, shut his right eye, flung out his left arm. '*Fath-Fith!*' he cried, '*Fith-Fath! Will I put on ...*'

Then the air was thick with arrows.

Deru abandoned the spell and ducked, Sam and Dion dropped the plank – and Zoe staggered. Slowly she folded and sat down with a sigh, both hands clutching the shaft buried in her left side. Roaring, Deru jumped to her.

Sam scowled, eyed the white ships again, then looked into the emerald – and in those depths he saw what Shem had been trying to tell him.

'The ships are ghosts!' he cried, squinting into the freezing radiance as they dragged Zoe back to shelter; as the charging soldiers were stopped by the unbridged gap. 'Quick! To the coracle! We'll paddle through them! They're illusions! The Beast's trying to trick us again!'

'You're crazy!' Deru was crying as he cradled Zoe. 'What are you talking about, Fool? I've thrown away Long Life for stupid dreams! But at least I'll die like a …'

'Dion,' Sam appealed, 'I'm right, aren't I?'

'Decide for yourself,' Dion said harshly. The nearest ship was only yards away now. The giant warriors, eerily silent and still, were radiant with corpse-light as the Beast's men flooded onto the causeway, shouting abuse as they slung ropes over the gap. Arrows flew over their heads into the village. 'You command. We're just here to help.'

Sam grimaced. He felt Shem's fire bloom in him.

'Then let's get on with it! Into the boat! Now!'

'Leave me here!' Zoe moaned. Her eyes were shut, her body soaked in blood. 'I'll die here. Go on, get away, all of you!'

'I'm not leaving you,' Deru insisted. 'You …'

'Idiot!' The Fool shook him. 'Nobody's leaving anyone. Come on!'

With the weird light of the silent white ships now upon them – a light like flaming milk – they scrambled into the coracle, arrows splashing into the water round them as Azazel's slaves swarmed over the gap. Sam grabbed a slat of wood and pushed off with Zoe groaning and writhing so violently that the coracle was nearly swamped before they were away from the jetty. Dion took the other slat; with his head down and his face calm he thrust powerfully into the water to bring them into balance again. Deru, with Zoe in his arms, glared up at the nearest ship. It loomed over them, so close now that they could hear the wheezing, stertorous breathing of those huge naked warriors lining the deck. Their eyes were black, dead buttons stuck in dough-like faces; their hair writhed like seaweed in a low-tide pool; their bodies were like lumps of wet clay, stuck together with no regard for symmetry or proportion … and the instant before the coracle drifted into the freezing light of that nearest ship Deru cried out in rage and fear, drew a knife from his belt, squinted, and hurled the blade.

The knife hit one of the giants in the chest … and flew on.

From the mists beyond came a splash as it struck water and sank. But the giant never moved, never noticed, did not look down … and Deru moaned.

'You're right, Fool! They're ghosts! They …'

Then, Azazel's men howling after them, Dion and Sam paddled the coracle into the mistily shining ghost-ship … and everything exploded.

* * *

There was blinding light and terrible pain as the fire seized them. 'Chrissa!' wailed Sam, flaming in the white inferno as he dissolved in an agony of dismemberment amid which he saw, prancing triumphantly before him, the Beast in his form of beautiful youth.

'*WELCOME TO THE FEAST OF LIGHT, YOU FOOL!*' crowed Azazel. '*YOUR LITTLE DAUGHTER CAN'T HELP YOU NOW! NOW YOU BELONG TO DEATH ALONE!*'

And down through fiery light he fell until, like a burnt-out ember, he drifted through depths of ocean where contrary unconscious voices squalled and fought, and he came to a tiny hot room deep in his soul where …

'You!' he cried, blazing with rage at the sight of his enemy.

'You!' said Shem with gloomy relish. Naked on a rock he sat, powerful legs crossed, brawny arms akimbo, his look wary, a gleam of emerald on his left hand. 'Are you here to talk at last? Or must we fight?'

Yet at the same time he seemed to hear another voice, oddly familiar. 'SAM!' it cried. 'SAM! ARE YOU THERE?' For a moment he paused as doubt invaded him. But then he knew: *it's a trick*! Clenching his fists, he glared at Shem. 'Get out of me!' I know you, you Beast!'

'Wrong!' said Shem. 'You've been a Fool since Ailma woke us up.'

'Woke ME up,' said Sam fiercely, stalking about, eyeing the ring.

'If we can't agree we won't ever beat the Beast,' said Shem calmly.

Sam laughed derisively. 'Join you and I'm dead! Give me that ring!'

Shem swayed back. 'Fool! You wear it already. See how Azazel …'

'YOU FAKE!' Sam screamed, and in a blind fury he fell to grappling with Shem, striking out at him and trying to tear the ring from his hand. 'YOU DON'T FOOL ME! BEASTIE DREAMS STILL LOST IN LIES!'

'Stop!' Shem cried. 'We must find Shemyaza! He can help …'

'SAM!' cried the other voice. ' LISTEN! WON'T YOU HEAR US? SAM!'

But Sam only attacked more fiercely. Yet Shem was as strong: back and forth they swayed, deadlocked until without him consciously hearing it, a new voice, harsh and grating, hissed in him: 'STRANGLE EACH OTHER!' His face contorted; his hands leapt to Shem's throat. 'NO! NO! SAM, DON'T LISTEN!' cried the other, oddly familiar voice, and angrily he ignored it – yet even as his grip tightened and Shem fought back he felt half-throttled himself; his grip weakened … but as it did he became stronger again. He renewed the attack … and as he did began to choke again …

'Why … die stupid?' Shem gasped, face purpling. 'This … is Beast-illusion. You … attack yourself! It's … part of his plan to … make us … kill ourselves. Listen! Can't you hear how … how the …?'

It was then he heard the music. And then, too, that …

'Diane?' he asked wonderingly. 'Is that you?'

31.
White Light

For there she lay asleep in her lonely room on Rankeillor Street that winter night when Chrissa came flowing from the light of the bright star, Sirius, that shone through her uncurtained window, and in her dream her daughter said: 'Diane! You must come with me! Dad needs your help!'

'Come with you?' Diane asked fearfully. 'What do you mean?'

'Easy,' said Chrissa. 'Give me your hand and I'll show you how.'

And Chrissa took her hand. Diane was seized by violent dizziness. Everything turned sickeningly inside out … but Chrissa was singing an odd, haunting song, and suddenly Diane found herself free of the sad arthritic envelope in which for fifty years she'd endured the world. Amazed she found herself floating through the walls of the house as if through smoke. *Like Peter Pan*! and girlishly she laughed as they whirled into the starry sky on waves of Chrissa's song; spinning ever higher into a field of light where stellar flowers bloomed. And up the Sinking Ways they flowed to the brilliant blue-white heart of the brightest star; to a gate where guardian lightnings flared. Then a tremendous shift! She was torn apart in fire!

'DON'T BE AFRAID!' cried a voice. 'OUR TRUE HOME! BUT WE FORGET!'

And into a brilliant garden (WE? US? IT? HE? SHE?) danced, spinning to the song of three great suns, swooning to orbit round a veiled star … and plunging to the planet of that star, into ocean depths where great grey ones swam; down to the coral hall where the Lost Stone's found. 'LOOK!' (WE? US? IT? HE? SHE?) whispered. 'DIANE,

LOOK!' Then bathed in healing emerald light one who never saw clearly before now saw the Hidden World.

So far below it floated, so dark and dense ... and from it poured a flood of images of war, death, plague and fear ...

'NO! NO! I WON'T GO BACK DOWN THERE AGAIN!'

'MUM, WE MUST! IT'S THE ONLY WAY! WE MUST FIND SAM! NOW!'

More pain. Plunging back. *Where are we going? Through the mirror to the Land of Obscure Desire! Why? To fight Lady Death who stole my Sam*!

'CAREFUL!' Chrissa sang. 'DON'T THINK OF HER! THINK OF SAM!'

WHY?' She was enraged. 'WHEN DID HE EVER THINK OF ME?'

'HE'S BEEN THINKING OF BOTH OF US! HAVEN'T YOU HEARD HIM CALL? CALL HIM! SAM! LOOK, LOOK DOWN AND CALL HIS NAME! SAM! SAM!'

Grimly as she fell back to the dark, time-bound world, Diane looked down to what reached up at her, and panic seized her. But no sympathy from Chrissa.

'YOU'VE LIVED WITH IT ALL YOUR LIFE, MUM! SO WHAT'S NEW? CALL HIM!'

She tried. 'SAM! SAM! ARE YOU THERE?'

Yet her call was faint. Weight enfolded her. But far below through the clouds she seemed to see the wailing face of ... of ...

'SAM!' she cried.

And in the darkness of the Womb-hall, Tiy – face naked and dull, right hand gripping left which until lately had worn an emerald ring; Her strength, confidence, and Long Sight lost – suddenly flinched.

For she sensed twin stars fall. She felt the fire of youth pour into Her weary body ... and briefly Her strength returned.

Far away on the Panting Cliff Azazel, dreaming Samjoyce's fall into his ghost-fire trap, sensed Tiy's sudden hope, and looked, and saw –

'Using Weak Ones against me?' he snarled at Tiy. 'I thought they were your enemy too. But don't crow yet! They're trapped! I'll suck them all.'

Tiy gasped. Uneasily She wondered: *Weak Ones? What's going on*? Then She knew: *Samjoyce's daughter*! She scowled. Then she saw what was happening, and Her scowl slowly changed into a smile.

For in that moment She knew the truth of what Dion had told her.

* * *

Down through the mists to the lake Diane and Chrissa plunged in their subtle bodies even as the four in the coracle paddled into a shining ghost-ship and howling men flocked onto the jetty of a ramshackle lake-village.

Then ... CONTACT! A blinding flash. White fire exploded; fog-drenched hills round the lake leapt into eerie relief; the lake itself seemed to catch fire as the two dream-visitors realised that the ghost-ships weren't ships at all but a vortex of greedy fire! Amid their shock they saw how, as the coracle seemed to explode, three of the figures in it reared up in agony, the fourth writhing on her back as, dazzled and terrified, the men on the jetty fell to hands and knees where they stayed as –

– Seven tall men and women in green deerskin rapidly descended a path from the hills to a stone, cut with El-marks, that stood the far side of the lake. Gazing into the cruel radiance, their fine-boned faces grave, their green eyes clear, Taishi and the Singers prepared their song as –

– A monstrous man, cruel face pitted with sores, greased black hair twisted erect in three foot-long spikes, strode up the causeway to the jetty where his dazzled men trembled. 'Bring the Death!' Sauriel snarled.

'SAM! SAM! ARE YOU THERE?' Diane called anxiously ...

–As in the flaming, still-floating coracle the three danced – burning, but not consumed! Their agonised cries shivered over the misty waters: one of them leaned imploringly towards the tall fair ones on the far shore; the hands of the second, twin shafts of fire, held a golden lyre as the third, right hand trying to pull a ring off the left, howled from a scarred face:

'YOU FAKE! YOU DON'T FOOL ME! BEASTIE DREAMS STILL LOST IN LIES!' –

'SAM!' cried Diane, 'LISTEN! WON'T YOU HEAR US? SAM!'

– From shore to jetty sweating men pulled a gleaming metal shell. In it Sauriel sat, a bronze band over his brow. His yellow teeth grinned; he gripped horn handles, squinted along a rod at the chaos of light offshore. 'DIE!' he whispered. 'DON'T YOU WANT TO DIE? FEED THE FISH! STRANGLE EACH OTHER! STAB YOURSELVES! DROWN! DIE NOW, SERVE MY FATHER'S DREAM!'

His hate poured into the fire. Murder! Suicide! Diane groaned. The right hand of the scarred man leapt to its owner's throat; the left (ring still on finger) tried to break the hold as the ugly man drew a knife and turned, shivering, on the man with the lyre who, unable to play, gazed at the sky. But as the ugly man tried to kill he tripped over the woman who, with blood bubbling from her side, writhed on her back. With a scream he fell overboard: fiery water swamped the coracle as the scarred man still fought to – ('NO! NO! SAM, DON'T LISTEN! SAM, WE'RE HERE!') – break his stranglehold on his own neck. Yet, as the death-wishing flooded them, the tall fair ones on the far bank assumed one-legged, one-armed, one-eyed spell-casting stance. NOW! Taishi the Seer cried, ringing a bell – and the chant of the Free Men and the ringing of their bell echoed out over the misty flaming waters into the heart of the vortex:

You sons and daughters of An and El!
Remember heights from which you fell!
See the Light shine through the door!
Hear the ringing of the bells!
Take up oar and come to shore!
TAKE UP OAR AND COME TO SHORE!'

The man with the lyre regained control, striking chords so sweet that the scarred one shuddered, fell to his knees, and pulled the ugly man from the water. The ugly one collpased over the wounded woman as the music sang out, light and high and clear, answering not the death-projections but the Free Men on the yonder shore. 'DIE, DAMN YOU!' Sauriel howled furiously, hurling the ugliest images he could summon from Azazel's dreamstore. He knew it was that bastard his father wailing through him; he had no freedom of his own, which only increased his hate for those who sought it. 'SLIT YOUR THROATS, SLIMEHUMPERS!' he roared. 'DROP DEAD, YOU TWITCHING TURDS!'

But the music answered him; about him his men writhed as, losing control, letting his hate flow where it would, Sauriel left the Death-shell and stamped away, muttering angrily. And in his dreaming Azazel groaned, damning the Free Men for their interference, damning the Weak Ones too as, from the midst of that fading, failing inferno, a voice echoed wonderingly:

'Diane? Is that you?'

32.
The Little Death

Still he fought himself. '*SAM!*' called another familiar voice. '*HEAR THE SONG*!' Then amid his madness he heard. Voices singing. The music of the lyre cut through his fog. Blinking, he saw Deru in the water. He reached out and pulled him to safety. He heard a howl of rage; in the emerald depths saw Azazel's cockerel-headed image fading … and then instead of the Beast he saw –

'Diane? It *is* you!' he cried in disbelief.

And in that moment he forgot everything else, forgot the war, forgot the rocking coracle, for he saw her clearly, asleep in bed, starlight cold on her face. But so thin and gaunt, aged by time and suffering. And he saw Chrissa too, aglow. In the emerald depths he saw them both. He gaped, as shocked as Diane. But Chrissa's face was serenely calm, and in Diane's gaze he saw pity, horror, awe. 'Diane!' he cried, and her eyes lit up.

'SAM! YOU DO HEAR US! YES, IT'S ME! AND CHRISSA!'

Bewildered he demanded: 'What's going on? How did you get here?'

'DON'T YOU KNOW?' Diane called back, her voice a distant, silvery sigh in his mind. 'YOU CALLED ME WHEN I WAS GETTING OFF THE BUS AT WAVERLEY!'

Then Dion's soaring music reminded him. *Last night amid the old stone men!* 'So I did!' he told her eagerly, unaware of the mad fire fading, of Zoe moaning below him, of Deru shaking him. 'But how did you find me?'

'She's dying,' Deru hissed. 'Help me, Fool! We must get to the …'

'I'M ASLEEP. I'M DREAMING. CHRISSA BROUGHT ME.'

'I'm glad!' he cried. 'You're just in time! The Beast had me! Are you okay? I'm so glad to see you, but … Shem wants to visit our father!'

'Help me paddle,' snapped Deru. 'She'll live if we hurry.'

'SAM, YOUR FATHER DIED NINE YEARS AGO! I WAS WITH HIM!'

'I mean Shemyaza, Diane. Look!' And as Dion continued playing, Sam sank back to the depths where Shem waited, not realising how he took up one of the slats and began to paddle. For as he joined Shem he saw before him Diane's amazed, shining face with Chrissa behind her. There in the depths he laughed with joy. 'Can you see it?' he cried. 'Diane! I'm Sam and Shem too! I was Shem! I was gored to death and sent to the Last Days, into Sam. I found the ring in the attic again, and Sam didn't know what was happening – but Shem did, and took me through the Gate, and Chrissa came after. Do you see? It's obvious now! So you went to Edinburgh? How many years have passed? Are things any better? Of course not! Azazel tricks us and bleeds us with Me-against-You!' Samshem laughed. But Diane and Chrissa had begun to fade. 'It's a hard fight! This is the Hidden World! Now the Shift's so near! But Shemyaza knows about the Beast! He knows how to beat Azazel! It's not over yet!'

'SAM! SAM! WE CAN'T STAY ANY LONGER. UNTIL NEXT TIME!'

Then he sensed them leave, leaping away to the Sinking Ways.

What if I forget when I wake up? Diane asked herself fearfully as she flowed with the subtle currents, and she cried out: 'CHRISSA! I MUST KNOW MORE OR I'LL FORGET, I'LL WAKE UP THINKING I'M AWAKE! CHRISSA! HELP!'

The veils of the Sinking Ways rippled in silence. Then –

'LOOK, MUM. I'LL TRY TO SHOW YOU.'

Diane looked, and sees brilliant, violent things that tear at her mind. A black isle heaving its way from ocean depths. Hundreds of subtle bodies soaring from an inferno. A tall woman in a gorgeous birdfeather robe who stalks an underground place back and forth, back and forth. And …

She screamed as the Beast-face loomed out of the void.

The emptiness of those eyes. The awful hunger, the …

For an instant the freezing chill of Azazel's gaze struck her, began to drain and destroy her with its ravenous emptiness.

'STOP!' an imperious voice cried. A sudden wind blasted that gaze and sent Diane tumbling back to her room in Rankeillor Street, to her body in its lonely room, to awake in a sweat in a grey cold dawn

... even as Samshem fell to the Hidden Place where Shemyaza lay bound in his ancient misery ... even as Chrissa plunged back to Montségur in the year 1243 and Azazel groaned, ranging through his vengeful dream. He'd had them! Something had driven him off. Tiy? Surely not! Quickly he Sighted the Womb-hall. It was in darkness. He sensed Tiy's exhaustion. No! Not her! Furiously he swooped back to the lake ... just in time to dream the coracle coming to shore ... in time to lose it entirely behind the dreamproof screens of the Free Men.

'Taishi,' he whispered, 'I'll have you and all your vermin yet!'

But in the Womb-hall Tiy laughed weakly.

'Fooled, you Beast! Fooled by Free Men and Weak Ones!' She muttered as the Long Sight left Her in the wake of Her effort and She fell onto the bed where only nights previously She'd soared with the Fool to such heights of remembrance ... and where that bright, fresh young mind of Samjoyce's golden blue-eyed daughter had invaded Her even as She shook the Fool in Her rage.

Her strength was gone. For hours She'd paced the Womb-hall, dragging weary feet through the raked red earth as She tried to follow and help the four. As washerwoman She'd met them, with failing power She'd summoned the owls. After that, darkness had closed in. She was tired – so tired that soon She'd experienced something unprecedented – the desire for the little death the Lullu called 'sleep'. Fearful, She'd made Herself keep walking, up and down, up and down – but inexorably the desire to shut Her eyes and let go had grown. 'I grow as weak as the Lullu,' She'd whispered hoarsely, walking, walking. 'I'm losing My power to that child.' And the more tired She got the more She'd brooded about Samjoyce's daughter ... and about a hope She couldn't yet admit. She'd recalled what Dion had told Her.

'*... Perhaps you're wrong to resist her ... for it may be that her nature is not so dissimilar to yours ...*' And it had occurred to Her: *I sent Hoel against the wrong target! But I can't call him off without the ring! It's too late! I'm so blind now I can't even see what's going on without ...*

It was then She'd sensed the twin stars plunge from the Sinking Ways; sensed Samjoyce's daughter and another Weak One, another woman. Bright in Her vision the child had flared, and it had felt so odd, for briefly amid that shining light She'd recovered Her own Long Sight and energy, almost as if – the thought made Her shudder – the child was somehow an extension of Herself. *Or is it the other way round?* What a shock! To be carried on another's wings! Carried to the lake, and into Azazel's dream. '*I thought they were your enemy too!*' the Beast had jeered. And then the battle! And Samjoyce, struggling with Shem, pulled out of it by the music of Dion and the Free Men, but most of all by his daughter and ... his Last Days wife?

Is that who it was? And then? *What did I do?*

Utterly confused now. Tiy slowly realised She was sprawled on the bed. Something important had just happened, but what? Frowning with the effort to remember, She fought weariness. 'They went up the Sinking Ways again,' She muttered. 'And ... I followed. And Azazel almost ...'

Then She had it. She laughed painfully.

'You Beast!' She whispered, wearily triumphant. 'I stopped you! I saved them! You almost had them! But I stopped you! Yes, I'm with them now. With *her*! And she's with Me! We'll beat you! You'll have to ...'

Tears welled from Her no longer ageless eyes as She realised what She'd done, what She was becoming. For a moment She seemed to see that blue-eyed child gazing at Her, soothing Her, telling Her that ... that soon ...

It was too much. She was exhausted. With a sigh, and for the first time in millennia, Tiy the Watcher shut Her eyes and let the soothing waves of the little death roll over Her, falling asleep even as, returning to Montségur, Chrissa stirred groaning from her long, nearly deadly journey.

... for the Beast had struck, and would have killed them both if not for the intervention of ... *was that the Old One? The Enemy?*

Slowly Chrissa stirred from her night-long trance and sat up, blinking. There was a ringing in her ears: she felt dazed and polluted. She took a deep breath, but the cold pure dawn air that swept the eastern end of this steep ridge did not clear the sense of pollution. Unseen behind her, the man who'd sat guard all night watched carefully. Mountains swayed about her; new snow on Tabor's upper slopes gleamed blindingly. At her feet began the precipices, plunging to the valley where for months now the tents of the besieging army had stood. Birds sang sweet in the woods, but as she rose to her feet she still felt inhabited by something unclean. *The Beast!* she realised. Azazel grinning in her, a lustful worm in her gut! *He caught me!* Slowly, blankly, she picked her way past Pierre. He turned, but she didn't even notice him as she went stumbling along the ridge back to the castle and the maze of huts on the terraces hugging the precipices on the north side of the keep.

Heavy-hearted he stood and followed, ducking under the branches of the stunted birch trees crowning the ridge. From the valley below trumpets rang, calling French soldiers to drill, to prayer, to breakfast.

'Not even a glance!' he muttered. But it was fear, not offence, that possessed him. She didn't ask him to guard her during these journeys … but somebody had to! Bernard was too weak now. And who else was close to her? *If anyone*, he thought, *can be close to her. How much more of this?* he wondered, thinking back over their three long years together since that dreadful night at Carcassonne. *What can I do? Should I have taken her as she wanted? But it would have been wrong! It's not time! All I can do is watch over her, like a shepherd over his flock! – eh, shepherd?*

Something made him flinch. A stir in his blood, in the air. It made him stop and look up as the Beast's trumpets belled up from the valley.

Then high in the heavens he saw that awful, wonderful light! It flared in his mind's eye, and from it he heard a voice singing, and knew it at once for that voice which had called to him at Carcassonne:

'*Beware now, shepherd!*' he seemed to hear. '*The Beast tries to seize her! Guard her with care! Be patient. The time comes.*'

Who are you? he wondered fearfully.

'*Look!*' sang the distant voice. '*Watch over her! Wait!*'

Then in the sky mistily he seemed to see, like some distant view of another world, two men setting out into summer woods from a dark door in a green hill. First the tall one with the scarred face and grey-streaked black hair, then the wiry dark man with blue eyes as bright as Chrissa-Joana's … and flickering on misty heights ahead he saw the titanic palace of illusion where the Beast lay slumbering, dreaming his dreams of death and decay … and he knew they went to face that Beast …

Then the vision faded into the dawn sky above Montségur as, not far ahead of him, Chrissa suddenly screamed in agony and collapsed.

33.
In the Rath of the Free Men

That night the Lodge of the Nine Doors was packed.

The shock of the battle on the lake was felt by Free Men throughout the hills. Long before the Seven Singers returned to the safety of the Lodge with the Fool and his companions, crowds were arriving in the full fearful knowledge that the Great Time had begun; that the Beast would never forgive Taishi for this open opposition. All who'd been outside safe places or off safe ways had suffered the battle with the death-wish dream like a battle in themselves. It had torn their nerves and sinews with fire, even breaking into some of the older raths where dreamproofing had worn thin. Many had been struck and drained by Azazel's hate, some severely, and in distress came hurrying to the Lodge of the Nine Doors, to the vast room under the hill where Azazel could not touch them. All that dark hot afternoon they arrived, green cloaks emerging from summer woods singly or in groups, on foot or horse, carts carrying those badly hurt, calling with the excited anxiety typical of their kind to each other as they converged on the small dark door into the green hill – the only door of nine kept open these days.

'Enki!' a blond smooth-faced man whose neck-beads told of two hundred years greeted another too cheerfully. 'Brother, the Shining Ones are back! Didn't you cry for joy when that glorious serpent-music broke Beast-fog?'

'Damu, I did not!' Enki gave his older brother a pale, jittery scowl. Tall, ashen, he led an ox-cart on which his three scared daughters tended his wife. Her back rigid, she stared unseeingly up at the flame-tinted evening clouds. He stopped, shaking his head in horror. 'I've never known such a shock! So our rath's old; we should have repacked the safety layers long ago, but it's still proof against normal Beast-dreams. I was knocked off my feet by that hate, and poor Elda …' – he nodded grimly back at his wife, now being unloaded by his daughters who, close to hysteria, were arguing with each other how best to handle her – "… has been Seized!'

'Seized?' Damu stared. 'Again?'

'What do you mean?' Enki flared. 'Do you imply …?'

'No, no, no! Dear Enki, please don't misunderstand …'

Enki glared at him. They passed through the door and under the outer layers, turf and mineral alternating, of the dreamproofing. Their relief was immediate: lingering Beast-hate still poisoned the air outside though they were hours and a distance from the battle. Yet Enki stayed angry.

'Damu, you live in one of the new raths; you wouldn't have felt …'

'I was outside Safety,' Damu declared grimly. 'I took the full force, and I can tell you: the Beast is not pleased.' He nodded back, lowering his voice. 'I meant no insult, I know Elda's a good women – but I heard that … well, lately she's been … *sensitive* to the Beast's dreaming …'

Enki's scowl deepened. The narrow passage pushed them close as they continued past ring-corridors and deeper into the earthy-smelling, torchlit lair. 'You'd be sensitive if you lived so close to the Panting Cliff,' he muttered, looking back at Elda. She walked, supported by his daughters, but her glazed eyes sank his heart as Damu gestured in exasperation.

'Then why didn't you move your family to one of the new raths?'

'We don't all run when the dreaming gets hard!' Enki said. 'Our clan has lived in that hill two thousand years. You do as you like, but I won't be driven out by a shapeshifting degenerate who denies the Light from which he fell!'

Then why are you seeking shelter here tonight? Damu wondered, but said instead with exaggerated tact: 'Have you farseen the Seven?'

Enki sighed. He knew what was coming. 'What about them?'

'Well,' said Damu, 'they bring not only Tiy's Fool – lost in himself – but Her Servant too, Zoe, near dead with an arrow through the guts. Phobel has her stable. *And* also that foul little half-free Deru …' Damu smirked 'Seems he's got a shine on Tiy's slave. Well, what can you expect? Not his fault, after all. *And* …' he went on, pausing for effect but angry now, for Enki was ignoring him as in a crowd they entered the great hall, vast and dim below the long low curve of its dreamproofed ceiling, '... *And* they have with them a stranger, Dion, who comes from the Shining Ones! Enki, don't you hear me? We're not abandoned! We should rejoice!'

'The Shining Ones?' Enki looked back at Elda, then in sudden rage he hissed: 'Keep your Shining Ones!' He smiled bitterly. 'Damu, the Beast is one of the Shining Ones. So who cares? What did they ever do for us?'

Damu stared warningly. Enki had raised his voice; dim faces stared out of the bustling, nervous crowd. 'Brother, Taishi led the Seven against the Beast today. Don't betray your mood when he returns tonight!'

Enki laughed. 'Damu, Long Life makes you a cowardly snob,' he cried aloud, attracting more attention, gesturing angry contempt. 'So, the Great Time! So, the Elohim are back! So what? You don't think they *care*, do you? They've got a game to run any way they can – us! All it means is we'll be swallowed in someone else's war that we don't need or want.'

There were mutterings. Agreement. Disagreement too. The mood was not happy. 'I warn you, Enki, take care!' Damu whispered, and, following his own advice, vanished into the nervous, shifting crowd. Enki stared after him then, ignoring the mutterings, turned to his tearful daughters. 'So I spoke my mind!' he said, pursing his lips at Elda's blank white face. 'Now, we'll find a corner and put her down – here, here will do – but GENTLY – and we'll take it in turns to queue for the Healers.'

But the queue for the Healers that evening was a long one. Many there had been Seized. And somebody must have blabbed, for a Sergeant of the Lodge got to Enki before any Healer got to Elda, and spoke angrily to him, about *treason* and *disloyalty*. Enki sneered. 'Why pretend?' he demanded. 'We're all scared out of our wits. We kept the Beast off our back only so long as we did nothing against him – but now? My wife's one of the first casualties. Just look at her!' He waved angrily. 'So do what you like. I don't care. I'll say what I say!'

There was a crowd round him. It cheered. The Sergeant retreated. No further attempt was made to subdue Enki and others talking like him. And by the time the Seven Singers reached the Lodge that night, Tiy's Fool and the other strangers with them, it was full. There was barely space to sit or stand, and the Healers were working flat out as the Elders of the Council and the Sergeants tried to keep some sort of order. But the mood was bleak and the Healers couldn't get to everyone: Elda was among those who didn't hear anything that night when Taishi at last entered the Lodge with one of the strangers rescued by the Seven – the Messenger, Dion.

Amid an utter tense silence Taishi stood up tall on the torchlit dais, wearing the green robes of Full Summer Oak, his wrinkled old face (how old? Some said five hundred, some said six) set in Respect for Honoured Guest – a mode unused in living memory. That alone caused consternation. Lodge Sergeants, feeling the trouble in the air, stiffened. But up on the dais Taishi seemed unconcerned. With the Seven Singers and the whole Council about him he turned to the stranger and went on, again with full Respect:

'So! You are Dion! You are welcome among us, sir.'

What he did next increased the consternation. In their packed hundreds the Free Men swayed and sighed as, with grand deliberation, down on his knees Taishi went ... and bowed his hoary head to the stranger Dion.

'*For you who created us have returned to us*!' cried Taishi as smoothly he came to his feet again ... and without any pause for argument (even some of the Elders were finding it hard to restrain their outrage) his theatrical voice flowed on in a passionate, apparently spontaneous eulogy which soon had everyone, even reluctant ears like Enki's, spellbound and held.

Dion stood silent as the words poured over him.

He was exhausted.

It had been a long day! Through the fog they'd come to the shore, the Fool and Deru paddling, himself resisting Beast-hate with his music until they were safe. But the weight of it! And though the Fool had helped with the paddling, he was lost by the time they were pulled from the water. Out of the coracle he'd gone staggering into the misty wood, bawling to himself even as Phobel called for help to draw the arrow from Zoe's side. All Seven had sung for her. The Fool had lurched back, howling in despair, tripping over the wounded woman. Deru had attacked him. What a business! *It's a wonder anyone in this world ever sorts anything out!* Dion silently told himself now. *But it's a good training for those who need it. Like me.* For it had fallen to Dion to understand and explain the Fool's mania. '*He must plumb his own depths before he can fight the Beast and win*,' he'd told Deru over and over until, with difficulty, but with Azazel trounced for the moment, they'd set out safely through woods and over green hills for the rest of the day, four Singers carrying Zoe, Deru never far from her side as the Fool stumbled along, mumbling aloud in his dream of reconnection. Some of the Singers had, despite their discipline, looked at him fearfully.

'He's just babbling!' Taishi had roared at them. 'It's a poor Fool who has to fight the Beast! Don't make it harder on him by asking him to be sensible!' Then, with a keen eye, Taishi had dropped back to Dion with a series of quiet propositions based on his understanding of things.

So now here Dion stood, playing politics, surrounded by hundreds of sophisticated Lullu pouring their emotions into him as he stood so still with Taishi making his pitch. Emotions. Tides washing over him so dark and bright. Dislike, open suspicion, nervous joy, fear of the future. The usual Lullu mix, though refined in these who remembered the El. Meanwhile (he abstracted himself as Taishi droned on) he sensed Deru at Zoe's side in a room where a Healer also knelt. More to the point, he probed and found Samjoyce still deep in the discovery of his own lost nature.

For at that moment Sam was wailing atop a hill under the misty moon, watched over by four Elders, men and women, who were adept in the journeys of soul-growth. To encourage success he's been fed a brew of the Hundred-Spotted Toad. Dion could feel he wasn't having an easy time of it. 'He'll be raving by now.' Taishi had told Dion with cheerful grimness as they'd entered the Lodge, 'but Fools learn best who rave most.'

Perhaps, thought Dion. *Samjoyce, may you marry your pride not only with the strength of Shem but also the knowledge of Shemyaza. For he has the knowledge of what makes the Beast tick, the Light that makes you laugh when you catch yourself out. Samjoyce, nobody can help you beyond this point.*

With a set face he waited as Taishi, head still bowed, went on in his booming, jovial voice that none in the Lodge could possibly not hear:

'We thought you Elohim had left us forever!' Taishi was milking his dubious audience expertly. 'Many Long Lives ago you brought the Serpent-fire of knowledge!' He bowed, ironic. 'You brought it, you woke us up – then you left us to the mercies of the Beast! Thank you! You left us to Azazel and Tiy, to ignorance and doubt! You forgot us! We did not forget you! We are Free Men who remember! Today we proved it, did we not?'

Dion grinned. 'You're an old rogue,' he said to Taishi alone. Then he set his face, and aloud, for the benefit of all, he said:

'We never left you! And haven't you dealt better with the Beast today than we in need of your help did? It's plain our mission to this world was not the failure that some among us claim. How else would you Free Men have remembered so well what we taught?' He clapped his hands and grinned wide. 'Your singing drove the Beast back to his dark dreaming hole,' he told them, meeting their doubting eyes with an easy charm. 'Good Taishi and your Council have kept the faith much better than we could have expected! Under such a weight of time and gravity! And with ...'

'Yes, all right!' hissed Taishi from the side of his mouth. 'Don't overdo it; these people won't buy too much; they're not happy at all.'

'... all the difficulties you've had to overcome to survive these hard and painful years in the shadow of the Beast,' Dion went on, and suddenly he was enjoying himself. 'The human life is not one that personally I'd adopt by choice. It has disadvantages! Yet spirit must seed dark matter, and that's what we tried here, to do as we were all done to once ourselves – but here with very mixed results. Yet you ...' – He spread his arms and started to laugh, and at his obvious enjoyment of an act both serious and absurd, others on their seated haunches about the place where the Council sat also began to laugh – '... I see you've fought for the survival of the spirit in a world that does not on the whole encourage it! Here we are, safe in this place from the dreaming of the poor Beast who once was one of us; who once came down to this world and found out that the bottom is easier than the top. But he – and his sister Tiy, who came from the same world – were granted a task that now they've forgotten. Yes, they forgot!

'But what,' he demanded, suddenly intent and serious, leaning forward, 'if the forgetting was planned? What if their task's a sort that brings no joy to anyone, least of all themselves? What if their corruption too is a part of that task? What if light has to fall to the uttermost rotten pit before it can know exactly what's what? Think about it! Who values an easy victory? Today your Seer Taishi led your Seven Singers out against the Beast. Do you think he did this out of simple impulse, or out of lack of concern for your welfare? Do you think the Elohim your enemy?'

'Yes!' cried a broad voice from the back, and it was Enki.

Dion laughed. 'No,' he said to the Sergeants running to grab the miscreant, 'leave him alone! Let him come and make his objection.'

'I will!' yelled Enki, and pushed his way through the crowd until he stood at the edge of the dais where the Council of Elders sat. Suddenly made uncertain by their threatening eyes, he paused. But Dion beckoned.

'Please,' said the stranger, 'Join me. Up here.'

Enki gaped. Taishi shrugged. Almost everyone else was aghast.

'If you think me your enemy,' said Dion, 'we must meet face to face.'

'But you'll blind me,' Enki muttered. 'It's not a fair fight.'

'Sirs!' Dion turned to the Elders. 'Did anyone mention a fight?'

'My wife was struck by the Beast today!' Enki said, loudly again.

'And you?' Smiling them down, Dion turned. 'You escaped unharmed?'

'I did not!' roared Enki, and hotly stepped onto the dais. 'Nobody here escaped harm!' he said, his arm embracing the entire Lodge as Dion saw Taishi covertly watching the nods and grimaces passing between various Elders. 'We're all disturbed! How do we know who you are? Even if you are of the Elohim, why should we trust you? Answer me that!'

Dion nodded. But for his sharp eyes he looked so ordinary – smaller, darker, even older than anyone else there. 'Do you sing?' he asked.

'What's that got to do with it?' Enki demanded. There were a few cheers, quickly hushed, from the back of the hall …

'Once,' Dion went on, scanning the Elders, assessing the range of their reaction from outrage through fear and cynical detachment to now-alert attentiveness, 'this land was free. And your ancestors knew who to trust and who not. Isn't that true, Taishi?'

It is!' Taishi rose, glad of the chance.

'Now wait a minute!' Enki protested, Sergeants waiting.

Dion said quietly: 'Let him speak. Then you speak again.'

'Very well,' Enki muttered. 'Age before sense as usual!'

With folded hands and his most severe face Taishi again addressed the Free Men. 'There was a time when the Beast and his vermin were locked up,' he declared. 'It was after the last Flood. An and El walked among us and taught us how to be Free Men. They taught us how to live long and how to think. They taught us number, measure, secrets of vision, the movements of the spheres. They said what is above is like what is below. They did not terrorise us; they brought us light.' He sighed. 'But then they left. The Beast broke out of his prison, and. …' – He shot an angry look at Enki – '… now see what we've got! Every man for himself; scared folk ranting like poor Beast-Seized Ones, calling power the same as right behaviour! But today – today! – the Singers of the Free Men fought for the Spirit!'

'And against themselves and their people!' Enki cried.

There was uproar. Three of the Singers immediately stood in protest as the hall erupted in abuse and agreement, but Dion quickly intervened.

'This is true,' he said apologetically, holding up his hands until the tumult died away. 'Action for the spirit is of course action against the self's security. This man is correct. Lately I was in Khem, where priest-kings called pharaohs now erect monuments in which number and measure are coded. Good work – but thousands suffer in the building. Just as …' – he smiled at the silent crowd – '… long ago the Lady Tiy, realising how badly Her memory failed Her, sculpted the land of the Whole Place in dimensions that show the true measure. Then She sent Her Fool to the Last Days to see the Beast's true shape. Now he's back. She has given him Her emerald ring and sent him against the Beast. She has abandoned Her own power, and for what? To aggrandise Herself? Hardly! No! She seeks Light too!'

He shrugged. The hall was silent. Even Enki was silent.

'So who is the Fool?' Dion asked. 'You've already shown you know. You came to our aid. Me? I'm no more than a big mouth – but in the Fool lies the lure that'll bring the Beast to heel and bring light to influence the fate of events as yet undreamed of – events in the far-off Last Days.' He held up a significant finger. 'At this very moment our Fool learns the knowledge he needs to unriddle the true shape of Azazel. That's his task. The rest of us, we must do what we can. If he fails, we suffer. If he wins …' And he nodded at Enki. 'This man thinks me your enemy …'

'No,' said Enki abruptly, 'I retract my remarks. I was upset. I say now that fate is fate.' And amid utter silence he left the dais.

Taishi eyed Dion discreetly.

They'll go with me now, said his look.

34.

The Toad

The mists had cleared. The moon sailed high amid soft summer stars; the massy woods rustled in the gentle breeze. No Beast-pressure on them tonight … but long before they came to the high place where the Four Elders assigned to watch him had taken him, Taishi and Dion could hear that the Fool was still wild-eyed and raving.

Sam had no memory of being made to drink the brew of the Hundred-Spotted Toad. He had no memory of being brought up here. He had no memory of anything in the external world since Diane and Chrissa had left him at the start of his exploration. But since drinking the Toad, his ravings and dancing had grown so wild that his guides (each had led many through Toad-delirium) had grown uneasy, fearing that in his holy madness he might harm himself seriously; that his heart or brain might burst, or that he might go too far into the hidden realms and never find his way back – or that, even worse, if he did return, he would do so Beast-possessed, wet eyes vacant, tongue bitten off, limbs shaking in a palsy that would cease only when (in a day or two) he died. All these fates were possible and sometimes befell novices, even Elders. There was aways risk.

Yet if this Fool failed to return brighter and stronger, charged with spirit-powers, it would (Taishi had made it plain) be a major disaster.

'We must risk it!' Taishi had insisted, the stranger Dion (his aura brighter than any had ever seen) nodding agreement. 'He has to plumb to uttermost depths and heights or he'll find nothing. He must drink full strength Toad, or ...' – he'd assessed the Fool's flushed, sweating face, and glassily inturned gaze – '... he'll not go far enough.'

So the brew had been prepared by old Erkigel from a mature mix which, having passed through many bodies already, was of maximum potency. 'Only a little,' he'd kept muttering as he measured the dose, 'only the tiniest amount! Any more, and ...' With a grim shake of his head he'd followed the Elders up the hill, mounting it sunwise with the Toad in a gold cup, stepping with the utmost care. To spill even a drop ... that would not augur well! And with difficulty, three of them holding the Fool as he sweated and strained, the fourth jamming his mouth open and his tongue down with a silver spatula made for this purpose. Erkigel had poured the brew down his throat. And the Fool, with a gasp and a gargle and a wild shake of his limbs that threw the Elders off him, had swallowed it all.

Soon after that his delirium grew violent as the Toad seized him, crushed him, dismembered and destroyed him – but not before, at some level in his mind, he saw them and realised what they'd done. 'You've fed me bloody amanita!' he'd wailed in an incomprehensible tongue, twitching and flopping on his belly across the hilltop like a stranded fish. 'Don't you berks realise I've got enough trouble already? Jesus, what a rush! Oh God, I'm dying! Fly agaric! You bastards, you've killed me!'

Then he was violently sick, over and over, retching in huge convulsive shudders, trying to throw off the restraining hands of the Elders, gasping out how at Nantgewydd one autumn he'd gone into the woods and gathered a sackful of this stuff, then chopped it and put it on the Aga to dry before powdering it, but the cat got at it, stupid brute, and died in foaming convulsion with Chrissa crying her heart out and Diane giving him hell.

After that he became still, to the relief of Erkigel and the Elders, and for a time seemed to sleep peacefully. At the four points round him they squatted, waiting, watching, Taishi and the stranger Dion down in the Lodge, no hint of the Beast in the ether tonight – then he began to jerk and moan, then suddenly sat up and, in a sane, reasonable voice, staring right through them, began a calm convers-ation with someone or something they couldn't see or sense at all, nodding his head as if listening, with little smiles apparently repeat-ing what he heard, but to himself alone.

That phase ended suddenly.

With a shudder he stopped in mid-sentence, looked up …

Then with a wild laugh he sprang to his feet and began running, dancing, leaping all over the hilltop so fast they had all their work cut out keeping up with him and heading him off as he charged from one point to another, continually laughing – or was it crying? – and calling out.

'COWARDICE!' he screamed, shuddering to a halt and pointing a shaking finger at thin air. 'Yes, of course! Always a coward! But they let you out! You slunk off and left him to rot! But I see you … COWARD!'

Then off again he whirled, until with another shudder he stopped and pointed again. 'VANITY!' he cried. 'Yes! That too! Love the sight of yourself in a mirror? Just like whatsisname – Narcissus!'

And away he danced … and as for the third time he stopped, again throwing out his accusing finger, the ring gleaming green in the moonlight, Dion and Taishi reached the top of the hill and saw him.

'GREED!' they heard him wail. 'Of course! You want to eat everything! And everyone! So you shall, my friend! Everything and everyone! You'll stuff it all down until your gut bursts! Then we'll see what you're made of! Your true shape in naked daylight! Then you'll do as She asks!'

And in peals of triumphant, cackling laughter he burst off again, the by-now exhausted Elders trying to keep pace with him as Erkigel came and with vast relief reported it all to Taishi and Dion.

'We thought he'd die! The Toad took him so deep his spirit nearly fled. But he found … something … and now … now you see … he …'

With a shriek the Fool came charging up at them through the moonlight, making as if to run straight into Taishi and Dion. But at the last moment he stopped dead … and started to laugh in their faces.

Dion began to laugh too.

Taishi stared at them as if they were both mad.

Suddenly the Fool stopped laughing. His face swam through a host of subtle changes. Emerald light seemed to come and go above his head. He looked at each of them with eyes from which all madness had gone – deep, calm, steady eyes. 'I see it,' he said distinctly, 'but I'm tired now.'

He yawned hugely. His shoulders slumped. With a sigh he let himself down on the ground and within seconds was fast asleep.

Dion smiled. 'All's well,' he said. Taking the lyre from his pack, he sat by the Fool and began to play, softly, gently.

'But what happened?' asked Taishi, immediately made nervous by those first plaintive notes. 'Has he found what he ...?'

'Sounds like it.' Dion yawned. 'Maybe he'll tell us tomorrow before we leave to meet the Beast. Maybe he'll tell me before I'm killed.'

'What?' Taishi assumed he'd heard wrong. 'You're going with him?'

'Some of the way,' said Dion calmly ... and then went on playing ...

For even before drinking the Toad Sam was deep in a journey that began when Diane and Chrissa left him. For even as his body paddled the coracle to the shore where the Free Men waited, he saw Diane attacked by the Beast and rescued (by Tiy, he dimly saw) to tumble back to Last Days Edinburgh. And memory made him follow, back, not to Edinburgh, but to his own Last Days ...

He's Samjoyce. In London, 1985. Abed at home, emerald ring on his finger, Diane uneasy beside him as he twists and moans, for NOW in dream he's caught amid the stone men on the moors above Gairloch ... caught in eerie vision of Shem mating with Her on the height of the Whole Place as the new moon rises, mind Toad-glazed, black bull awaiting him in the Womb-hall, ready to hurl him through death to the Last Days ... to Samjoyce again.

'*You see?*' Shem whispers. '*Full circle. I became you; you became me! We possess each other, we are one another! Now look!*'

For NOW amid pandemonium of warring voices Shem and Tiy seize him; at last he plunges through the Gate ... back to the Whole Place, appearing just in time, for the Beast's at Her throat, Her battle's almost lost ... but he turns the tide as he runs raving from the height ... NOW to become the Fool in the grove, ignorant and naked, singing his happy song, by day building his dam and tearing it down, by night speaking with his friends Fox, Brock, Hawk and Badger – until Ailma breaks taboo, awakening him as Hoel attacks – until the Wild Women tear Hoel to pieces and Tiy shows Her face – the face of his nightmares; the face that laughed as he was gored to death in the Womb-hall ... the Womb-hall, yes!

For NOW from Tiy's cup he drinks elixir ... and together, silver bells ringing remembrance, they soar to that ocean of light where the Elohim glide, to the Emerald Gate as Shemyaza warns of the

Hidden World: NOW down the Sinking Ways they plunge into agonies of time and weight; and NOW at Kharsag Azazel approaches the Lullu woman; NOW the fall of the Watchers; NOW Tiy's thrown into the Valleys of Fire as Shemyaza, resigned, and the Beast, raging, are taken west in a black ship skimming the sea until NOW it descends into the depths, great grey ones escorting it. 'WHO ARE YOU?' he cries, and in him they sing as the ocean deepens: 'WE ARE THE GUARDIANS OF THE SUNKEN ISLE, THE SOMETIMES ISLE, THE HIDDEN PLACE. NONE BROUGHT HERE CAN ESCAPE, FOR THE STARCHAMBER'S CLOSED AND CANNOT BE OPENED UNTIL LOVE CONQUERS THE SHIFT!' And NOW a submarine cliff with a door in it; Azazel and Shemyaza are shut in the Hidden Place, the door closed so that ...

Total blackness. Soul-crushing weight. He tries to flee ... but hears a sad voice, singing:

'SHEMMM! COME TO ME NOW, HEAR ME, FOR I KNOW THE SECRETS OF THE BEAST, I KNOW HIS TRRRUE SHAPE AND WHAT HE CANNOT ENNNDURE!'

But another voice laughs:

'*MR SAMJOYCE, EH? COME TO VISIT DADDY? THINK HE'LL TELL YOU HOW TO BEAT ME, EH? BUT I DON'T THINK YOU CAN! WHO EVER DEFEATS DEATH IN THISS WORLD! LOOK AT ME! CAN YOU SEE MY TRUE SSSHAPE? EH? LOOK! LOOK!*'

And NOW before him whirl Beast-faces. The mocking youth; the cockerel-headed monster; a vast cyclops – his heart freezes, for each way he looks the Beast faces him, mocks him in a mob of hideous forms, flickering from one to another so fast that NOW he's overwhelmed, driven from the depths, Shemyaza's voice fading mournfully away as –

He's on a rocky hill. A moonlit night. He fights the Beast. The Beast has ten hands. Six hold him, two tear open his mouth, two pour foul brew down his throat. He roars, chokes, swallows it; and the poison seizes him. 'You've fed me bloody amanita!' he wails, twitching and flopping as the cramps and nausea take him. 'You bastards, you've killed me!' and he throws up, weirdly remembering how their cat at Nantgewydd died foaming. Then with a great cry he sinks down, down, down again, this time surely for the last time. Dying. Dying. Dead.

But Azazel's laughter's stilled, for NOW ...

Of a sudden and unexpectedly ... PEACE.

* * *

Peace. He sleeps. From the dead he rises. In Toad-vision he walks an enchanted land. Moon and stars dance in the soft night sky; dark friendly trees sway amid many-coloured shadows; the air sings with sweet energy – and on the branch of a great old oak perches Owl, blinking sleepily.

'You look bewildered, man,' Owl hoots.

'I seek my father,' he says, not knowing who speaks.

Owl peers benevolently. 'What is his name?'

'Shemyaza. He's shut in the Hidden Place. I must find him.'

'Ah. I was told to expect you. Perhaps I can help. Follow me.'

Owl takes to the air, and through the wood Sam follows ... until out of the shadowy undergrowth a sleek sly form materialises.

'Where are you going, man?' asks Fox, red tongue lolling.

'Fox!' He's overjoyed. 'But you said you'd never speak to me again after Ailma got me hard! You said I smelt like other men and I'd betray you and skin you and ... horrible things!'

'Nothing personal, pal.' Fox eyes him sardonically. 'If Owl brings you here then you're still a Fool I can trust. So what's up?'

'He seeks his father,' cries Owl. 'Can you show him the way?'

'I can lead him to one who can,' grins Fox. 'Follow me, man.'

He follows Fox until at last the forest gives way to the shore of a moonlit bay of ocean where Dolphin plays, far out on the silver waters.

'Here we are.' Fox grins again. 'Now you have to get your tail wet.' And turning his head to the bay he barks: 'Dolphin! We need your help! This man seeks Shemyaza! Can you take him in the right direction?'

'Of c-c-course! I've b-been waiting.' Dolphin laughs and swims in close to shore, frolicking in the breakers. 'Get on my back, man.'

'Thank you, Fox,' Sam says warmly. 'I'm glad we're friends again.'

'Don't mention it.' Fox vanishes into forest shadow. Gingerly Sam wades into the foam and straddles Dolphin's broad smooth back.

'Hang on t-t-tight!' Dolphin chirps, and surges out to sea, leaping with friends and mates, chattering with peeps and whistles until, with land far behind he urges: 'I'm not one for the d-deeps where Shemyaza lies, so now I'll call Big Cousin. Don't be s-s-scared. He's always grumpy!'

Dolphin whistles, shrill then amid huge turbulence the great grey one rises from the deep. Sam gazes up in awe at Leviathan towering above them in the moonlight. Leviathan turns his rolling eye down on Dolphin.

'What is it, little one?' he rumbles. 'It had better be important!'

'This man seeks his f-f-father Shemyaza.'

'Shemyaza? His father?' rumbles the great whale, and slaps the sea so angrily with his fluke that Sam's nearly washed off Dolphin's back. 'A man with a Last Days aura? Little playful one, don't you ever think? Trust men and they'll have you in a cage jumping through hoops! As for us ...'

'That's the Beast in us,' Sam cries, clinging on for dear life. 'It's to beat the Beast that I must talk to my father!'

Leviathan pauses in his violent rolling.

'Did I hear the man SPEAK?' he asks in amazement.

'I th-th-think so,' says Dolphin, giggling fearfully, for the rest of the school has scattered. 'They're, you know, c-c-capable of it.'

'Capable of SPEECH?' Still Leviathan seems amazed.

'Yes,' Sam says firmly, 'I fight the Beast so that we'll overcome the next Shift. Shemyaza knows the Beast's true shape – so take me to him!'

'A speaking man?' Moonlight gleams on the great grey back. 'Wait, little one. I must speak to race-soul. This is ... unusual.'

'Damned right it's unusual!' says Sam. 'Take me to my father!'

'How do we know he's your father?' Leviathan demands, vast eye rolling.

'If you serve the Elohim,' Sam counters, 'you'll do as I ask.'

'The Elohim? What do you know about them?'

'They sent me here,' Sam insisted. 'I'm sorry we're stupid. I don't like it, and I want to stop it! So will you take me to my father?'

After a pause Leviathan announces dubiously:

'It's most irregular ... but race-soul raises no objection. Get on my back and hold on. But are you strong enough? Won't fear drive you mad?'

'I've swum the heights that the Elohim swim! That spark is in me! I'll endure the depths! I must, or I'll never find Light again.'

'Well answered! Little one, bring him to me!'

The difficult transfer is made. Up on the vast back Sam scrambles from Dolphin. 'Thanks!' he cries, clinging uneasily to Leviathan as Dolphin slides away in agitated relief. 'Ready?' demands Leviathan.

'Okay!' Sam grits his teeth. 'Get on with it!'

Then Leviathan up-ends and dives ...

Deep and deeper still they plunge into darkness and weight until at last they reach the black cliffs of the Sometimes Isle ... and there, amid the gloom, the compressed point of pain that is Sam senses rather than sees the wall of huge basalt blocks before them, pitch black in the blackness, and set in that wall, darker still, an opening the height of a man and the width of two ... and fearfully knows he sees the door to the Hidden Place.

The door is open.

'There! You'll find Shemyaza within ... if you dare enter.'

'Why's the door open?' Sam asks uneasily.

'The Beast left it open when he escaped,' comes the answer.

'... NONE BROUGHT HERE CAN ESCAPE ...' thunders a memory-voice.

'But how did he escape?' Sam demands, suspicious.

'That's for Shemyaza to tell you, two-legs.' Leviathan rolls an impatient eye. 'I've done as you asked. Here you are. Now I leave you.'

Clumsily Sam slides off that great back to stand before the forbidding door as Leviathan glides away, leaving him alone. Then into his mind swims the tale his great-grandfather Captain Davey told; of finding the strange black isle in mid-Atlantic in the year 1882 ... the black isle with the room buried in the shattered cliff, and the three crumbling figures within.

Who are they? Who will they be?

He fears he knows.

Groaning with weight and fear he forces himself into the Hidden Place. Down a passage, through a second door he goes, heart in mouth ... and stands and stares ... for there before him, against the far wall of the chamber, sees what at first he takes to be a great man-shaped rock, crusted with weed-festooned chains and pressure-flattened shell-creatures.

Then Shemyaza, with a huge groan, moves one hand just an inch.

And the echoing sad slow voice sounds in him:

'SHEMMM! HOW LONGGG I'VE WAITED! HOW MUCH I'VE ENNNDURED SINNNCE THE BEEEAST BETRAAAYED ME ANNND TIY SOWED MY SEEED! HERE YOOUU ARE AT LAAAST! NOWWW! LISTENNN! I HAVE MUCH TO SAYYY ... BUT SPEEEECH COMES SO HARRRDD!'

'Yes, father,' Samshem whispers. 'Speak! I'm listening!'

Then he hears that old slow voice deep in him; he listens, he questions Shemyaza his father, he learns what he needs to know ...

* * *

It was then on the hilltop that Erkigel and the Elders heard and saw him begin to speak to something or someone they couldn't see or sense at all ... until with a shudder he stopped in mid-sentence, looked up (as if at an uninvited guest), then sprang up and began leaping, laughing, running about like a lunatic even as Dion and Taishi approached. Still laughing and shrieking, he came up to Dion and into those deep blue eyes he looked, his laughter joined by Dion's, until suddenly he realised where he was and what had happened. Then the power of Leviathan's unchained depths flowed through him, and the emerald light haloed him.

'I see it,' he said distinctly, 'but I'm tired now.'

After that he slept ... with Dion watching over him.

Taishi eyed Dion uneasily. What had the singer meant. '*Before I'm killed*'? And the music ... Dion played his lyre so softly over the sleeping Fool that the music, felt rather than heard, made Taishi shiver, for though it was quietly reflective, images of huge violence shimmered in it.

The Great Time's on us, Taishi knew. *The Beast must be fought. But if this Fool fails, he'll be rampant, unstoppable, and utterly cruel.*

He turned. 'Erkigel! Prepare Toad. We'll be up all night.'

'Taishi ...' Erkigel paused uncertainly in the night.

'Yes. What is it?'

'This Fool – has he any chance of taming the Beast?'

'If not,' said Taishi grimly, 'all the dreamproofing in the world won't help us. We must make ready. Get on with it, old man!'

So who's old? Erkigel was exhausted. The Fool's ravings ... he nodded and left. Taishi gave other orders. 'Lavellan, stay here, tell me if anything happens. Milel, go down to the Radiant Pool, tell all who haven't come in to get here or flee north. Roth, call every Healer you can reach to join us in Council, quick. Hillel, go to the half-free Deru; tell him to prepare himself to face Council. Stay with him, bring him when I call.'

When they were gone he again eyed Dion and the Fool. Neither seemed aware of him. Now the music was ineffably sad. With a sigh he turned on his heel and descended the hill, but that music pursued him all the way, whispering in his mind as he returned to the Lodge and came into the Council of Elders for a meeting which, he knew, might yet end in chaos.

Zoe moaned. It was after dawn. She tried to move, to remember, but could not. Only one face, one name. 'Deru,' she whispered. 'Deru …'

'Hush.' A cool hand touched her brow. She thought it was Deru. With difficulty she opened her eyes and focussed in the lamplight on three dim figures. The Healer. And the Fool. And Dion.

'Deru!' She moved: her side flamed with pain. 'Where … is he?'

'Be still,' said Dion. 'He'll be here soon. You and he can stay here. But the Fool and I must go now. So get well. Be happy.'

'But …' – She tried to sit up, but could not – '… She said I must …'

'She can no longer tell you to do anything,' said the Fool.

And by the time she realised who'd spoken – for his voice was not the voice of a weak or unsure man – they were gone. To fight the Beast.

Later Deru came back, and she wept in his arms.

Gradually he'd stirred, head splitting, cold and wet and aching, with no idea who or where he was, nor what had happened. Stray flashes of crazy vision flared in time with the pounding of his skull; the echoes of a vast voice boomed. He tried to open his eyes but his leaden eyelids were glued to his cheeks. His mouth tasted of stale vomit, his gut felt like a cement mixer in motion. He sat up in bed (it felt like cold wet rock) and with an effort brought his hands to his head. 'Jeeze,' he groaned, 'I must really have tied it on last night.'

Seated on a rock a few feet away in the cold dewy dawn, Dion put down his lyre and turned. 'How do you feel?' he asked.

Somehow Sam thought it was Diane, in bed beside him.

'Okay, Okay!' he barked irritably. 'So I'm an idiot, and I'm paying for it now, and I swear I'll never touch another drop, honest!'

'It's time we got going,' said Dion.

That's not Diane! Sam realised, and then: *Where am I?*

He managed to open his eyes. A blurred face swam before him. At last he knew who it was. Then it all came back in a flood that made him gasp. And without thought he asked a question that told Dion everything.

'Why did you lot help the Beast escape?' he demanded.

Dion, not at all taken aback, smiled gravely.

'If you know that question then you know the answer.'

The Fool shook his head. His eyes cleared. He stared accusingly.

'You knew they'd fail, didn't you? Apart from Shemyaza they were all novices. You sent them knowing full well how they'd react. You planned it! Azazel and Tiy in particular …'

'Not in particular,' Dion said. 'But if not they, then others would have done as they did. And yes, we planned it.'

'So you punished them for doing as you knew they'd do!' Sam laughed, his face weirdly underlit by the glow of the emerald ring. He tapped it. 'You were the one who gave this to Tiy. And probably put the idea in her head of getting Shemyaza's seed that fathered me.' Again his bitter laugh. 'And you arranged Tiy's release, and the Beast's escape! Why? To try us? To put us Lullu up against it? To ...?'

'Don't you think we'd better get going?' Dion repeated.

'Get going?' Sam sneered. 'Oh, I see you now, Dion, Messenger of An and El to this Hidden World! And yes, Shemyaza told me how to beat the Beast.' Aching all over, he staggered to his feet. 'So you're right! Let's go. No time to waste! Oh no! Only centuries and millennia wasted already, and four thousand more years to the Shift!'

And with a curt nod of his pounding head Samjoyce started down from the hill, Dion following him thoughtfully as Lavellan the Elder, watching from a discreetly distant hiding-place, tapped his brow with a finger and sent silent warning to Taishi.

'*They're coming down now*!'

35.
Beastie Dreams

Taishi was exhausted. Council, Toad-stimulated, had argued all night, examining entrails, questioning the spirit-world about the possible fate of Dion and the Fool, until it grew plain that most Elders put the short-term interests of the Free men first. *Fear of losing Long Life makes us weak,* Taishi thought disgustedly as the final damning vote was taken. *What's worse, it takes a half-free to tell us! And don't we love him for that?*

For Deru's plain speaking had not endeared him to many. Brought from Zoe's sickbed the half-free had been questioned harshly. His loyalties and rights had been called into question by speaker after speaker.

'*You were sent to serve us. Why now do you serve the Watcher Tiy?*'

'I'd be dead if I'd refused! And don't you remember the times before the Beast last drove Her out? Did She ever hurt us as the Beast does now?'

'*You led these three here and exposed us to the Beast's hate! Now many are Seized, yet you fear more for a slave-woman than for your own people!*'

'Not even Free Men can avoid fate!' Deru had sneered. 'Don't you see yet that men must stand together or die?'

'*Arrogant cretin! Agent of fate, are you?*'

And so on, until at last the half-free told the Elders exactly what he thought of them. 'If you didn't want to help, why bother?' he'd cried, at which many eyes had turned accusingly on Taishi. 'You can't bargain with the Beast! Don't you know what happens to collaborators? You despise others as *slaves*, but when they ask your help all you see is a threat to your precious Long Lives! let me tell you ...'

Yes, Deru had his say, but it did no more good than Taishi's argument that the Great Time demanded new thinking and risk-taking. Word of the vote reached the waiting crowd even as Lavellan alerted Taishi.

So, when Dion and Sam came down to the Lodge they were not let in. The mood of the crowd as they approached was warning enough. Sam, still angry at Dion, saw handsome faces twisted by fear and dislike, pushing against Lodge Sergeants and crying anxious questions:

'Why did you come here and turn the Beast against us?'

'If you're so smart why do you need our help?'

The two men held their tongue as they fought their way through the crowd to the door of the Lodge where they met Taishi.

'No!' Taishi extended clenched fists. He stood surrounded by grim Elders, Milel and Erkigel among them. 'You can't come in.'

'What?' Sam laughed. 'Not even for breakfast and an Anadin?'

'I'm sorry,' Taishi muttered. 'Council says we've helped you enough; we wish you luck, but we must consider our own.' With a scowl he added: 'Because we helped you many raths were dream-blasted, and last night many were alarmed by your ravings on the hill, and ...' – stiffly he turned to Dion – '... by your too-sad music. I'm bound to put my folk first.'

'So you think I'll fail,' Sam said flatly.

He met Taishi's eyes, and Taishi saw the new power in him.

'The Beast can't be dismissed just like that.'

'Nor I,' said Sam. 'But I get your point.' He eyed Taishi, then Dion. *Who can I trust?* he wondered. 'Thanks for poisoning me last night,' he went on. 'We'll go now. But first we'll see Deru and Zoe.'

'You can't see the half-free!' Milel blurted.

'Oh?' Sam looked at the Elder. 'Why not?'

'He's under arrest,' said Taishi, his disgust plain. 'Council voted to try him for consorting with a woman of inferior species. With a *slave*!'

Sam spat, then grinned angrily. 'We'll not go until we see him! We'll stay, and force the Beast to come against us *here* – which he will!'

This was heard by the crowd. An anxious babble broke out. The Elders looked at each other as Taishi, judging the situation, said quickly: 'Very well. Come with me,' and the Elders reluctantly parted as he led them into the Lodge, down dark passages to Deru's cell. As the door opened Deru jumped up. 'I *demand* to see Zoe!' he cried, and then, 'Oh. You.'

'Yes,' said Sam. 'Me. So, your fine folk don't appreciate you.'

'My fine folk!' Deru laughed bitterly. 'All my fine folk appreciate is how to keep shit off their fingers.' He glared at Taishi. 'I *demand* to see her! And I swear if she's harmed I'll call down such curses as …'

'You heard the vote,' Taishi rumbled. 'As soon as she can walk – if she recovers – she's expelled from this Lodge and the protection of it.'

'Then expel me with her!'

Taishi sighed. 'You must stay to face trial.'

'Do something!' Deru appealed wildly to Dion and Sam.

Sam told Taishi flatly: 'Tell your Council that when I've defeated the Beast I'll see that every *slave* in the lands learns what cowards the *Free Men* are! Then where will your people be, for all their Long Life?'

'I will tell Council this,' agreed Taishi, betraying no emotion.

'Also you'll drop the charges against Deru, grant him access to Zoe *now*, and let them *freely* decide if they'll stay here or leave.'

Taishi stared. 'It isn't yet clear if she'll …'

'I – and the Lady Tiy – will hold it against you if she dies.'

Taishi smiled faintly. So did Dion, while Deru gaped, amazed.

'You give us no option,' Taishi said smoothly. 'I'm sure Council will take your points.' He stopped smiling. 'But only if you succeed.'

'Yes,' said Sam. 'But in the meantime you'll lodge Deru with Zoe to help her recovery.' And at Taishi's curt nod Deru laughed wildly. 'Fool, what's happened to you?' he cried. 'You seem to have found yourself!'

'Yes, and my name's Trouble.' Then they said farewell to the half-free and Taishi took the two of them to Zoe where she lay, delirious.

'I'll be back,' said Taishi, leaving them with her.

When they emerged Taishi was waiting, holding something wrapped in oiled cloth. He beckoned Sam aside and unfolded the cloth.

It was a sword, jewelled, intricately basket-hilted, that the old man part drew from its scabbard. Sam drew breath at the sight of the curved, rune-inscribed blade. Wrapping it again, Taishi pressed it into his hands 'This was my father's sword,' he whispered. 'Take it, but don't let anyone see you with it: hide it until you've gone … and when you beat Azazel down to his true shape, cut off his head for me. No!' He raised a hand at Sam's protest. 'I'm shamed by my people. It's the least I can do – and if it tastes Beast's blood, my father's shade will rejoice.'

So Sam took the sword, but as he hid it awkwardly under his cloak he met Dion's eye, and a sense of approaching disaster afflicted him.

After that, with no more ado, Sam and Dion left the Lodge and started west into the hills ... towards the Panting Cliff ... towards the Beast.

It was near noon before they spoke so much as a word to each other.

Sam had limped through the hostile crowd and away from the Lodge as if struck by sudden lameness. Only when they were well away and hidden deep in steeply climbing birchwood did he stop. With a sigh he withdrew the concealed sword, and stuck it through his belt. As he did he looked at Dion, but the Messenger merely stared back at him, blue eyes opaque. Sam had been about to explain what Taishi had said, but something in that look made him keep his mouth shut. Instead he pointed questioningly on up the slope, and Dion nodded. So they continued, climbing out of the wood onto a high wet moor, now wading waist-deep through emerald acres of long grass and newly unfolded fern as the horizon before them widened out to hazy bare hills dreaming under broken grey cloud drifting under a veiled and intermittent sun. The day grew warm and humid: for miles about nothing moved or made a sound save for the buzzing of bees at heathery cups and the horse flies and other pests that tormented them. To the west they continued past stagnant peat-pools and outcrops of rock, and never a word they spoke, Sam brooding on many things, his hand on the hilt of the sword Taishi had given him, Dion striding behind him as they left the threatened lands of the Free Men and approached Azazel's palace of illusion. Yet though the Beast was surely aware of their approach, nothing moved. Both land and sky remained empty of any clear threat ... but still they did not speak; their silence now lasting so long that it grew ever harder to break, its very endurance a growing barrier to communication ... a threat in itself.

How can I talk to this man? Sam wondered, resisting the urge to look round and see if Dion watched him. *He's not even really a man. It's just a form he assumes for convenience: he can come and go as he pleases. He's one of those who manipulate us all through history. What are we to him but creatures in a zoo? They engineered all this! Tiy and Azazel* (he thought how the Beast had tried and failed to tear him away from Shemyaza) *are as they are as because of Elohim scheming as much as because of any decisions they took themselves. So what's all this to him? An interesting game? Sociological survey? Research project? And me! I'm half Elohim too! But so are we all. All the Lullu! They MANUFACTURED us, for godsakes! Take an ounce of dumb primal man and stir! From Australopithecus to Peking Man to Neanderthal and Cro Magnon.* He laughed bitterly inside himself. *Yet for all their knowledge they've fucked up! Is that how the universe grows? According to the fuck-up theory of history? So why feel bad when we fuck up? – except that it does us no good. Born to suffer and die! Is that all? What idiocy! And what am I thinking?* he brooded mordantly, glancing back at Dion. *So now I know how to beat the Beast! Cowardice and Vanity and Greed! Sounds like fighting myself! And ...*

It was then that Dion increased his pace and came up alongside.

'There's something I've decided to tell you,' he remarked.

'Great!' Sam said. 'You mean about the Forty-Nine Heads?'

'Before today's over,' Dion said casually, 'you'll kill me.'

Sam stopped dead. He stared at the blue-eyed man.

'What did you just say?' he demanded.

With a pleasant smile Dion repeated what he'd just said.

Sam shivered. 'Why are you winding me up?' he asked. 'How can I kill you? Why should I? We're on the same side ... aren't we?'

'Oh yes,' Dion readily agreed. 'But it'll happen, and I tell you now so that when it does happen you won't be fooled into false sentiment. The situation'll be tight, and if after it happens you make the wrong decision, everything's lost: the Beast wins as sure as night follows day. Now come on! Don't stop! I tell you now because it's essential you understand.'

'Who the hell are you?' Sam growled at him. 'Christ seeking crucifixion?'

'Death,' said Dion, 'is tragic only when it's a waste. In any case the spirit goes on. But if this world dies, the waste is huge. Now let's move on. And if you will, please tell me what you learned last night ... before the Beast starts his next attack. Because then we'll have our hands full.'

Sam shook his head in amazement.

'What *is* all this?' he demanded.

'Didn't Shemyaza tell you?'

'Oh, he told me plenty!'

'Well?'

'Among other things he told me to keep it to myself!' Sam barked.

Dion smiled. 'Discretion's a virtue,' he said, 'but in that case, why did you go screaming all over the hill last night? Cowardice and Vanity and Greed? So the Beast's scared; he tried to break it up – but why then did you go running about telling him precisely the grounds on which you'll attack?' And though Sam glared at him Dion took his arm and moved him on ... on towards the rising western hills, towards the Panting Cliff. 'Very well.' Dion shrugged at Sam's instinctive resistance. 'But what about your daughter? Do you know where she is and what part she plays?'

'All right,' Sam snapped, hand on sword. 'So you tell me!'

'My knowledge doesn't matter,' said Dion. 'It's what you know and do that counts now. And how well you understand her part. Because surely by now you realise that without her none of this can succeed?'

'All I know,' said Sam despite himself, 'is that she's with the Weak Ones. The Cathars. In the thirteenth century after Christ. Is he one of you?'

'But have you seen her there? Have you visited her?'

Sam stopped again. 'What are you talking about?'

'She's visited and helped you here. Hasn't she?'

'So what?' Sam scowled. 'How do you know all this?'

'The same way I know you'll kill me before the day's out.'

Sam swallowed. *Vast depths and heights appal him.*

'This is getting beyond me again,' he said miserably.

'It had better not. If it does, you're lost. So don't you think it's time ...' – Dion smiled engagingly – '... you looked in the emerald and tried for the wider point of view? Because after tonight it's going to be all up to how you and she can communicate. And if you depend on her to reach you all the time, then what happens when she's weak and in need of you?'

'Wonderful!' said Sam, waving his arm at the sky. The clouds were clearing. The sun shone bright. 'What's this? The Open University?'

'Well?' said Dion. 'Aren't you going to try it?'

'Get lost!' Sam snarled, and strode away ahead. But surreptitiously he peered into the emerald ring, murmuring Chrissa's name, Shemyaza's depths rumbling in him as, far beyond moon and horns, scenes began to appear.

Then, without warning from the cloudless sky, the deluge struck them.

Azazel had begun his attack again.

Within seconds they were drenched. A violent wind whirled hail at them. The horizons vanished. Sam's gaze was torn from the emerald: he cursed and shook his fist at the storm: his hand fell to Taishi's sword, he drew it and in incoherent rage began waving it at the buffeting sky. Dion eyed him remotely … and of a sudden he caught himself, shuddered at the sight of the blade in his hand, and lowered it down to his side.

'What do you mean: I'll kill you?'

Dion, shaking his head, gestured sadly.

'What counts is what you do after that.'

With shaking hands Sam scabbarded the sword.

'Where do we go now?' he bawled into the storm.

Dion took him by the arm again. 'Come on, Fool'

'Don't call me that! I'm sick of being called that!'

'That's your name until you beat the Beast.'

'And then what?' Drenched and staggering, Sam stared. 'Tell me!'

'Then,' Dion cried, tugging him onward, 'you command him to do as Tiy your mother has commanded you! To lead you both to the Sometimes Isle.'

'So She *is* my mother? She fed Herself with Shemyaza's seed?'

'She no longer remembers. Don't blame Her for that, Sam.'

'Who said I blame Her for anything? What's the point?'

'The point is that She is becoming your daughter.'

'What?' Lightning flashed. 'Explain it to me!'

'You must bring your Chrissa through to here.'

'What are you talking about, you lunatic?'

Dion laughed. Took his lyre from his pack.

'Listen, Fool!' And he struck a bright chord.

Under blue sky the storm raved about them violently.

Sam wept at the sound of that music. Bright depths and heights.

'You Beast!' he screamed, drawing the sword again. 'Why should I have to endure all this? Haven't I been through enough already? Speak sense!'

'Don't confuse me with the Beast!' Dion shouted. 'See sense!'

'How can I see sense where none exists?' Sam wailed, and suddenly –

As if from above he sees himself striking down, sword-bright –

He stopped the blow at the last moment.

Tears burst out on his cheeks and he sank weeping.

In his mind's-eye he saw the Beast, laughing.

'You see what we're fighting?' asked Dion.

'But how can we resist it?' Sam wept.

'We go on,' said Dion calmly. 'That's how.'

So on they went. Stumbling through the Beast-storm, supporting each other, fighting their way through the darkness the Beast threw at them all that afternoon, Dion never taking his fingers from the strings of the lyre and Sam's right hand rarely far from the hilt of Taishi's sword ... for each time there was a pause in the music Sam found his mind overwhelmed and his hand again on the sword with the desire to strike down the messenger ... as from the high storm-drenched moorland they followed a leaping rock-bound brook down between high bleak crags with the smell of the sea ahead ... and increasingly into Sam's mind crept the vision of fantastic architecture crowning those crags. He saw before him now the spires, pinnacles, domes and gardens of a vast and glittering palace that reached from the valley below them to the sky above. He saw a marvellous civilisation with cities clustered green in sweetly designed parkland round the base of that palace; he saw before him all that scientific progress ever promised; he saw the systems of public transport in gleaming operation with torpedo trains to pull contented multitudes from sparkling galleries of art and commerce to their contented family homes; he saw the faery promise of the Last Days now realised, and though in him Shemyaza rumbled warning, his desire to believe in what he saw became overwhelming, so that when Dion cried: '*Watch that root!*' or '*Duck that branch!*' he felt insulted, held back in his eagerness to embrace the shining Utopia that lay just ahead – and so on down the mad brown moorland stream as it leaped on its way past the crags of the Panting Cliff he slipped and slithered under the ash and silver birch, his mind by now so taken that he saw nothing of them: he saw only what Azazel dreamed.

And so they came down to the flood-plain under the Panting Cliff, not three miles from the sea, where what Dion saw and what Sam saw were not the same at all. For ahead of him the Messenger saw a tangled and briar-thick wilderness through which the stream they'd followed wound muddily over grey salt-flats to a bay hemmed in by ponderous cliffs ... but Sam beside him saw a Last Days waterfront city as bright and magnificent as Sydney or San Francisco. He saw streets and sparkling high-rise towers; he saw the wealth of man; with new hope and with pride in his era of origin he walked those streets, gazing up at the soaring heights of a high-tech future ... and then, from the urgently-moving sidewalk crowd through which they weaved, he looked aside across the busy street, by now completely fooled ... and through the four-lane flow of traffic on the far side he glimpsed ...

'Chrissa!' he cried in joyful amazement. 'What are you doing here?'

'Dad!' She was equally amazed. Tall and bronzed in jeans, golden hair flowing free over a rainbow-coloured blouse, she heard his voice, stopped and cried back: 'Is that you, Dad? What are you doing here?'

And with her eyes fixed on him, not looking right or left, seemingly so overcome by the sight of him that she forgot all danger, she stepped off the kerb and straight into the path of an on-coming ...

'Chrissa!' Sam screamed. 'No!'

Without pausing he whirled to make a desperate dash through the traffic to reach her – but a firm hand caught his arm. '*No!*' shouted a warning voice. '*It's Beast-illusion! Ignore it! Another step and you're dead!*'

'Let me go!' he screamed, heart bursting with fear.

'Dad, Dad!' cried Chrissa, her eyes fixed on him, burning with hope and love as he fought the restraining arm, as she ran. Then –

A terrible screech of brakes –

Chrissa screamed –

Sam saw blood fountain –

He saw an arm, torn away from her body, fly up in the air, fingers reaching limply for the sun –

Then a sick rage seized him, so violent it had him almost fainting as he swung about to see the mocking, smiling face of –

'You! You bastard! You Beast!' he screamed, in hot thoughtless blood drawing the sword and swinging it hard and flat and –

'*NO! NO. DAD!*' cried another voice, in his head, but too late, for the sword sheared through flesh and bone, and as Dion's head leapt from his shoulders everything changed: the gorgeous city vanished; Sam found himself shuddering on the edge of a salty quicksand under high bare cliffs, staring in horror as Dion's head struck the ground, bounced slightly, and rolled upright, the blue eyes gazing up at him.

Then Dion's body crashed down alongside his head, and Sam dropped the sword and fell to his knees, wailing in horror and mortification as the Beast's mocking laughter echoed down from the Panting Cliff above.

'MR SAMJOYCE! WELCOME TO MY SHOW! SO YOU'VE CHOPPED THE WRONG HEAD WITH TAISHI'S SWORD! TUT-TUT! NOW WHAT? I'M FASSCINATED TO FIND OUT! AND YOUR LOVELY DAUGHTER! SSSO SWEET AND TASSSTY, AND NOW SHE'S MINE! MY SSSTAR ATTRACTION! GOING TO TRY TO FREE HER, EH? COME ON, THEN!'

But Sam scarcely heard.

On his knees he stared at that severed head.

For still the blue eyes were open and fixed on him.

'*Azazel's got your daughter! You must save her*!' he seemed to hear.

'But how?' he whispered, appalled by himself, appalled at how easily he'd been beaten despite all he'd learned and all the help he'd received. *You told me I'd do it*! he thought, amid the Beast's laughter.

'*Dad, the Beast infects us all*!' An agonised voice whispering in him. '*The Old One's not the Enemy! Don't let him blind you*!'

'But how!' he cried again to the severed head

'*Fool*!' From those blue eyes, still open and unblinking, Dion's voice rang clear in his mind. '*Quick! Use the ring, the lyre, your head – and my head too! Pick me up, meet my eyes, seek Chrissa in them! Play the lyre and hear her voice! Then look in the depths! Ignore the Beast or we're lost! Look deeper and higher! Remember the Shining Ones! Look to the Cathars, call Chrissa, see her where she is and make connection beyond the Beast-dream! Then climb the Panting Cliff and take me with you! It's time, Fool! I'm the first of the Forty-Nine Heads you have to cut! Don't waste my death! Don't panic! The Beast hasn't won yet! Cut the Forty-Nine Heads and you'll beat the Beast! But seek Chrissa first*!'

And Samjoyce did as he was told. Fighting the Beast-visions he set Dion's head on a rock and met those eyes, he took the lyre, he called Chrissa's name as he struck a chord. And that shimmering chord cut away the Beast-vision of slaughter at the Lodge of the Nine Doors as into the emerald depths he swam … seeking Chrissa … seeking Montségur …

36.
High Pastures

Autumn storm raved round Montségur. Chrissa moaned in delirium.

Azazel's second onslaught had come before she'd recovered from the first. Exhausted she'd emerged from trance, narrowly surviving Azazel's attack on Diane and herself in the Sinking Ways. Then, dazed and still vulnerable, she'd began stumbling back to the castle, when …

She's snatched. Clammy blue dream-hands seize her, squeeze her, hurl her into a vast black opening mouth through which –

'SSSWEET CHILD, AT LASSST YOU'RE MINE! COME WITH ME!'

Drowning, spinning through filthy corruption! Black visions, and –

NOW she walks a street in a shining Last Days city, traffic rushing past as a sly voice asks: 'LOOK, CHILD! WHO'S THAT?' – and over the street and through the traffic she looks to see Sam. An explosion of joy fills her: without thinking she leaps into the traffic and … and …

A sword flashes. A head leaps from shoulders –

Sam's face, aghast –

The hideous mocking laughter –

'Dad,' she cries, 'the Beast infects us all! The Old One's not the Enemy! Don't let him blind you!'

Azazel howls at her as she twists from his grip and sees –

Blue eyes! Brilliant blue eyes into which she swims, the radiant light of the sea where the great grey ones glide, and before her stands a tall masked woman in a robe made of the feathers of many bright birds, holding a severed blood-dripping head, the head of a blue-eyed man. A living head! Smiling at her! And those blue eyes … spinning bright … so bright –

'*Look! See your shepherd! Trust him! Remember how he saved you!*'

Time like a dream. Confused shadow-play! A groaning man held on a table by three soldiers. A surgeon pulling a crossbow bolt from his thigh then cauterising the wound with boiling pitch. The shepherd screams –

Briefly her eyes opened. She saw faces swimming above her like white clouds. But so vague, so very far away! Moaning she shut her eyes again. *Pierre, why wouldn't you love me when I asked? I scare you and you won't take me. Now I'm lost in this madness. Too many worlds! But is it wrong to want a kind man who'll stop me hurting like this? Oh Pierre …*

Pierre! Escaping from Carcassonne! Bloody commotion! Ringing swords, flashing faces, a horse's fearful whinny. 'Mother Fabrisse!' she wails …

Amid the confusion, a shining face.

Down its cheeks flow fiery tears.

Black wings beat in her head, driving out all light.

In time she awakens. Heat. Dust. Smell of horse dung, wood-smoke. The sound of hooves. Flies droning. A hand stroking her brow. She opens her eyes fearfully, dazedly. Coarse red-and-blue striped canvas. A tent! Where? What? She tries to sit up … she has no strength; falls back on the rough camp bed, panting, pupils dilated. A hard hand gentle on her brow. 'Rest!' Above her a thin dark face with goatee beard. A pewter goblet floats to her lips. 'You're safe. But drink! You must sleep more.'

'Mother Fabrisse!' she sighs. 'Where …?'

'You're safe in the Lord Viscount's camp. Calm down. Drink this!'

The opiate slips down her throat. A gaping fiery face yawns wide and engulfs her; Mother Fabrisse cries from the flames; darkness swallows her into worse confusion; for NOW she stands by a bed looking down on the face of … of … 'MUM! YES! THAT'S DIANE!' –

The hideous mocking laughter again as Mum rears up in her bed, and it's not Mum, it's the Beast again, looming, leering –

'DEAR CHRISSSA, LET MEEE SHOW YOU JUSSST HOW I …'

But again the severed head! And those blue eyes spinning bright –

Plunging back. To the tent. Evening. Red sun slants low through the canvas. Horses whinny. Slowly she opens her eyes, utterly confused –

'Water! Drink now!' A man's voice. Cup at her parched lips. With gratitude she drinks. Looks up. A hard brown face framed in chain mail and fine gorget; body clad in black iron-studded leather; more chain mail all the way down from knees to the tip of his pointed toes.

'You must be hot in that,' she mutters faintly, in English.

He starts at her voice. 'So it's true!' he says.

'What's true?' She drinks again. Cool water! 'Who are you?'

Raymond Trencavel introduces himself. The name means nothing. With difficulty she lifts her head. 'Father Bernard?' she croaks, 'Mother Fabrisse?' But Trencavel looks uneasy. 'The old man and the shepherd are safe,' he mutters, then, looking aside, asks: 'Can you ... see the future?'

'What?' For in his face she sees: MOTHER FABRISSE IS DEAD!

'You're virgin?' he demands, hectically eager. 'Can you tell the fate of our cause? The shepherd swore to me you can! You must tell me! Now!'

She hears the Beast laughing. She shudders, shuts her eyes.

'What is it?' he asks. 'What's going to happen?'

'Don't you know already?' she says. 'Don't ask!'

He clenches his fists. She sees Azazel licking his lips.

'I must!' he cries. 'Tell me! What will become of the faith?'

Walls of flame. Roasting flesh. Burnings, massacre, madness.

'The faith?' asks a voice. Her voice. Where am I? A weak, grim little laugh. Suddenly before her she sees a book, open. She lies on her bed in Berkeley Road, reading about the Cathar crusade. 'Oh, it'll live,' she says, her head spinning, 'but not in the light of day. It'll be driven into dark places: its believers burned and scattered.'

Trencavel's jaw works grimly. He glares at her.

'And this siege? Will I take back my city?'

A mocking laugh bursts from her. Appalled, she hears herself cry: 'No, you fool, you won't! Soon you'll be driven back to exile! In a few years you'll be crawling to King Louis, serving in his army, begging his royal forgiveness so you can get some land to die on. That's your future!'

'My friends died for you!' he snaps, trembling so violently that for a moment she fears he'll hit her, 'and in reward you tell me this?'

'I only tell you what'll happen,' she says, exhausted.

'You and your shepherd will leave this camp by nightfall!'

'And Father Bernard?' she asks.

Trencavel's face a dark, Beast-ridden storm.

'We'll see him back to Montségur. But you and the shepherd ... I swear, if both of you aren't gone by tonight, I won't answer for my acts!'

Above her gloats the Beast. She opened her eyes. *Mother Fabrisse! No, it's Esclarmonde de Perella. And Father Bernard! And Pierre!*

Utterly lost and confused, she cried: 'All lies! All illusion!'

* * *

It wasn't. Bernard and Pierre and Esclarmonde were there. She lay in one of the tiny huts hugging the terraces under the keep of Montségur. The hut (thatch roof supported by a beam running between two rocks round which stood the drystone walls) held her cot, a wooden chest, cooking utensils and an oil-lamp. There was no window: the door opened on a grey shroud of wind-blown mist that hid everything. Through the wind sounded the honking of geese and bleating of goats from a pen on the edge of the drop to the valley where the besieging army camped. On the stool, lame leg stretched stiffly out, sat Bernard de Laurac – skeletal now, quite bald, skin like luminous parchment, eyes fixed on Joana (still he called her Joana) where she lay in her fever. Esclarmonde de Perella, the Seigneur of Montségur's daughter, knelt by her side, wiping sweat from her brow. Pierre Belot stood awkwardly by the door, cap in hand, craggy face dripping rain. Esclarmonde looked severely up at him.

'What happened?' she said, pale face anxious. 'Didn't you watch her all night? Surely you saw something!'

Miserably Pierre shook his head. 'When dawn came she got to her feet, and started back still in trance. She looked weak and lost. She didn't see me. Then suddenly she cried out and collapsed.'

'Didn't she say anything?' Esclarmonde insisted.

'No. She never does. Not now. Not since . . .'

'But you must have sensed something!'

'I had another vision,' Pierre admitted.

'What was it? Tell us!' Esclarmonde demanded, sharp-eyed.

Pierre eyed the goodman. Bernard nodded. Uneasily the shepherd said: 'There was a great light – that light I saw at Carcassonne. And a voice came from it and told me: *The Beast tries to seize her!* It told me to guard her with care and be patient.' He eyed Chrissa in despair. 'And it told me the time comes, whatever that means. Then I saw her father and that blue-eyed Shining One. They were setting out from a door in a green hill. Then she screamed and collapsed – and I carried her here! And . . .'

Chrissa's eyes suddenly opened, her face white and terrified.

'All lies!' she cried harshly. 'All illusion!'

'You disturb her!' Esclarmonde hissed. 'You'd better leave us.'

And as the healer laid hands on her temple Pierre, agonised by his failure to protect her, ducked out of the door, shaking his head in self-condemnation as Bernard whispered sharply: 'Shepherd, good friend, you've done your best, and all know it. Don't blame yourself!'

But Chrissa laughed again with that terrible grating sound, and when from outside the door he dared look back at her white face he saw such a rictus of hate and Beast-possession that he cried in pain. Past huts and the goose-pen he stumbled to the brink of the drop to the valley below, the wind whipping him as he looked into the grey writhing shroud that hid the Enemy troops waiting, waiting, waiting month after month at the foot of the pog. *How much longer?* he wondered, and shuddered. *It can't go on like this! The whole world hates us!* And the wind mocked him. YOU'RE RIGHT, SHEPHERD! I LIKE A MAN WHO CAN SEE SENSE! YOU FIGHT FOR A LOST CAUSE!

With tears and rain streaming down his cheeks he nodded in violent agreement, for a moment wanting to throw himself into the abyss. YES, WHY NOT? But then in his mind's-eye he saw blue eyes and, teetering, stopped himself. 'No!' he shouted into the murk. 'If we fall there's nothing left! The Beast'll take everything! I'll do my best! Yet what's my best when it leads to this? When I don't even know what my best might be? Why didn't I take her when she wanted me to? But I couldn't! I couldn't!'

And staring into the mists he sees . . .

*Shepherd, shepherd, time's a dream! Pierre, do you remember it all? When Trencavel kicked us out? I could hardly walk and she'd lost her mind. No wonder! But she was raving! Those woods. We found that hut and slept that night and all next day until the pain of my leg woke me up with her still asleep. So pale and thin and filthy. I hated her! Blabbing to the Viscount like that! And after they died for her! But I told the goodman I'd look after her, so I set snares, caught a rabbit, lit a fire, and the stink of roasting flesh woke her up. And did she come at me? Like a Fury! Half the night we argued. I called her Joana: she said she was Chrissa; I asked why she'd told Trencavel such bad news: she said why had I told him she could see the future, and I said: 'How else would he agree to help you escape?' I said I'd take her here but she said: '*NO! *I've had enough of that holy stuff!' And I got angry and would have slapped her, but my leg gave way, I fell over, and she . . . she touched my shoulder. 'You *ARE* hurt!' she cried . . . and when I snapped that better men than me were dead because of her she turned white; she stared at me, then ran for clay and bark and herbs, and as she dealt with my leg she sang that song the goodman found. Quant lo bouie! The Herdsman's Song! I cried to hear it! Stupid Pierre, always weeping! But her touch! So gentle! That's when I knew I loved her. Her breath on my neck. I could have had her then. She wanted it! Why not? But she scared me. She still does! Yes, she's a woman, but – she's from nowhere, from the world of the aeons. It's not her fault, but it's not mine either. I do the best I can! Haven't I looked after her and kept her free? She got her health back.*

And when Trencavel fled I asked again if she wanted to come here but she still didn't. But I didn't lose patience. Where did we go? Oh yes! To that hermitage in the Gorges of Galamus, then up past Quillan to the high plain . . . but then the French took Roquefeuil and the high plain wasn't safe any more, so we went deeper into the hills; and when winter came I took her to Flix. What else? I had to make a living; I'd wintered Na Borrel's flocks for years. And it was the safest place to go. Over the hills and far from the tales. We couldn't avoid people forever just because some wanted to bow at her feet and get a blessing and the rest wanted to turn her over to the French for the reward. Nobody can live like that. And I thought Gargaleth and Guillaume would understand. Well, Guillaume, anyway. Saracens you can never tell. After all, they were both there when the goodman came and got me to lead him to the Gate of the Stone. They knew me! But I'd changed. They hadn't. They couldn't see why I hadn't taken her as my woman. I knew what they thought! Poor Pierre! Moth fluttering round her flame, not even getting his wings burned! I couldn't tell them why. I couldn't even tell her! The way she looked at me sometimes! Yes, so it was hard on them. It's not custom to have women on the pastures. And I was moody. But she kept her mouth shut, as I begged her. So sometimes asleep she cried out in her Last Days tongue – everyone has their quirks – and when that started she slept out in the cortal with the sheep. And still cooked and washed. And she was good with the sheep! May the Good Spirit witness that she'll have the ugliest-minded old ram eating out of her hand! A natural! And when Gargaleth fell over that cliff and broke his arm she healed him. Was he grateful? I saw his look. He'd have tried, she'd have taken – but he didn't dare. He sensed it too. Her strangeness. And they resented my bringing her. It disturbed them. But there was nobody and nowhere else I could trust, with a price on her head and the French all over the highlands. Gargaleth – I see why he thought as he did. But old Guillaume? Blethering on how the tales about her scared him? How she came from a spirit-realm, drove the black friar mad, told Trencavel his siege would fail! Give her a chance, I said. She may be strange . . . but she's still a woman, like any other. And his answer? So, Pierre, why don't you do her, as that's what she wants. Augh! What could I say? He had a point – but I'm the way I am, and I'd sworn to . . .

And from the edge of the abyss Pierre looked up at the hut where she raved in Beast-seizure. He saw nothing, and through the wall of the wind heard nothing as Esclarmonde de Perella and the goodman tried to calm and quiet her – but he could imagine well enough, and his imagination was a torment! Ragged nails bit into his palms, he screwed his eyes shut –

I've done my best! How DARE Esclarmonde tell me I distress her? What does she know? Good woman, no doubt, but so holy she's juiceless! She has no idea! Oh Sweet God! Leaving Flix solved nothing. Back north we came, and for months met nobody. We had the flocks, and she was so strong and beautiful I groaned every time I looked at her! But she was sad. She felt bad about avoiding Montségur. And me not . . . well. As for her dreams . . . I heard all of it. Her FATHER, *and the* LAST DAYS, *and the* OLD ONE, *and the –*

And the Beast. Oh God, let us defeat that Beast!

The goodman says the Beast conquers through fear and greed and lust. But how did he get into Lady Chrissa? Was he there all along? I can't bear to think it! But what if that's it? Fear? She was always afraid of what she sees must happen here. Very soon! Is that it? She didn't want to face it. She used to get so angry. The way she looked at ewes suckling their lambs, and at women with babes-in-arms! Sometimes I nearly lost control. But it wouldn't have been right. The Shining Ones told me to protect her, not take advantage of her. They told me to become greater than I am, not to give in to lust. They said I must 'save us all from the Shift'. Whatever that means. I don't get it. I'm simple, and it's best that way, or the Beast'll get me too and I won't be able to help her.

But HOW *can I help? What happened? I wish she'd confide in me. Is it my fault? She doesn't talk to anyone! Never did. Not even the goodman knows her; he said so. 'She has a Last Days mind,' he said. 'We're of a different age.' You can say that again! But what happened? Where's her father and that blue-eyed Shining One? I saw them before she fell. So why don't they* DO *something?* NOW!

Chrissa, your fate's too high for me! Remember that night you talked to the bright star? How you cried to the sky for a SIGN? *To overcome your fear of Montségur and the terrible burning? You told me often enough! Now here we are, and I'm here with you to share it. Lady Chrissa, I'll live for you, die for you – so don't you dare give up to the Beast! Don't you dare! Do you remember that night?* he implored, trying to reach her where she lay delirious. *Two years ago! How time flies! Please remember!*

And she did. She was there again. Round the fire on the high pasture, Pierre insisting: 'We MUST go to Montségur now! Why are you scared? The siege is over! I won't spend another winter with you at Flix.' But still she won't go, still she fears that final step . . . and the Beast grins in her, turning her fear to anger. For Pierre won't even look at her. *Why treat me like this?* she cries silently. *I know why you won't take me with you to Ax tomorrow. You're going to visit the whores in the Bassin des Ladres. I'm sick of it! I know how you eye me when you think I don't see!* And then suddenly, in clumsy heat and nervous haste, she throws herself at him.

With an incoherent gasp he pushes her away.

'Lady Chrissa! What are you doing?'

'Do I smell bad or something?' she demands . . . and as the anger takes her she feels foul Azazel upon her, cockerel-headed, pumping and grabbing, trying to force her legs apart, hissing: 'HAVE YOU NO LOVE FOR A POOR OLD MONSSSTER WHO ONLY WANTS JUST A LITTLE-LITTLELITTLE AFFECTION?' – and with a gasp she shuts her eyes, in such fear that Pierre, thinking himself to blame (for who else is she staring at?) in agony mutters:

'Lady Chrissa, all see the light in you! It says don't touch! It'd be like fire meeting water!' Anguished he waves at the starry sky. 'We'd put each other out, leaving only ashes and steam. Then where's your cause?'

'But...' – breath shudders out of her: tentatively she opens her eyes and it's Pierre she sees – 'you risked turning to ash when you rescued me.'

'You scare me,' he admits. 'All your talk of Last Days, and the dreams that seize you ... how can I be your lover?' And at his doleful smile she freezes. 'Embracing you I'd see that dreadful Gate of the Stone you came through, with Her teeth that bite men in half. I can't do it! I can only serve you the best I can, and learn what part I'm meant to play.'

'You don't want me,' she says, her eyes flashing.

'You know I do!' he protests. 'But it's ... it's not time.'

'Rubbish! I disgust you! I'm a burden! I'll leave!' And with Beast-fumes heating her brain again she jumps to her feet. 'All you men are the same,' she cries hotly. 'Half of you call me witch, the rest call me holy, but none of you dare to touch me! It's no good! We're too different!'

'Where are you going?' Alarmed he rises from the fire.

'No! If you don't want me, don't follow! Leave me alone!'

Furiously uphill she runs to a limestone crag and by starlight climbs it, hauling herself from one ledge to the next in blind sad rage, darkness crowding her until at last, at the top, she finds herself facing the bright star. Low above the south-west horizon it shines, and at the sight of it her fingers seek the emerald pendant Fabrisse gave her. So pure! So near yet faraway... abruptly she feels a crushing sense of loss. Trapped in the pit of an endless dark well! In despair she lifts the pendant to her brow and seeks the green ray for the first time in – how long? Over a year? – as appalled she cries: 'Mother Fabrisse, where are you? And where am I?'

DAUGHTER, WHAT'S WRONG? whispers the tiny distant voice.

Mother Fabrisse? She stares into green depths. *Is that you?*

WHO DO YOU THINK IT IS, CHILD? WHAT'S WRONG?

'Everything! All I see ahead is death! Pierre won't take me! Why am I here? Why didn't I go straight after Sam, to the Old One's world?'

YOU'D HAVE BEEN TORN TO PIECES, CHILD! YOU CAME HERE TO LEARN HOW TO SEE OUR SISTER THE OLD ONE, NOW YOU'RE BORED, AND THE BEAST TOUCHES YOU. TIME YOU WENT TO MONTSÉGUR TO START THE REAL WORK AGAIN.

'But why? Father Bernard never sends for me! Why go there? For what? The burning? Why can't I forget it? And why is Pierre so ...'

CHILD, BERNARD WAITS – AND HE KNOWS HOW PIERRE IS! DON'T YOU KNOW YOUR SHEPHERD YET? IF YOU WANT HIM TO ACT, ASK THE OPPOSITE!

A shout breaks the spell. 'Lady Chrissa! Are you all right?'

CHILD, YOU DON'T NEED ME ANY MORE FROM NOW ON SEEK YOUR TRUE MOTHER AND FATHER AND BE PATIENT WITH YOUR GOOD SHEPHERD!

And the green depths are empty as Pierre calls again. Reluctantly she answers, gazing at the bright star. Uneasily he joins her ... for he sees her glow in the night. 'You cried out.' He drops to his haunches. 'Why?'

'Montségur.' Sighing, she feels his face with her hand. 'You and I ...'

'It's not the time.' He bows his head, then surprises her by adding: 'Not yet, anyway. I've been waiting for this. I'll take you.'

'No!' ASK THE OPPOSITE! 'I'll go on my own.'

'Impossible!' He shakes his head stubbornly. 'I'll take you.'

'What did you mean, not yet?' she asks in a small, careful voice.

'Don't know.' He shrugs, tense again. 'It just came out.'

'You're telling the truth?' Then she says: 'You usually do.'

'I follow the path that seems right to me,' he mutters.

'But not what anyone else asks, eh?' she flares, her desire surging again. 'Can't even hold a woman who asks for a little comfort, can you?'

'Why insult me? Of course I can!'

Then he hugs her, but awkwardly, as if embracing glass.

'You're not hugging an angel!' she cries. 'It's just me!'

He says nothing, but his eyes are wet and his face taut as he lifts his head to the bright star. *Not yet*, it winks at him. *Not yet, shepherd ...*

She lays her head on his shoulder ... but hears the Beast again ...

NOT YET! she hears, NOT YET, SILLY GIRL! NOT YET ... NOT YET ... NEVER!

37.
The Siege

So that over a year after escaping Carcassonne at last she'd come again to Montségur, climbing through the scrub of pine and privet to the fortress where it floated almost amid the swirling clouds. And at her first sight of Father Bernard she was appalled, for he'd grown much weaker; he could walk only with Imbert's help as he emerged from his hut to meet them. Yet his eyes were bright enough as he greeted them warmly.

In this he was virtually alone.

There had been changes in this high rare place since her last visit. Esclarmonde de Foix had died, Bishop Guilhabert too: spiritual leadership was now in the hands of Bishop Bertrand d'En Marti, who ten years ago had conferred the *consolamentum* on Bernard and Fabrisse.

Bertrand was not a seer. He was an administrator, and in charge of a nightmare. One siege just over (Raymond of Toulouse had been half-hearted about it, but a siege is a siege); five hundred pilgrims and refugees on the rock, many more in the village and woods below and about, plus the garrison under Pierre-Roger itching to hit out at their persecutors. When Joana arrived late that day in 1241 he had quite enough on his mind without Bernard's confidential revelation that she foresaw tribulation and death for the faithful at Montségur in little over two years' time. 'Does she need such a *hot* fire for her purpose?' he'd asked, lifting an eyebrow.

Yet the night she arrived he received her, Pierre, and Bernard in a small room over the North Door: a room cluttered by desks piled high with books, letters, accounts of grain transactions and monies gathered from the faithful. By the smoky light of a *calelh* set on the desk behind which he sat she saw a grave, rugged, gentle, unsmiling man ... and he saw a tall young woman of great natural force and beauty, sun-bleached hair a cloud of gold on her shoulders. Yet he saw something unfulfilled in the sadness of her face, and wild depths in her startling eyes, and her gaze was not quite steady. Several times she turned to the shepherd beside her, and he drew his own conclusions. 'Daughter,' he asked precisely, steepling his fingers before him, 'how do you think we're to deal with you? I must be frank. There are tales. You unsettle people. There is talk of ill luck. I'm sure you know it.' He raised his hand to forestall her. 'Brother Bernard tells me things I'd find incredible ... had not Bishop Guilhabert and Dame Esclarmonde both told me the same before they left us. That your purpose and our fate are linked ...' – he looked at her sternly – '... but that you fear your purpose too much to know how to carry it out.'

Flushing, she said quickly: 'I know I must stay here to ...'

'Yes,' he answered, 'and so, for formality's sake, as your spiritual director I impose a retreat on you, to be spent on this rock, its length indeterminate. I will not be involved in the, um, *subtle* training you require. As for you, shepherd,' he went on, 'come and go as you will – but please make yourself available as guide for our purposes when we require.'

To this Pierre agreed. And that was that. Now Bernard, watching her as she twisted and moaned, shook his head sadly as outside Pierre waited in the wet, wind-wracked mist. *Those early days were hard on you,* he thought. *Poor child, the Beast put his finger on you eight long years ago, when we first received you here ... and you've made such great strides since then. Yet how angry you were when you returned! With Pierre, with yourself, with all of us! You wouldn't learn, you made it plain you wanted to go, and oh! How you'd eye us, as if we were all burned to cinders already! I know it was difficult – hard looks in your back, suspicious words you were meant to hear – well, by now you know we're not all saints even in this pure and holy place. And whenever the dark mood came on you I scolded you and told you: 'Work, don't think! You can't walk away now! Did Fabrisse die for nothing?' Oh yes, I bullied you, and you hated it, but you knew I only spoke the truth ... and you began your green ray work again ... and it leads to this ... but you will beat this darkness, child, and when the time comes you will tell me exactly how I must call you in your Last Days dreams!*

Yet as she moaned in Beast-delirium on the cot he felt helpless, and for the first time fearful, for he had no idea what had happened and no way to reach her. He could only wait and see, hope and pray –

a situation not unlike that confronting Montségur itself.

For he remembered well how the siege began. That lovely May morning, sitting in the warmth, watching the ant-like troops crawl into position so far below – six thousand of them, led by Hugh d'Arcis, the new seneschal of Carcassonne. It had been no surprise: the siege had been inevitable since Ascension Day last year. On that fatal day Pierre-Roger, hearing of eleven inquisitors in Avignonet, had gone there with his men. The gate of the bailiff's house had been opened to them by night; with axe and sword they'd broken into rooms where the inquisitors slept, smashing their brains out in retribution for all the victims those holy men had sent to the stake. So Montségur was ready when the army came, with huge supplies of grain and water, and the wild terrain made encirclement of the castle impossible. Six months it had lasted so far: it was a nuisance but hardly a threat, hot summer days punctuated by indecisive skirmishes as those of the faith came and went at will … and now with winter near many were sure that soon the besiegers would give up and go away, as others had done before them. All assaults had failed; there was no siege-machine in the world that could hurl rocks even halfway up the mighty crag defending them! Bernard knew morale was good! *But our fate was sealed then*, he also knew, his gaze fixed on her wild, sweat-beaded face. *You told me about it, child. You told me, and I saw the guilt eating at you, though I told you time and again that the Beast feeds on guilt, and that foresight doesn't make you responsible for what you see. All this must be! It was sealed long ago! But where you see tragedy I see the triumph of love. The trial to which we're called will free a Light that ripples through this Hidden World, and on its wings you'll soar. Our sacrifice will help you on your way. If you come through this! Yes, you've gone too far, tried too much too soon, let the Beast get a grip – but he fears you! And if Pierre …*

Suddenly she was seized by new frenzy. In a terrible change her face twisted into a mocking dark mask. Her eyes glittered, she convulsed as a laugh not her own burst from her – then, her arms flailing as Esclarmonde struggled to hold her, she cried out in a harsh, vicious, grating voice:

'*Fool! Think you'll get her back ssso easily? You're beaten, and all those Weak Ones will burn, and you and your sssweet Mummy Tiy …*'

She shrieked. She choked. And in horror they eyed each other as the Beast-mask collapsed and before them whimpered a terrified child:

'Dad! *Dad! DADDY! WHERE ARE YOU?*' Chrissa wailed.

* * *

Not yet. Not yet.

Alone and horrified by the quicksands under the high bare cliffs on the edge of a western sea Sam gazed into the unblinking blue eyes of a severed head as Beast-storm raged in him. Worms crawled under his skin, unclean breath swirling down from the cliffs choked him, mad eyes glared and unseen nails scratched him ... but he saw only Dion's dead-but-living head and those blue eyes so bright with confidence, hope and intention:

Not yet. Not yet. But soon! So find her! Now!

'Yes!' And he shuddered, fighting the chaos of death-wish dismay that flooded him; refusing to see the bloody sword or Dion's body at his feet – accepting only Dion's blue eyes ... Chrissa's blue eyes.

'Dad! *Dad! DADDY! WHERE ARE YOU?*'

'Chrissa!' he cried, clumsily striking a chord on the lyre, seeking her face ... and the note rang clear as a bell, sharp as a sword, slicing apart the mists in his mind. Yet still in him Beast-voice hissed mockingly:

'CUT OFF A HEAD! CUT OFF A HEAD! BETTER DEAD, BETTER DEAD! OH, MR SSSAMJOYCE, WHAT'S THE USE OF RESISTANCE? GIVE UP! I'VE GOT YOUR SSSWEET DAUGHTER, I'VE GOT YOU, AND TIY'S MINE TOO! YOU'VE LOST! LOOK!'

Again she's tossed in the air, broken by the traffic –

He paid no attention. Deep into blue eyes he stared. A high-pitched singing in his head now. Colours flashed. He saw her! He –

'COWARDICE, VANITY AND GREED, EH?' crowed the Beast –

'Chrissa! Chrissa!' With the image of her desperate face fixed and growing brighter he turned from blue eyes to emerald depths, he struck the chord again ... and her face exploded, blinding, dazzling, a vortex of white light that spun him like a leaf and hurled him to the Sinking Ways ...

And he sees Chrissa! He sees Diane! He sees Tiy! He sees –

That chill freezing gaze. Wings beating, claws tearing at his heart as mad thoughts crawl in him. 'DESTROY YOURSELF! DESTROY YOURSELF!'

But the shining light! Chrissa's shining face! Shining –

'*No!*' shrieked Azazel. '*YOU CAN'T GET AWAY FROM ...*'

Then he was free, winging high, seeking amid the lightnings and dark gulfs below, seeking from sea to plains to a landscape of rugged mountains from the heart of which the white light of her face came flaring to meet him ... and down through the image-storm Azazel hurled at him he plunged, calling out her name, down to a stormwhipped crag towering so high above the fog-drenched valleys, his gaze fixed on a long narrow castle that – like the Ark on Ararat – crowned the highest point, dark precipices verging the grey, mist-shrouded walls on all sides but one. 'Montségur!' he cried. 'Azazel, you won't stop us now!' And like an hawk to its nest he fell, his gaze spearing through fog to the cramped narrow courtyard within the walls; to stables and soldiers' quarters built against the rectangular keep that rose like the fo'c's'le of a ship; to black-robed men and women at communal prayer under the sky; to bent forms washing clothes under wind-blown canvas awnings; to mounted soldiers coming and going along the misty beech-thick ridge; to the maze of tiny stone huts packing the steep narrow terraces outside the north walls where people with calm quiet faces milked goats or carried stone for masons who, despite the storm, were strengthening the walls and outworks along the ridge. And in the valley below through the swirling mists he saw the tents of the besieging army, soaked pennants of the command pavilions tossed by the wind as ill-equipped local levies sourly drilled in muddy ground alongside knights at practice on makeshift tilt-yards, smiths hammering at their forges, engineering gangs building machines of war ... and also he saw men who, hid in mist, climbed a steep wooded gully up the craggy southern flank, dragging equipment with them, unseen by the lookouts set along the narrow spine of the summit ridge.

But this meant nothing to him, not then.

For he heard a silent, mournful whispering.

Not yet. Not yet. Not yet.

And there, by a goose-pen below a hut on the precipice edge, he saw the gaunt tall grey-haired man who with grieving face gazed down into the misty abyss, shaking his head in despair. *Not yet, Pierre!* he thought as Sam touched his mind and knew him. Chrissa's guardian! The shepherd!

Pierre didn't sense him. Not yet. For then –

'Dad! *Dad! DADDY! WHERE ARE YOU?*'

The shriek of pain burst from the hut. To it he turned, and was struck by a blast of poison hate. For there at the door lurked Azazel – shadow in shadow, darkness in darkness. '*I WARNED YOU, MR. SAMJOYCE!*'

'Drop dead!' Sam laughed angrily, holding up Dion's head as he pushed through that poison mist. 'You deny light and love! We deny you! Get out of the way! You've done your worst, but I haven't done my best yet!'

And into the hut like cool breeze he flowed past the lame old man and the pale slender woman who knelt by the cot where Chrissa lay.

The sight of her shocked him. She gasped in Beast-torn agony.

'Chrissa!' he cried. 'Chrissa, can you see me? Can you hear me?'

And he heard her little-girl whimper: 'Daddy? Daddy? Is that you?' And knew that Azazel and she alone saw him.

'YES!' Shemyaza in him demanded. 'AND WHO ARE YOU? REMEMBER YOURSELF!'

That voice roared in her, shaking barriers of self-doubt aside ... and it was Tiy in her who sat up with such force that the black-robed Weak One tending her was thrown back; with blazing eyes She saw and knew Shem Her Fool; She saw Azazel too. 'Get out, Beast!' She cried furiously. 'My Fool has you beaten; now you'll do as I ask and help us through the Starchamber. And I'll plead for this world before those who can ...'

Then as She saw the emerald ring on Sam's finger confusion seized Her. She felt the pendant about Her own neck. At the touch of it Her fears came back. 'Where is everyone?' She cried, staring wildly, blankly about. 'Why can't I see? Where am I? Who called Me? Fool Myself, to give him My ring and let that child invade Me! What am I doing here? This isn't Me! Where are you, Zoe?' And lost in the Womb-hall She wept, fighting the illusion that Shem (*Or is it Dad?*) was with her as Azazel attacked again. And Bernard and Esclarmonde saw Her eyes widen in horror as in despair She wailed and fell back. She began an infantile giggling. 'CUT OFF HIS HEAD!' She croaked in a dragging voice. 'STUPID, STUPID, CUT OFF HIS HEAD AND GO TO BED, CUT OFF HIS HEAD AND BETTER DEAD, CUT OFF HIS HEAD AND SUCK ME INSTEAD!' Yet still they saw only her.

And Azazel danced in triumph as again her face froze into his mask. With mocking, lifeless eyes she stared up at Sam, sucking her thumb like an idiot child.

'*YOU SEE, SAMJOYCE?*' she croaked. '*TWO BIRDS WITH ONE STONE, EH?*'

But Sam was unimpressed. 'Who's the real Fool?' he asked and – holding up the lyre as Esclarmonde and Bernard eyed each other in amazement – he called loudly to the shepherd outside:

'Enough self-pity, shepherd! Act now! Start to play your part!'

He struck the chord ... and Pierre cried out in agonised ecstasy as the white light burst in him and his doubt fell away. He turned even as in the hut Bernard seized his head in both hands and Esclarmonde shrieked: their minds blazing with unbearable brilliance as they heard the voice singing from the inferno. '*Use this, daughter!*' sang that mighty voice, '*Use this pain, use this fire, soar on its wings to the Starchamber Gate!*'

And as the echoes rippled and lingered Pierre rushed into the hut, face ashen, looking neither right nor left as he made straight for the cot where Chrissa lay witless. 'No!' he roared, throwing himself down on his knees by her, brushing Esclarmonde aside as feebly she tried to fend him off. 'Don't you see?' He went on with utter conviction in a voice which Bernard had never before heard from him, 'It's my absence that distresses her, not my presence! So no more NOT YET! Now all of you, get out of here, leave her to me! And that …' – sticking out his tongue he threw up crooked fingers on either side of his head – "… includes YOU, you Beast, you Lie, you filthy unseen thing! Go on, GET OUT!'

Then Chrissa began to sob as Pierre drew her to him. Esclarmonde protested shakily. But Bernard, with difficulty rising to his feet, said:

'Goodwoman, the shepherd's right. Let's leave them.'

So, though looking back dubiously, Esclarmonde helped him out.

Sam grinned at the furious lurking shadow. 'What are you waiting for?' he cried, holding up Dion's head and shaking it at him. 'Now I'll meet you and defeat you: you'll take us to the Sometimes Isle!'

'*DEFEAT ME?*' Like smoke Azazel writhed, but as he faded he cackled, '*DO YOU THINK SO? LOOK!*' Then Sam looked and saw how, even as Chrissa sighed in Pierre's arms those soldiers, unseen in the fog, had scaled the heights and seized a ledge just eighty yards from the fortress walls.

'*FOOL! YOU CAN'T DEFEAT DEATH!*' cried Azazel, fleeing to the Sinking Ways and back to the Panting Cliff with Sam in furious pursuit.

That night the enemy held their position on the ridge … and began to build a trebuchet. A week later the bombardment started.

She plunged through an abyss of dizzy green depths, that high-pitched singing in her head … back to weight, back to clamour and pain as sense returned and she found herself in the known-but-unknown arms of …

'Pierre?' she asked amazed, still in a dream. 'Is that you?'

'You're back!' he whispered. 'Thank God!'

Slowly she focussed. First his gaunt, anxious face … then past him, through the door. Mist swirling clammy and grey outside. Her head ached. She was free of whatever had seized her, but it was hard to … to …

Dad? she wondered. *Are you okay? You were here, weren't you?*

She heard the noise of men fighting. Her eyes widened. 'What ...?'

'Hush!' he whispered, and carefully kissed her. 'There's enough noise in the world already. Rest now.'

Lifting a finger she weakly traced his face, then sighed. 'Pierre, it's starting! Everything I saw in my Last Days dreams! From now on ...'

'I know,' said Pierre. 'So let's rest while we can.'

She relaxed. She slept. But after that there was little sleep.

The terrible time. The time of the trebuchet. No time to think. She was herself. She wasn't. *WHO AM I?* Gasping she ran through smoke and dust amid the screams of wounded men; her dress a rag torn for bandages, her hair a tangle, her face dust-dark with sweat-tracks gleaming as she ran towards the keep, in her haste slopping water from the wooden bucket she carried. A roar, a crash: stone splinters sprayed her, behind a mangled door she threw herself ... then on under the battlements where a trumpet blew, sounding retreat from the eastern outworks. Panting she climbed steps to a covered platform where Esclarmonde and other women worked with the wounded, bandaging and soothing the horrible mushy wounds caused by stone from trebuchet and mangonel. Without thought she set down the bucket, tore another strip from her dress, and turned to the work.

Esclarmonde looked up. 'Goodman Bernard would like a word with you.'

'Later. Later,' said Chrissa, dipping cloth in the water.

'Why not now? You haven't stopped since dawn.'

'Neither have you! Later! Later!'

After sunset she came to his hut where he sat between earth and sky. Wordless, she sat at his feet. By lamplight he saw dried blood under her nails, ice in her eyes. They watched the night. They heard the crash of rock from the trebuchet. It hit the defences every ten minutes, regular as clockwork. She met the goodman's eyes. 'You wanted a word with me.'

'It's time to tell me how to reach you in the Last Days,' he said.

Her smile was faint. 'Full circle,' she murmured slowly.

So thin, he looked at her steadily. 'You're ready, Joana?'

'Yes,' she said. 'Since we fought the Beast. Since Pierre ...'

She let it hang delicately. Bernard raised sparse brows.

'You have not yet ...?' asked the Burning Man.

'No,' she said, 'That's for ... IT. He was right all along about that, but the Beast got to me; I didn't want to see why he wouldn't.'

'And your father. Have you had any ...?'

She bit her lip as another rock crashed into the east walls.

'No time or chance,' she said. 'I went too far last time. I brought the Beast here.' She gestured. 'This!'

'What?' Bernard applauded. '*You* caused this war? Well I never!'

She breathed hard, then relaxed, even smiled.

'Father Bernard, you were saying?'

'I want you,' he said, leaning forward on his stool, 'to summon me up as I came to you in dreams before you went through the Gate; when you were twelve-years-old Chrissa in London. Show me through the inner eye. Then I'll know how to reach you ... when the time comes ...'

So again she slipped into the spirals of time and memory ...

Chrissa. Twelve years old, thirteen soon, on holiday in Scotland with Mum and Dad, and Dad so odd lately, wearing that weird green ring with the weirder tale of how his great-grandad Captain Davey found it. She's out on her own, following a burn tumbling down to the sea, following it without care, rushing downhill in fresh-air glee until – terror! – she loses her feet and falls headlong, gasping, grabbing at the flaking trunks of stunted silver birches, to land with a bone-jarring thump on a brief grassy ledge some feet above a deep dark pool into which the burn cascades.

And there he is.

The burning man of her nightmare, gazing calmly up at her.

She catches her breath ... then slowly relaxes. He's hideous, yes, but it's not how he looks that scares her now; but his fate and whatever he wants from her. For there he lies, plain as day, apparently floating just under the surface of the water, his horrible wounds healed by it, and the gown he wears not in flames but placid about him like a lily. And he's smiling.

'My child,' he seems to say softly in her, the wounds of his suffering body like blossoms of blood. 'My sweet child, I bless you.'

'Who are you?' she asks aloud in a wonderment, again seized by the disturbing sense of inhabiting two worlds simultaneously. 'I mean, I know who you are in my dreams, but ... I think I know you ... I mean ... you know?'

'So you do.' Still he smiles. 'But the lower worlds are thick, and it's hard to remember clearly. Soon you will. Start now, if you like!'

'Remember what?' she asks reluctantly, for at this talk of memory the fear seizes her again. 'Do I have to?'

'I suppose you do,' he gently says, 'since you already did.'

'But that doesn't make any sense!' she exclaims.

'I can call you only because you told me how to. Now look!'

Then despite herself Chrissa looks past him into the deep green depths of the pool . . . and abruptly, with no time to wonder what was going on, finds herself falling through blinding light into . . . into another world.

No time to think. She's herself. She isn't. WHO AM I?

Gasping she runs through smoke and dust amid the screams of wounded men; her dress a rag torn for bandages, her hair a tangle, her face dust-dark with sweat-tracks gleaming as she runs –

For a moment, confused by recognition, she came half out of trance, but the goodman whispered: 'Look again, child! Look again!'

A shift. In horror she watches . . . from another place. What place she can't tell, for it's dark and bright at once, and from it she sees a wild grey mountain dawn; she sees her friends all chained together, herded from the castle and forced down the rock to a stockade at the bottom, driven by soldiers with the scarlet cross on their white surcoats . . . and at the bottom wait the faceless ones, robed and hooded in black, holding crosses, begging her friends to recant. Begging begging begging! Her anguished fury in the dark place (WHO AM I? WHERE AM I?), yet she knows it's part of the plan as she seeks her friends into the high, tinder-dry stockade; as the hooded ones advance behind their crosses, chanting their hypocrisies as flaming torches loop over the stockade walls.

Then she sees him. With loving eyes he gazes on her as flames begin to roar about him; with his great voice he sings that sweet sad song even as (I'M BURNING TOO! I'M BURNING TOO!) she shrieks in horror – but he cries: 'Use this, daughter! Use this pain, use this fire, soar on its wings to the Starchamber Gate! See through Her night and bring back Her day; find your father to kill the Lie; wear the Stone to free yourself; sing the song to quench the fire! Go where the Shining One waits! Go NOW!'

Everything blazes up into brilliance, into a song of pure creation, and she's dissolved in that brilliance, many worlds and faces swirling round her. And among the faces is Sam's. Screaming. Pleading. Falling.

And there's another face. A terrible face.

Both dazed they swam out of that brilliance back to Montségur. For a while they said nothing. They looked at each other. Then Bernard sighed.

'To think I'm so inventive!' he said drily. 'Burning in water!' But at her look he added: 'It still troubles you, doesn't it? You think it a sin that our dying brought you here and will send you on again.'

But Chrissa only said: 'I saw that black friar. Coming here.'

'Our bold Brother Jean.' Bernard nodded. 'I saw him too.'

'Father, I love you,' Chrissa said, and stood. 'But I must go.'

Then she left him, returning to the wounded.

38.
Midwinter

No friar but a furtive vagabond trudged up the steep road, stepping aside whenever soldiers or mounted men came past. Barefoot, hair tangling over filthy face to sackcloth shoulders, all he had in common with Brother Jean who'd terrorised this region was the stink of his worms. As well for him. Many remembered him and would have been happy to reward him suitably.

He'd escaped Carcassonne during Trencavel's final attack a month after mad Sybille brought the honey-cakes even as riot broke out in St Vincent.

The delivery of the cakes was a miracle. All night during the riot and after the heretics escaped the parcel lay forgotten at his unguarded door.

There was no guard because of the riot and because Guillaume d'Ormes, raging at the escape, called the whole garrison to the stake in the Citadel where Fabrisse had died, singing psalms until smoke overcame her. Two other stakes being unused, the seneschal made his men watch the slow death of the Sergeant of the Guard blamed for the debacle. Whipping and partial strangulation plus slow drawing and quartering encouraged them wonderfully. It was near noon before a guard returned to the black friar's door outside which the parcel lay. He was opening it when the man on duty the night before came by. 'Them's for 'im.' He nodded at the door. 'That mad crow brought 'em before the trouble started. 'Oney-cakes, she said.'

The new guard hefted the leaf-wrapped parcel, opened it, and eyed the heavy half-baked lumps within, prodding one with a dubious finger.

‘Don’t fancy ’em meself. Weigh a ton. ’E might as well ’ave them.’

‘Suit yerself. Not ’is fault them friggin’ ’eretics got away, is it?’

So Brother Jean got the cakes and learned of the escape. For hours in his rage he howled. At last he took a bite. The pain as his tooth snapped on the file hidden in the cake was nothing. Indeed, he welcomed it ... and when he found the file his mad eyes gleamed.

‘I’ll have them yet!’ he hissed that night as he started on the lock. ‘I’ll see Christ save them yet!’ As for Sybille, he forgot her.

A month later he escaped amid Trencavel’s last attack. With both sides slinging stones he opened the door, knocked his distracted guard off the parapet, slipped into the tilt-yard between inner and outer walls then, lurking in shadow, waited until an undermined section of the outer wall collapsed with a roar. Amid the melee he ran. In the suburbs he coshed a drunk and stole his rags. And as Jean de Beaumont came to lift the siege, Brother Jean disappeared: Crazy Jean came to the rugged Corbières, avoiding roads, obsessed by a golden girl who’d twice destroyed him ... and though now She never tormented his dreams (he no longer dreamed), everywhere his rage grew on rumours of Joana-called-Chrissa. For a year he sought her, madly pretending he was mad; that she alone might cure him. ‘Where is she?’ he whined in every hamlet, eyes wet and empty. ‘I must find her!’ After over a year he heard she was at Montségur. Nearly he went there as a refugee himself, to get into that Dragon’s Head and kill her ... but mad wisdom won.

No, he decided. *I’d be recognised before I can strike ... and if I can’t strike, then who can? I’ll bide my time. The world will help me.*

The world obliged. Montségur’s destruction was decreed. This time, a strong army! Under Christian command! It was hard not to join the siege when it began ... but again mad wisdom won. He was a tramp, might be taken as a heretic himself – especially if the siege failed. *Wait till success humours them*, he told himself. *Be patient!* So he lurked, and everywhere heard that Montségur was impregnable, heard how Imbert de Salas had fought his way through with reinforcements, and cursed to hear this killer called a hero. ‘Yes, I love the faith!’ he cried when challenged. ‘May God strike us dead if we don’t die for it!’ Thereafter he stayed in woods, avoiding people ... especially as royal soldiers, bored by the length of the siege, took to plundering and terrorising. Crazy Jean had no desire to entertain them. So he waited, lurked, slipped about ... until one day on a hill near Freychenet he met an angry man who told him the news he awaited.

'It's all over.' The man wept, and spat. 'Bishop Durand's men climbed the pog in a mist and set up a trebuchet. Now the faithful are bombarded behind their walls and the rats who don't care have got out!'

Crazy Jean also wept to hear this … with gratitude.

'Hoel!' he muttered continually as he came to the pog and stared up there where rocks crushed walls and bodies in the service of God. 'Hoel, you'll be revenged yet! Hoel, I can *smell* her up there … can't you …?'

Chrissa smelled him too. Another hate-filled lurking mind. Yet now it meant little. The attack never let up. Mangonels, brought up to support the trebuchet, kept up a continual hail of smaller stones between the ten-minute punctuation of the big rocks. It was so unrelenting that she, like everyone else, had trouble remembering life before. The continual smash of rock smashed into their minds as well as the walls. Every impact further deadened hope. When she did snatch sleep, when she did dream, nothing in the dreams was as bad as daily reality; nothing in them suggested focus on anything but the here and now … the here and now of death and dying.

Yet Montségur had been built not as a fort but a temple, a nerve-centre in the giant invisible body sprawling through mountain ranges and deep valleys from the Gate of the Stone to Bugarach – a body patterned after a greater body, to open up doors to the higher worlds. The spiritual pattern of the place – even the arrow-slits in the keep were oriented to solsticial sunrise-and-set – elevated the mind, did not drag it down. Once Montségur had shimmered high above the dark, teeming world, protected by its cliffs. Now the enemy had scaled the cliffs; Bishop Durand had installed his deadly toy; the advantage was altogether lost. Now amid the unending din of war Chrissa sometimes thought on what Esclarmonde de Perella had once told her.

That pale, dedicated woman! Pierre didn't like her. 'It's because you don't know her,' Chrissa had told him.

'No,' Pierre admitted. 'And I'm happy to keep it that way!'

'I don't know her either,' said Chrissa. 'She grew up here.'

'*Light has been acknowledged here since time began*,' Esclarmonde had said one fine summer night long ago. '*Here we celebrate the equinoxes and pray at sunrise and sunset because then the fight between dark and light is fiercest. Such times affect us powerfully. Place and angle are important too.*' From the battlements she'd gestured. '*See how the walls run! All planned! Bishop Guilhabert told my father how to rebuild to make it a true centre. Joana, this temple lives to increase the spirit that ebbs and flows so strong between Light and Hidden World! Learn to read this book!'*

She had. Now this book was being smashed – thoroughly, unrelentingly, without mercy or passion. The endless pressure of attack removed existence into another sphere altogether. Night and day and night again; lurid with the clamour of falling rock and fresh assaults. The weak eastern outworks were long since crushed with too many men crippled or dead. Some knights owned chain mail; the footmen had only tunics strengthened with strips of leather – no protection against flying rock. So Pierre-Roger had withdrawn every one behind the eastern barbican and castle walls. Now these too were crumbling under the trebuchet's attack. Morale was failing. Many hundreds still crowded behind the walls and on the western heights beyond range of the trebuchet, but many had slipped away by night, leaving the rest tight-lipped or repeating desperate rumours. Corbario the Catalan coming to aid them! Raymond of Toulouse (even the Holy Roman Emperor!) sending an army to lift the siege! Meanwhile, men died in every new skirmish.

Chrissa knew. She said nothing. She worked, soothing, binding, doing the best she could. And nobody came. Nothing came but the unending smash of rock. And Bishop Bertrand, who did not believe in miracles, organised the exodus of the treasures of the faith. One day he called Pierre Belot.

'I know that your work with the goodman Bernard and the Lady Chrissa's essential,' he said, gently enough, 'but so are our needs now. I want you to do as I asked before: I need you as a guide to come and go.'

'Well, then you must!' agreed Chrissa flatly when he found her outside the keep amid the dust and din. Despite or maybe because of her exhaustion her eyes shone with sharp bright light and Pierre, now oddly feeling more alive than ever in his life before, heard himself laughing.

'Yes! So I must! But what about our work?'

'This is part of it!' She squeezed his arm.

He lost his humour. He stared about. Wounded men groaned.

'What if I'm killed or captured, and miss my part when it counts?'

'What if the sky was green with pink spots?' And, tentative, for so much lay unconsummated and in the balance, she hugged him. 'Have faith!'

'Faith!' he grunted sourly. 'Give me an easy life and good meals!'

'Don't be so dramatic.' Slowly she turned away. 'Pierre, I must ...'

'Yes,' he said, grimacing. 'Don't we all!'

Three times that dreadful mild winter (wet and windy, but no severe cold or snow to dislodge the enemy) Pierre slipped out by night, leading goodmen out by steep paths down the scrub-thick north-west face. In this way money and proscribed books – by Plato, Plotinus, Porphyry and other ancients whose arguments were anathema to God's self-chosen ones – were safely hidden in the Ariège caves. Each time he returned alone, stalking night-slopes under black skies, brooding on the approach of the terrible end that goodmen called beginning ... and on his own part in it. So little time to learn! And Chrissa! Who could know her? Still he felt a fool beside her, especially in the mind-work! Who knew where her Last Days will would lead? So headstrong and – she'd said it! – independent! And so each time he came back he feared what he'd find.

One starry windy night in early January he evaded the patrols and for the third time climbed the north-west face, following a familiar route that brought him up to a ledge wide enough to stretch out on. There, a thousand feet of empty space below him, he went over the work of holding-shapes-in-the-mind that he'd been doing. Silently amid the mountain night (yet even here he heard the *crump* of falling rock from the trebuchet) he repeated to himself the words they'd taught him, the outer formulae of inner growth:

'*My mind is not my own alone*,' he mouthed, '*but is ...*'

Suddenly he was seized by a sense of acute alarm.

'*WAKE UP!*' he heard her cry. '*HURRY UP! SHEPHERD, I NEED YOU AGAIN!*'

He leapt up on the ledge, staring into the night. Nothing. Only the wind, the distant crash of rock. He shivered. 'Pierre,' he told himself urgently, 'you were named after the rock! Now here you hang over the abyss – yet have you ever felt so free? So they'll kill us and try to wipe out what we stand for. But the spirit lives! Now the Lady Chrissa calls you! On the green ray again!' He shut his eyes in despair. 'Why didn't she wait for me! Quickly, now! Climb, shepherd! Climb!'

As fast as he dared, an agony eating him, he climbed to the dark bulk of the beleaguered castle, came past huts still safe from cross-bow snipers or falling rock. He found neither Chrissa nor Bernard. At the North Door, face gaunt-lit by the torch flaring in a niche, he declared himself and his pass to the guard-patrol – doing so loudly, for the *tramontana*, though blowing hard, was outdone by the unending clatter and crash of stone rain from the mangonel. The bar of the door was raised from inside. Over the landing and through the door he ran, and up an alley between workshops and lodgings to the long, narrow, overcrowded courtyard of Montségur.

And stopped. The Bishop was preaching.

He stood blinking in the light of open fires. Hundreds of people sat, many praying as Bishop Bertrand walked among them. The Bishop didn't stop preaching even when a mangonel-load smashed into the walls over his head. Pierre saw that few even looked up. 'The Light grows strong!' he muttered, amazed ... and then, even as he searched for Chrissa among those calm firelit faces – many so thin and lucently refined! – he knew that the Enemy was not now the threat of death; was not Church of Rome or King of France: the Enemy now was loss of faith; was giving in to adversity and the fear of it.

'... All bodies die,' Bishop Bertrand was exhorting them in a calm quiet voice as he walked about. 'Ours die soon. Here we face faceless ones who will destroy our bodies. No doubt of it! But they can't destroy us!' And Pierre's fury of impatience to find Chrissa was calmed – but not much – by that serene voice. 'For the soul is immortal! Forget this, or feel alone and abandoned, then the Beast will rack us. But how can we be alone? Look to the stars!' And up he raised his hands to the midnight winter sky where constellations bloomed like needle-fires in velvet. 'Do the aeons care?' he asked, his face so grave, his gaze holding all those so trapped yet free in that place. 'Do they? Do they care what happens to our bodies?'

Then – the first time Pierre ever heard it – Bertrand laughed.

'We know the answer!' he said. 'Or we'd not be here! So let's ignore ordinary talk: we're here by choice! We all know there's more to life than the safety of a body that in any case lasts only a painful season or two! Why cling to it? So now our bodies suffer – but our souls surge high; and our Enemy's a Friend despite himself, for by persecuting us he aims us at the Light! What else? How can we endure this save by growing stronger? How can we accept persecution but in charity? And you, sir ...'

Without a pause he turned up to Pierre-Roger the garrison commander, who with his wife and father-in-law had emerged onto the high covered walk that entered the keep. And Pierre groaned. *She's in danger! Why can't I just interrupt this and find out what's happened?*

But he couldn't. He didn't. The tension was too great as the Bishop went on. *Something's happened! What? To do with Chrissa?*

'... I ask you: can force against force bring wisdom? Is Beast better for attacking Beast? Violent means: violent ends! But ...' – he raised his hand as Pierre-Roger, beefy hands flying to beefy hips, started to protest and the next rock came, smashing into stables. Horses screamed shrilly as Bertrand continued – '... Sir, no blame. no BLAME! You've done your best – but what do we do when faced with extinction? Kill our killers? The hurt child stung by a wasp wails that nobody else ever knew such pain! But now here we learn that the pain is universal! How else would we still be here, fighting for what in the eyes of the world must seem a lost cause? What foolishness keeps you here, my lord commander ... but a love of truth?'

'You know I sympathise with the faith,' Pierre-Roger cried harshly, 'but I won't turn the other cheek when someone hits me – nor waste my life! We'll fight for you so long as there's hope – militarily speaking. When that's gone, my *love of truth* will constrain me to tell you! That's all I can offer you now! And that woman ...'

'That's more than we ask, and we thank you for it!' Bertrand called back, his voice rising above the hubbub of argument that came as much from soldiers as civilians. 'May you join us in the Light when we are called!'

But Pierre-Roger turned on his heel back to the keep as Bertrand, his hands lifted in peace, saw the shepherd waiting. 'My Lord!' Pierre cried as the next rain of stones came, and down on his knee amid the moans of those hit he went as women – Chrissa not among them – ran to help, 'The books are safely away. But where's the Lady Chrissa? I sensed danger. Is she ...?'

Bertrand eyed him with a grave forestalling hand. It told him all he needed to know. He groaned and struck his thigh.

'She's on the green ray,' the Bishop said. 'She couldn't wait.'

'She *should* have!' Pierre breathed deep. 'Where is she?'

Bertrand gestured at the keep. 'Come. Quickly!'

Pierre ran. Ran for dear life. *Her* dear life.

'I *must* go!' she'd insisted. They sat together at Bernard's door. Far below and to the north distant plains were fading as night came whistling in. She'd touched the pendant. 'There's a battle. Sam needs help.'

'What about your shepherd?' Bernard asked.

'He's out herding other flocks,' she said.

'You're sure it's not a trick? What if the Beast . . .?'

'I won't think like that!' she flared. Then she realised her agitation and sighed. 'This time I'm ready for tricks. Yes, I wish Pierre was here! But he isn't, and I can't wait. There's no time to lose. I must go NOW! But if he feels betrayed by my going without him,' she added, exasperated, 'it'll damage our unity when we have to rely on each other. Just thinking like this damages it. So will you tell him I had no choice?'

'I'll watch over you,' he said quietly. His face told him she wouldn't be dissuaded. *But after last time?* He thought quickly. 'Listen. Before you go, there's a secret you must know – but only the Bishop, as guardian of the faith, can reveal it. Now get Imbert for me, and then wait here.'

'What secret?' She shifted. 'What do I need secrets for?'

'Girl, if you hadn't forgotten you wouldn't ask!' Bernard barked. 'Now get Imbert for me then stay here. Will you do as I say for once?'

So she did. Imbert helped Bernard off to the Bishop. *What's going on?* she wondered, impatient as the wind blew stars into the sky; as in the wild night she saw and heard Sam fighting the Beast. *I must go now! Why agree to wait?* Yet despite her fierce clear readiness a softness ached in her; she set the pendant to her brow and sought Pierre . . . *and sees him trekking down a rocky slope* . . . and fought her old doubts, telling herself: 'He finds strength for this . . . or not. The same's true for me. No sentiment!'

Yet she shivered, and when Bernard came back, she was staring into the abyss. But Pierre wasn't there. 'Nobody's fault,' said Bernard.

'I know,' she said, 'but it doesn't help.'

With the wind howling Imbert helped Bernard over the sill of the West Door into the keep. There Bishop Bertrand, pale thin Esclarmonde by him, beckoned Chrissa aside. He stood stiff and his eyes were like slate.

'You're sure about this, daughter?' he demanded.

'Goodman Bernard spoke of secrets.' With the briefest of genuflexions she met his gaze. 'How can I be sure of *secrets* and things I don't know?'

'Then,' said Bertrand mildly, 'you *are* sure. At last. Come along.'

Intrigued yet irritated by the delay she followed him past stone cistern walls into a barrel-vaulted, torch-lit hall. Here Raimon de Perella sat with Corba de Lanta and with Pierre-Roger and his wife at a plain, not-overladen table.

Raimon de Perella, Montségur's owner, tall and heavy with a mournful eye, did not rise. Nor did his and Corba's daughter Philippa. Browner than Esclarmonde, she eyed her sister apologetically, for Pierre-Roger, staring at Chrissa like a hungry house-trained bear, would not stand nor let her do so either.

But Corba stood, raven-browed in her black robe. 'I apologise for the disrespect shown from this table,' she declared forthrightly, and bowed to Chrissa. 'Especially, my dear, to you.' Her brows dared denial as Pierre-Roger, bristling, half-rose: she cast a quick eye at Raimon's saturnine downcast face. 'You and I,' she went on, 'hardly know each other, but I – forgive me! – have seen you grow strong despite the words and suspicions against you. We all know you're not of our time and ways, and some of us – even some big strong men among us, believe it or not! – are scared of you!'

And her nod in Pierre-Roger's direction was so pointed that Chrissa wanted to but dared not laugh as she met that woman's eyes.

'Yes,' said Corba pointedly, 'it's clear to me that our fears of you belong to the Beast. You carry my prayer with you, child.'

'My mother says bluntly what we all think,' said Esclarmonde.

'I'm glad!' Chrissa's brow creased. 'But can we get on with it?'

'Yes,' said Bertrand from the door to the stair. 'Come along.'

'I'll join you.' Corba pushed back her chair, severely eyeing the man she'd given up to become *parfaite.* Raimon de Perella sighed and stared at the ceiling; Pierre-Roger scowled at Philippa; Esclarmonde shook her head ever so slightly. *What's going on?* Chrissa wondered, ever more perplexed and made none the wiser by Bernard's enigmatic face.

You know, child. You know very well! said his face.

So, with icy fingers of wind sneaking through clattering shutters, up the tight helical stair they climbed, the Bishop leading, iron key in one hand and horn-cased lantern in the other, then Chrissa, Esclarmonde and her mother, and last Imbert helped Bernard. At the top Bertrand came to an iron-studded door. Mating the key with its lock, he turned without opening the door. 'Thank you, brother,' he told Imbert, handing Corba the key and Esclarmonde the lamp, giving Bernard his arm. Imbert bowed and went ... and as Corba opened the creaking door Chrissa saw such clarity in Bernard's gaze that her heart shivered. *I only just begin to see you. The rest of you may wither, but it all goes into your vision!* And as she stared she was sure she heard him singing that song, that Song of Joana:

Prendran aigo senhado
E diran: que es morto ayssi
Aco's la paura JOANA . . .

But the Bishop gave her such a look that her mind turned to ice.

So you think you know it all, said that look. *We pray that you do!*

All so strange, she thought as she entered the tiny room beyond the door. *Father, why do I feel so cold and faraway?* And as Bernard was helped to an antique chair she looked at him again, her plea veiled.

You need your shepherd, Joana, to help you with your goats.

Her heart sank. *Maybe.* She eyed the room with its rows of pigeon-holes from which the most precious manuscripts had already been removed. *Maybe . . . but all my warmth's gone into mangled flesh and war!* She dug torn nails into her palms. *But I must accept it! In the Light of the Emme Ya! For Sam, for Dad! For these good friends! And for . . . for . . .*

Sensing her pain Esclarmonde encouraged her with a well-meant look. But to Chrissa it was as cold as the wind that howled. And as the Bishop bent to an iron-hooped oak chest he saw her shudder. *So I'm wrong*, he thought, unlocking the chest. *Her soul knows the danger. Pray God I do right. If not, our accounts are at a loss!* And he said to her quietly:

'Few know what's in this chest. You're not baptised, you're not even of the faith as we know it, but . . .' – he eyed Bernard – '. . . I'm told you're a Light-Bearer whom we must help whatever the cost. Very well! But before I open this chest you must know that what it holds, though but a fragment of finer essence, will blast whoever makes dark or selfish use of it.' And as he lifted the lid he added: 'Some say that evil entered the world in the mineral kingdom, when matter grew dense enough to trap aeons of light which strayed too close. There's Light in this Treasure – but Darkness too! So beware! It's our greatest treasure, though some claim it fell from Satan's brow. But others say good spirits gave it to us to combat dark Watchers.'

Even as he took out the box she knew what was in it.

'The ring of moon and horns,' she said flatly.

She heard Bernard chuckle. But the Bishop looked at her in amazement as he opened the box. For there it was. So plump on its velvet couch, set with raised oval boss on a band of bronze, its facets gleaming in lamplight with inner radiance ... and in the topmost facet the tiny bronze sphere flanked by slender crescents. 'That's it,' she whispered. 'But how? How did it ...?' She tore her gaze away. 'I've worn it,' she told Bertrand. 'It brought me here to you; it sent my father to the Old One. But how, because ...?'

She shrugged, accepting the mystery, and without more ado took the ring and set it carefully on her left hand. There it sat, heavy and warm and whispering in her already, proof of paradox still beyond her grasp. *Now I know it'll all tie up*, she thought. *It's when things you need just turn up.*

Remotely she heard the Bishop's dazed voice.

'This Stone brought you here? Then I don't need to warn you!'

And he grimaced as urgency seized her.

'I must act now – or all the good in the Old One whose soul I ...'

Shaking her head fearfully she slid the ring onto her finger.

Green fire roared. Through it her gaze fixed on Bernard. She heard a voice cry out: '*Now Joana goes to heaven with her goats! AEIOU!*'

'Bring Pierre,' she said distantly. 'Bring Pierre if I'm still gone when he returns! Watch me, but stop nothing!'

Emerald flame consumed her. She fell. Corba caught her and set her in a chair. She had gone. And as Bertrand went to preach Bernard said:

'Let us pray for her ... and for her shepherd.'

39.
Beat the Beast?

'Ready or not, here I come!' Sam howled wildly, pursuing the Beast from Montségur, through emerald gulfs of Sinking Ways to Panting Cliff, still so furious at Azazel's attack on Chrissa that he ignored the voice hissing in him: '*Don't let his false shapes fool you!*' Instead as he flowed after the coiling darkness ahead he grew cocksure, now so convinced he had the Beast on the run that momentarily he relaxed, found himself thinking he was Dan Dare chasing the hideous Mekon! Then he wondered: *Ten years old, reading the* Eagle*?* And even as the Mekon's deadly glaring eyes turned on him he shook himself out of that. Another Beastie dream! Another delusion! But he knew he could see through them all! See through those false shapes and pin down the Beast! A sure thing! Hadn't he seen through other disastrous delusions to rout (though at what cost?) Azazel from Montségur? 'So you fooled me; I cut off Dion's head!' he cried as the Mekon shredded, mouthing horribly, back into that cloud of fleeing darkness. 'A head wiser off its shoulders than on! Eh?' And he shook the blue-eyed head, clutching it by the curly locks as down he fell to the Beast's chosen battlefield, so over-heated by wrath and apparent success that he took no account of what the Beast set up against him. He failed to remark on the fact that the world taking form below him now was covered not by green forests but by grey cities, by endless streets leading to motorways that sliced through fenced and beaten land. He was driving. On both sides a violent yellow harvest bloomed under a wet June sky. The yellow of the rape was dazzling. At the wheel of the Volvo he had a pounding headache. Strange voices muttered in the back of his skull, and on the passenger seat beside him was a canvas bag hiding something that terrified him, something that …

'*DON'T THINK WE DON'T KNOW*,' whispered a voice, '*MURDERER*!'

Too late he realised, made a violent effort to break free, the tyres screaming into a skid, a container truck looming above … then everything breaking, tumbling, smashing into glaring yellow, into –

'Jumbo Shish with hot sauce and everything,' he slurs, leaning heavily over the red formica counter of the Ali Baba Kebab Kave on Seven Sisters Road, setting down the heavy canvas bag carefully between his feet, not liking the way the Arab kid cook eyes him. Outside the lights change: dense midnight traffic surges over the intersection where fools score quick kicks and slow death. He feels listless, on the run, but from what? He can't seem to remember. It'll come back. Unsteadily he meets the kid cook's calm stare. 'How you doin'? Whatsyername? Abdul? Sinbad?'

'Pissed old fart!' Gleaming, the kid with the Cap'n Sinbad tee-shirt and cocked hat gives him a superior look. 'You don't remember?'

'Tonight I don't remember any names,' says Sam tragically.

'Too bad.' The kid sticks a loaded skewer of fatty mutton cubes over the coals, gives the packed-meat doner torso a whirl against the electric grill, breaks open pitta bread shells with gut-wrenching twists, stirs up the salad and hot sauce, then turns and says –

'Hey Sam. You've got a nice little girl. I'm seeing her Thursday.' He leers with myterious East End wisdom. 'Garlic dressing for Sir?'

Rapping the counter hard, Sam cries: 'Listen, you little sod, if you lay a finger on my daughter I'll …'

'Nice ring you've got there, Sam.' The kid nods at Sam's left hand. 'Now where'd you get that?' Ice-cold he smiles into Sam's eyes. 'Hot?'

Sam's heart pounds. 'What do you mean?'

'Wanna deal?' Grinning broadly now the kid spreads his hands. 'So lemme relieve you of the anxiety and you get free Jumbo Shish at the Kebab Kave every night for life. Can't say fairer than that, eh?'

And his eyes bore into Sam's so that suddenly –

Gotta get out! Ducking his head, Sam turns to leave.

'Scrap that order! And if you touch my …'

'Forgetting something, are we?' asks the kid.

The bag. Almost at a run Sam snatches it up and makes out of the door in such heart-pounding hurry that he collides head on with a buxom black woman who shrieks as he knocks her over and falls with her in a tangle of arms, thighs, torn fishnet stockings, orange peel and coke cans in the gutter. Nails at his eyes, shouting, screaming, hands dragging him off, shaking him, a fist in the kidneys, the cries of a crowd gathering, behind him a voice in wonder saying: 'Hey now, look what's in here?' and the Cap'n Sinbad kid saying in bored disgust, 'Knew he was a freak!' as people press round and the outraged woman, on her feet now but still screaming abuse, puts in the boot. In the distance a siren wails as eyes goggle into the bag, disbelieving and disgusted –

'What's innit? Hey! Whaddidedo?'

'Man, it's a ... I swear to God I never ...'

'Yeah, but *what* is it?'

'Sweet Jesus! I think I'm gonna throw up –'

Screech of tyres as the white police Transit slams into the kerb. The crowd scatters as twelve Met regulars in riot gear bounce out in wedge formation, using their shields and batons, weird behind their visors.

'Right, break it up. You! What's going on?'

'This guy, sir, he comes running outa here and knocks my lady right over but you wait, that's not all, just you take a look at this, sir, right here in this bag he's carrying, enough to make a man –'

Pushing back his visor the sergeant, hairless face cold blue in the streetlight, takes a good long look at Sam.

'You mean this one?'

'Yessir, that's him.'

'Roughed him up?' The sergeant glares about.

'Hey, just doin' your job for you!' cries a cheeky voice.

'Sir, just take a look in the bag, right here.'

The sergeant snaps a finger: six of his men charge into the crowd and drag the cheeky bugger to the Transit. Nobody else moves. The sergeant takes a look into the bag. A long look. He rummages about with a hand.

'This your bag?' he asks Sam.

'My bag?' Sam protests faintly. 'Never saw it in my ...'

'Liar,' says Cap'n Sinbad. 'He tried to leave it wiv me.'

'Going to take you in, son.' The sergeant eyes him grimly. 'Can't have folk running about with heads in bags, can we? And what ...' – from the bag he plucks Dion's lyre –' ... is this?'

'A lyre.' Sam tries. 'If you'll just let me ...'

'No, son, I don't think so!' The sergeant holds it out of reach.

'And ya see that ring?' calls Cap'n Sinbad.

Yes. The sergeant sees it. He grabs Sam's wrist and pulls the ring close to his eyes. In its light his face glows green, seems almost to dissolve, as if . . .

Oh God, thinks Sam, *I've been* . . .

'Yours, eh? Like the head? And the . . . lyre?' Mocking he stares into Sam's eyes. Sam tries to speak. He's frozen by hate and contempt. The best he can manage is a dumb nod. 'Right.' Inexplicably the sergeant throws down his hand without taking the ring. 'Break it up. Let's move.'

Amid jeers and curses the crowd disperses, the cheeky bugger released with a caution to watch it. Soon, siren wailing, the Transit weaves into the station past high razor-wired walls, searchlights and Dobermann patrols. Doors slam: up steep steps to photoscan entrance they run him into a busy echoing hall. Giant video-screens on the steel-grey walls show the action on every street for miles around. In a side-room they give him the works. Strip-searched, cards and ID found, left naked (but for the ring, why didn't they take the ring?) he huddles bare-arsed on a moulded plastic chair. In the ring he sees nothing. No light. No depths. Nothing.

The sergeant, helmetless and bald, enters. From the bag he lifts the head and puts it on a table. It sits level, the neck sheared perfectly. The eyes are dead – dull and glazed. There's a dribble of blood from the mouth; the tongue is twisted between clamped teeth. The sergeant grins without mirth. 'One head. Provenance unknown. Start talking. So you're Samuel David Joyce of 15 Berkeley Road, N8, Where did you get this head?'

'Why not take the ring too?' Sams asks thickly, finding it hard to speak. Somewhere along the line someone burst his lip.

'Good question.' The sergeant nods. 'Well, son, the truth is I can't take it. Wouldn't be right. Wouldn't be ethical. You'll have to give it to me before I can accept it. Now. Where did you get that head?'

'Can't . . . remember . . .'

'You won't rest until you do, son.'

And so on. All night long. All day long. Who knows how long? That gleaming bald face, that dull slack head, both swimming before him, and the questions, the questions, until at length there's only one question:

'*THE RING, SAMJOYCE! GIVE ME THE RING AND I'LL FREE YOU!*'

No! No! Never give him the ring! If you do you're lost!

Over and over, on and on, but no dice, until he's so exhausted he can't see, hear, or think straight. Lights glaring in his face. The sense of being taken somewhere else. New faces before him.

A TV huckster voice bellowing:

'*SO YOU THINK YOU CAN BEAT THE BEAST? SO HAVE A GO! STEP RIGHT UP RIGHT NOW! FOLKS, LET'S GIVE MR SAMJOYCE A BIG, BIG HAND!*'

Sudden cut to studio audience howling and booing. Sedated and still bare-arse-naked Sam sits in the moulded formica chair, blinking under hot close-range spotlights. TV eyes zero in on his blank face as the host – dapper in crushed blue velvet, Elizabethan ruff and pantomine mask (left profile black, the right quite white), mimes extravagant greeting:

'*SO HERE WE ARE AGAIN, FOLKS: TIME FOR THIS WEEK'S . . . WAIT FOR IT . . .*' – with a flourish of lacey wrists he conducts the audience's roar of ritual response – '. . . "*BEAT THE BEAST*"! *AS YOU ALL KNOW, EVERY WEEEK ON THIS SHOW WE GREET A CONDEMNED MURDERER DUE TO DIE IN A FEW SHORT HOURS . . . AND THE GAME WE PLAY IS . . . WAIT FOR IT . . .*' – and again the Von Karajan bit with the audience – '*YES! LIFE AND DEATH! THAT'S RIGHT! HERE ON "BEAT THE BEAST"! ONE IN TEN OF OUR GUESTS WINS A FREE GOVERNMENT-APPROVED PARDON TO ESCAPE THE GALLOWS – AND WHY NOT? WE ALL HAVE MOTHERS! WE ALL MAKE MISTAKES! ARE WE HUMAN WITHOUT MERCY? IS LIFE WORTH IT IF WE CAN'T SOMETIMES – YES! YES! . . .*' – again he counts down the audience roar – '. . . "*BEAT THE BEAST*"!'

'*QUIET, NOW, FOLKS,*' he goes on. '*I WANT TO INTRODUCE OUR GUEST THIS WEEK . . . MR SAMJOYCE! YES, THE CELEBRATED HEAD-IN-BAG CASE! AND HERE HE IS, ALL THE WAY FROM WORMWOOD SCRUBS MAXIMUM SECURITY! HEADED FOR A STIFF NECK IN JUST EIGHT HOURS – HE'S COMPLETELY OUT OF IT, FOLKS, SO DON'T WORRY YOUR PRETTY LITTLE HEADS, AND NOW LET'S HAVE A WARM HAND FOR – MR SAMJOYCE!*'

A storm of boos, catcalls, rotten tomatoes and bad eggs (bought at the kiosks in the foyer) shower the stage from all angles. Paralysed Sam sits, dribbling egg-yolk frying lightly on his skin under the grill of the spots.

'*THANK YOU, THANK YOU, HE DESERVES NO LESS! BUT DOES HE DESERVE MORE? CAN MR SAMJOYCE . . . "BEAT THE BEAST"? REMEMBER: ONE IN TEN MAKES IT . . . YES, ONE IN TEN, FREE PARDON, FULL CREDIT REINSTATEMENT . . . PLUS, FOR THE ONE-IN-A-HUNDRED WHO NOT ONLY BEATS THE BEAST BUT "WINS THE QUEEN" TOO: A CAREER AS DULY-ELECTED MP IN ANY ONE OF A BASKET OF GUARANTEED SAFE CONSTITUENCIES IN THE SOUTH-EAST! HOW ABOUT THAT? SO! MR SAMJOYCE, WE INVITE YOU TO . . . "BEAT THE*

BEAST"!' And Sam just sits there, numb naked statue melting in the heat, stupefied with egg and tomato dribbling from him as the host, straddling a chair back-to-front and rocking forward mask-to-face cries:

'*BUT FIRST THE QUESTION EVERYONE WANTS TO ASK: MR SAMJOYCE, HOW DO YOU FEEL ABOUT SNUFFING IT AT EIGHT ON THE DOT TOMORROW MORNING?*'

'I ain't done nuthin',' Sam hears himself whine in hideous Hollywood cockney. 'It wiz all a frame-up, honest. Dunno wot I'm doin' 'ere, but don't tell me old mum, it'd bryke 'er 'eart, stryght up, mister.'

'*HIS OLD MOTHER!*' The host whirls, a crystal tear flies parabolically out of the eyehole of his mask, clearly visible onscreen nationwide. '*HOW ABOUT THAT? DON'T TELL HIS OLD MUM, IT'D BRYKE 'ER 'EART!*' And whirling back he cries: '*WELL, MR SAMJOYCE, MAYBE SOON SHE'LL "REJOYCE" WITH HER BOY BACK SAFE AND SOUND AT HOME, BECAUSE THE PEOPLE ARE GIVING YOU A CHANCE TO REDEEM YOUR HEINOUS CRIME AND . . . WAIT FOR IT . . . "BEEEA-TTT . . . THE BEEEA-SSST"!*'

'Good on yer, guv,' Sam mumbles, '"*Re-joyce*" – litery, that is.'

'*NOW, TO "BEAT THE BEAST" YOU HAVE TO ANSWER JUST THREE SIMPLE MORAL QUESTIONS! READY? ONE! WHAT ARE THE BEAST'S THREE GREAT WEAKNESSES?*'

'Easy, mate!' Sam's head lolls, eyes glazed as he sways in the heat, mumbling into the mike. 'It's greed an' cowardice, innit? An' pride . . .'

'*YOU'VE GOT TWO! GREED AND COWARDICE! AND THE THIRD? TEN SECONDS!*'

'Yeah, well . . . lust?' asks Sam feebly, a Victorian idiot.

'*A VICE, YES – BUT NOT THE ONE WE WANT! FIVE SECONDS . . . FOUR . . .*'

'Three! Two!' the entire audience counts down, '. . . One . . .'

'Then wot abaht vanity?' Sam cries out, the creature in a cage.

'*VANITY! HE'S GOT IT! GREED, COWARDICE, AND VANITY!*' Jubilantly the host punches the air. '*GREAT! THE BIG HAND FOR MR SAMJOYCE!*'

Amid boos, more tomatoes and rotten eggs fly from the big hand.

'*AND NOW FOR NUMBER TWO! GETTING INTO IT, EH? BUT FIRST, TELL US WHY YOU CUT OFF THAT POOR GUY'S HEAD WHEN HE WAS SUCH A GOOD FRIEND TO YOU?*'

'Dunno, guv. I got confused. Thort 'e was the Beast.'

'*THOUGHT HE WAS THE BEAST! HOW ABOUT THAT! MR SAMJOYCE, YOU REALLY DO WANT TO "BEAT THE BEAST"! SO HERE'S NUMBER*

TWO: IN WHAT AGE OF HUMANKIND DOES THE BEAST FINALLY TRIUMPH? YOU HAVE FIFTEEN SECONDS TO ANSWER!'

'Easy,' Sam mutters slackly. 'Yer Last Days 'ere an' now. This shit!'

Audience explodes with catcalls and insults. Amid his sedated haze he glares into blinding light at the masked face which chants: '*TWO! TWO OUT OF TWO!*' the host wails rapturously. '*HOW ABOUT THAT? NOW! THE BIG ONE THAT DECIDES IT! WILL YOU SWING, OR WILL YOU ... "BEAT – THE – BEAST"!*'

The life-and-death mask swoops down to Sam's vacuous face; glazed eyes are impaled on eyes like needles. '*HERE WE GO! THIS IS IT! A QUESTION ABOUT VIOLENCE AND OUR MORAL RESPONSE IN AN UNCARING SOCIETY! MR SAMJOYCE! NOW! FOR LIFE OR DEATH: IF A LOONY GOES FOR YOUR HEAD WITH AN AXE, WHAT IS THE MORALLY CORRECT RESPONSE? FIFTEEN SECONDS ... FROM NOW!*'

'Turn the other cheek doncha?' says Sam as programmed.

'*FOURTEEN ... THIRTEEN ... WHAT? – WHAT DID YOU SAY?*'

'Turn the other cheek,' Sam repeats, voice zombie-flat.

'*YES! YES! YES!*' Trembling in ecstasy, the host sinks to his knees in prayerful thanks. '*PRAISE GOD! MR SAMJOYCE, BY YOUR CHRISTIAN FAITH IN THE FACE OF AN UNCARING, GRABBING, GO-GET-IT SOCIETY YOU HAVE "BEATEN THE BEAST"! HOW ABOUT THAT? MARVELLOUS! RUTHIE! PLEASE!*'

Amid passionate moans a buxom lovely teeters centre stage. She wears high heels, seethru skimpies, a fixed smile, and carries a gilded tray from which the host snatches the pardon and golden key of freedom. '*YES, FOLKS!*' he cries, waving them over his head. '*"BEAT THE BEAST" PARDONS MR SAMJOYCE! – BUT THAT'S NOT ALL!*' Still on his knees, fluttering the pardon before Sam's glazed eyes, he asks eagerly: '*DO YOU TAKE IT AND RUN LIKE A RAT, MR SAMJOYCE – OR WILL YOU GAMBLE IT ALL AND TRY TO "WIN THE QUEEN"?*'

'Reckon ah jest hev to try!' Sam drawls in fake Texan, sweat gleaming on his brow as he fights it. 'Man's gotta walk tall or die small.'

'*WHAT – ABOUT – THAT??? "MAN'S GOTTA WALK TALL OR DIE SMALL"!*' The host springs to his feet, leading a burst of genuine spontaneous applause. '*HALLELUJAH!*' he cries, ripping up the pardon and cheekily popping the key down Ruthie's cleavage. '*DON'T NEED THOSE NO MORE, NOSSIR! BECAUSE TONIGHT – NOW! – WE – ARE – ON-LINE-WITH: "WIN THE QUEEN". AFTER THE BREAK!*'

Headsplitting trumpet fanfare. Bustle of activity. Purple drape thrown over Sam's nudity. Back on the air the host gets going again:

'*"WIN-THE-QUEEN"! YESSIR! AND LET ME TELL YOU NOW! JUST BACK FROM AN EXHAUSTING ROUND OF POLICY-MAKING IN TOKYO, BEIRUT AND MOSCOW, WE HAVE WAITING FOR US NOW, IN THE PRIVACY OF HER OWN LOVELY HOME HERE IN LONDON, OUR VERY OWN QUEEN OF HEARTS! YES, THAT'S RIGHT, SHE OWNS OUR HEARTS HERE IN METROPOLITAN ENGLAND – GOOD TO SEE YOU AGAIN, YOUR MAJESTY!*'

Suitable silence as band strikes up 'I Vow to Thee My Country' alias Holst's 'Jupiter' . . . and all but Sam bow as Her Royal Features flood every screen, austere and arcane, a forever-middle-aged miracle of medical science in royal blue and strawberry rinse, seated by the fireside, holding out a glass with the name of a famous distilling firm emblazoned on it in red.

'*I am so glad to be able to be with you all tonight,*' she says in that famous husky voice, '*but it was a close thing. I have been carrying our British values – the Torch of Freedom itself! – among races and persons with whom . . .*' – she pauses significantly; from a dozen screens her two dozen imperious eyes drill into Samjoyce – '*. . . we do not always see eye to eye! I think I have earned this drink – don't you?*'

The audience erupts as she takes a businesslike swig from the branded glass; as a young flunky pours her another, label prominent:

'IF GLEN SKEAN DHU WILL DO FOR HER THEN GLEN SKEAN DHU WILL DO FOR YOU!' thunders a vast voice that echoes on from every angle.

'*THANK YOU, YOUR MAJESTY! LET'S HEAR IT FOR HER MAJESTY! FLYING THE FLAG ABROAD AMONG DEPRIVED NATIONS – IT'S TOUGH AT THE TOP!*'

The audience erupts with glad patriotic cries. She cuts them off with a peremptory hand. '*So kind. I have to be orf again soon, to California. They're having so much trouble with that unmentionable disease. Do you know: since we stopped mentioning it here we've had no more trouble? I do believe they're ready to pay for our British expertise at last!*'

The audience erupts again, and again her gaze transfixes Sam.

'*So you're the one who wants to play "Win The Queen"?*' Leaning forward to eye him more closely she purrs huskily, '*Hmm. You look a bit bolshie!*'

'*HE'LL TURN THE OTHER CHEEK!*' says the host in a confidential roar.

'*Yes? Very good. What has he done?*' she demands.

'*WALKING ROUND TOWN WITH A HEAD IN HIS BAG, YOUR MAJESTY!*'

'*A head? What on earth was he doing with it?*'

'*HAUNTING HIMSELF WITH GUILT, YOUR MAJESTY – HE'S A SCOT.*'

'*You, fellow!*' she barks at Sam. '*What were you doing with it?*'

'Jest wantin' tae get aheid, ye daft sassenach sourock!' Sam howls in cod Scots. 'Ye bauld glinchin' limmer, div ye no ken whit . . .'

Saxon outrage drowns him. Shouts off: 'Get awa' hame, Jimmy!' and 'Fuck off Jock!' The Queen raises a hand. '*Quiet!*' she orders, peering at him. '*Fellow,*' she scolds, '*you're rude and recalcitrant! But I never blame a person for their background. I think we must seek the best in everyone, don't you?*' And closer still she peers at him, her face exploding double life-size from every monitor round him. '*So you want to get ahead, eh? So tell me: where did you get that ring?*'

Her eyes expand through the screens at him like whirling ice-drills. 'It's nae yer question tae ask!' he cries, face twisting ferociously.

'*Well, fellow, to "Win The Queen" you must give it to me!*'

'Fook aff, ye scraichin' howtowdie witch! Back tae yer byre!'

The ring on his finger burning now as he stands, shaking his head, lost in storm of delusion amid appalled silence and thunder on the royal brow.

'*You will give me that ring or you will . . .*'

'. . . LOSE THE QUEEN . . .!' chants the audience gleefully.

'*HE DIDN'T MEAN IT, YOUR MAJESTY!*' The host turns to him, hissing for the world to hear: '*GET IT RIGHT, ASSHOLE! GIVE THE RING – OR SWING!*'

At last Sam breaks the chemical shackles and finds part of himself.

'Nope!' he shouts in his own voice at last. 'Shove it!'

An even longer appalled silence. Then –

'*Orf with his head!*' she cries, hurling her glass at the screen.

And as the screens all shatter and the audience takes up the cry: 'ORF WITH HIS HEAD! ORF WITH HIS HEAD!' a roaring invades him, a swooning hot vortex of a million eyes all glaring and a million mouths all chanting: 'ORF WITH HIS HEAD! ORF WITH HIS HEAD!' as in an utter faint he swims amid the advertised dramas of Beast-dream back to the condemned cell where he awakes, head splitting, to find he's sharing his cot with a naked budding girl-child, blonde and wriggling up against him with her thighs open.

'Alice!' he cries, starting with the shock of recognition.

'No, Dad,' she sighs. 'Wrong again! It's me! Chrissa!'

40.
Cap'n Sinbad's Mask

As grim as an arrow Chrissa shot through the Sinking Ways after Sam and the Beast, a green scream in her bones as she plunged into the abyss of the sleeping world-mind, quickly thickened by its recalcitrant weight, drenched in its Beast-dream maelstrom of pains and joys and doubts and sorrows.

Down through alleys of memory she plunged, fighting distraction . . .

Dad! she called. *Where are you?* –

. . . as Sam bursts through her door roaring 'CHRISSA!' and only just in time she covers up the drawing of the burning man, and through the tidal wave of sound from her speakers she swings, white with shock at his . . .

She caught herself, dismissed the juvenile delusion, looked back to see Father Bernard by her side at Montségur. He looked troubled. *I'm not the Joana of your song!* she called. *I won't be dead at the foot of the fire when the shepherd comes in!* Then she saw Pierre climbing the crags, and groaned with doubt, and Montségur was gone, the scream in her bones much shriller now, like a voice crying: 'Sister! Sister!' – and she saw Tiy writhing alone in the caverns of the Whole Place; blind but somehow helping her; old but dying to be young; dead and dying to be born again. Then she went winging over forests, over hills, until abruptly she found herself above a seashore under barren crags. Amid a violent storm a man danced howling. At his feet lay a headless corpse and a golden lyre. In one hand he shook a severed human head, in the other a bloody sword. 'ORF WITH HIS HEAD!' he was screaming as the cruel wind threw him this way and that – then he tripped over the headless corpse, falling so hard he lost both the sword and the head. Instantly the wind snatched the head and whirled it away up the crags. Back came the wind, eagerly attacking, spinning him round so that she saw his shocked glazed eyes …

'Dad!' she cried, but he didn't hear … and she saw how, on the finger of the hand that had held the head, sparkled the emerald ring!

It swooped at her. *It's on my finger too!* A bright mouth opened, Beast-wind raging in it, Sam wailing 'ORF WITH HIS HEAD!' as she found herself staggering alongside him. Without thinking she grabbed the sword. 'ORF WITH HIS HEAD!' they wailed together, staggering through the green scream to the cliff, Beast-storm beating at her as through them she realised:

The Stone's found itself! But …

The scream reached a crescendo. The Beast-mouth opened. Into it she shot to a deeper depth of forgetting, of Beast-dream.

Clouds swirl black over miles of red-shot city roofs and towers that pack the roads to exhausted horizons. On rushing wind like a broomstick witch. Into the past of Last Days memory. Looming faces. Doctor Isaacs asking her about her burning man dreams. Creep! Wet spaniel eyes agleam. '*And does he DO anything when he, um, embraces you, Chrissa?*' YUK! And pounding, pounding. The green scream strobing. King's Head disco Thursday night with Jane and Clara. They sit at a table with the lightshow pulsing, flickering over their faces, some lank old leather creep monopolising the videojuke with Springsteen's 'Born in the USA'. 'My Dad calls it "penile swagger"!' she howls. Jane and Clara collapse in giggles. Yet she's nervous, hanging onto her tight-wrapped brolly as if for dear life.

'Hullo, sweetness.' A voice in her ear, as slick and hard as oil on iron. With a start she looks up into the fierce dark eyes of the kid who's always bothering her, the kid with the Cap'n Sinbad tee-shirt.

'You can bugger off for a start!' she retorts in his face.

Smiling, he leans closer. 'Saw your dad tonight, sweet thing.'

She sways away. Yuk! His hair gleaming slick with wet-look gunk!

'He's in trouble, your dad is. The Old Bill's nicked 'im!'

'What?' Clutching her brolly like a sword she jumps up, pulls him away from Jane and Clara. He stinks of rotting roses. 'Well, go on, tell me!'

The kid grins, evil. 'Had a bloke's head in a bag, dinne?'

'Creep!' She raises the brolly … *and was suddenly on a mountain ledge waving a sword at – she heard a distant voice. 'Joana! Joana!'*

She lowers the brolly, shivering. 'I don't believe you, creep!'

'Check the Blackstock Road nick. See if I'm wrong. That's a

pretty ring on your finger, sweetness! If you want to …'

She flees home. Dad's not there. Mum's out. Thursday. Peace Group. Soon in a daze she finds herself at the door of the Blackstock Road Police Station. Rain drizzles through dim light shed by twin gaslamps. A beefy bobby on duty under them smiles and tips his helmet. He's bald.

'Sergeant Dixon, miss. And what can I do for you?'

'Please sir …' – Chrissa furls her brolly – '… My Dad's here.'

'Your dad?' beams the bobby. 'What's his name, then?'

'Please sir, his name's Mr Samuel Joyce, of …'

'Sorry miss.' Sergeant Dixon frowns. 'Afraid he's got to swing. Eight prompt tomorrow. Nothing I can do. Better run along home.'

'Swing? what do you mean?'

''Ang by the neck till 'e's dead, miss.'

'But …' – she gapes – '… there's no more hanging in England!'

'Where 'ave you been, miss? Times've changed. Sorry!'

'I must see him!' she cries … and his eyes gleam on the ring.

'What a pretty ring!' He smiles. 'Where did you get sssomething like that? Give me that ring, sssweet miss, confidential-like, and maybe …'

'No!' She jumps away, ready to flee. The bobby's smile broadens.

'This way, miss.' He holds out a hand. 'Take your brolly?'

'No! I'll carry it myself!'

What am I doing? Clutching the brolly she follows the bobby through empty yellow corridors to a door which he opens with a giant iron key.

'In here, miss.' He smiles. 'Ten minutesss.'

'*CHRISSA, BE CAREFUL!*' cries a voice. '*SEE WHAT'S GOING ON!*'

'What's the matter?' asks the bobby. 'Don't you want to sssee daddy?'

'Of course I do,' she says coldly. Into the cell she marches … and as the door slams behind her she's fully aware that she walks into a trap.

And there, naked and bruised on the floor under the dim cobwebby light in the attic at 15 Berkeley Road, Sam lies moaning, empty whisky bottle by him, eyes glazed, right hand slack, left clenched tight over the emerald ring as he mutters: 'ORF WITH HIS HEAD! ORF WITH HIS HEAD!'

Dropping the brolly, she throws herself down by him amid the clutter of three-legged chairs and broken tennis rackets, shaking him hard –

Then his eyes focussed on her –

And through them she fell into –

... The huge wave curling above her head, high above the skeletons of fire-blackened buildings, frothing lip black with debris, its roar louder even than the wind that came in the wake of the fire in the night. So high in the sky, crashing down on her, on all the dead who lie about; it'll wash the whole world clean! Terror seizes her as, with the wave plunging, the wind before it blows a face at her; a poster from the Last Days ... and as it falls she reads: SOON! CAP'N SINBAD IN 'BEAT THE BEAST' AT DINGWALLS!

Then Cap'n Sinbad peels off his black-and-white mask and –

Hissinggrabbingpumping!

A bruising blow. She's on her back, Sam naked astride her with the eyes of a beast, tearing the clothes off her and –

A bright light burst in her like a starshell –

'*CHRISSA!*' she heard. '*THE EYES OF THE BEAST! SEE THROUGH THE ...*'

Remembering, she looked ... and found herself on her back on a ledge on a crag of the Panting Cliff, Sam astride her, but no, not Sam, Azazel, at her with his lust, beady cockerel eyes wet and wide, forked tongue flickering from quivering beak, knee trying to force her thighs apart as jelly fingers slobbered on her and the stench of rotten roses made her gag.

'*GIVE ME THE RING, CHILD! THAT'S ALL I WANT!*'

Then she saw Cap'n Sinbad unmasked as he slobbered and pumped. She saw Sam's face lost in his leer like a frozen wail. *Absurd!* she told herself. She made herself smile. 'Oh stop!' she whimpered, 'You're so strong! I'll give you the ring ... if you'll show me your true, your handsome real shape!' At which Azazel leaned back and howled (if in pleasure or pain she didn't know or care) as she tore her hand free, got the ring to her brow, and –

From the Sinking Ways she looks.

First she sees the bloody sword, lying where she let the brolly fall.

NOW she sees further. NOW she sees Tiy, weak and blind and cold at the Whole Place, the Beast's army at Her gate ... and Tiy, touched by the warmth of Chrissa's youth, smiled ... then moaned as she left Her to Her despair.

NOW she sees Diane in Last Days Edinburgh!

Diane, tired from sleepless nights, temping in an office today ...

And Diane choked with shock. For suddenly through McRae PLC's sales forecasts for 1999 on her green screen she saw Chrissa – the NEW Chrissa, black-robed, hair a mess, that awful ring on her finger – and Chrissa was fighting a writhing mist from which faces glared . . . and one of them was Sam's face! But as soon as it appeared, the vision faded. Left with the sales projections Diane stared, first at her VDU screen, then through the grimy winter window up at the obdurate bulk of Edinburgh Castle on its rock – then, gorge heaving with shock, she stumbled to the toilet as . . .

NOW – hunting, hunting – Pierre! Where are you? And she finds him, also on a mountain ledge, but so far away at Montségur, and caught in a dream! 'WAKE UP,' she cries, 'HURRY UP!' she cried. '*SHEPHERD, I NEED YOU AGAIN!*' And Pierre started, looked up, and got to his feet as . . .

. . . the green scream wails too loud, tearing her back to the war.

Through chaos she falls . . . past a severed head. In a field of light it floats, blue eyes so bright! And its lips move, it speaks urgently . . . but amid the clamour she can't hear a word as sudden stench invades her . . .

'WHAT ABOUT FATHER BERNARD?' crowed Cap'n Sinbad, panting triumphantly above her where she lay on the ledge. '*CAN'T HE HELP YOU, SWEETNESS . . .?*'

'Oh no!' she cried – and again she lost control, falling back to –

'ORF WITH HIS HEAD!' Sam chants madly. 'ORF WITH HIS HEAD!'

On her back in the attic she finds herself fighting with Sam's mad, sweating, Beast-ridden face above her. '*SWEETNESS!*' he hisses, red eyes hot with lust, and beating at him she shouts: 'I hate you!'

So the black tide drowned her deeper. Beast-voices gleefully shouting 'HATE! HATE! HATE!' engulfed her. Feebly she clawed at his face –

The ring flashed. '*WAKE UP, CHILD!*' cried her deepest voice.

In its depths like a lifeline she saw those bright blue eyes.

So who fears who? the Shining One demands. *Take a good look!*

She took a deep breath; again she faced that monstrous face heaving above her . . . and behind the mask of lust she saw the self-contempt, the battle going on . . . and the fear . . . of her.

I'm the Beast to him as he is to me! she realised, utterly astonished. *The Beast wins by making us fight each other. But then how can we . . .?*

'Your head!' the head whispers. '*Like mine. It's the only way!*'

What do you mean? But she knew. And she was terrified.

And Dion's smile says what has to be can only be if she has . . . faith.

Absolute faith. She groaned, and saw the face of Mother Fabrisse, not supernal and shining at all, but screaming with pain . . . and the agony wasn't just in the fire, it was in the DOUBT! That the sacrifice meant nothing!

But as the Beast tore at her Chrissa realised:

If there's nothing, then there's nothing to lose!

She told herself, *Chrissa this is it. Ready or not . . .*

Summoning her strength, into the slathering idiot face above her she said, very calmly: 'Sam! Wake up! The Beast apes us! To me he's you, to you he's me! What you see's not me, it's Beast-projection. Illusion, Dad! You must slay it to beat him!' She laughed in sheer terror. He gaped at her. 'So take that sword and cut off my head and keep cutting, whatever you see! But start with me! Dad, do it! Cut off my head! Now!'

Then Sam broke out. He'd found himself shocked and naked on the cot in his attic cell, riding his own daughter! Even as he'd found himself on her he'd thought: *This isn't me. This isn't her. It can't be!*

Yet even as he'd rejected this incestuous vision the sweet child below him had turned into a terrible splendid furnace, fired from head to toe in the blood of red ochre ... and there he was again in the depths of the Whole Place, riding Tiy, riding to glory, exploding from the constrictions of the Hidden World so ecstatically that all his moral doubt and horror was lost as soon as found. '*MORALITY'S FOR WEAKLINGS!*' the Beast in him had roared. '*RULES MEAN NOTHING TO THE STRONG. DO AS YOU WILL – THAT'S THE LAW! TAKE HER! SCREW THE WEAK ONES! THAT'S WHAT THEY'RE FOR!*'

But then she met his eyes and offered her neck.

'Cut off my head!' she cried. 'Now!'

And then for the first time Azazel lost him. But –

'ORF WITH YOUR HEAD?' he asked, and cackled stupidly –

'Dad! Did you hear me?' Crushed by his weight she lay. On the ledge. On the cot. 'Do you see the sword? There! Use it. Now!'

He looked. He saw the sword. But mist obscured him, wind tore at him. He fought to remember. Bit by bit, fighting something he couldn't see, it came back. Azazel fooling him with Chrissa crossing the road. Dion's death. Chrissa at Montségur. Leaving her with Pierre; chasing the Beast into ... Beast-trap. Losing Dion's head – and his own. Pandemonium on the street. Now ... storm-wrapped high on a windy ledge astride a scared young woman, angry ocean waves breaking far below. *Where am I?* And he told himself: *At the Panting Cliff! I came here to beat the Beast.* But ... and a voice had ... The sword! Yes! There! And as if down the wrong end of a telescope he saw himself now, straining for it, the wind fighting him every inch. He saw how he turned *his* head, pushed out *his* arm and *his* fingers.

Now he has it! Hand round the hilt. The left hand!

The ring. On his index finger it flared into sudden focus, the emerald a hungry eye. It leapt at him, blinding, expanding, and –

A massive electrical jolt. Then he was fully awake.

On a ledge, clutching a sword, astride her.

On her finger as on his the ring sparkled.

He stared at her in disbelief. Chrissa stared back … real, solid … her skin brown with wind and sun, eyes as blue as Dion's, hair a mess, black robe torn, hands rough with work. *No*, he thought. *Another Beastie dream. It must be. She's at Montségur! Another projection. That creep!*

Yet even as he cursed he realised what she'd said.

'ORF WITH HER HEAD! ORF WITH HER HEAD! ORF WITH …'

With the bloody sword in his hands he eyed her wildly. Again he grew giddy. Again he finds himself in the attic. With a hot grin he rubs the silken brolly down her thigh. '*A PRETTY SWORD, SSSWEETNESSS!*'

'Dad!' Desperately, seeing him still lost, his so-solid form astride her writhing between Sam and the cockerel-head, she tried again. 'Dad, I'm no more here in the flesh than we're in the attic,' she said firmly.

Sam flinched, drew sharp breath, looked at the sword in his hands and then at her. But his face twisted and she knew the Beast had seized him again.

'*DO THIS TO ME AND YOU'LL SUFFER FOREVER,*' Azazel muttered.

She laughed. She held the ring up to his face:

'Dad!' she shouted. 'Samjoyce! Wake up! Do it! Strike now!'

He snapped out of the attic. He saw her. Fear seized him. 'You can't mean it,' he said. 'Cut off your head?' – and he pinched her arm.

'O ' she cried crossly. His eyes widened in horror.

'But … Chrissa …' he managed, 'you're really here! I can't …'

'No! It's a projection. Part mine, part yours! The Beast uses our own dreams! Dad, I'm here, but not – you know – in the flesh! Now do it!'

Yet as she said this she felt all too present in the flesh. Hard rock digging into her back, sour salt storm whipping spray in her face, his body so heavy astride her … and the ring … the ring … but …

Am I still at Montségur? she wondered. *What if the Stone's brought me all the way through without need of a Gate? Maybe I've never been properly earthed. Oh, Pierre … where are you?*

'I think you're really here,' he said harshly. 'I can't …'

'No I'm not!' she moaned, shutting her eyes. 'Do it!'

'How can I?' he demanded incredulously, fearing that he could.

'I can't stand this! Drop the questions and do it!'

MAN WHO CUT OFF HIS DAUGHTER'S HEAD ON "BEAT THE BEAST"! – TONITE!'

That did it. This foul place where Azazel roosted – and even as she cried out and Sam with a terrible answering cry raised the sword, his eyes fixed on her now, she saw Cap'n Sinbad laugh, and wondered: *Oh Chrissa, what have you done? It's finer than I thought. If he strikes as Sam, that's right. But if he's the Beast in the moment that he …*

Above her now the flickering faces and forms …

'No!' she heard Sam roar. 'No! You won't …'

'Pierre!' she cried out as the sword came down, and then –

41.
Cutting Through

'Where?' demanded Pierre, pulling Bishop Bertrand after him up the stairs in the keep. 'Where is she? Why did she go without me?'

'The spirit called her,' said Bertrand.

'Which spirit? The Beast? Why didn't you stop her?'

'Stop her?' Bertrand asked as they reached the top landing. 'Haven't *you* tried often enough?'

'So I have,' Pierre admitted angrily. 'But where is she?'

'In here.' The Bishop nodded. 'Be calm now.'

But Pierre was not calm, and became less so after he threw the door wide open. With a cry he threw up his arms, reeling into the Bishop who, white with shock, staggered and almost fell back down the staircase.

'In the Name of God what have I done?' Bertrand muttered, swallowing.

For the room was ablaze with green fire. It crackled and danced from every corner and form and shape, hissing a song that hurt the head. It was so blinding bright that initially to Pierre the four human figures in it seemed no more than dark two-dimensional negatives. Three were on the floor, two unmoving, one crawling feebly for the door. The fourth ...

'She's opened a gate!' Pierre cried in terror. Dropping to his knees with a hand over his eyes he crawled into the furnace, making for the heart of it where Chrissa sat slumped in a chair. For in a whirling dance from the ring she wore poured tongues and sheets of emerald fire, flaming about her like a living robe, coruscating into a vortex above her head ... a vortex sucking her out of this world. For though amid the fire her face remained lividly visible, congested with rapidly shifting, violent emotions, it and her entire form appeared increasingly evanescent, ghost-like, and somehow *elongated* – as though her physical substance were being drawn into that coronal vortex through which her soul had already departed.

'Why didn't you wait for me?' Pierre cried, his searching hand meeting Bernard's prone form. But no reply came. Clenching his teeth he crawled deeper into the green scream, enduring the pain in his bones until it grew so bad that briefly he lost his wits and found himself back at the Gate of the Stone, crawling over Her teeth with Her visions driving him mad . . . then with a shake of the head he drove out the past. Again he snatched a look. Her ghost-face was twisted in fear and rage, silently wailing. 'Serves you right!' he shouted. 'Bitten off more than you can chew again, eh?' He crawled closer, sobbing with pain. 'So is this it? Off without so much as a goodbye and thanks-very-much, Pierre?' But still she writhed, her dissolution continuing apace. Falteringly she raised her transparent, elongated left hand . . . and as the ring screamed at Pierre's he forced himself to his feet and shouted: 'It's not good enough! You said we'd work together, and so we must! Chrissa! You can't go without me!'

Then Bertrand, praying at the door, saw the shepherd lurch up against the emerald light, momentarily eclipsing it – and plunge into it with an incoherent yell. The fire roared up brighter than ever . . . and the Bishop saw the two of them outlined, silhouettes embracing in the heart of it – one pale and almost gone, the other solidly dark. Peering through shaking fingers he saw one feed the other with substance at a loss to itself, and he marvelled, thinking with his usual remote calm: *Shepherd, it's as well you're unlettered. The Evangelist might have dissuaded you! 'Do not hold on to me, because I have not yet gone back up to the Father.'*

His thoughts were interrupted.

As if the walls of Montségur and this world itself were suddenly ripped away he found himself gazing at a wild sea-grit place, at a man's grim face, at a shining sword, flashing down . . . then in Pierre's arms the Chrissa-form twisted violently as briefly (the Bishop saw it) her head leapt mouthing from her shoulders into the whirling emerald vortex. But Pierre (what did he do? Later he couldn't tell, nor could Chrissa) seized it back as he pulled her closer and cried: 'No! No! That's a demon! Here you are! You're here! With me! With Pierre! I'm here with you at Montségur!' Yet even as, eyes shut, he dragged her back to safety, he heard Bertrand cry out. He opened his eyes . . . and yelled in horror. For both of them saw the livid scar that leapt round the whiteness of her back-flung neck. A snake striking from nowhere; a sudden black-welted necklace. Her eyes opened, she choked, her hands leapt to her neck as if she was being strangled. In fear they waited. But there it stopped. 'She lives,' Pierre cried, aghast 'but if I hadn't got here! Why did you let her go? Why did you ...?'

Again she spasmed, writhing more solidly now in his arms as the fire from the ring began to fail, bursting out in darkening clots, soon ceasing altogether. The lamplit room returned to normal. With a sigh of relief Pierre relaxed, briefly shut his eyes, aware only that though Chrissa lay limp she was solid and breathing again. He laid her down in the chair. That sword flashing down. That writhing form from which he'd snatched her in the nick of time. 'I thought you were gone,' he whispered. Behind him Corba stirred ... though Bernard and Esclarmonde lay still as he looked accusingly up at the Bishop.

Bertrand met his glare. 'She insisted on it,' said the Bishop. 'She didn't want to go without you but said she must. It was plain she couldn't survive unaided. I agreed with the goodman that the Stone must be risked.'

'The *Stone* must be risked!' Pierre laughed madly. 'And her?'

Bertrand's smile was thin. 'She wore it before. It's the Stone that brought her to us! The Stone that lets us see what the Watchers do!'

Pierre scowled at her scar. Though hideous, it had grown no worse. And on her finger, the ring. 'It nearly took her head,' he said.

'So it did,' said Bertrand. Corba sat up. 'So it did. And don't we all face that? And worse.' Esclarmonde groaned. A sudden gust banged the shutters ... and through the wind from the far end of the castle Pierre heard the distant crump of rock from the trebuchet. Belatedly he remembered the other battle they fought, here at Montségur. And what was to happen. Soon. Dizziness seized him as he tried to make sense of the many spheres of this war.

Of course she couldn't have gone this time, he told himself. *First she has to fulfil what brought her here. But ...*

'... Barbican ...' croaked Chrissa, eyes flicking open and shut again.

'What?' Pierre started. 'What's that, my ...'

'The barbican,' she croaked again. Distress twisted her face; her left hand went to the scar round her neck ... and Pierre's jaw dropped to see how, as the emerald brushed it, the scar vanished as rapidly and mysteriously as it had come. She breathed deeply; as she exhaled her eyes opened again, startlingly present. She saw Pierre. Quickly she reached up to touch his unshaven cheek ... then gasped, shuddered, and sat up. By lamplight she took in the room, saw Corba and Bertrand trying to revive Bernard as Esclarmonde sat up, rubbing her head. 'Is everyone all right?' she asked nervously, in her normal voice, and again unconsciously her hand touched her neck and her head, as if at some level not sure of either. 'Oh my goodness but that was too much for a Friday night!' she told Pierre with a shaky laugh. 'You know I never could stand Cap'n Sinbad, and ...'

Again Pierre heard the crash of rock from the trebuchet.

'What did you say about the barbican?' he interrupted.

With a sharp intake of breath she pulled herself together.

'They've taken it,' she said bleakly. 'I saw as I returned. Men up the cliff, knifed the sentries, and took it. They're at the walls now.' Her eyes glazed, again she touched her throat. 'I hear the Beast laugh!' she whispered, and shook off Pierre's hand. 'No, I'm all right! Pierre, he knows he can't be beaten in this world. Trump him and he cheats. He's everywhere!' Tears squeezed from her eyes. 'He's here now, outside! He took the barbican as Sam and I fought him! And he had us fooled! He had us so wrapped up that ... Pierre, if you hadn't ...'

'You shouldn't have gone without me,' he said.

'I couldn't wait.' She met his eyes. 'I had to go.'

'And did it work? Has your daddy seen through the Beast?'

'We'll only know when IT happens and we go,' she whispered.

IT. He knew what she meant. It meant more and worse than this. It meant something still so vague in his understanding that even after these events he scarcely knew if he believed in it, or in his part in it.

They fell silent, caught ever closer to the fulfilment of her dreams of the burning man as Bernard stirred at last. Through the wind and the crump of the trebuchet they heard the clamour of war. And they knew that Pierre-Roger would not recapture the barbican on that or any other night. For now the time of the Feast of Light approached.

'Mad!' Diane muttered, trembling in the office loo, aware she couldn't stay too long. But what if when she returned to the VDU she saw more wild stuff through the sales figures? Sam and Chrissa and God knew what. She knew she'd just have to face it. The work was awful but all she could get since her nerve had broken that fearful night of the battle on the lake, of the Beast-attack. Temping for a firm making tartan condoms! With winter near she'd need every penny for the electric ... if the grid didn't overload and break down for a week in January like last year. The worst January since records began ... pensioners had died in thousands. New Ice Age, freak storms, all of it. Something to do with the circumpolar vortex and the last hundred years being unusually fine: back to normality, etcetera. She'd read about it, and it was nice, knowing it was all you could expect and a fate common to all, glaciers soon grinding down Scotland again – though no doubt they'd leave the south well alone. Just typical! But that didn't help keep a body warm ... though there were plenty of folk about to tell you that hating the English on a half-bottle of Highland Mist was a whole lot better than no fire at all on a wintry night with the wind doing a jig on the stair.

Oh, what are you on about, Diane? she thought irritably, head in hands as she sat in the stall. Someone rattled the door.

'Are you planning your holiday in there?'

'Just a minute and I'll be out.'

'Don't hurry yersel, hen!'

I'll HEN you! she thought even as she realised that what really scared her was not what she'd seen on the VDU but the fact that she'd seen it while incontestably, indubitably awake; three coffees already down the hatch on a dreich grey day in a shabby office on Lothian Road.

One moment, sales forecasts for tartan condoms.

The next, Chrissa fighting the Beast.

And Sam's face ... and the sword ...

Still she felt weak. 'Now get a grip,' she told herself as the doorknob rattled again and a loud voice outside said:

'She must be dead, she's been in there that long.'

'I'm coming!' she called.

'Well now, you're safe with this firm, hen!' – and giggles broke out, abruptly stifled as Diane marched out and down the shabby corridor back to her VDU, face like thunder as the office manager intercepted her.

'Is everything all right, Mrs ... um ...?'

'Joyce,' she supplied, rapidly re-entering the file she'd been working on. 'Mrs Diane Joyce. No, everything is not all right. I know I'm only temporary here ... but I do expect to be able to go to the ...'

She stopped. Her mouth hung open. She stared at the screen. 'Oh my God!' she muttered. The manager peered close. He saw only figures.

'Oh no!' she said, and her hand flew to her mouth. 'Sam, don't ...'

'Mrs Joyce, is something the matter?'

She didn't hear him. With terror in her eyes she stared at the 1999 sales forecasts. Ten minutes later, even as the manager rang her agency, she was on Lothian Road, bewildered and out of work again.

42.
The Forty-Nine Heads

For highlit in blazing emerald through the figures on her VDU she'd seen Sam agonised amid the writhing mist, cutting down at Chrissa's neck with the sword. A wonder she didn't scream.

Sam did. The moment he cut he knew: *Fooled again! This IS Chrissa!* But too late. He was committed. Taishi's father's sword cut as easily into Chrissa's neck as it had through Dion's. Yet even as he struck and the Beast's laughter echoed round the Panting Cliff, a gaunt tall man appeared from nowhere. Into the blazing radiance he stumbled, wrapping his arms round her and pulling her away with a furious cry … and abruptly Azazel's laughter was stilled, for the stranger seemed to … to *dissolve* her in his embrace, to spin her round some unseen corner into invisibility. For suddenly she was gone. Just a sparkle of emerald to show where …

Shivering Sam sank to the ledge, sword in his lap. Owned by the Beast! Sadistic lust to see blood gout. But he had no chance to rest or work out what had happened, for immediately Tiy appeared before him, regal in Her Gown-of-the-Feathers-of-many-bright-Birds, solid and glaring. 'Failed again, Fool!' She cried, dark eyes flashing. 'Didn't I tell you to …'

Yet even as She mocked him he saw blue eyes and heard: '… *So take that sword and cut off my head and keep cutting, whatever you see!*' And he realised: 'You're not Tiy!' He tensed. 'Just more Beast-projection.'

'Fool!' She reached out. 'Now give me the ring and …'

With a shout he leapt to his feet and swung the sword. Tiy's head fell at his feet. Everything changed. Blood spattered the cackling *tricoteuses* knitting below the guillotine. '*Two down!*' whispered a voice.

Bewildered he saw blue eyes. '*Forty-seven more! Don't let his false shapes fool you. Cut! Keep cutting.*' And hooded in black he stood on the scaffold as from the tumbril Diane came up, arms bound, neck bare, red hair neatly coiffed and capped in white ... and she knew him. Quietly laying her head on the block, she whispered: 'May God forgive you, Samjoyce, for I cannot!'

'VIVE LA REVOLUTION!' he yelled – and a roar went up as the bright blade plunged and Diane's head tumbled into the gory basket, the gorgeous wig, her last vain secret, falling pathetically away as it did ...

He wiped his brow and groaned for now before him ...

'Glad to see we're still headhunting, Mr Joyce,' she said in that well-known husky voice, 'but what are we doing with the capital? Using it to get ahead and make Britain great again? – or are we a moaning minnie?'

'Fook aff!' screamed McSam the Tartan Terror. Lurching he cut – once, twice, three times. Blue blood welted in gouts – but now before him –

Stood himself. Samjoyce. The fool who walked about with severed heads in carrier bags, who'd Beaten the Beast but insulted the Queen. Now as the prison clock struck eight he came to the scaffold surrounded by warders and the governor and a muttonchop whiskered minister droning from the Book of Common Prayer. They led him up to the trap; his hands were tied; the noose was set about his neck as the minister begged him to repent. The governor met him manfully in the eye and said: 'You can still save yourself. Give Her Majesty the ring and she'll grant you her royal pardon.' Then his composure broke. 'Save yourself, man!' he cried.

But Sam shook his head. He stood calm without apparent fear ... and as they set the black hood over his head he eyed his executioner and said:

'Do your business well, Mr Pierrepoint.'

'*Now!*' urged the blue-eyed voice. '*Make it five!*'

But for the first time in his career Sam Pierrepoint hesitated. With his hand on the lever he began to tremble and sweat.

'Do it, man!' cried Samjoyce. 'For the sake of my soul!'

'Amen!' cried the minister as the trapdoor opened. He fell. Searing pain leapt across his throat; gripping his throat he staggered and choked into the parlour of the Kebab Kave where Cap'n Sinbad shrugged and said:

'Listen, mister, it's time we worked something out.'

'Like an *ex capita* payment?' yelled Sam, enraged – and Cap'n Sinbad bit the dust. Sam subsided gasping. Taishi stood apologetically before him.

'My father's sword,' the old man said. 'It's not meant to be used for this sort of passionless mass execution; it was meant for nobler …'

'Not you too,' groaned Sam, but nonetheless he did the job – then he groaned again, for now Zoe lay before him, pale on her sickbed.

'Why did you lead us into this, you Fool?' she cried. 'Don't you see? – you're just a Fool, you can't beat the …'

And Sam cut, and weeping he cut again. Then he saw Deru.

'*Eight down, forty-one to go*,' the blue-eyes whispered.

'She's right!' the half-free insisted, misshapen face pleading. 'You can't kill Death! The best you can do is reach a temporary arrangement.'

'I PISS on your temporary arrangement, Azazel!' Sam panted. He cut Deru down then rested on the sword, giddy and delirious. 'Come on, you vain, stupid, greedy coward! Stop hiding behind others! Show yourself!'

'Names, names! Tut!' From the wind-torn mists, a scolding voice … and there before him lounged the beautiful naked youth, eyeing Sam with cold disapproval. 'Do you mean all that?' he asked. 'You'd chop me too?'

'Damn right!' Breathing hard Sam advanced, and swung, and missed.

'No, really,' said Azazel complacently, 'you didn't quite under …'

Sam howled, and swiped, and missed again.

'… stand,' the Beast went on, shaking his head sadly. 'You're so negative about me! I just do a job. You think I cause all the pain in the world? That's stupid! How could I persuade the human race that …'

He paused. His eyes widened in alarm. Samjoyce was staring not at him but into the depths of the emerald ring.

Blue eyes. Dion. Chrissa. Keep cutting, they told him.

'Listen,' he said, extending a hand, 'I think you and I could …'

'Take a cut!' roared Sam as he sliced again, this time with such power that the head of the beautiful youth sprang off his shoulders … but the mists writhed and the giant blue Beast appeared, cockerel head and all.

'*GETTING TIRED, SAMJOYCE?*' Azazel hissed down at him, his

beady eyes glinting. '*YOU'RE SSSAVING ME TIME AND EFFFFORT BY DESSSTROYING YOURSELF!*'

'You bloody oversized broiler!' Sam shouted, and reaching up he cut and cut again. But with every cut two new heads leapt from the gouting neck of each head severed. Soon twenty writhed about him, each bright-eyed with new delusions. Yet he cut. He cut and cut as from the shore below belled trumpets: looking down he saw Azazel's army through the mists. '*Ignore it! Keep cutting!*' said the blue-eyes in him, '*Sixteen down! Thirty-three to go!*' And he saw that the army below was oddly vague; realised that the trumpets might only be gulls mewling from offshore stacks ... yet as he cut each new head he grew more exhausted and sick in soul. dreaming madly that he was the executioner of human progress, a murdering Fool of terminal Last Days self-celebration. Yet though the Beast laughed still the blue-eyes cried: '*Cut! Twenty! Twenty-one! Keep cutting!*' – and, staggering as his delirium grew, he cut. '*DEATH GUARANTEES LIFE!*' hissed the dying heads. '*YOU'LL HAVE TO CHOP FOREVER TO BEAT ME THIS WAY, FOOL!*' Yet on and on he hacked, eyes gleaming, body slimy with gore; and as he hacked he heard his own voice sing: 'Death needs Life to kill and eat! And Life needs death to grow! Death needs life up on its feet, or supper cooks too slow!' And with a horrified cackle he added: 'Always cut below the bud, create vigour through denial! For the life of man, like a rose from mud, finds its meaning in Death's Trial!'

Before him a sun blazed bright. White light seared him. Dazed he saw standing nearby a tender, terrified boy-plant in Pharaonic robes.

He cut without mercy at that royal throat.

'*YOU JUST CUT TUT!*' cried a voice. '*THAT'S HOW WE PUT THE SUN TO BED!*'

He stood before a blazing house and roared:

'I am Cylon! That is the house of Pythagoras, and he's in it!'

Yet from the inferno he heard Pythagoras call back:

'*FOOL! I HAVE SEEN CAMBYSES INVADE EGYPT! I HAVE SEEN THE DAUGHTER OF THE PHARAOH CLOTHED IN RAGS! IN PRISON IN BABYLON I SAT WITH THE MAGI! I HAVE RUN WITH THE SERPENT AND ...*' – emerald light flashed from the inferno – '*... I HAVE THE EMERALD TABLET OF HERMES! FROM THE DEAD I HAVE SEEN THE LIVING SPRING! SO HOW CAN YOU HURT ME, YOU BEAST?*'

'Like this!' howled Sam the Beast, and charged, and as Pythagoras fell in delirious succession new heads appeared. He gave Cleopatra the asp; tore Hypatia's flesh from her bones; in Persia he flayed Mani; in Rome he began to lose his wits. Sent to assassinate a King Dagobert he did it but later in guilt slit his own neck. '*Twenty-seven! Twenty-eight!* cried the blue-eyes. '*Keep going!*' So he gagged, lurched, spun about on the ledge of the Panting Cliff, striking now without sense or reason, chopping whatever appeared. By its very existence it must be hostile! CUT CUT CUT! Nothing is true! Hashishin sneaking into Damascus to kill the caliph, the Old Man promising paradise. Striding up the choir of Canterbury to chop the head of the meddlesome priest! Sacking Béziers, Toulouse, Carcassonne! Seizing the barbican at Montségur where . . .

A flaming man appeared before him.

'Joana's safe,' said the burning man. 'She'll meet you when it's time.'

'*CHOP THAT HEAD TOO!*' cried the Beast.

Sam lowered the sword but not his eyes.

'No!' he cried as the blue-eyes burst in him. 'Not him!'

'*Cut! Cut! Cut!*' cried the blue-eyes. '*Make it thirty-three!*'

'Let's get on with it,' Sam groaned . . . and so the Beast came on again, every head with a new persuasion as Sam wearily cut. Revolution, freedom movement, the liberty of man. ORF WITH THE HEAD of King Charles, Admiral Byng, Charlotte Corday. In peeler's blue he found himself ranked against Chartist crowds; as the Boche charged he went up over the wire. '*Forty!*' blue-eyes confided as he sank the ice-pick in Trotsky's skull; '*forty-one!*' as he shelled Allende's palace to ruin. '*Another eight to go! Seven sevens – that's the number to beat the Beast. Now . . .*'

'NO!' Megaphone bellow over the world. 'ENOUGH! TOO MUCH!'

His mother appeared. He cut. His father. He cut. The heroes of his youth, his first lover: he cut and cut and cut . . .

'*NO!*' Again that roar of pain. '*ENOUGH! YOU'VE BEATEN ME, SAMJOYCE! NOW WHAT DO YOU WANT? YOU'VE CUT ME SEVEN TIMES SEVEN!*'

'*Not so!*' cried the blue eyes urgently as the wind dropped and before him now Sam saw no more opposition. He was alone on the ledge. A path led up. Below, the shore was empty. There was no army. He sighed in relief, ignoring the blue-eyes as he started up the path. '*Don't let him fool you! That's only forty-eight! You'll have to cut again!*'

'Get lost!' Sam sighed, and climbed to the top of the Panting Cliff.

He stood gazing over dark boggy moorland. For a moment before him he saw, superimposed glamorously on this land of bare rock and peat-hag, the bright fantastic towers, gardens and winding galleries of a palatial city.

For just a moment it enchanted him. Then he shook his head.

'It's not like that,' he shouted at the moor. 'Now show yourself!'

Nothing happened. Nothing moved but gulls mewling on updraughts from the ocean far below. A crow flapped slowly across the dreary sky.

Leaning on Taishi's sword he shouted again:

'Come on! Show yourself, if you dare! You said you'd take us to the Sometimes Isle if I beat you! Now keep your word and let's make a deal!'

'Stop shouting!' demanded a bad-tempered, crabby old man's voice from behind him. 'What do you mean, I gave my word? I said MAYBE!'

Sam whirled, sword at the ready. *Careful!* warned blue-eyes.

'Yes, all right!' the old man said testily, waving him back. 'So you've made your point; here I am; and whaddaya want?'

Sam gaped. *Surely not ...!* Quickly he looked in the emerald ... and in the depths saw the same rheumy-eyed old man, fists clenched, brows knotted in grievance against the world, spindly shanks clad in stinking goatskin, no shoes on his bog-brown feet. *His true shape?* Sam wondered, perplexed –

In that moment of doubt Azazel attacked, physically, with a desperate but agile skill, throwing Sam off balance, grappling for the sword.

'*Get him off the ground, or he'll have you!*' cried the blue-eyes.

But Sam was exhausted. 'First the sword ... then the ring!' the old man panted, spraying him with triumphant spittle, throwing Sam on his back and half-wrestling the sword from his hands. 'You did well, Fool, but not well enough! Can't you count? Forty-eight is NOT seven sevens! We MUSSST obey the Rules, mustn't we?' He grabbed for the ring. 'Now give me ...'

'What rules?' gasped Sam as he heaved and tried to throw the old man off. 'What rules did you ever ...?' – but with every second Azazel weighed more, his shape shifting, growing gigantic again as he pinned Sam down, tugging at the ring. 'Sorry, Mr Samjoyce!' he crowed, forcing Sam's arm across his face so that the emerald floated before his eyes, and –

The white light burst! Blue-eyes! Sam's head roared; he found himself deep in Shemyaza's cell, deep in the Hidden Place; he saw Chrissa and the shepherd in tight embrace on a black rock amid a dark pool. Emerald and violet they flamed even as faces screamed from another fire, a mortal fire from which a great voice cried: '*Hear me, Joana! Hear me in the Light of the Shining Ones!*' Then it cried: '*WE BURN WE BURN WE ARE BURNING MELTING WE ARE OH CHRIST!*' – and the fire of the Feast of Light poured through Sam as he lay pinned down by Azazel. From the earth below it erupted through him, it burst from him as he bellowed angrily and heaved; as he surged to his feet gripping the old man round the waist, as he staggered and held on though Azazel beat at him with increasingly feeble blows as gulls mewled on the wind above – until with the old man light as a feather Sam dropped him and, before Azazel had the chance to shift, seized the sword and chopped.

'*Forty-nine!*' cried blue-eyes. '*That's IT!*'

And the flames roared up as Sam, panting, saw the headless corpse of the old man fade, to be instantly replaced by ...

'Oh no,' he groaned, and wearily cut again. Azazel's head bounced off and ... again the same old man. Sam stared. Bared his teeth and cut again. And again. And again. And every time the same old man until at last Azazel snapped: 'ALL RIGHT! Enough! So whaddaya want anyway?'

Sam eyed the Beast cautiously. *Too good to be true*, he thought.

'Whaddaya mean, too good to be true?' Azazel glared and sat down on a wet heathery bank. Plucking a stem he began to chew it. 'I'm tired of games! Thisss is me!' He spread ragged arms. 'Whaddaya want? Satan with hooves and horns? Prince of Darknesss in blue velvet?' And mumbling he produced a bottle from his filthy pocket. 'So have a drink!'

'No, thanks,' Sam spat, and – one more time – again he hacked ... but it was still the dejected old bum there. 'Do me a favour and drop this head-chopping,' Azazel mumbled. 'What you sssee is what you get.' He stabbed a horny thumb at his chest and took a swig. A tear trickled down his cheek. Sam raised the sword. He backed off. 'No! I can't hurt you now. You've won. Rules!' But at Sam's look he spat in contempt. 'Wonderful! He does me over and doesn't even know how he did it! Thinks I'm free of rules and I chose all this. Know why I got ssstuck with this job?' he croaked. 'I showed you Lullu how to get ahead, that's what!'

'Thanks,' said Sam, 'You're a real friend.' Again he threatened. 'Now – the Sometimes Isle! The Starchamber! You'll take us!'

'All right! So I'll take you.' His eyes gleamed as he took another swig from his – Sam began to realise – bottomless bottle. 'But I just want you to know that if not for me …' – he wagged a maudlin finger – '… you'd still be an ape in a tree. I give folk reason to live, to grow, to think! If I wasn't around they'd have nothing to rebel against, no injussstice to conquer, no enemy to ssslay! They'd have no guts, no heart, no nothing!'

'You sound like a Tory headmaster,' said Sam bleakly, and shivered. It was cold. Night and rain began to fall. 'Now! Tiy sent me to …'

'Still loyal to that old bat?' The old man cackled. 'She's finished sssince she gave you the ring. Take a look!'

Sam looked through the emerald depths to the Whole Place, and there he saw the wrinkled old woman who wept silently. Yet he saw Chrissa too.

'You'll take us to the Starchamber,' he said steadily.

Azazel guffawed and smote his brow. 'You believe the crap Tiy told you about stopping the Shift? The Elohim won't lisssten! And if you think …'

Sam grabbed his bottle and smashed it. 'Listen!' he yelled as Azazel sank glumly back. 'You'll keep your word for once. You'll take Tiy and me to the Sometimes Isle – and we start for the Whole Place right now!' He yanked Azazel to his feet. The old man mumbled querulously. 'First, call off your sons! And what happened to Dion's head?'

'My sons?' Azazel grinned and tapped his scabby skull. 'Here are my sssons! Fool, you cut most of them off without even knowing it!'

'Projections?' Sam stared. 'Bortibel? Sauriel? All of them?'

'You don't think I'd trust any ssson of mine, do you?' Azazel snarled, and irritably jerked his arm free.

'What about your armies? Call them off too!'

'Whaddaya mean, call off my armies? Whaddayya think I was fighting you with? Look in the ssstone and check it.'

Sam looked into the ring. He saw a land that was suddenly, mysteriously quiet. No armies raged. No killing went on. Exhausted men bathed in streams and drank. But … deeper … that Feast of Light. BURNING BURNING! Chrissa and her shepherd. Anxiety touched him. *What if …?*

'What about Montségur?' he demanded. 'And Dion's head!'

Azazel grinned. 'Montségur's mine. The Last Days are mine. As for your Dion, he's gone back to where he came from. Your hope is futile. I'll take you and Tiy to the Starchamber – but that's all.' He shrugged and started trudging east. 'So let's get on with it.'

43.
Feast of Light

With the seizure of the barbican it was clear that Montségur was as good as lost. By night a company of Basque volunteers had outflanked the defences by scaling the precipice. They'd knifed the sentries and taken the tower before the alarm could be raised.

During the following days all attempts to regain the barbican failed. Rumour and false hope proliferated among the exhausted defenders as their supplies ran low. The bombardment continued at ever closer quarters. So the final weeks began. One night Chrissa and Pierre with Bernard met three other men chosen to play a part in the last act – Amiel Aicart, Poitevin and Hugo. Pierre heard what he'd have to do quietly enough. If he felt terror he didn't show it. Terror had grown mundane.

'So,' he sighed later, 'Back to the depths, eh?'

On the first of March trumpets blew. Pierre-Roger led out his men on a last desperate sortie to dislodge the enemy from the barbican. It failed. Many died. That night he came to Bishop Bertrand. His face told it all.

'The time has come,' he said heavily. 'My men demand that we surrender now. We can do no more. There is no hope. We've done our best, but ...'

Bertrand eyed the dusty, ragged, exhausted man, then said:

'Yes, you've done your best. You have our blessing and thanks. But one thing – we must remain here for another fifteen days. Until the Feast of Light ... There's a task to be completed.'

'About ...' – Pierre-Roger scowled – '... Joana?'

Bertrand nodded, then began telling the soldier something of the why, what, how and when. But Pierre-Roger shook his head.

'Give me no reasons,' he said. 'I'll do what I can, but it's best I know no more than I must.'

Wild-eyed in his rags Crazy Jean hung out on the fringes of the camp next day when the heretics came down to negotiate surrender. All day long Pierre-Roger and Raimon de Perella met with the new royal commander, Gui de Lévis, and his advisers. By sunset the terms were agreed. Montségur to be forfeit to Church and King. The garrison to leave unmolested. All those baptised in the heretic faith to be given up to the stake. Yet first, a two-week truce. No action against the castle, no fighting by either side until that time was up, upon which Pierre-Roger guaranteed to hand over both castle and heretics, on surety of hostages from his own family.

This news ran round the camp. It amazed and disgusted the rank and file. 'Never heard of nothing like this,' Crazy Jean heard a man grumble. 'Why don't we just burn 'em now and get it over?' Crazy Jean hurried away to his shelter in a wood to think (as best he could) on what this truce might mean. He was in poor shape, regarded with suspicion even by other camp-followers. All thought him mute: he had not spoken once since his arrival four months previously. Yet now, safe in a windy thicket, he squatted on his heels and anxiously stared at the castle, stark on its rock against the fading sky. 'Hoel, Hoel, Hoel!' he muttered. 'She'll not escape Hoel again! No, she will not!'

Gui de Lévis had trouble justifying the two-week truce to the furious Bishop of Narbonne. 'Please see,' he said wearily, 'that surrender in two weeks is better than dragging it on and on. This way we get a castle in good order and keep the costs down.' And when the Bishop snapped that bargaining with heretics was bargaining with Satan, the general grew cool. 'My lord, today I bargained with soldiers like myself! And why not let them make their peace? Heretics, yes, but brave men too, and with this damned war now nearly over surely we can afford a little Christian charity – we've shown precious little to date. My order stands!'

That night ghostly silence reigned. Trebuchet and mangonel had fallen silent. An air of unreality blanketed both the pog and the valley below. During the succeeding days and nights of truce this unearthly atmosphere intensified. Prayer and sermon were continual as those about to die made ready. Nearly two hundred of the elect faced the flames. All knew what lay ahead. None protested the capitulation. Instead their fervour grew so jubilant that some soldiers – all with a free pass soon to life and liberty – were overcome enough to receive the *consolamentum* and condemn themselves to the stake … for this exaltation of the soon-to-die was a palpable force, hard to resist. It shone from them, disquieting or shaming those who did not share it. As the time approached, their exaltation increased. Few slept any more. What point, with the Feast of Light so near?

Few knew of the special mission. Chrissa's secret had been well kept. During that last fortnight her training with Pierre went on all the time, and Pierre grew ever more silent and philosophical. *Not just through Her snapping teeth this time,* he thought. *This time it's all the way to Her womb. Pierre, you were better off with the whores in Ax.*

Yet he knew he wouldn't turn away. He knew it every time he looked into Chrissa's eyes. Sometimes sky blue and warm; at other times so icy and remote. They weren't bound for the stake – but they both knew that their transformation would be as absolute. To avoid disaster the timing and every other aspect had to be precise. In trance with Bernard she spent many of those last hours ensuring he knew how to contact her in her dreams at Berkeley Road. She thought little about her battles with the Beast, how nearly she'd perished. There was no time. As for Sam … she nearly lost control again one night. Out she went on the green ray – and down through swirling angry clouds she came to a ship in a raging sea. A strange ship, sleekly black as ebony, its surfaces carved with images of the myriad forms of life killing and coupling. It had no masts, no visible means of power, yet glided through the storm with utter smoothness. The deck was flat and featureless save for one small cabin set amidships. Outside this cabin sat Sam, head in hands, his back against the wall. He was watching a sour-looking old man who sat alone at the stern as if at a tiller … except there was no tiller. And in the cabin …

In the cabin she saw the Old One, tossing in fever.

Confusion seized her. *Madame Pédauque?* She withdrew rapidly.

'They're on their way,' she muttered to Pierre. 'So are we!'

Meanwhile the Spring Festival was prepared. The Feast of Light. Amid the unearthly exaltation atop the mountain Chrissa and Pierre worked on, increasingly washed clean of the world and its problems. The time of fear and doubt was past. Now there was only what had to be done.

Before the celebration and a day before the truce expired, the garrison marched out, leaving Pierre-Roger and a few others to oversee the final hours and protect those civilians left. So the weary soldiers departed with their families, receiving presents of spice, money and food from the doomed ones for whom they'd fought so long. The farewell was so intense that the most hardened had trouble turning away to walk down to the world again, and some who'd meant to leave found at the last moment they could not. Amid joyful cries and embraces they stayed to receive baptism and die. The rest, fifty or so men, followed by their families and baggage, went with brave show of order. From the valley below, Crazy Jean watched anxiously as they descended the steep zigzag trail; knights on small hardy mountain horses; men whose poor armour was scuffed and dull. Yet they held their heads high and were not humiliated. In silence the royal ranks parted: marshals waved them out of the cold wind into tents where paperwork was completed. Church imposed light penances, State processed them back into the daily world. Then, so slowly, singly or in groups, they trudged or rode away from Montségur. Most could not look back. Some passed a bare rock where a mad wretch waited ... and when Crazy Jean at last broke silence and began jabbering questions few even noticed him. Some glared; an old knight threatened to kill him if he didn't shut up; the rest ignored him. Only one man responded at all.

'Golden hair? Yes, she's there. God knows why. Never found out. Who are you anyway? Get out of my way. I'm going home. If it's still there.'

And that night as he lay on the stony ground Crazy Jean heard the passionate calls and massed responses of the heretics celebrating their Feast of Light in the castle above, and his teeth chattered, for the night was alive with their joy, thrilling and vibrating to it. Then he saw a blue-eyed face smiling at him, and he stood and screamed with rage:

'I'll get you yet! Oh yes I will!'

All night and all next day the celebration of the Feast of Light grew in intensity. To many in those last hours the physical world was no longer substantial; their bodies were temporary garments, about to be given up. Night and day then night again, but few of them noted the passage of time. In a great circle in the courtyard they prayed without ceasing as twice the moon succeeded the sun; building themselves up to such a pitch that the very rock below them seemed to shiver with the power they invoked, and the cloudy grey heavens above them rippled with light, yawning wide in readiness to receive them when the sun rose again.

When darkness fell that last night the plan was set in motion.

At sunset Pierre, Chrissa and Bernard met in the keep with the Bishop, Pierre-Roger, and Esclarmonde. Amiel Aicart was there too, with Poitevin and Hugo. These three, all strong lithe men born to the hills and sure in the faith, knew their part and what they had to do. Without sentiment the practical details and timing were discussed one last time. Sacks holding the last of Montségur's treasures were checked and securely tied on four broad backs. Lengths of hemp rope were tested and coiled; the faces of the five about to leave were blacked with charcoal. 'Hands too,' said Pierre. 'But what about grip on the rocks?' objected Amiel Aicart. 'You're right,' Pierre acknowledged, finding it hard to focus on detail. Covertly he eyed Chrissa ... and the ring she wore. She seemed utterly calm. *Yes,* he told himself, *but what have I got to give? If it destroys me, well, that's the fate of it.* For still he couldn't really believe in what she'd told him of their destination. And even as he thought it a sombre mood came over them all. The night was darkening fast. 'Let us pray now,' said Bertrand.

After they'd done this, Bertrand offered Pierre the *consolamentum.*

The shepherd thought hard before shaking his head.

'But you are a believer,' said the Bishop, 'and ...'

'Yes.' Pierre sighed, glancing at Chrissa. 'But in this trial ahead I'll see things I never saw before. With the weight of baptism received so recently I might see nothing clearly. But I ask for your blessing.'

Yet as Bertrand blessed each of those about to leave Pierre-Roger grew impatient. 'Enough!' he said harshly, stalking up and down, and gestured out of the window. 'It's dark now. Time you were gone. You'll need all night. Light a fire on the Bidorte when you're clear. Godspeed.'

Then for the last time Chrissa turned to Father Bernard. Wordlessly they drank each other in. His eyes, shining so bright from that skeletal face, said: *Sister, soon we'll hear the Song!* Deeply moved, she bent and quickly kissed him on the forehead then, eyes glistening, she turned away and embraced Esclarmonde, genuflected to Bishop Bertrand, bowed to Pierre-Roger, and beckoned sharply to Pierre and the other three. 'Come along!' she said in a strained voice. 'Let's go! Guide us, shepherd!'

And so, faces as black as the night, they quickly left the keep and descended past the terraced huts to the lip of the steep north-west drop. The night was cloudy; there was no moon yet. The first length of rope was secured round a stunted pine. Without ado, Pierre first, Chrissa in the middle, Amiel Aicart last, they began lowering themselves into the abyss, kicking their way down drops more than two hundred feet at a time.

So they left Montségur and vanished into the gulf.

Two hours later Pierre-Roger stood with Raimon de Perella at a window. A fire twinkled through the night from a height far across the valley. 'So they're safely away,' the garrison commander murmured, and felt relief that shamed him. By breaking his vow to deliver up all the elect he'd risked the lives of his wife and children, held hostage in the royal camp. *Oh,* he thought woefully, eyeing Raimon de Perella sideways. *But this man ...*

Montségur's owner didn't hear. Staring into the black night he heard not the wind but the doomed ones gathered in the courtyard. With Bishop Bertrand leading them they chanted the first seventeen verses from the Gospel of John, his mother and wife and one of his daughters among them.

'That's just a little fire,' he whispered. 'The fire at dawn will sweep us all away, not just our brothers and sisters, our wives and ...'

He stopped. He said no more. He eyed the night sightlessly.

Together the two men awaited the dawn, the red dawn.

Crazy Jean didn't wait. At nightfall a lethargy came on him. In his thicket he slept. Soon his first dream in three years had him wailing so loud that a sergeant, irritated beyond measure, sought him out and dumped a bucket of freezing water over him. Spluttering he leaped to his feet.

'Quiet, idiot! Unless you want something hotter at dawn!'

'Hoel, Hoel!' howled the madman as he ran off into the night. 'They've gone without you! Where? Yes! Deep and deep and deeper still!'

'Thought you were mute!' the sergeant roared, then forgot him.

Soon afterwards there was commotion in a cleared pasture where horses were staked out, not fenced. Urgent need of dry wood had required the dismantling of all corrals. In any case they weren't needed any more. So tonight the beasts were staked, and their guard wasn't watchful, but drunk in anticipation of a hot fire at dawn to warm his hands before at long last going home. So it wasn't hard for Crazy Jean, even with his teeth going like castanets, to sneak up on a bay mare at the bottom of the pasture. He was a poor rider, but dared not look for harness. As quiet as he could he led the mare by her halter into the woods … but the stink of his fear alarmed her. She snickered loudly. 'What's that?' cried the guard, jumping up with crossbow cocked. 'Who's there?' At random he fired a bolt. It thunked into a tree above Crazy Jean's head, so alarming him that he found the energy to half-jump, half-scramble up on the mare's broad back.

With clumsy determination he rode away, obsessed by visions of the hags who'd torn him to pieces, of that blue-eyed golden-haired child … of a cold snowy day on the banks of the Ariège over ten years ago. As fast as he dared he descended the steep road north round the hills, then went west and south towards Tarascon, towards the Gate of the Stone. Meanwhile the guard couldn't be bothered to raise the alarm. 'Just some poor bastard saving his hide,' he told himself, yanking the wooden stopper from his bottle. 'Well, we can let one go, can't we?'

The end was made as quick and impersonal as possible. Everyone wanted it over and done with. The dawn was cold and grey. As soon as it hinted, royal troops marched up to take possession of the castle. With them came others to march the heretics down to the fire. The great South Door was opened. Without fuss those about to die were marshalled in the courtyard. There was no time to dress them in the white penitential shifts and paper mitres demanded by the inquisition. In their black robes and just as they were, the martyrs were shackled together amid an eerie silence that remained absolute save for the whine of the wind and the jingling of chains. In a whisper a soldier apologised as he nipped a woman's ankle. From the keep Pierre-Roger de Mirepoix and Raimon de Perella watched with the Frenchman – a saturnine Norman – come to dispossess them. The man seemed moved, and kept shaking his head. They saw the goodman Bernard de Laurac carried into line by his companion Imbert de Belesta. 'I can walk!' Bernard insisted, 'if I can just have your shoulder to lean on.' And he hobbled into line behind Imbert, demanding to be shackled like the rest. Bishop Bertrand, already chained, saw this and called a French sergeant.

'No need to shackle this man,' he said quietly. 'He's lame. He wants to walk to his fate, but he cannot do so chained.'

They show no fear at all! thought the sergeant with amazed despair. It was the same man who'd drenched Crazy Jean a few hours earlier. *Are they human? Not even one of them bawling for mercy?*

'Here, old man,' he said gruffly, offering Bernard his arm, not knowing why. 'Lean on me. I'll see you there, if it's what you choose.'

'It is.' Bernard smiled at him. 'Thank you, brother.'

Pierre-Roger and Raimon de Perella came down among them before they were taken, to be given thanks and little gifts. Among them were Raimon's mother, and Corba, and Esclarmonde, and he must have said farewell to them, but he never remembered it, nor the fire that followed, not even when hauled up before the inquisition two years later. As for Pierre-Roger, the simple violent soldier who'd slain the inquisitors at Avignonet, he went free.

Under fast dull cloud the two hundred were brought slowly down the steep winding track from the pog to the stockade built on sloping pasture on the south-west side. Sliding down through tight-clinging pinewood they came to the pyre. Round it the staring army waited. Priests and friars moving through the ranks cried out praise to the Almighty, exhorting Him to guard his flock against unseemly pity for heretics. For now as the doomed ones were brought ever closer to their final Feast of Light it was heard by all how they chanted the Lord's Prayer – their version – over and over without ceasing. And as the ranks parted to let them through it was clear that many were in trance. They saw and heard nothing at all. Pale with fasting, their faces glowed with otherworldly light, but – who could tell which world? 'No pity!' shouted angry priests, slapping the faces of men who seemed too impressed. The heretics, assembled at the gate of the stockade, continued to pray. Shackles were struck off their ankles as the Bishop of Narbonne, in a huge voice and as quick as he could, roared out official excommunication and abandonment against every name on a long list. Halfway through it his voice gave out: irritably he gave the list to his new prior, Ricard de Capdenier. The prior finished it swiftly then cried out:

'Do any here recant? This is your last chance to save yourselves!'

None of the two hundred paid any attention. They huddled together, their eyes staring into space as they continued to chant and pray. Stiffly the Bishop gestured to Gui de Lévis, waiting on horseback nearby.

'Right, let's get on with it!' the general bawled. 'Now!'

With anxious brutality the soldiers who'd brought the heretics down from the castle herded them into the hastily built stockade. It was hardly big enough. Those first in were forced by those behind to scramble up the haphazard pyre, slipping between the piled-up, pitch-smeared logs, praying aloud as best they could. 'Right!' And the sergeant who'd so tenderly helped Bernard all the way down now pushed the old goodman roughly into Imbert's arms. 'Get in there! Go on! Move!'

'Thank you again, brother,' whispered Bernard, his smile remote yet beautiful, and the sergeant, with fearful disgust on his face, shut his eyes and turned away as the pushing and shoving continued. Soon all had been jammed in. Packed body to body on the slippery logs they helped each other to stand, but as they prayed they kept swaying and falling. Those on top of the pyre could see over the stockade wall, those lower around them could not. But all heard the final order shouted from the outside world.

'Now! Get on with it!'

A dozen flaming torches looped over the wall and fell among them. Amid a brief silence, their bodies instinctively flinching away, they stared as the bright blooms of fire sprang up. Eyes met eyes in sudden terror – then in a great voice Bishop Bertrand began the Lord's Prayer again, and as the smoke began to twist and coil other voices joined him. The flames began to catch the logs. More torches looped over the wall. Esclarmonde de Perella found the hem of her robe on fire and was amazed. The air shivered with a gust of heat. She embraced her mother. Sheets of flame roared up from the pitch-smeared logs, were fanned by the wind. Black smoke billowed. Prayer turned to agonised shrieking. Bernard, still held up by Imbert, felt the hair in his nostrils crisping as a wave of heat struck him. Into his lungs it seared. *Now!* he realised. *Now!* And as the flame snatched at him with its greedy roar he raised his head and cried out: 'MY CHILD, MY SWEET CHILD, I BLESS YOU! NOW HEAR MY SONG!'

Then he was one of two hundred writhing in a sea of flame, the reeking black smoke choking prayers and screams alike as the ranks drawn up about watched with mouths agape, priests and friars stalking among them with harsh exhortation, those closest flinching from the heat even as with long poles they beat back the blackened, pain-maddened hands clutching at the top of the stockade, itself now well on fire.

Yet as heat became ice and with his skin peeling and cracking, Bernard sang. He sang the songs of his youth, not aloud, for he could no longer speak and he was blinded – yet he sang, sang the Song of Joana . . .

Quant lo bouié ben de laura
Planto soun agulhado
AEIOU!

... and on wings of fire he went seeking one whom he found ... singing until she heard him, saw him, woke up to him! *Hear me, Joana!* he cried. *Hear me in the Light of the Shining Ones!* – and saw her in the Last Days, and at the Gate of the Stone with the shepherd. And at the last he knew that she saw him and heard him. Now the Light, the Light, the Light! 'Fabrisse!' he cried aloud with a last effort of his lungs ... then fell with all the others as the roaring pyre caved in.

Then pain had murdered itself and all was done but for a voice crying:

'*WE BURN WE BURN WE ARE BURNING MELTING WE ARE OF CHRIST* –'

It was amazing to those outside how long some of them lasted.

44.

At the Gate of the Stone

All night the five travelled steadily. Evading the siege they found mules awaiting them on the crest of the Bidorte. They lit a signal fire and continued silently over the high reaches under the cloudy night, in time descending steeply down to the Ariège by way of the snowless Col de Font Albe. Still deep in the night they came to the river and followed it north to Ussat. There they crossed and started up the craggy high western slope, Pierre hunting by feel and memory until he found the narrow, shrub-hidden entry to the caves that he and Bernard had taken ten years earlier. Then leaving Hugo with the mules, Poitevin and Amiel Aicart (staggering under a double load) followed Chrissa and Pierre down the long dark tunnel to the great cavern. There, torches flaring, they found the first of the cross-in-circle, cup-and-dove symbols marking the way to the greater depths. Pierre and Chrissa waited as Poitevin and Amiel Aicart grunted and heaved, stowing away three of the sacks they'd brought with them in a hidden side-chamber above head height. The fourth sack, left outside with Hugo, contained designs called Rota or Taro. These they'd take with them into Spain.

They made hurried farewells. Poitevin and Amiel Aicart were not sad to return to the outside world. Amiel Aicart looked back once. With a sigh he sucked in his breath. He saw the shepherd holding a torch – but as for Joana-called-Chrissa … she glowed. There in the dark cave some way from the shepherd she stood … and she glowed, shone with a faint soft sheen of emerald about her. And Amiel Aicart shook his head as he left them.

'Brother, we'll never speak of this,' he told Poitevin.

'A sad night,' said Poitevin after a while. 'Our meaning's lost.'

Amiel Aicart was silent, then said as at last they saw before them the dull night sky framed where Hugo waited: 'No. Not so.'

When they were gone Pierre and Chrissa stared at each other, both keyed up to such a pitch it was hard to speak. *I no longer know who I am*, thought Pierre, awed by the light shining from the ring . . . and from her.

'You took me from here before,' Chrissa said. Her voice echoed flat with the fight to contain herself. 'Is it far?'

'Deeper,' Pierre managed, wondering if he could fulfil what was so long awaited, long delayed. 'Much, much deeper!'

'Then let's go.' She felt as if carved from the rock that weighed on them. Fear and love, both frozen. *Father Bernard!* 'Lead me, Pierre.'

So through that great cave past calcined forms that loomed like beasts Pierre followed the daubed symbol, hunting the way past forks, over house-sized slides of rock, chest-deep through a silent lake where blind albino trout preyed on blind albino shrimps. On and on they went, deep and deeper until – to Pierre it seemed forever – they reached the cave where stick-men hunters chased shaggy beasts across smooth black walls. *Already She begins to mutter!* he thought, imagining Her cruel mouth ahead. And by torchlight he saw Chrissa eye those rock paintings: he shook with the sense of a great mystery about to be revealed. 'You were so frail when I brought you out,' he muttered. 'Now look at you as you go in again.'

She turned. 'Yes!' she said. 'We must be quick.'

But with a dazed face he shrank back.

'What is it?' she asked. 'What's the matter?'

'Your face. It . . . shines brighter every minute!'

'So does yours, if you really want to know,' she said, and dismissed it. She touched his arm. 'Now. How do we go from here?'

The touch of her fired him. Raising the torch he showed her the narrow ledge above them. It curled away to a dark hole in the wall. 'There,' he said. 'That's the way. Into the maze. To the Gate.'

'Courage now,' she said. 'Remember our friends.'

Wordlessly he heaved her up on the ledge, then chinned himself up. Beside her he put out the torch, jamming the stub of it in his belt. In the sudden utter darkness he sidled round her. 'It's all feel from now on,' he hissed. 'The rope that goodman Bernard put down when we got you out should still be here.' And to the mouth of the maze he crawled. The rope was there. *I'm leaving the world forever!* he thought, appalled as he began his crawl into the maze again. *I'll never see the sun again! I'll never . . .* Fear seized him and he stopped. Behind him she said urgently: 'The rose! See the rose!' Breathing in deep gasps he focussed on the image he'd been taught – and saw it before him. The rose. It was on fire. It was dripping blood all over him. *Go on, shepherd!* he insisted as shrill spirit-voices began muttering in him. *The Lost Stone again!* they cackled. *The Pierre Perdue! The Peyrepertuse! But can he breathe blood? And who's this he's got with him?* Gasping, he forced himself on. Along the narrow, twisting wormhole he crawled, following the rope Bernard had laid down so long ago . . . yet with every turn the bloody tide mounted, thick and gelid. He was drowning in it! It clogged his mouth, his nose. *I can't breathe!* Again he began to panic, and cursed as he bashed his head on the rock only inches above in a vain effort to escape it. 'Chrissa!' he said.

Behind him she was attacked by the same delusion. '*DAD! DAD! HELP ME! I'M SINKING!*' Again she was drowning in that bog at Gairloch, Sam before her in the circle, writhing in a field of unearthly fire!

The Old One's fire! she thought. *But now I'm the . . .*

'Pierre, it's coming true,' she muttered, heart beating hard as she reached out her left hand to him . . . and at her touch he trembled. 'Be still!' she soothed him, touching the ring to his head . . . and he saw a river of bright emerald spirit pouring from a celestial pitcher, a shining star. Down, down, down so rich with life it plunged into the writhing weight of this Hidden World, to mingle with the bloody tide, light with dark, dark with light. Gasping in a rush of desire he breathed hard. 'Now move on!' she said. 'We need what my sister offers. She seeks Light too!'

Then Pierre forgot his fears. Instead his passion surged. With a sigh he crawled on. Ahead now, utter silent darkness. No screaming vibration or pulsating, blinding emerald light. *No*, he thought, excited by the glow that followed him. *The Light shines for us now!*

Soon the passage grew almost wide and high enough to let him stand.

'Her Gate!' he said, and struck fire to light the torch. And even though he knew what to expect he still drew a sharp breath at the sight of Her squatting haunches, Her dreadful teeth. 'It's still open! But now be careful! Touch these teeth and Her mouth snaps shut!'

'Which is the one that opens and shuts it?' she demanded.

'This one.' He pointed at the lower right dog-tooth, askew in its gap.

'Let's hurry,' she whispered – then turned her head.

'What is it?' Pierre felt alarm.

'Can't you hear? That scuffling?'

'I thought it just another ...'

Tapping the emerald against her brow she looked into it – then made a face. 'An enemy!' she said, her face weirdly lit. The scuffling from the tunnel behind them was louder. Her eyes burned. A scent came off her that gripped his heart. His lips parted. 'Now come on! Quickly!'

Gingerly he straddled the deadly teeth of the Outer Gate. A fire-red glow began to pulse from the chamber beyond. Closer came the scuffling sound; below him gleamed the deadly white teeth. *So sharp and erect! Why not fall on me now?* He gasped at that voice; found himself frozen as his belly sagged to within an inch of the nearest point. 'Lady Chrissa!' he said numbly. 'Help me!' Again the ring's touch fired him. With relief he rolled over those teeth into the ruddy glow of the grotto where the black pool dreamed. His blood pounded as he turned with a hand she didn't need. Deftly she swayed past the teeth to the smooth black floor, holding the hem of her long black gown, and his blood pounded harder as –

'Ailma!' croaked a voice from the tunnel. 'I'll not let you ...'

The grotto pulsed scarlet as Pierre held up the torch.

Approaching the Gate on hands and knees they saw the gleaming eyes and torn, ragged form of Jean d'Aubigny.

... through the maze he'd followed them, panting, hissing, teeth bared in the darkness, following not the rope but the trail of blood that glowed before him; the trail he'd followed from the mouth of the caves, maybe all the way from Montségur. He had no memory of the journey, nor how in grey pre-dawn he'd hid behind a tree until the coast was clear; nor how he'd found the place of the stick-men ... where he'd twitched like a dog until he got the scent, saw the blood-trail glowing on the ledge above him.

Now, sniffing, sniffing, he crawled through the maze, following a trail that promised ... what, he didn't know. But soon he would! Very soon! For now the blood coated his arms, filled his mouth, swamped his mind in mud where fat worms crawled ... and now through the blood he saw Her!

Blazing emerald bright he saw Her through the blood as She ducked through the teeth of the Gate before him ... into a room pulsing red.

Then a panic seized him. *What if I'm too late?*

'Ailma!' he croaked, crawling faster. 'I'll not let you ...'

Chrissa's face shone implacably. Pierre found himself fearing her.

'You're here just in time.' Her voice had an eerie, ringing note. She took hold of the dog-tooth and twisted it to the vertical.

With loud gnashing and grinding the Outer Gate began to close, top and bottom jaws together. 'But now we'll never ...' Pierre cried in horror as scarlet lights whirled from the grotto walls and Crazy Jean, screaming, came to his feet and threw himself at the emerald blaze of Her, standing amid the bloody glow beyond the rapidly closing gap.

'You killed me once!' he cried. 'Now ...'

He was far too late. With a heavy clunk Her jaws snapped shut on his neck. His eyes bulged: bloody foam flew from his still-working mouth as his head, neatly severed, fell to the smooth black sloping floor ... and with increasing speed rolled through the whirling pulses of scarlet and emerald down to the pool of still black water dreaming at the centre of the grotto.

With barely a ripple the head of Jean d'Aubigny vanished into the pool. Pierre gaped. First at the pool, then at the closed Outer Gate, then at the pool again. The strange meaning of this death ... he was on fire inside and out. 'What did you mean, just in time?' he demanded. But Chrissa was unmoved. 'Put out the torch,' she said, and began to disrobe. 'Here we are! See the black isle?'

He did. Beyond the shores of the inky pool, gleaming as bloodily now as the water and the smooth rock underfoot, he saw the flat black rock, the isle amid the pool. The vortex of the Gate. He turned. An incoherent sound escaped him. For she stood naked, wearing only the ring! And the wild scarlet light pervading the rest of the grotto was tamed by her! He saw emerald hair cascade over emerald shoulders, curl over emerald breasts – he stared, hypnotised and nonplussed by contrary urges, his face suddenly wide open and childlike as she stepped forward and tugged at his shirt.

'Pierre, wake up! We must hurry. It's time. Can't you feel it? At Montségur. We must go on the wings of their Song of Fire, their Feast of Light! Now it's time! Now you take me, we mate and merge and –'

Yet still he gaped, despite the heat in him by now so used to denying desire he no longer knew how to release it; even now seeking moral excuses for a reluctance he knew might destroy the whole work entirely.

'But ... but ... isn't this *Her* way?' he cried.

'Her way? Pierre, *Her* way is *My* way now! Be quick!'

Clumsily, wrapped in her light, he tore off his shirt.

'Hurry!' she begged. 'The passion! It starts!'

For she felt flame leap up. She saw screaming faces amid swirling black smoke. She heard the prayer of the Song, and the power leaped up in her as Pierre's resistance broke, his body knotting, convulsing, stretching as the fire leaped through him too. Tearing off his leggings he stumbled after her into the black pool. Emerald and scarlet zigzagged on wavelets as the shock of it ran up through him: he gasped as he stubbed his toe on Hoel's drowned head – then he joined her on the black islet, plunging into the flame of her amid the emerald light as the pulsing scarlet took on a richer ruby aspect, and through fire and ice she gazed and drew him deeper into her, hurling her cry into the vortex now opening to the Starchamber Gate; and both of them burning, burning, burning with Father Bernard and all the others; burning as he sang from the pyre –

Planto soun agulhado
Trobo sa henno al pé del foc
Tristo descounsolado
AEIOU!

And now they moved together in the whirling blaze as emerald and ruby combined beyond violet into the piercing white light of the aeons outside time as a girl in London awoke screaming from her dream of a burning man – '*Hear me, Joana! Hear me in the Light of the Shining Ones!*' And out of the Hidden World they burst as the two hundred died – '*WE BURN WE BURN WE ARE BURNING MELTING WE ARE OH CHRIST!*' And a great flower of which Pierre was part spiralled up to the heights as she cried: '*SAM! NOW! CALL ME!*'

45.
Starchamber

But as they neared their destination the storm grew worse and Sam heard nothing. Outside the cabin in which the old woman moaned feverishly he sat with head in hands on the gleaming jet-black deck, eyes shut as lightning stabbed down from the roiling violet above. Behind him billowed ragged red cloud: ahead the horizon was black, thunder inaudible amid the rage of wind and sea. Savage cross-currents broke continually short and reared up in spume-tipped towers from which the wind creamed sheets of spray ... yet where he sat feeling sick Sam stayed dry. This was odd enough, but more alarming yet was how, whenever he looked, he saw the ship rolling and pitching with violent, sickening irregularity – yet his body told him they were on a calm and even keel. proceeding across a flat sea without deflection from a dead-straight south-westerly course.

And Tiy in the cabin, always crying querulously. He heard Her now:

'Fool! Where are you! Come and keep Me awake! Talk to Me!'

Two days and nights this had gone on. The storm had begun even before they'd left Ys, where every warm year more land was lost to the sea. Tiy had been put to bed; brooding silently Azazel had taken his place at the stern and there he'd remained with his bottle, always staring at Sam as by unknown means he steered this odd black ship. No mast, sails, oars, crew or rudder – no sense of engines vibrating in its sleek, sealed hold – yet on and on it surged, even-keeled amid the wildest gusts as they neared the edge of the world. Just Azazel seated unmoving. And now Sam sneaked a look. Through the weird half-light he saw Azazel there, the never empty bottle at his lips. Just like some crabby old bum from Camden Town or the Bronx. Yet that look of menacing benevolence in his rheumy eye made Sam shudder. *Like a butcher eyeing up a lamb! What does he want? What's the game?* He groaned. If only the storm would let him think! Shutting his eyes did no good. He couldn't stop the wind shrieking, or the Beast's cold gaze on him, or Her endless cries. Mercifully in the night She'd fallen briefly silent: exhausted, he must have slept, to awaken with a start at dead of wailing night. Since then he'd sat wondering how he could feel so sick with no food in his belly. And about everything else. If only he could think! Mysteries coming to heads that swallowed their own tails! The ring back on Tiy's finger, but dull, cold, dead, and Tiy so old and feverish in the cabin. Feverish in the cabin en route to the Black Isle! Like Madame Pédauque! Ring-destiny all coming full circle! Davey Joyce had come this way on the *SS Heaton* in 1882. Nearing the smoking black isle newly burst from the depths he'd gone ashore as the mystery Madame Pédauque retired with a fever, delirious on her bunk. And Captain Davey heard …

'*I am La Reine Pédauque! Here you'll find a key to what's lost – but be quick: I cannot endure this weight for long!*'

He saw Her tossing, sweating in the cabin, naked, caked all over in slimy red mud that dripped to the floor and coagulated like blood. And Her feet … with a shiver he realised: *They're not human feet!*

'No!' he said. In sick frozen calm he shook his head. 'That's what Davey saw, not me!' For so his great-grandfather had seen Her and heard Her cry before finding the emerald ring … on the crumbling finger of one of three in birdfeather robes who sat in the …

'Fool! Fool! Where are you? I need you!'

He shook his head, shuddered, looked west. Teetering atop the waves then plunging madly (so his eyes told him) he saw before him an ever-deeper blackness into which violet lightnings poured unceasingly, casting up a sulphurous underglow. *Burning!* he thought … and again in a flash of white saw faces screaming from a fire, saw Chrissa and her shepherd joined in flaming, spiralling embrace on a black isle that thrust its way up from the – and suddenly recalled a visitation. Last night. In seasick misery he'd ignored it. Now he thought: *Chrissa, was that you? You came and went so fast. We'll be there soon. What's to happen?*

We come to our father, said Shem in him.

'Yes.' He nodded sternly. 'I keep forgetting, don't I?'

He sniffed again. Yes. The wind. Hot and charred. Burning.

'Time we had a word,' he muttered. Then he stood and stamped up to Azazel, ignoring the apparent pitching and tossing as best he could.

The Beast did not move. More than ever he looked and smelled like a wino, a dead loss, a weak and pathetic old man. But his rheumy eyes never left Sam as he took another swig from the bottomless bottle.

'We're there soon, aren't we?' said Sam flatly.

'I hate your attitude,' Azazel whined.

'I don't give a damn,' said Sam.

The Beast grabbed his gut and belched. Sam flinched. 'So be like that!' barked Azazel. 'Don't you think I need my pleasures too? Who got you here? Who fixed it up?' He jerked a thumb at his ragged chest. 'Me. I did. Got you and that old bitch to Ys. Endured the humiliation. Got this ship fixed. Any thanks? No. Then I set up for the isle's next lift and sit here a century while you ignore me! Now here you are at last and it's: "*We're there sssoon, aren't we?*" Bleaugh!'

And the Beast spat a thick gob of disgust between Sam's feet.

'What do you mean, a century?' Sam snapped.

'Here we go!' Azazel groaned. Lifting his eyes to the flashing sky he took another swig. 'Is it any wonder I drink? This man!' he told the sky, 'He beats me using the forty-nine head routine, no idea what it is – and now he thinks this is easy! Sail calm seas and here we are! The Sometimes Isle just happens to rise as we just happen to arrive! What a Fool!'

'Listen,' said Sam, 'I don't need you to ...'

'You listen!' The old man's gaze was intense. 'You think you know it all. I've been around longer. I got stuck here because I was a fool too. Know why? I had expectations of you Lullu. Thought you could handle the knowledge but you messed it up. I took the rap.'

'You took the women too,' said Sam.

'The women, the women!' Azazel shrugged. 'The Elohim knew it would happen!' He eyed the cabin angrily. 'Tiy and me were just out of a Hidden World ourselves. Why did they give us the job? Ask yourself!'

'Yeah,' said Sam, 'fascinating. But when do we get there?'

'Typical!' The storm whirled violet, black, filthy sulphurous yellow as the black ship glided smoothly on through huge waves. Sam grew dizzy as the Beast glared at him again. The stench. 'You sit at her door like a sick dog for – let's call it two days and nights – yet you think *when* you get to the Starchamber it'll all be easy . . .'

He shrugged, shook his head, took another swig.

Shemyaza's there too,' said Sam. 'Waiting for you.'

'The Starchamber's not the Hidden Place,' Azazel growled.

'Not if you insist on separating them.' Forcing a smile, Sam stood his ground as the old man angrily gestured with the bottle.

'Go away!' Azazel snarled. 'You disgust me! You all disgussst me!'

'What's the problem?' said Sam. 'Why must you screw everything up?'

'Because I see how it is!' Azazel shouted, and made a big pantomime of sticking a finger up his backside then sniffing it. 'It ssstinks!'

Sam laughed. 'What! Everything? What about the rose in bloom?'

'Sssweet while it lasts,' hissed the Beast, 'but it all rots.'

'And feeds its own return!' cried Sam excitedly. His eyes smarted. 'You've got it wrong! All life on earth dies – to be reborn!'

'A philosopher,' Azazel told the storm. '*Now* he gets what I'm up to!' With an evil cackle he turned. 'Who knows?' he said. 'Maybe they'll open the Starchamber just for you and Tiy . . .'

'And why not you too?' said Sam steadily. 'If only you'd . . .'

'Believe? Have faith?' Azazel gawped. 'In what? Know what you'll find up the Sinking Ways? Round the Emme Ya ssstar? A bunch of bourgeois do-gooders who say they serve the universal prime directive by stirring up the broth in every world they find. In their own image! I tried to break that . . . bu don't worry about it,' he ended, mocking Sam's doubting face. 'You'll find out – or trip over your feet and break your neck. I hope you find out. Then you'll see why this planet's better wiped when the next Shift comes. Who needs it?' With a drunken grin he drank again and waved casually past Sam's shoulder. 'There. Ansssswer to your quessstion.'

Sam turned, his eyes streaming with tears. From the crest of a wave he blinked and saw how the deepest blackness ahead was now resolved into an island of sharp, smoking mountains, their peaks etched in a bloody yellow glare of eruption – a glare reflected in the roiling sky above from which lightnings poured down to the sulphur reek of new-born earth.

With a shudder he left Azazel and ran past the cabin to the bow. *A hundred years and a day? If I went back now I'd crumble to dust the moment I touched lesser earth!* Of a sudden there was a quick, febrile lightness in him. Clutching the Medusan carving at the head of the bowsprit he eyed the scene with pent breath as through a bubbling muddy sea the black ship slid. Ahead, the mountains shuddered as the depths again shook: boiling geysers burst up; showers of charred fish rained about … but none fell on the shining black deck. Lightnings flared down as the burned sea tossed and the black ship glided closer. Now he saw eerie violet lights playing amid the smoking peaks. Lava flowed in broad effulgent tongues down lower slopes, black and sheer and gleaming. Above him loomed these cold dripping cliffs as the black ship came through the maddened sea into a surging bay.

Then he saw Dion's head before him, and those blue eyes were bright.

'SHEM,' murmured a deep vast voice, 'MY SON, I AM RISEN AGAIN!'

And he saw that hoary shining head arising from the ocean as the great grey ones weaved about it in intricate dance that told him:

'NONE BROUGHT HERE CAN ESCAPE, FOR THE STARCHAMBER'S CLOSED AND CANNOT BE OPENED UNTIL LOVE CONQUERS THE SHIFT!'

Then again he saw Chrissa in flaming embrace with the shepherd, and a huge pain tore his heart as through them he saw a great wall of monolithic basalt blocks loom up as the black ship slid within feet of the oppressive new-born shore. And there in the violent sea amid the storm it stopped in perfect equilibrium. Sam stared at the wall behind which the Starchamber lay as Azazel left the stern and came to the cabin where Tiy lay in Her fever. *Chrissa!* he called even as behind him Azazel entered the cabin, shutting the door behind him.

The Beast stood amid the gloom. He looked down at the sick old woman. Her eyes were shut. She mumbled feebly. She was no more substantial than a tracing on rice paper. Her hair had withered and fallen away. Her face had fallen into hollow caverns. Her hands so limp above the sweat-drenched sheet were shrunken into claws. Even the emerald in the ring that the Fool had given back to Her was dull. Yet Azazel's eyes gleamed to see it.

'Medicine,' he whispered, producing his bottle. 'We're there now. Drink this. It'll wake you up.'

'There? Where?' She croaked from a cracked sore mouth, blind old eyes hunting the source of the voice. 'Are you My Fool? I feel so cold!'

'That's time,' said Azazel. 'It does that. Now, drink!'

'What is it?' Alarm in Her voice. 'Who are you?'

'Your brother, sister,' said Azazel – and forced the bottle between Her lips. She struggled weakly, gagging on the foul stale spirit even as Sam burst in and snatched the bottle away.

'I knew I couldn't turn my back on you!' he cried in a rage. 'Now what are you trying to do?'

'Look,' said Azazel equably. 'Isn't She better already?'

And She was. Or certainly seemed to be. As Sam stared She sat up, Her body firmed and filled, Her face fleshed out and Her hair grew back –

'Are we there?' She demanded sharply.

'Yes, Lady,' said the Beast, bowing like a servant.

Sam groaned. Her eyes shot to him. 'What is it, Fool?'

'My Lady,' he cried. 'This is a false recovery. You ...'

'False recovery? How can My recovery be false?'

'Exactly, sssweet sissster,' murmured Azazel. In a sudden motion he snatched back the bottle and offered it to Her. 'Another little drop?'

She drank, then stood. She seemed Her old self. 'Well! So we're here! Where are the robes? Why are you two just standing? Quickly!'

'Come on, brother,' said Azazel silkily, 'we must do Her will.'

Sam ignored him and faced Her. 'Lady,' he said, 'you must ...'

'I must what? Who are you? Get out and get us ashore!'

Azazel had gone out. He returned with the birdfeather robes. He was wearing his already. With an ironic bow he left two and returned to deck.

'Put it on and join him and help us,' Tiy scolded.

'*Do as She says!*' the blue-eyes whispered, and Sam did.

Outside the clamour was tremendous. Again at the stern, Azazel quickly had the ship hovering steady by a shelf of gleaming rock just below the great black wall. In it Sam now saw a door, the height of a man and the width of two, just as in Captain Davey's tale. Everything seemed to be in juddering, shaking motion: the noise of the storm was enormous as Azazel, coming up behind him, seized him by the scruff of the neck and threw him onto that rock-shelf. The force of the throw sent him skidding helplessly up against a jagged wall. He lay dazed in the bedraggled robe. Before he could regain his wits She was there beside him, again apparently regal and proud, Azazel behind Her. With difficulty he got to his feet. The island was shaking violently. Even as he swayed a huge section of the cliff above broke off and crashed into the angry sea, missing them by feet.

'Well, you Fool!' She cried, and looking into Her eyes he saw drunken madness. 'Here we are! Better hurry, for My strength won't last. Your little girl won't get you out of this! Yes, she had Me fooled with all her sweetness and light! Why did I fear My brother?' And She clapped Her arm round Azazel's shoulder. On Her finger the ring gleamed with a cold light. *Why did I give it back to Her?* Sam wondered as She told him eagerly: 'He's got us here, and you've given yourself as My witness! Your heart will feel a great remembering, a great awakening! Be glad! Come along!'

Yet as he opened his mouth to rage Azazel said:

'Got a problem? Have a drink. Relax. Got you here, haven't I?'

He said nothing. Yet in him he felt a rumbling, bubbling, swelling pressure as the Beast, grinning wide, pushed him after Her. 'Amazing, her powers of regeneration!' Azazel taunted him. They came to the basalt wall. Black as the cliff itself, it was built of massive, close-fitting blocks that trembled continuously as the island shook. More stone came down and Sam automatically ducked. But Tiy cried out in mad exhilaration and the Beast grinned, took another swig, and offered the bottle. 'Sure you won't? Protects against evil, you know,' he said, bleary eyes agleam.

'NO!' Sam shouted as lightning split the sky. Thunder crashed and a torrential red mud-rain full of dead fish plunged, immediately drenching, from the roiling violet clouds. Plastered wet they reached the outer door of the Starchamber. Sam knew it from Captain Davey's tale. The tapering side pillars, the spiral carvings on the lintel ... the flat, utterly opaque slab of the door itself, reflecting the raging sea behind and below them. There was no sign of keyhole or handle or any other way to open it. Tiy, dripping red mud, the Gown-of-the-Feathers-of-many-bright-Birds clinging to Her, opened her mouth ... then staggered and almost fell amid a fresh tremor as Sam was struck hard by something that came out of the sky. He did fall, even as Azazel bellowed with laughter and held up by the tail the thirty-pound bass which had struck him. 'A big Fool felled by a bigger Fish!' roared Azazel, 'and a cooked fish too!' With grimy hands he tore chunks of flesh from the sea-baked bass and stuffed them into his mouth as Sam groaned and Tiy for some seconds stared dazedly at the door. Her mouth worked but nothing came out. At last She turned in a rage.

'The code!' She snapped at Azazel. 'What is it? Say it!'

'Anything for you, sssweet thing,' Azazel murmured through a mouthful of fish. Contemptuously chucking the mutilated bass at

Sam as the Fool got onto his hands and knees, the old bum stepped up to the door, spat out fish and drank deep, then rasped out a long, complex string of sounds that in accumulative effect produced a further, special shivering to add to the trembling of the island already … and as Sam, still shaken, got to his feet he saw the outer door dissolve into nothing.

Tiy stalked angrily into the short inner passage. Azazel pushed Sam after Her. The rock trembled as She came up against the inner door.

'Again, Lady?' asked the Beast, prodding Sam in the back.

'He's got you pissed,' said Sam with an angry effort. 'Don't listen!'

'Get lost,' the Beast muttered as She turned, 'it's not your business, you turd. You don't know anything about my sssweet sissster and me!'

'Get it open, brother!' She cried, ignoring Sam completely.

'*Get it open!*' Sam mimicked Her in furious sadness. 'My Lady, don't you see that it can't, it *mustn't* be opened until love conquers the …'

Azazel kneed him hard in the groin. He gasped and doubled up, and as he did the bubbling rage in him threatened to explode. But then again as the Beast called out the inner door code he seemed to see the blue-eyes again, and they told him: '*Act weak! Listen and wait! The Feast of Light comes! You must invoke and invite Her at the right moment!*'

The slab before them trembled and dissolved, and Sam, still doubled up, gasped and turned away from the gust of foetid air that rushed out of the long-shut chamber beyond … and in the same moment, even as the isle shook so hard that only Azazel stayed on his feet, a sulphurous stench flooded into the passage on the pulsing waves of a glaring, violent light from the sky; a stream of lava began pouring down from the heights outside the door as the Beast, grinning, yanked first Tiy then Her Fool to their feet.

Both were retching and labouring for breath in the foul mix of sulphur and dead air, but Azazel was breathing deep.

'Almost like old times,' he croaked. 'We spent so many happy hours breathing this sssweet air … didn't we, sissster?'

'Happy?' She snatched at the bottle as the violent light beat past them into the tiny corbelled chamber beyond the second door. 'I'd rather forget,' She said viciously as Sam, left to one side, looked dully into that dark hidden place. *Shemyaza?* he asked without passion. *Father?*

But the chamber was empty. Just a stone table and stone benches about it. Nobody on them. 'What did you think you'd find?' the Beast asked him genially, prodding him in the kidneys as Tiy, regaining her false drunken hauteur, stepped through like a queen reclaiming her kingdom. 'Did you think Shemyaza was waiting here with net and trident to rescue you?'

Still Sam said nothing. Pushed, he entered that tiny dark place and stood leaning against the stone table. *You poor fools!* he thought with a sudden flash of irony. *You both use me, but you're like jugglers with too many balls in the air. Can you hold them now? Of course not!*

Then, without any consultation, Azazel turned and spoke the opening codes in reverse. The pandemonium and strident light of the outside world were abruptly cut off as both doors rematerialised in place. Tiy flinched in the sudden utter darkness. She felt dazed and vague. She could remember nothing clearly since giving the Fool Her ring and sending him away against the Beast with Zoe and blue-eyed Dion of the Elohim. Since then all was a dark mad dream, full of haunting echoes and hopes that seemed like no hope at all. Now here – *WHERE AM I?* – She stood in a black shaking place that stank of death. The emerald ring was on Her finger, but no light came from it. Then by the bloody light that began to pulse from the shivering walls She saw before Her the luridly highlit forms and faces of the Fool and –

'Why are you here, brother?' She asked uncertainly, twisting the dull dark emerald round Her finger, trying to remember exactly what and where and why with Azazel's age-wracked human face floating before her. His eyes grew brighter every instant. 'I mean … it's so long since we …'

'Have another drink, sissster,' Azazel roared, thrusting the bottle at her, sly face gleaming scarlet in the blood-light as a high-pitched humming began to sing from the walls. 'It's the essence of the elixir! The Elohim accept you again, sissster! All division and separation are over forever – when you drink this drink again!'

She looked at him and saw the crafty jackal in a shining hall where all was curve and pulsation. She felt flat and sick at the sight of the bottle he offered. Fearfully She eyed Her Fool. Tight-lipped, Sam shook his head. 'No good,' he said. 'The Beast bends the truth. Don't listen.' At which Azazel laughed. Torn, She stared into the emerald. Beside Her, Sam stared too. The shake of the floor and the scream of the hum made it hard to see, to think. Still the emerald was dark and dead. 'Why can't I see?' She muttered anxiously. 'Why can't I see? It must get brighter! Brighter!'

Then the entire island lurched. The air screamed. Sam was thrown hard against Her. Behind them Azazel drew a long obsidian-bladed knife from his rags. Neither of them noticed, but as Sam fell against Her the blue-eyes cried: '*Now! The ring! Touch the ring and call her!*' And as Sam crashed into Her he grabbed Her left hand, his fingers closed around the ring ... and blazing green fire leapt out of it.

His huge inner pressure exploded.

Shem and Shemyaza leapt up from his depths.

His vision cleared. In those emerald depths he saw Chrissa and her shepherd whirling up into a great white light; he felt the dizzy whirling in him too as he heard Chrissa cry: '*SAM! NOW! CALL ME!*'

But even as he opened his mouth Tiy saw too late what was happening and tried to throw him aside. From the ring or the knife. Perhaps She didn't know Herself. But She was too weak, too drunk. Azazel stabbed him in the back, triumphantly crying as he struck:

'FOOL, I TOLD YOU, YOU CAN'T BEAT DEATH!'

Distantly he heard Tiy shriek as pain exploded him, as a black shaking roar raced through him and tumbled him into the Hidden Place.

'Chrissa!' he cried with the last light in his mind, 'Chrissa!'

And with that –

With that –

The white light burst.

'NOW WE DANCE THE DANCE OF THREE-IN-ONE!' cried the mighty wind that came on the Light; its huge voice exploding brilliantly in the Starchamber and throwing the Beast aside as, snarling, he stabbed at Tiy, who was swept down over Her Fool's writhing, bloody body ... and as the ring on Her finger poured out the Light She screamed, and Azazel roared as he too was stripped of self-conscious sense ... then all three were lost in the dizzy white dance of transformation; all lost in the fire of the Feast of Light. In it they whirled as its echoes rippled through the world of time and place to touch them all before and lead them on to this ... touching a child in her London dreams, and Diane in Edinburgh; Tiy in the Womb-hall, Joana in the death cell; the Beast in his lair and Pierre on the pastures. They blazed from Montségur to the Gate of the Stone; through the fusion of Light reflecting and merging, increasing in strength, from one black isle to another ...

Now from some distant height of soul where Sam and Shem and

Shemyaza dance their own three-in-one, (WE? US? IT? HE? SHE?) looks down the Sinking Ways to the reactivated Starchamber in that depth of the Hidden World; looks down to see how, stripped to ghostly X-ray skeletons, Samjoyce and Tiy and Azazel writhe amid the vortex, lines of fire erupting from the depths of the emerald ring, whirling round and through them as they flop and shriek on the shaking floor ... and sees how, gradually, steadily, where the skeletal Tiy rolls in agony a new form now builds upon her amid flashes of gold, violet, emerald ... a resurrected body, blue-eyed like the summer sky, golden hair like the harvest sheathes ... and Azazel too transformed as the black isle thunders and roars in its shaking-apart. Now where Azazel groaned and cursed lies a tall gaunt man, foetally curled ... and next to him the murdered Samjoyce has taken on a deeper, older aspect ...

And she laughs. In a sudden peal of light she laughs as in her Gown-of-the-Feathers-of-many-bright-Birds she finds herself and rises to her feet in the Starchamber ... and her laughter's a music that heightens the joy of the Feast of Light as there in the Starchamber she raises the Fool and the Shepherd to their feet and brings them in their Gown-of-the-Feathers-of-many-bright-Birds to their seats around the stone table as the Black Isle bucks like a mad horse about and below and above them. The shock of a huge explosion tears through the island like blast-off fire as spiralling, twisting, whirling up like fiery serpents in the Dance of Three-in-One they go. Barely substantial their hands knit and fuse in circle; their eyes meet like a myriad mirrors all falling through each other; the rumbling of the world rumbles in their hearts with pain, love and hate for fuel as they abandon their envelopes and go up to the Whirling Castle where another great door opens. Immigration checks unsuspected as such are conducted, and then through the radiance, through the lightnings, through time and space the new body soars away through the Sinking Ways to the shining ocean world that circles the Emme Ya star in the Sirius system. And into the great dance of the grey ones who ever glide in the patterns of their ocean mind. And so through further inspection to the ranks of the Company that prepares a return to the Hidden World in the Time of the Shift ... the Company of those who have been born, have lived, seen, understood and emigrated.

And as heaven meets earth the black isle sinks, bearing down to the hidden depths again a room that's hewn from the rock and sealed behind two closed doors. A thousand fathoms deep it falls again upon its elevator of the Light and Dark. And in it as the island sinks still sit the empty, abandoned bodies of two men and a woman. They're all strangely dressed in gowns made of the feathers of bright tropical birds. Hand in hand they sit around a stone table in that hermetic chamber. Their eyes are open, their pupils turned up. One of the men, dark and saturnine with a shock of hair that turned white in the final moment, still smiles in ecstatic glee. The other, tall and weathered by mountain life, gazes up in loving awe, his hand gripping that of the woman between them.

And she ... she is bright, blue eyed, golden haired ... but her eyes are as dead as theirs. Their spirit is gone as the island sinks to the pit of the Hidden World again. Yet on a finger on her left hand is the emerald ring, glowing steadily in the darkness of depth and night as the Feast of Light spirals away to the shining ocean-world that circles the Emme Ya Star.

Glowing. Glowing in the night with a bright and steady fire.

Through the centuries it glows in the hidden depths.

And in the Year of Our Lord 1882 ...

Epilogue: Edinburgh

. . .Davey Joyce sails from Sicily with Madame Pédauque on board . . . and over a century later in November 1999 Diane Joyce sits alone in her room on Rankeillor Street, well wrapped up in bed with the electric fire on full, books on Catharism, apocryphal mysteries and other odd subjects stacked up about, watching TV this freezing night with snow deep on silent streets outside.

Whirling off the highlands, the storm fell on Edinburgh this afternoon, blanketing Nicolson Street as she came home – walking to save the bus fare and afford a bottle – after another futile effort to find work . . . any work.

For word has got around. Every agency has an excuse.

'Yes, Mrs Joyce, your record's fine, just fine, but . . .'

'But I see things I shouldn't,' she mutters resentfully, sipping from a tumblerful of unwatered Haig & Haig, watching the ten o'clock news on STV and trying to ignore her sense of huge disaster looming. Trying to ignore her fear that something other than the news might appear. 'The way they react you'd think I was HIV Positive.'

The news. The usual stuff. First the weather. Roads blocked. Sheep frozen to death. Worst November since records began. Assembly still split over extra relief for the sick and aged. Expert explaining how the shift in the Gulf Stream accelerates the return of the ice. Meanwhile abroad. Five Knights of the Purple Heather caught red-handed in London about to blow up the Metropolitan House of Commons. Three shot dead, the remaining two face the death penalty. In Germany, new Wotan cult excesses involving human sacrifices to propitiate the AIDS-demon. In Brussels, NEC ministers still haggling over agricultural policy. In Brazil, thousands flee leaking reactor. In Luzon, thousands at mass spiritist rally see Virgin Mary come down from skies. And now the continuing crisis in the Middle East. League of Islam armies entrenched outside Istanbul. Russian warships in the Black Sea and the Yanks in the Med. 'Amerislav interference' denounced by jihad leader Muhammad Al-Khash. UN arbitration denounced by everyone. And from Washington the sly face of Abraham Lincoln Daley III, Leader of the Senate, most powerful man in the west. 'Lemme assure citizens of the free world we ain't gonna stand idly by and let this fanatic upset the international balance of payments. And lemme also tell you I've been onto Moscow and the General Secretary feels exactly the same as me.'

'And now a roundup of other items before we return to the weather here in Scotland. AIDS deaths are reported still on the increase in . . .'

'I can't stand it,' Diane tells herself softly. She turns off the TV and pours herself another drink. Her hand shakes. Since that vision on the VDU, since she lost her job, she's been getting through a half bottle a night. It keeps the dreams at bay. The fact she can't afford it only makes it more necessary. It's over a month since she last went down to Portobello, to the Church of the Second Coming. The thought of facing Augustine Farquhar . . . 'Oh my dear, I can tell by your aura that a terrible psychic force has struck you!' No thanks. But my God what do I do next? *she wonders in a dull frenzy.* I mean I saw all that happen! Sam cut off Chrissa's head, I saw it! I'd know I was mad if not for all that other stuff. I've been there. It's real – as real as here and now. *And with frightened eyes she stares out of the half-curtained window. The snow has stopped, the sky has cleared . . . and there, low above an opposite rooftop, shines the bright star. Sirius. And the white light flares through her.*

'No!' she cries, flinching away, tumbling out of bed to draw the curtains tight shut. 'I've seen enough! I've had enough! I don't want any more! Why don't you both go away and leave me alone?'

But again the star flashes. With a gasp she stands and stares, and seems to see a blue-eyed face hanging before her in the night.

Diane! *a voice coaxes her,* Diane! Put that bottle away! That's the Beast's trick! Put it away and sleep! We've got a lot to show you!

'Who are you?' she shouts aloud, alerting residents through the house. Someone bangs the floor above. She doesn't hear that.

'We're all here in the Emme Ya. Diane, there's work to do, the Shift is near, we must return, but to return we must be invited by those like you who remember us. Now, sleep, and let us show you!'

'But are you Chrissa?' she cries at the severed head. 'What . . .'

'All's well, Diane. Now sleep, and let us show you.'

Weeping softly, Diane returns to her bed with the curtains still open, the brilliant star shining in her face. Reluctantly eager she turns out the light. 'Show me what?' she sobs. 'What can you show me that you haven't already shown me? Don't you know what it's been like for me? What do you want, the pair of you?'

For a time she lies there restlessly, unable to relax with the light of that star so blue-cold on her face. Twice she reaches for the bottle and twice withdraws her hand; the third time, cursing, she unscrews the cap and gulps ... but the whisky's foul, her stomach turns, convulsively she sits up and retches, blowing it out of her mouth.

'No!' she wails, gagging, disgusted at herself. 'I can't ...'

Diane, relax. Please, Mum. Relax. Lie back. Sleep now ...

With a tiny moan she does as she's told, her eyes wet with tears as she sighs and lies back, her heart hammering dreadfully. On her side she lies, facing the bright star. Gradually her heartbeat slows down as through her tears she sees Sirius swim ... then from that star she sees a silver arrow leap like a highway of light, pouring through her window ...

The white light explodes at the foot of her bed. And there amid it flame the three of them. Yes, three, though united in one shining body of light. Three forms, wearing brilliant robes made from the feathers of many bright birds, their eyes so clear and bright. Sam, and ... Chrissa, and ... a tall gaunt man with a pleasantly ugly face.

'Chrissa? Chrissa? Is that you? But what's Sam doing here? And –'

'Yes, Mum, it's me, and Dad, and Pierre. We're all ...'

'Pierre? Who's Pierre? What are you?'

– 'We are (WE! US! IT! HE! SHE!).'

– 'We are a cell in the Company.'

– 'Diane, come with us now and –'

At the third voice she explodes:

'How dare you talk to me, Sam Joyce!'

'Diane, everything's all right!' the Chrissa-voice assures her.

'But I saw him cutting off your head! I saw him ...'

– 'It had to be done, Mum.'

– 'To beat the Beast, Diane.'

– 'Madame, we are now one in the Emme Ya!' *And the form called Pierre gives her a roguish bow, a lopsided smile.* 'Madame Joyce, we ask you to come with us now. Please!' And from the core of light Pierre extends his calloused hand. 'Come with us!'

She senses no danger, yet she hangs back. 'Last time I went with you,' she tells the Chrissa-form, 'that ... that Beast ... I was in bed for a week!'

– 'We've beaten the Beast, Mum.'

– 'But he still owns the Earth and that's why ...'

– '... We ask you: come with us now, Madame Joyce!' *And still that rough honest hand's extended, and this time she takes it.*

Briefly it feels like a hand, a human hand, flesh and blood. Grateful for its solid reassurance she grasps it. Yet as she does the white light dissolves her in its song. 'AEIOU!' *a great voice cries: she sees a fire burn up to heaven as* (WE! US! IT! HE! SHE!) *pour out of weight and night into the Sinking Ways, through guardian lightnings to vast blazing light, golden and silver and violet, of the Suns behind our sun . . . and through the emerald gate to the ocean where the Elohim glide in an elegant dance.* 'YOU'VE FOUND US AGAIN!' *murmurs the vast grey one floating beside them, and in that rolling eye of Leviathan they see the severed head of Dion.* 'WELCOME TO THE COMPANY OF LULLU WHO'VE SEEN THROUGH THE BEAST AND FOUND US HERE!'

'YES! YES! YES!' *wink many stars flowing in the deep of this great dance, and images of their lives on earth now approach, reel, and retire, all in quick succession, all through the ages, dancing.* 'BUT HAVE YOU COME TO STAY? OR WILL YOU JOIN US? FOR WE MUST GO DOWN AGAIN! LOOK!'

Then through the emerald gate (WE! US! IT! HE! SHE!) *look back to see the Hidden World, the beautiful Earth lost so deep in gravity's abyss, so caught in densities of time and the teeming desires of death and life.*

Red and black clouds roll round it and on them squats the ever-shifting image of the Beast. And Azazel laughs.

'I CAN AFFORD TO LOSE A FEW,' *he cries,* 'BECAUSE I'VE GOT THE GAME SEWN UP! SOON THE LAST SHIFT!' *Savagely he mimics:* 'LOOK!'

And there below them: history and herstory, all confused from beginning to end, from birth to death in every land; impermanent intelligences with the Beast of Fear on their backs to blight their sight; every advance won in such a way that soon it's lost again; new ideals unconsciously sprung from the same old idols that they denounce. And increasingly the sweet air turned to poison and clear water into slime: the singers of peace admired for a season before their tongues are torn out by derison, pincer, or rank incomprehension. 'FAMINE OUT OF PLENTY!' *cries the Beast, squatting on the planetary mind, keeping the orb unconscious as it rolls on to a new crisis of astrophysical conjunctions.* 'TRIGGER THE SHIFT!' *he whispers in the raw hot screaming minds of millions.* 'WHO GIVES A DAMN? HERE TODAY AND GONE TOMORROW, SO WHO CARES ABOUT TOMORROW? IF YOU DON'T GET IT WHY SHOULD ANY OTHER FUCKER? WHO CARES IF THE SEAS ARE DEAD? JUST CRAP IN 'EM SOME MORE, AND PISS ON THE SKIES AS WELL! WHO TOLD YOU SUCKERS YOU HAD A RIGHT TO LIVE ANYWAY? HAVEN'T YOU HAD ENOUGH? SO VOTE DEATH – NOW!'

'But people don't buy this, do they?' asks (WE? US? IT? HE? SHE?) *in horror before, staring at thistory, realising that they do.*